D0948470

THE YEAR'S **BEST**
MYSTERY AND
SUSPENSE
STORIES
1994

Other Books by Edward D. Hoch

THE YEAR'S **BEST**
MYSTERY AND
SUSPENSE
STORIES
1994

EDITED BY **EDWARD D. HOCH**

 **Walker and Company**
New York

ONCE MORE, FOR **PATRICIA**

First published in the United States of America in 1994 by Walker Publishing Company, Inc.

Published simultaneously in Canada by Thomas Allen & Son Canada, Limited, Markham, Ontario

Library of Congress Catalogue Card Number: 83-646567
ISBN 0-8027-3192-9

CONTENTS

CONTENTS

INTRODUCTION

The year 1993 was an unusual one for the mystery short story. There were about four hundred new stories published in America, and a few dozen more in a number of British anthologies. This was only a slight falling off from previous years, but in reading through them one was struck by two impressions: Last year's stories were longer than usual, and fewer women mystery writers were represented.

Perhaps it's not too unusual that authors prefer longer stories, in which there can be greater character development without a sacrifice of plot essentials. Certainly both *Ellery Queen's Mystery Magazine* and *Alfred Hitchcock's Mystery Magazine* are more open to stories in the 9,000- to 18,000-word length than they were just a few years ago. One publisher, Dark Harvest, has launched a *Criminal Intent* series, with each volume containing three new novellas in the range of 25,000 to 35,000 words. Four of five nominees for the Mystery Writers of America's Edgar award for best short story were over 9,000 words long, and the Fish winner for best first story was over 13,000 words long.

Looking again at the list of Edgar nominees in the short-story category, we note that for the first time in seven years there is no woman nominee. In these pages, only three of the twelve stories are by women. Looking over the list of anthologies, we observe that the year saw no new *Sisters in Crime* volume, and a promised *Deadly Allies* sequel, combining the talents of Sisters in Crime and the Private Eye Writers of America, was postponed. Several popular women writers, in both America and England, simply failed to publish new short stories during the year. We hope this will make for a bountiful 1994.

Last year was also one in which we lost an unusually large number of mystery writers, and my necrology at the back of the book has never approached this length before. Leslie Charteris,

Lillian de la Torre, Dorothy B. Hughes, Helen McCloy, and the rest are talents that will be sorely missed. We grew up reading their stories and novels, and we may never see their like again.

Another trend in short stories during 1993 seems to have been an increasing popularity of series characters. Both British authors represented here, Julian Rathbone and Peter Tremayne, write about series sleuths, as do Americans Lawrence Block, Bill Pronzini, and I—although Block's Keller is more accurately described as a series hit man. Interestingly enough, the stories by Rathbone, Tremayne, and me all feature women sleuths.

Again this year there are many people to thank, especially Douglas G. Greene, Janet Hutchings, Marvin Lachman, Bill Love, and my wife, Patricia. Without them, this would be a far lesser book.

—*Edward D. Hoch*

DOUG ALLYN

THE GHOST SHOW

*As he has done occasionally in past stories, Doug Allyn draws
here upon his musical background and his experiences touring
through the Midwest with his band. The result is a vivid portrait of a world we rarely see, with its memories of past stars
who are dead—and maybe not so dead. Readers of* Ellery
Queen's Mystery Magazine *voted this their favorite story of
last year, bringing Allyn his second EQMM Readers Award.
"The Ghost Show" also brought him another Edgar nomination from Mystery Writers of America.*

That guy onstage is the sorriest-lookin' Elvis I've ever seen,"
Wardell grumbled as I eased down on the bar stool next to him.
"Elvis never wore no horn-rims."

"He's supposed to be Buddy Holly, chump." Doc sighed, giving me a what-do-kids-know look behind Wardell's back. "He
may not look much like Buddy, but he moves like him. Like he's
been dead a helluva long time. Wonder where they dug him up?"

"They held auditions in Chicago," I said. "Cohen ran an ad in
Variety, hired a hall, the works. The black guy who's doing the
Jimi Hendrix act is great. Overall, the show's pretty good."

"They're all just actors, though," Wardell groused. "We're the
only real band on the bill."

"So we are," Doc said. "Stoney and the Bones are the only
real band in a dead-stars revue, and the actors are gettin' paid
more than we are. That tell you anything, Wardell?"

"Yeah. We'll be makin' steady money for a change," Wardell
said sourly.

I caught the bartender's eye. "Jack Black on the rocks," I said. "Do it twice."

"I thought you were on the wagon, Stoney," Wardell said.

"Singing's dusty work," I said. "Need a little lubrication for the pipes. How'd we sound, Doc?"

"Not bad for a first night, but Wardell's piano was a little loud and your guitar was thin. The bass and drums were solid. I'll tweak the sound setup tomorrow. How's your hand holdin' up?"

"Good as new," I lied. It hurt like hell, a painful reminder that motorcycles and trees are a bad mix. The bartender parked a double bourbon in front of me and I knocked back half of it at a single gulp. It cut a gully down my throat and exploded in the deep south. Velvet napalm. I sipped the rest of it slowly, scanning the room. Not a bad crowd for a show bar in Omaha. A mixed bag. Mostly stag flyboys from the air base down the road, some cliques of yuppie singles and divorcées on the make. Doc wouldn't have any trouble finding temporary true love. His rugged puppy looks and shaggy blond mane would make him a trophy in a herd of half-smashed brush cuts.

The audience had applauded politely after our set, but I doubted that many of them knew who we were. Stoney and the Bones are strictly a golden-oldies footnote now. People remember us as the band that introduced Bonnie McGee to the world. If they recall us at all. This crowd came for the beer and the rock-'n'-roll ghost show: Elvis, Buddy Holly, Jimi Hendrix, and a brand-new act, the late, great Bonnie McGee.

"Anybody met the chick who's doin' Bonnie's act?" I asked.

Wardell shook his head.

"I stopped by her dressing room," Doc said. "You know, to say howdy, wish her luck."

"So?" I prompted. "Does she look much like Bonnie or not?"

"Not much." Doc shrugged. "Same size, I guess, but she ain't a redhead. She's got Bonnie's voice down pat, though. I heard her singing in her room. Thought it was a record until I knocked."

"What's she like?"

"Neighborly. I said howdy, I'm Doc Feeny, road manager for the Bones. She told me to take a hike."

"Proves she's got taste, at least," I said.

"Maybe you shoulda worn a T-shirt without holes in it," Wardell said. "The grunge look's passé, Doc."

"The hippie look's comin' back," Doc said, "and so will the Bones. A hit song, a break or two, and we'll be big-time again."

"Sure we will," Wardell said. "But while I'm waitin', think I'll crash back at the motel. We at the Holiday Inn?"

"Third floor," Doc said. "And don't smoke anything nasty in your room. They've got security."

"What? And blow my chance at stardom?" Wardell smirked. "See ya, Stoney." He sauntered off.

I waved good-bye with my glass.

"That punk needs a personality transplant," Doc said.

"He may not be Mr. Warmth, but he can flat play a piano. And it's not like we're married to him. He'll move on. The Bones have always been a revolving-door group, players come and go."

"Everybody but you and me," Doc said.

"Which blows the theory that we get smarter with age."

"Amen." Doc smiled and we touched glasses in a toast to nothing in particular. The pseudo–Buddy Holly ended his set with a lame version of "Peggy Sue." The Bonnie McGee act was next. I killed my drink and ordered two more. Insurance. I'd seen dead-rocker shows before, but never a ghost act of anyone I'd actually known. Or cared about. I caught Doc's eye and he slipped me a couple of Quaaludes under the table. I gulped 'em dry.

Len Cohen, the emcee/manager of the show, had worked with all the big acts at one time or another, including the Bones. He sprinted onstage, tall, dark, and geeky. His slicked, thinning hair and black tux made him look like an anorexic undertaker. "Ladies and gentlemen, here she is, the baddest biker mama of all time, back from her last tour in the land down under, and I mean *waaayyy* down under! The one, the only, BONNIE Mc-GEEEEE!!!"

The backup band kicked into the riff from "Ridin' the Iron," and Bonnie bopped into the spotlight. No problem. I felt nothing at all. For about five seconds. And then my heart stopped and my eyes were stinging, blurring my vision. I could barely see the stage. Which reinforced the jolt I'd felt that first instant. Time travel. It was Bonnie onstage. Sweet Jesus, it really was. Fiery red hair, black leather vest and spandex hotpants, tattoos on her arms and thighs, the way she moved . . .

I knocked back my second double without even tasting it.

She jumped into the first verse of the song. Doc was right: She sounded a lot like Bonnie. Exactly like her, in fact. I tried to pick out a flaw: tone, accent, anything. I couldn't find one. She was perfect. Perfect.

I closed my eyes, letting the music wash over me, and the memories. Feeling the buzz from the bourbon and the drugs kick in, letting Bonnie's voice take me higher than I'd been in years.

The ghost singer did Bonnie's set, song for song, note for note, exactly the way I remembered it. The way I'd heard it in my head a thousand times over the past ten years. And somewhere midway through the set, in the muddle of my mind, the germ of an idea took root and began to grow. A boozy fantasy that gradually solidified into a conviction.

I was hearing an encore. It really was Bonnie up there. Somehow she'd found a way to come back. She'd fought her way through the darkness or whatever was on the other side. And she'd returned to the place she was most alive. On a stage, in the spotlights, a band jamming behind her, amid the smoke and din of a rock-'n'-roll saloon. She'd come back to it. And to me.

I knew it was crazy, but between the booze and the Quaaludes and the pain of loss I'd been carrying all these years . . . Each song intensified the idea, until I was almost sure it was true. Almost.

"Doc?" I said quietly. "Do you hear what I hear?"

"What do you mean?"

"Nobody's that good an imitator. Nobody could be. I think that's really Bonnie up there."

"You mean a tape? Nah, I helped Len's crew set up the PA system. It's not rigged for a lip sync. She's singing live."

"I know. That's what I mean. Check her out. Her voice, the way she moves, everything. I really think it's her, Doc. Somehow she . . . I don't know. She's come back."

Doc scanned my eyes, looking for a smile. We've got a history,

Doc and me. He can read me. "What the hell?" he said slowly. "You're serious, aren't you?"

"Yeah," I said, swallowing. "I think I am."

Doc swiveled to face the stage, frowning. He seemed suddenly uneasy.

"Well?" I said.

"I don't know, man," Doc said. "I admit it sounds a whole lot like her, but . . . Hell, Stoney, that's crazy. Dead people can't come back."

"Sure they can. Happens all the time. We call 'em ghosts," I said, standing up. Too fast. The room wobbled on its axis. "And this *is* a ghost show, right?"

"Yo, partner," Doc said, steadying my arm. "You okay?"

I pulled away from him and threaded my way through the crowd toward the stage. Slow going. The floor was pitching like a cruise ship in a rough sea. Tables kept blundering into my way. She saw me coming. She seemed to be singing to me, drawing me deep into her eyes. . . .

Her eyes. They seemed different. Darker than I remembered. Colder. I couldn't seem to focus on them. I needed to get closer. I vaulted up on the stage, stumbled to one knee, then stood up.

"Hey, boys and girls, look who's here," she said, grinning at me across the stage. "It's my old singing partner, the guy that gave me my big break, Mr. Keith Stone. Give him a hand; maybe we can do a few of our hits together."

One of the stage crew shoved a microphone in my hand. I eyed it stupidly for a moment, then dropped it. It hit the stage with a thump amplified into a thunderclap. Bonnie froze and the room fell silent. Up close her face seemed to be wavering, as though I was seeing her through a waterfall. I shook my head, trying to clear it.

"Bonnie?" I said.

"He's trashed," a stagehand said. "Get him the hell off." Somebody grabbed my arm. I tried to shake loose and couldn't quite manage.

"Bonnie?" I said again, squinting at her through the fog in my head. "It's you, isn't it?"

She hesitated a moment, glaring at me. And then she smiled.

5

But with no warmth. "Yo, Keith, *maty bracie*. You didn't think you'd get rid of me that easy, did you?" Bonnie said. And in that instant I *knew*. Knew it to the core of my soul. It was Bonnie. But I couldn't seem to bring her into focus, or even stay on my feet. The stage was revolving like a wobbly turntable, picking up speed, spinning. And I was going down. . . .

My left eye wouldn't open. It was gummed shut, as if somebody'd licked it and tried to mail it to Seattle. The right one worked, though. I could see my feet. Socks. Somebody'd taken my boots off and tossed a blanket over me. Doc, probably. Motel room. Right. Holiday Inn. Omaha. I risked a slow look around.

Len Cohen was hunched into a question mark, scowling over a newspaper at the dressing table. He'd traded in his tux for a rumpled sport coat, knit tie, cotton Dockers. Doc was sprawled across an armchair reading a *Mad* magazine. He was wearing faded jeans and a T-shirt. From last night? Hard to say. He seldom wears anything else. Sunlight glowed around the window blinds. Morning sun? Afternoon? Couldn't be sure.

"Good morning, butthole," Len growled.

I sat up, slowly, slowly. The room lurched. So did my stomach. I felt flat as a road-killed possum in a truck-stop driveway. I wanted to groan and die, but wouldn't give Len the satisfaction. Doc unfolded himself from the chair and poured me a cup of coffee from a carafe on the nightstand. It was lukewarm. Black, with triple sugar and laced with amphetamines. Doc Feeny's surefire cure for a morning after. I gulped half of it down and felt the amphetamines kick in. And decided I might just survive after all. And it'd serve me right.

"So," I croaked, "Doc said we sounded a little rusty last night."

"You sounded adequate," Len conceded. "It was the show you put on afterward that's bothering me. When I offered you the gig you promised you'd stay straight, Stoney. What the hell happened?"

"It was tougher than I expected," I said slowly, remembering. "Hearing those songs again and especially . . . seeing Bonnie again."

"Yeah, that chick does a heckuva job, doesn't she? Her name's Carol Anspach. Best imitator I've ever seen, and I've seen 'em all."

"But that's the thing, Len. She seemed real to me. Not an act at all. It was like Bonnie'd come back somehow."

"Get real. That wasn't Bonnie onstage last night any more than it was Elvis or Hendrix. Or were you so wrecked you thought they were real too?"

"I know it sounds crazy but, look, you know me, Len. I may be a little wild, but I'm not nuts. I swear I thought it was her."

"Correction. I used to know you, Stoney, back when you were still somebody. But in case you've been smoking something extra heavy-duty, here's a reality check for you. Forget the tabloids that claim she's been spotted everyplace from Nome to Armpit, Idaho. Bonnie's long gone. She died of a drug overdose in Australia ten years ago. I even had the dubious honor of identifying her body afterward. If you hadn't been in traction from cracking up your 'cycle you could have attended her funeral yourself."

"I know, I don't mean it was *really* her, but . . . Dammit, Len, I'm telling you there was something uncanny about her voice, her moves, everything. Doc noticed it too. And when I got onstage she said something to me."

"Like what?" Len asked.

"I . . . can't remember. But it was definitely Bonnie's voice. Do you think I wouldn't know her voice?"

"Maybe she was possessed," Doc offered dryly, winking at Len over the top of his magazine. "Maybe Bonnie took over what's-'er-name somehow. You know, like Linda Blair in *The Exorcist?*"

"*The Exorcist,* right," Len echoed. "Very funny, Doc. Only I'm not laughing. Now listen up, you two burnouts. That wasn't Bonnie last night, and it wasn't her ghost or whatever. She's an actress from Chicago named Carol Anspach. She did a Janis Joplin act in Vegas for a while, and now she's doing Bonnie. She's damn good, audiences like her, and I think we've all got a shot at making some serious bucks here. But you'd better get this straight: Carol's the headliner for this show, not the Bones. I signed your group on because I figured the show'd be more realistic with you as an opening act, but my God, if you give me any more trouble I'll fire your sorry butts in a New York minute."

"So why don't you?" I said.

"Because believe it or not, that little episode last night actually got us some pretty good ink," he said, waving the paper at me. "The music critic of the *World-Herald* said Carol's so good she even fooled you. So if you want to rave at reporters about how Bonnie's really come back, be my guest. But don't try it as an excuse for getting wrecked again, Stoney. You stay straight from here on or you're gone. And just to show you I'm serious: Doc, you're fired."

"No, he's not," I said. "He's been with the Bones from the beginning and in the old days there were plenty of times you were damned glad Doc was along. How many shows did he get us through when we were in no shape to play?"

"You really don't get it, do you?" Cohen sighed. "Maybe if your pal Dr. Feelgood isn't around to pick you up when you're too wrecked to play, you won't get wrecked quite so often."

"Don't blame that on Doc. We've all been legal grown-ups for a while now. And unless you'd like me to tell that music critic last night's little scene was your idea, Doc stays."

"Fine, have it your way," Len said, unfolding himself from the chair. "But we'd better be clear on this, Stoney. The old days are gone. As dead as Joplin or Hendrix or Bonnie. It's all show biz now. You want to work, you stay straight."

"I will. It won't happen again."

"It better not," he said, pausing in the doorway. "You know, you could be right, though. Maybe Bonnie did come back for a minute last night. To remind you what happens when dopers get careless."

"Screw you, Len," I said.

His face darkened and for a moment I thought I'd pushed him too far. But he must've figured the Bones could still make him a few bucks. He slammed the door on his way out.

"Thanks," Doc said.

"*De nada,*" I said. "I mean it. You're the best roadie in the business and you've saved my tail more times than I can count."

"You want some pills?" Doc said, reading my eyes. "You look like you need 'em."

"Nah, I'd better pass, Doc. Len was serious and we definitely need the work."

"Whatever. Look, what you said before about Bonnie comin' back. Do you really believe that?"

"I don't know," I said slowly. "Len's right. I was blown away. That's probably all it was. A bad trip."

"Maybe," he said doubtfully. "I didn't wanna say anything with Len here. But I was straight, Keith, and she seemed so real she scared the hell out of me, too."

"C'mon, Doc, after that monster Texas biker caught you with his mama I didn't figure anything'd ever scare you again."

"That dude was porky enough I figured I could outrun him," Doc said, smiling faintly. "How do you outrun a ghost?"

He was half serious. I know Doc's face as well as my own. I can't always tell when he's kidding. But I know when he definitely isn't.

"All right," I said slowly, "maybe we'd better settle this one way or the other. What did Len say that chick's name was?"

"Which one is she?" I asked, scanning the crowded restaurant.

"There, in the corner booth, readin' the book," Doc said, glancing at me curiously. "You saw her last night."

"Not very clearly," I said. "She looks different in daylight."

"Don't they all. Look, I gotta make a phone call," Doc said. "I'll catch up with you later."

"Whatever," I said absently as Doc faded into the crush. The girl in the corner didn't look anything like Bonnie. Same size maybe, same slender build, but her hair and eyes were dark, and her oversized glasses and Cornhuskers sweatshirt made her look like a college coed. Pre-law. I worked through the crowd toward her table. She had a good face: wide-set eyes, aquiline nose, hair cropped close. Not punk, just short. She glanced up as I approached. If she was concerned, she hid it well. Good for her.

"Hi," I said. "I think I fell on my face before we were properly introduced last night. I'm Keith Stone."

"So I gathered," she said. "I've heard a lot about you. Mostly bad. And you certainly lived up to your reputation. What do you want?"

"For openers, to apologize," I said, sliding into the booth across from her. "I'm really sorry about what happened."

"Apologies don't cut much ice with me, Mr. Stone. Opening nights are tough enough without having a drunk crash my act."

"I know," I said, feeling myself flush. "I, ahm . . . I was upset. I guess I went a little heavy on the anesthetic."

"From your rep, I take it you get upset quite a lot. What was the problem last night?"

"I saw a ghost. Or thought I did. You must be really terrific at what you do, miss. You actually made me believe . . ." I swallowed, and looked away.

"Len told me what you said," she said, cocking her head, looking me over for the first time. "I thought he was joking. Maybe I should be flattered, but in the shape you were in, you would've seen Easter bunnies next."

"No," I said, "it wasn't just booze. It was your voice, the way you moved onstage, everything."

She shrugged. "I'm an actress. An interpretive artist. I used to do Joplin, now I do Bonnie. Maybe I'll never be as good as they were, but I try. I do research, I rehearse like a dog, and I take my work seriously. Which is more than you ever did."

"You don't like me, do you? And I get the feeling that it's about more than just last night. What's your problem?"

"Maybe I just resent what self-destructive jerks like you do to yourselves. And what you did to her."

"Did to *her*? Lady, you've got it exactly backwards. She was nobody when I met her. Joining the Bones was her big break. We had a few hits together, made some serious money. Then I cracked up a motorcycle and she quit us to go solo while I was still in the hospital. Didn't even say good-bye. Not that I hold that against her. It was the smart move, and Bonnie was always smart. Still, if anybody owed anybody, she owed me."

"Did she? When you hired her, you hadn't written a hit in quite a while and your band was on the skids. She helped put the Bones back on top again. And she was dead within a year."

"And you blame me for it? Figure I led her astray or something? Lady, why do you think her arms and legs were tattooed? Sure, it gave her a terrific rock-'n'-roll image. But it also camouflaged needle tracks pretty well. I've got my flaws, but I've never turned anybody on to drugs in my life. She was a user when I met her, and I was ten thousand miles away when she overdosed."

"Methinks the gentleman protests too much."

"Bull. I just got steamrolled by some heavy memories last night. Maybe it was because I never got the chance to say goodbye, or even to go to her funeral, I don't know," I said, sliding out of the booth. "Look, I've apologized and that's the best I can do. And don't worry about it happening again. Up close, minus the red wig, you're nothing like her. Nothing at all."

"You're right, I'm not. I'm just good at what I do. And so are you, when you try. I caught your set last night. I was impressed. If you think you can stay sober long enough maybe we can work up a couple of the songs you and Bonnie did together. It could punch up the act."

"No thanks, lady. I may be a has-been working in a damned ghost show, but I'm not down to mooching off a dead girl's talent like a freaking graverobber."

She flinched; her face reddened as though I'd slapped her. She stared down at the table a moment, focusing on the pattern in the Formica. And when she looked up, she'd changed. Her eyes were burning, transformed, as though something was ablaze in her soul. "Yo, Keith, *maty bracie*. You think you'd get rid of me that easy? I'll be back."

It was Bonnie's voice. Unmistakably. My blood chilled, freezing my heart in place. And then her eyes seemed to melt. And she spoke again in her own voice. "You see, Mr. Stone," she said coldly, "it's not just wigs and makeup. It's art. And the only crime in art is to piss away your talent, the way you have. Or to destroy someone else's. Now take a walk."

For a moment I couldn't speak. "What the hell is this?" I managed at last. "Who are you?" She ignored me, staring out the window as though I'd already gone. I turned, and bumped into Doc. I didn't know how long he'd been there, or what he'd heard, but his face was ashen. He looked as shaken as I felt.

* * *

The show finished the week in Omaha, then moved south for a weekend stand in Lincoln. Opening night was rough. My guitar amp shut down on me twice. The second time I kicked it halfway across the stage. The audience loved it. Len wasn't amused, but I felt a bit better. Temporarily.

The next night was a lot worse. As we finished our set and the curtain came down, the lights winked off for a moment. And Bonnie said, "You think you could get rid of me that easy? That easy?"

It was Bonnie again. I swear to God it was. Her voice was muffled, but it seemed to surround us. Then the backstage lights came on. The whole thing hadn't taken three seconds.

Len's crew was already shifting the equipment, getting ready for the Hendrix act. Doc stalked onstage from the wings and I tossed him my guitar. "Where's Anspach?" I snapped. "I've had enough of this garbage!"

"Forget it," Doc said grimly. "It wasn't her."

"What do you mean? Of course—"

"Stoney, she was standing five feet from me talkin' to Len when it happened. Besides, that was Bonnie's voice. And we both know it."

"But . . . Dammit, Doc, what are we gonna do?"

"Do?" he echoed. "Nothing. We do nothing, say nothing. Just keep on truckin' like it didn't happen. If somebody's runnin' a game on us, eventually they'll get bored. And if they're not . . . Hell, if Bonnie really comes back we'll work her into our show, tell Len to cut Anspach loose and give the rest of us a raise."

He was grinning, but there was an edge to him, a wildness in his eyes I hadn't seen in years. He was definitely spooked, but there was no dog in him. He wouldn't run scared. And if he could handle it, so could I.

I sighed. "Right. Maybe we oughta set up an extra mike for Bonnie. She wasn't very loud."

"She was loud enough," he said, his smile fading. "I heard her just fine."

The show finished the run in Lincoln without any more incidents; then we packed up and rolled east into Iowa for a string of one-nighters. Des Moines; Sioux City; after the third or fourth town I lost track. A shakedown cruise, working out the glitches in low-rent saloons and concert halls, getting ready for bigger dates in Chicago and Vegas.

Usually the players on a tour coalesce into a kind of extended family, a kinship of the craftsmen, all in the same bus chasing a neon rainbow. It's one of the pleasures of life on the road. It didn't happen with this show.

We were a house divided. I avoided Carol Anspach, and vice versa. We didn't talk or catch each other's acts. The Bones opened every show but I'd split as soon as we finished. I told Len Cohen I was staying out of the bars to avoid temptation. But the truth was, I was ducking Anspach like a dog who'd been kicked. And the bars weren't the real danger, anyway. It was the sense of déjà vu, as though touring with Bonnie's ghost had revived my own private demons. And brought the crazy days back. I found myself falling back on old standbys, booze and poppers. But I didn't have the constitution for it anymore. Often I was too high or too low to do the show. Without Doc and his stash I couldn't have made it.

Len knew what was going on, of course. But he didn't say anything. He wouldn't, as long as I could do my act. Hell, maybe he was hoping I'd OD too, so he could hire an actor to play me. Someone easier to control. Another square peg for his square new order.

He was right: Times had changed. The people in the ghost show didn't drink or smoke. They read, or listened to self-improvement tapes on headsets. They did calisthenics at roadside rest stops. The guys in their road crew even wore matching coveralls with the show's logo on the back. Clones, the lot of 'em.

The Bones? We'd sit in the back of the bus and play high-stakes pinochle, or jam for hours on battered guitars, playing old songs or working up new ones. But mostly we played the old songs.

Doc was as edgy as I was. He hid it behind a wall of wisecracks, but I knew this thing was chewing at him. I'd catch him staring at odd moments, looking off to another place, some other time. We went back forever, Doc and me. We'd survived bar fights, bad dope, bum gigs, and crooked promoters. We were hardened rock-'n'-roll road warriors. But being part of a ghost show made us feel ancient, like dinosaurs blundering through a blizzard. Doc tried to kid me out of my funk. He said it was like *Invasion of the Body Snatchers* had happened for real, and the Bones were the last people on earth who hadn't popped out of pods. The truth was, the Bones clung together like ragtag remnants of a defeated army. Surrounded. And outnumbered.

Until Doc evened the odds a little. He hired a new guy, an honest-to-God hippie throwback we picked up at a rest stop in Iowa. He called himself Gopher. I doubt he could remember his real name. His eyes were as empty as the bottom of a beer mug, but he was a free spirit, willing to work for food, a place to crash, and an occasional pop out of Doc's bag. He flatly refused to wear road-crew coveralls, called them fascist. So Doc quit wearing them too. Maybe the Bones weren't stars anymore, but by God we had our own road crew again, in torn denims and headbands and hair down to their waists. Scruffs defiant.

The one thing Doc wouldn't talk about was the ghost. I brought the subject up a couple of times but he blew me off. Said he didn't want to encourage my delusions. And he was right. Hell, I knew it was all a scam and Anspach was just an actress. I *knew* it. She'd learned to sing like Bonnie the way a parrot learns, by listening to records and mimicking the nuances. But what she'd said to me in the restaurant, and the voice we heard onstage in the dark . . . Remembering it raised the hair on the back of my neck.

Haunted or not, the ghost show's bad luck continued. The bus broke down on Highway 80 just west of Moline. We were stuck waiting for repairs most of the day and barely made it to Peoria in time to set up for the show. Len had booked a weekender in an American Legion hall, a barn of a place with hardwood floors and acoustics like the inside of an oil barrel. There were no dressing rooms, and the hall was jammed, standing room only by nine o'clock.

The Bones opened the show and got a pretty good response. It was an older crowd, definitely Geritol generation. They remembered us, or freaks like us, from their lost rock-'n'-roll youth.

The rest of the band split for the bus to play cards, but I stayed.

I'd been stuck in the bus long enough for one day, and anyway, I was curious. I was ready to see how real Anspach's act would seem if I watched her from the wings, cold sober.

I didn't get the chance to find out. Len gave his usual spiel, the backup band kicked into the first song, and Bonnie/Carol came bopping out. I focused on her with every atom of concentration I could muster, trying to see past the wig, to remember the face of the woman I'd talked to in the restaurant. But I couldn't seem to separate them. Memories of Bonnie kept superimposing themselves on her imitator. If Anspach saw me standing there, she gave no sign. She spun to face the audience, grabbed the mike stand. And froze.

For a moment I thought it was stage fright—nobody ever truly loses it. But then I saw a faint wisp of steam from her fist where she was holding the stand. And realized she was burning.

"She's frying! Kill the power," I yelled at the roadies as I sprinted onstage. I slammed into Bonnie's shoulder first in a flying tackle, spinning her away from the microphone, knocking her into a heap in the corner. Her eyes were glassy and her palm was seared from the electrical shock she'd received. She wasn't breathing. I tried to start mouth-to-mouth but one of Len's road crew thought I'd freaked and dragged me off. I took a swing at him, and then went down under a pile of clones in blue coveralls.

Len caught up with me at the motel desk, checking in.

"You oughta get that knot on your temple looked at," he said, eyeing me critically.

"I've been hurt worse falling off bar stools. How's your star?"

"The emergency room treated her for shock, second-degree burns on her hand, and bruised ribs. Did you have to hit her so hard?"

"I didn't have to hit her at all. I could have let her toast to a golden brown. What the hell happened?"

"That burned-out roadie Doc hired back in Iowa, what's his name? Gopher?"

I nodded.

"He pinched a frayed power cord underneath the mike stand.

Carol caught a hundred and twenty volts as soon as she touched it. She was lucky you were handy."

"If she was lucky it wouldn't have happened at all. And what makes you think it was Gopher's fault? It could have been one of your crew."

"Nah, it was Gopher. Doc admitted it and even apologized, which is a first. He's already cut him loose. But from now on, if you want to hire the handicapped, clear it with me, understand?"

"Yassuh, Boss. Is Anspach still in the hospital?"

"Nope, they released her. She's up in her room, resting. She feels pretty rocky."

"Yeah," I said. "I'll bet she does."

It took her nearly ten minutes to answer my knock. She looked like a train wreck, but somehow no less attractive for it. Wearing an oversized bathrobe, her dark hair a tousled shambles, she could have passed for her own sickly sister. Her left hand was wrapped in greasy gauze and her eyes were dazed. Good.

"Hi," she said. "I guess I owe you a thank-you. Thank you. And good night." She started to close the door, but I caught it.

"Sorry, but it ain't gonna be that simple. First, let's get you back in bed where you belong," I said, pushing her gently into the room. "Then we have to talk. It's important."

"If it's about your friend being fired—"

"It's about him and a lot more. I need your help. Please." She let me lead her to the bed. She eased down on the edge of it, blinking, trying to collect herself.

"Are you okay?" I asked.

"I don't know," she said honestly. "My hand hurts and I'm half in the bag from the painkillers they gave me at the hospital. Which is an average day for you, right?"

"That's more like it," I said. "For a minute there I thought you were going to be civil."

"A lapse," she said, eyeing me warily. "It won't happen again. Now, what do you want exactly?"

"I'm not sure. I guess I want you to break a mirror for me."

"Come again?"

"A mirror. Like in a fun house? I feel like I'm lost in a roomful of mirrors. People are getting hurt and I can't see what's happening or find my way out. But somehow I think you know the way out."

"Are you high or something? You're not making any sense."

"Look, I know you've got no use for me, but dammit, I saved your neck tonight. You owe me, lady. At least a mirror's worth."

"I see. And which mirror would that be?"

"Just explain one thing to me. That first night, I thought you sounded exactly like Bonnie. So much that I thought she'd— I don't know. Come back for one last encore or something. It was crazy, but I was stoned and that's what I thought. The next day, though, I was straight, more or less, and you still sounded exactly like her. Even called me molly brochia, or something like that. Hell, I can't even pronounce it, but you could. Bonnie used to call me that sometimes. But only in private. You couldn't have gotten that off a record."

"No," she said. "I didn't. And before you ask, that bit back in Lincoln, when you heard the voice in the dark? I had one of the stagehands rig a cordless mike to play through one of your amps. Consider it a payback for messing up my opening night."

"You mean that was your voice?"

"No, it was Bonnie's. Look, explaining it would take more energy than I've got right now," she said, wincing as she tried to take a deep breath. "But I can show you. If you're sure you're up to it."

"Lady, at this point I'm ready for anything."

"There's a box in the closet. Get it for me."

"What's in it? A Ouija board?"

"No," she said, easing back against the pillows. "Something much better."

It was a portable VCR, and a few videocassettes. I glanced the question at her, but her eyes were closed.

"The tapes with numbers on them are bootleg videos of Bonnie when she was still with the Bones," she said without opening her eyes. "The third tape is the one you want. Len bought it from Bonnie's brother. *Mały bracie.*"

"What?"

"That's what it means. 'Little brother.' In Polish."

"Bonnie was Irish."

"Her mother was Polish," she said. "An immigrant straight from the old country. Very uptight, which is why the family would never talk to the press about her. They were ashamed of the way she died." She sagged back into her pillow, pursing her lips against the pain in her hand. I hooked the VCR up to the TV set, turned the volume down, and inserted the cassette.

The tape was a pastiche, a collection of 8mm home movies transferred onto videotape. They weren't in any particular order and they'd been hacked up pretty badly to delete segments without Bonnie. It opened with her eighth-grade graduation, cut to Bonnie and another girl singing country music in a high school gym, cut to a church picnic, Bonnie watching a mob of kids in plaid shirts and overalls play softball, cut to Bonnie singing in a local folkie bar, one of the songs she'd mailed to my record company. I'd liked the tune so much I asked her to come out to L.A. for an audition. . . . I stopped the tape, swallowing hard.

And realized Anspach was watching me. "Jesus," I said, "she was just . . . a hick. The tattoos, all that biker mama stuff, it was just a front. I don't understand."

"You might if you were a woman," Carol said. "She was coming out for a tryout with the Bones, right? A group with a reputation for being stone rock-'n'-roll crazies. She knew it was her big break and she'd have to fit in to make it. So she tried life in the fast lane. Your life. And it killed her."

"Look, I know it may look that way, but I swear she was already heavy into drugs when I met her. I didn't turn her on to anything. Hell, before she left she was stumbling around like a wino after every show."

"And did your pal Doc help her out?"

"She never hit on Doc for so much as a speeder that I knew of, and I would have known. Whatever happened to her, she did to herself."

"It doesn't matter now," she said, leaning back, closing her eyes again. "There's only a few minutes on the tape. You'd better see the rest of it."

I switched the VCR on. Bonnie finished the song. . . . Cut to the Bonnie I remembered, tattooed arms, hair cut short and spiky. She was sitting in a dressing room, holding a guitar. "Yo, Stoney, *maly bracie*," she said, to the camera, and to me. "You think you can get rid of me that easy? I'll be back. But first I've got some thinking to do. And so have you. We've got a lot to talk about, you and me. Meanwhile, I've got half a song here. It needs a bridge and a final chorus. Give a listen." She played a brief introduction to the song, then sang two verses. "That's as far as I've taken it. Give it your best shot and we'll polish it up together when I get back. And don't worry, I'll be back." She reached toward the screen to turn the camera off. . . .

Cut to Bonnie, age thirteen or so, walking hesitantly into a living room, wearing a white confirmation dress. I stopped the tape and sat there a few minutes, getting my breathing under control. Then I turned and met Carol's eyes.

"You've had this all along?" I said wonderingly. "Knowing she made it for me? That's cold, lady. Damn, but that's cold."

"Maybe it is. Actually, I intended to give it to you, but after that first night I changed my mind, decided to use it to run a game on you instead. Besides, it's obvious from the clip that she left the group to get away from the life you were in. Only she didn't make it. Whether you meant to or not, you destroyed her."

"That's not true," I said.

"Perhaps you just don't want to believe it."

"It's more than that. And anyway, there's something wrong with this film."

"What do you mean, wrong?"

"I'm not sure, but . . . Something's missing. Or there's something I'm not seeing. Can I watch it again? I'll take it back to my room if you want to rest."

"Watch it here," she said, closing her eyes. "I'd rather not be alone and the tape won't bother me. I know it . . . by heart."

Her voice faded. I think she was asleep before she finished speaking. I rewound the tape and watched it again, beginning to end. And then again. But it wasn't until the fourth or fifth time through that I realized what I'd missed earlier. Two things really. The twenty-year-old Bonnie singing in the little saloon didn't have any tattoos. But when we met a few months later, she looked like the biker mama she pretended to be. Tattoos on her arms and thighs to cover needle tracks. But even more important, in the last segment, of her confirmation day, if I looked past her carefully, I could see into a bedroom.

The room was out of focus, and I couldn't be sure it was hers. But I think it was. Because there was a kit on the nightstand beside the bed. A shooting kit. Cotton balls, a small bottle of alcohol, and a hypodermic syringe. And at the time, Bonnie couldn't have been more than thirteen years old.

Len opened the door in his pajamas, blinking. He looked at me with disbelief, then at his watch. "What the hell, Stoney, it's five in the damned morning. What's wrong?"

"Everything. I need to talk to you."

"About what?"

"About Bonnie," I said, pushing past him into the room. "I need to know what happened to her, Len. Exactly."

"Now? Can't it wait until morning?"

"No, it's waited too long already. Please, Len. It's important."

He hesitated, reading my eyes, and either figured I was dead serious or completely around the bend. "You know what happened," he said sourly, stepping back into the room. "Everybody does. She overdosed. Collapsed onstage. Ambulance took her to a hospital, but she died the next day without regaining consciousness."

"Died of what? Specifically, I mean? What was she on?"

"Hell, I don't know, some kind of heroin speedball mix."

"Where did she get it?"

"What do you mean?"

"The tour was just starting. You'd only been in the country a few days. Where did she get the stuff?"

"She walked it through customs. Damnedest thing I ever saw."

"Walked it through? How?"

"She had some official paperwork that said she was diabetic and had permission to bring some vials of insulin into the country. She had the harder stuff mixed in with it. The cops found it in the fridge in her dressing room. The hell of it was, the coroner who did the autopsy said she really was diabetic. Apparently had been all her life. She was the last person in the world who should have been using. Did you know?"

"No," I said, shaking my head slowly. "I guess there was a helluva lot I didn't know. Or was too buzzed to notice. Why didn't all this come out at the time?"

"The local law clamped a lid on it. Didn't want to publicize how easy it'd been to get drugs into the country. Which was okay by me. All I wanted was to get the hell out of there. Funny, I thought getting Bonnie away from you would be good for her. Thought you were a bad influence, that she'd be okay on her own. But I guess you weren't the problem after all. Or at least not the way I figured."

"Meaning what?"

"Nothing," Len said, glancing away. "Forget it."

"Jesus, don't jerk me around, Len. It's too late for games. Dammit, I have to know!"

"Fine, you want it all, sport? Here it is. Bonnie was pregnant!" he snapped. "Nearly three months along. They said she probably misjudged her fix because her body chemistry was changing."

"My God," someone said softly. Me, I guess. I sat down slowly on the edge of Len's rumpled bed.

"I'm sorry, I didn't mean to hit you like . . . Ah hell, we were all a little crazy back then. The mistakes we made, we just have to live with 'em. They're history, Stoney. It's over."

"But that's just it. It's not over. I've got this awful feeling that it's all coming back, Len, and it's going to end just as ugly. Maybe it's bad karma or something, hell, I don't know. Bonnie getting hurt tonight helped me see it, but I think it's been there all along."

"Stoney," Len said carefully, "Bonnie didn't get hurt tonight. Carol did."

"Right," I said. "That's what I meant."

I found myself walking along a side street. Wasn't sure where I was and it didn't matter. I've been in hundreds of towns that I've never seen in daylight. You roll in, do a show, move on. It's the life. After a while it seems normal. Almost. But I felt disconnected now. Like I was finally an honest-to-God member of the ghost show. My own ghost, drifting like smoke.

The videotape. It kept replaying in my head, frame by frame, superimposing itself on darkened shop windows and the sides of passing trucks. I glimpsed Bonnie's smile in gutters, the glow of her eyes in alley shadows. At times I heard the song. Two lonely verses repeating endlessly like an old 45 stuck in a groove. Or it'd just be a whisper of her voice on the wind. Her last message to me. Nothing profound, just a few sentences. But it troubled me. There was something unfinished about it, something . . . And after a while I realized what it was.

She hadn't said good-bye to me. Not in life, or on the tape. The last thing she said was: "I'll be back."

"I'll be back."

I could hear the drone of the television through the hotel door. I rapped twice, then again once, our signal for all clear. Doc peered cautiously out past the chain lock, then unhooked it and let me in.

"What's up?" he said, blearily massaging his eyes. He was barefoot, wearing briefs and a T-shirt. I'd seen him this way before countless times. It seemed oddly intimate now. "Kinda early, isn't it?" he said.

"I went to see Anspach," I said, glancing around the anonymous room, the rumpled bed. "We had a long talk."

"Looks like you musta talked all night. Next show's not till nine. I can do you a couple downers if you wanna zone out."

"You've got a stash here?" I asked, surprised.

"With all the excitement I didn't have time to stow it proper. It's in the tank. You want some 'ludes?"

"Why not?" I trailed him to the john, watched as he popped the toilet top and took out a flat, book-sized parcel sealed in a waterproof plastic Baggie. He expertly flicked the bag open with a fingernail and popped the box top. "Two enough?"

"For now," I said, cupping them in my palm. "Funny, whenever I need to get up or down you're always handy. Like the power company or something."

"The power company?"

"Sure. When you turn on the lights, you never think about where the juice comes from. You're like that. Doc Feeny, Dr. Feelgood. The power company."

"That's one way to look at it," Doc said warily, reading my eyes. "Somethin's up besides us, isn't it? What's wrong?"

"Not much," I said. "Just my whole damn life."

"That's a relief." Doc snorted. "For a minute there I thought it might be serious. Wanna narrow that down a little?"

"Sure. Let's start with Gopher. Len said you fired him."

"Had to. Hated to roll over on a buddy, but he was too far gone, man, a total screwup. He coulda killed that chick. I shoulda realized how blown he was. Never shoulda taken him on."

I stared at him a long time, reading his face. His very familiar face. "C'mon, Doc, all the time we've been together, I probably know you better'n your mama. Lie to her if you want, but not to me. You knew exactly how blown away Gopher was. That's *why* you hired him. To take the fall for Anspach's accident. Hell, he's so burned out he probably thinks he really did it."

"But you don't?"

"I know he didn't. Because I know you. You're an ace roadie, one of the best in the biz. Much too good to make a mistake like that—or let some screwup make it, either. That was no accident. You set her up to get burned, maybe killed. I knew it from the first. I just couldn't figure why you'd do it. Ghost show or not, we're makin' more money than we've seen in years. It didn't make sense. Until I realized it wasn't her you were trying to get at. It was Bonnie. Wasn't it?"

"That's crazy! Bonnie's dead, dammit."

"But sometimes the dead come back. Hell, Doc, it's what we've both been thinking. That the ghost in our show is real."

He nodded, swallowing hard. "That day in the restaurant . . . We both saw it, heard it, in broad daylight. And then that night in the dark . . . That was Bonnie. No question. I haven't hardly slept since. Afraid to. Doin' speeders till I'm startin' to see the walls crawl. I hadda do somethin' about it or flip out altogether."

"Relax, Doc. It's over. There's no ghost. At least not the usual kind. Anspach got a videotape from Bonnie's family, a bunch of home movies cobbled together. That's how she made her act so perfect. That and pure talent. She's really good. Good enough to make us both believe in ghosts."

"You're sayin' she's been fakin' it? But that voice we heard in Lincoln couldn't have been her."

"She had a stagehand run a tape of Bonnie's voice through a cordless mike. Simple. If we'd had our heads on straight we'd have figured it out. But we haven't been straight. Either of us. It was easy for Anspach to mess with our minds. Or what's left of 'em."

"Sweet Jesus Jenny on a bicycle," Doc said, slumping to the edge of the bed, burying his face in his hands, "I swear to God, Stoney. This thing's makin' me crazy. All I could think of was if I could run Anspach off, Bonnie'd go with her."

"I figured it had to be something like that. Pretty risky, though. You might've killed her. And that bothered me. The idea that you were scared enough to risk killing somebody. Hell, Doc, you've got the guts of a burglar. Or a dope dealer. I could only come up with one reason you'd be afraid of Bonnie, dead or alive. Because you thought she'd come back for you. Didn't you?"

"You know, don't you?" he said slowly, looking up at me.

"Most of it," I said. "It's there on the video if you know what to look for. Tell me the rest."

"Bonnie lit into me while you were in the hospital. Blamed me because you were stoned when you cracked up your bike. Called me a damn cancer. Like it's my fault you like to cop a buzz once in a while. And you know it's not true."

"No," I agreed. "When I get trashed it's nobody's fault but mine. So what happened?"

"She got the offer for the solo tour. Said she was gonna get some bucks together and get you straightened out when she got back. And get rid of me. So I decided to run a little game on her. I found her stash. She had it hid in some medicine bottles in the fridge. Probably thought she'd get it past customs that way. I boosted the dose on a couple of 'em. Christ, I swear I never meant to really hurt her. I just figured she'd conk out or freak enough to get busted by the law. She'd draw a little slam time and forget about us. We'd go on like always."

"An accidental overdose?" I said softly. "Is that it?"

"That's exactly what it was, man. I still can't figure out how it went wrong. I didn't boost 'em much."

"It didn't take much. The medicine you found wasn't fake, she really was diabetic. I'm guessing she'd lost out on things all her life because of it, and didn't want to risk losing her chance to work with us. So she camouflaged it with tattoos. And fit right in. The boost you gave those bottles was probably the first fix she ever had. It killed her. And the baby she was carrying. My baby, Doc."

"But sweet Jesus, Stoney, I didn't know. It wasn't my fault. You know me, Dr. Feelgood. I get people up or down sometimes, but nothin' heavy. I'd never hurt anybody on purpose, you know that."

And he believed it. Bonnie was dead. And our child with her. And my life was a ghost show. Elvis and Jimi and me. We'd all died the same way. And Doc really believed that he hadn't hurt anyone. Dr. Feelgood. Dr. Death.

He was already spinning halfway across the room before I realized I'd hit him. He slammed into the wall and crumpled to the floor. I snatched up the chair from the dressing table. Doc looked up at me, dazed, cowering. He was crying and his nose was bleeding. And I couldn't hit him. Hell, he was right. In a way I was as guilty as he was. But I had to hit something.

I pitched the chair through the window, exploding the glass out on the street. And then I walked out. And I didn't look back.

I was packing. Len rapped once on my open door. "The cops busted Doc," he said, glancing around. "There was some trouble in his room and hotel security called the law. They caught him holding a couple grand worth of goodies." He paused, waiting for me to react. I zipped my shaving kit closed.

"Cop said his bail will be at least ten large. You got that kind of money?"

I shook my head.

"If you want an advance, maybe we can work a deal. Say a contract extension? At a slight pay cut?"

"No," I said. "I'm out."

"Out? You mean you're leaving? What about Doc?"

"He's on his own."

"Then what about the show? We've got contracts."

"Hire another ghost. Any street bum can play me in the shape I'm in now."

"What's wrong with you? What the hell's happened?"

I didn't answer. I couldn't.

"All right," Len said slowly. "Go on ahead. Maybe some time off the road will do you good. But remember, when you get ready to work again, you still owe me six months."

"I won't have to remember, Len," I said. "You will."

His beeper went off. "Duty calls. See ya, Stoney," he said, and trotted off to find a phone. I didn't even look up.

When I did, Carol was there, watching. She looked a little shaky, but better than she had earlier. She was pale, dressed in patterned jeans and a peasant blouse. Her left hand was wrapped in a clean gauze bandage. "Len says you're leaving," she said.

"I'm going home. To Indiana. Hang out at my granddaddy's farm awhile. He can use the help. So can I."

She smiled. "Sounds dull."

"I hope so," I said.

"Are you coming back?"

"Not to this show, no. I may have flushed my talent, I don't know. But I'm not a ghost yet. At least I hope I'm not."

"You look real enough to me. This farm you're talking about, does the house have a porch?"

"A porch?" I frowned, thinking. "It used to have. I haven't been there in a while. Why?"

"The show has a break scheduled in a few months. Maybe I can pop out to wherever it is. And we can sit on the porch, maybe sing a few songs. You've never heard me sing, you know. I mean, in my own voice. I'm pretty good."

"I'll bet you are," I said. "I'll let you know. I don't know if I'm going to be singing anymore."

"You will," she said positively. "Anybody who's survived the life you've been in can get through anything. Would you like a copy of that video? The one with the song on it?"

"No," I said. "I'm not likely to forget it. Thanks anyway."

"No charge," she said, straightening. "Well, have a safe trip."

"Hey, Anspach," I said. "There is one thing you can do for me, if you wouldn't mind."

"I guess I owe you one. What is it?"

"This may sound kind of odd to you, but . . . You see, we never had the chance to say good-bye. Bonnie and me. Could you . . . say good-bye to me? In her voice, I mean."

She stared at me for what seemed a very long time. Her dark eyes were a mystery. I thought she was going to run a game on me one last time. But she didn't.

"No," she said at last. "I guess not. I'll see you, Stoney. Good luck." And then she was gone.

I finished packing the last of my things, snapped the case shut, and carried it to the door. I glanced around to make sure I hadn't missed anything. The room was neat, anonymous. The bed was still made. Like no one had been there at all. Not even a ghost.

"Good-bye, Bonnie," I said.

LAWRENCE BLOCK

KELLER'S THERAPY

Lawrence Block, honored this year as a Grand Master by the Mystery Writers of America, went on to win their Edgar Award for best short story of the year with this gripping novelette about his series hit man, Keller, last encountered in our 1991 volume with "Answers to Soldier." For most authors, the story that follows would have enough plot twists for a lengthy novel. For Block, it's a splendid example of why he is truly a Grand Master of the American mystery.

I had this dream," Keller said. "Matter of fact, I wrote it down, as you suggested."

"Good."

Before getting on the couch, Keller had removed his jacket and hung it on the back of a chair. He moved from the couch to retrieve his notebook from the jacket's inside breast pocket, then sat on the couch and found the page with the dream on it. He read through his notes rapidly, closed the book, and sat there, uncertain of how to proceed.

"As you prefer," said Breen. "Sitting up or lying down, whichever is more comfortable."

"It doesn't matter?"

"Not to me."

And which was more comfortable? A seated posture seemed natural for conversation, while lying down on the couch had the weight of tradition on its side. Keller, who felt driven to give this his best shot, decided to go with tradition. He stretched out, put his feet up.

He said, "I'm living in a house, except it's almost like a castle. Endless passageways and dozens of rooms."

"Is it your house?"

"No, I just live here. In fact, I'm a kind of servant for the family that owns the house. They're almost like royalty."

"And you are a servant."

"Except I have very little to do and I'm treated like an equal. I play tennis with members of the family. There's this tennis court in the back."

"And this is your job? To play tennis?"

"No, that's an example of how they treat me as an equal. I eat at the same table with them, instead of with the servants. My job is the mice."

"The mice?"

"The house is infested with mice. I'm having dinner with the family, I've got a plate piled high with good food, and a waiter in black tie comes in and presents a covered dish. I lift the cover and there's a note on it, and it says, 'Mice.' "

"Just the single word?"

"That's all. I get up from the table and follow the waiter down a long hallway, and I wind up in an unfinished room in the attic. There are tiny mice all over the room—there must be twenty or thirty of them—and I have to kill them."

"How?"

"By crushing them underfoot. That's the quickest and most humane way, but it bothers me and I don't want to do it. But the sooner I finish, the sooner I can get back to my dinner, and I'm hungry."

"So you kill the mice?"

"Yes," Keller said. "One almost gets away, but I stomp on it just as it's running out the door. And then I'm back at the dinner table and everybody's eating and drinking and laughing, and my plate's been cleared away. Then there's a big fuss, and finally they bring back my plate from the kitchen, but it's not the same food as before. It's . . ."

"Yes?"

"Mice," Keller said. "They're skinned and cooked, but it's a plateful of mice."

"And you eat them?"

"That's when I woke up," Keller said. "And not a moment too soon, I'd say."

"Ah," Breen said. He was a tall man, long-limbed and gawky, wearing chinos, a dark-green shirt, and a brown corduroy jacket. He looked to Keller like someone who had been a nerd in high school and who now managed to look distinguished in an eccentric sort of way. He said "Ah" again, folded his hands, and asked Keller what he thought the dream meant.

"You're the doctor," Keller said.

"You think it means I'm the doctor?"

"No, I think you're the one who can say what it means. Maybe it just means I shouldn't eat Rocky Road ice cream right before I go to bed."

"Tell me what you think the dream means."

"Maybe I see myself as a cat."

"Or as an exterminator?"

Keller didn't say anything.

"Let's work with this dream on a superficial level," Breen said. "You're employed as a corporate troubleshooter, except that you use another word for it."

"They tend to call us expediters," Keller said, "but troubleshooter is what it amounts to."

"Most of the time there is nothing for you to do. You have considerable opportunity for recreation, for living the good life. For tennis, as it were, and for nourishing yourself at the table of the rich and powerful. Then mice are discovered, and it is at once clear that you are a servant with a job to do."

"I get it," Keller said.

"Go on, then, Explain it to me."

"Well, it's obvious, isn't it? There's a problem and I'm called in and I have to drop what I'm doing and go and deal with it. I have to take abrupt, arbitrary action, and that can involve firing people and closing out entire departments. I have to do it, but it's like stepping on mice. And when I'm back at the table and I want my food—I suppose that's my salary?"

"Your compensation, yes."

"And I get a plate of mice." Keller made a face. "In other

words, what? My compensation comes from the destruction of the people I have to cut adrift. My sustenance comes at their expense. So it's a guilt dream?"

"What do you think?"

"I think it's guilt. My profit derives from the misfortunes of others, from the grief I bring to others. That's it, isn't it?"

"On the surface, yes. When we go deeper, perhaps we will begin to discover other connections. With your having chosen this job in the first place, perhaps, and with some aspects of your childhood." He interlaced his fingers and sat back in his chair. "Everything is of a piece, you know. Nothing exists alone and nothing is accidental. Not even your name."

"My name?"

"Peter Stone. Think about it, why don't you, between now and our next session."

"Think about my name?"

"About your name and how it suits you. And"—a reflexive glance at his wristwatch—"I'm afraid that our hour is up."

Jerrold Breen's office was on Central Park West at Ninety-fourth Street. Keller walked to Columbus Avenue, rode a bus five blocks, crossed the street, and hailed a taxi. He had the driver go through Central Park, and by the time he got out of the cab at Fiftieth Street, he was reasonably certain he hadn't been followed. He bought coffee in a deli and stood on the sidewalk, keeping an eye open while he drank it. Then he walked to the building where he lived, on First Avenue between Forty-eighth and Forty-ninth. It was a prewar high-rise with an art deco lobby and an attended elevator. "Ah, Mr. Keller," the attendant said. "A beautiful day, yes?"

"Beautiful," Keller agreed.

Keller had a one-bedroom apartment on the nineteenth floor. He could look out his window and see the UN building, the East River, the borough of Queens. On the first Sunday in November he could watch the runners streaming across the Queensboro Bridge, just a couple of miles past the midpoint of the New York Marathon.

It was a spectacle Keller tried not to miss. He would sit at his window for hours while thousands of them passed through his field of vision, first the world-class runners, then the middle-of-the-pack plodders, and finally the slowest of the slow, some walking, some hobbling. They started in Staten Island and finished in Central Park, and all he saw was a few hundred yards of their ordeal as they made their way over the bridge and into Manhattan. The sight always moved him to tears, though he could not have said why.

Maybe it was something to talk about with Breen.

It was a woman who had led him to the therapist's couch, an aerobics instructor named Donna. Keller had met her at the gym. They'd had a couple of dates and had been to bed a couple of times, enough to establish their sexual incompatibility. Keller still went to the same gym two or three times a week to raise and lower heavy metal objects, and when he ran into her, they were friendly.

One time, just back from a trip somewhere, he must have rattled on about what a nice town it was. "Keller," she said, "if there was ever a born New Yorker, you're it. You know that, don't you?"

"I suppose so."

"But you always have this fantasy of living the good life in Elephant, Montana. Every place you go, you dream up a whole life to go with it."

"Is that bad?"

"Who's saying it's bad? But I bet you could have fun with it in therapy."

"You think I need to be in therapy?"

"I think you'd get a lot out of therapy," she said. "Look, you come here, right? You climb the stair monster, you use the Nautilus."

"Mostly free weights."

"Whatever. You don't do this because you're a physical wreck."

"I do it to stay in shape. So?"

"So I see you as closed in and trying to reach out," she said. "Going all over the country, getting real estate agents to show you houses that you're not going to buy."

"That was only a couple of times. And what's so bad about it, anyway? It passes the time."

"You do these things and don't know why," she said. "You know what therapy is? It's an adventure, it's a voyage of discovery. And it's like going to the gym. Look, forget it. The whole thing's pointless unless you're interested."

"Maybe I'm interested," he said.

Donna, not surprisingly, was in therapy herself. But her therapist was a woman, and they agreed that he'd be more comfortable working with a man. Her ex-husband had been very fond of his therapist, a West Side psychologist name Breen. Donna had never met the man, and she wasn't on the best of terms with her ex, but . . .

"That's all right," Keller said. "I'll call him myself."

He'd called Breen, using Donna's ex-husband's name as a reference. "I doubt that he even knows me by name," Keller said. "We got to talking a while back at a party and I haven't seen him since. But something he said struck a chord with me and, well, I thought I ought to explore it."

"Intuition is always a powerful teacher," Breen said.

Keller made an appointment, giving his name as Peter Stone. In his first session he talked about his work for a large and un-named conglomerate. "They're a little old-fashioned when it comes to psychotherapy," he told Breen. "So I'm not going to give you an address or telephone number, and I'll pay for each session in cash."

"Your life is filled with secrets," Breen said.

"I'm afraid it is. My work demands it."

"This is a place where you can be honest and open. The idea is to uncover the secrets you've been keeping from yourself. Here you are protected by the sanctity of the confessional, but it's not my task to grant you absolution. Ultimately, you absolve yourself."

"Well," Keller said.

"Meanwhile, you have secrets to keep. I respect that. I won't need your address or telephone number unless I'm forced to cancel an appointment. I suggest you call to confirm your sessions an hour or two ahead of time, or you can take the chance of an occasional wasted trip. If you have to cancel an appointment, be sure to give twenty-four hours' notice. Or I'll have to charge you for the missed session."

"That's fair," Keller said.

He went twice a week, Mondays and Thursdays at two in the afternoon. It was hard to tell what they were accomplishing. Sometimes Keller relaxed completely on the sofa, talking freely and honestly about his childhood. Other times he experienced the fifty-minute session as a balancing act: He yearned to tell everything and was compelled to keep it all a secret.

No one knew he was doing this. Once, when he ran into Donna, she asked if he'd ever given the shrink a call, and he'd shrugged sheepishly and said he hadn't. "I thought about it," he said, "but then somebody told me about this masseuse—she does a combination of Swedish and shiatsu—and I have to tell you, I think it does me more good than somebody poking and probing at the inside of my head."

"Oh, Keller," she'd said, not without affection. "Don't ever change."

It was on a Monday that he recounted the dream about the mice. Wednesday morning his phone rang, and it was Dot. "He wants to see you," she said.

"Be right out," he said.

He put on a tie and jacket and caught a cab to Grand Central and a train to White Plains. There he caught another cab and told the driver to head out Washington Boulevard and to let him off at the corner of Norwalk. After the cab drove off, he walked up Norwalk to Taunton Place and turned left. The second house on the right was an old Victorian with a wraparound porch. He rang the bell and Dot let him in.

"The upstairs den, Keller," she said. "He's expecting you."

He went upstairs, and forty minutes later he came down again. A young man named Louis drove him back to the station, and on the way they chatted about a recent boxing match they'd both seen on ESPN. "What I wish," Louis said, "is that they had, like, a mute button on the remote, except what it would do is mute the announcers but you'd still hear the crowd noise and the punches landing. What you wouldn't have is the constant yammer-yammer-yammer in your ear." Keller wondered if they could do that. "I don't see why not," Louis said. "They can do everything else. If you can put a man on the moon, you ought to be able to shut up Al Bernstein."

Keller took a train back to New York and walked to his apartment. He made a couple of phone calls and packed a bag. At three-thirty he went downstairs, walked half a block, hailed a cab for JFK, and picked up his boarding pass for American's five fifty-five flight to Tucson.

In the departure lounge he remembered his appointment with Breen. He called to cancel the Thursday session. Since it was less than twenty-four hours away, Breen said, he'd have to charge him for the missed session, unless he was able to book someone else into the slot.

"Don't worry about it," Keller told him. "I hope I'll be back in time for my Monday appointment, but it's always hard to know how long these things are going to take. If I can't make it, I should at least be able to give you the twenty-four hours' notice."

He changed planes in Dallas and got to Tucson shortly before midnight. He had no luggage aside from the piece he was carrying, but he went to the baggage-claim area anyway. A rail-thin man with a broad-brimmed straw hat held a hand-lettered sign that read NOSCAASI. Keller watched the man for a few minutes and observed that no one else was watching him. He went up to him and said, "You know, I was figuring it out the whole way to Dallas. What I came up with, it's Isaacson spelled backward."

"That's it," the man said. "That's exactly it." He seemed impressed, as if Keller had cracked the Japanese naval code. He said, "You didn't check a bag, did you? I didn't think so. The car's this way."

In the car the man showed Keller three photographs, all of the same man, heavyset, dark, with glossy black hair and a greedy pig face. Bushy mustache, bushy eyebrows and enlarged pores on his nose.

"That's Rollie Vasquez," the man said. "Son of a bitch wouldn't exactly win a beauty contest, would he?"

"I guess not."

"Let's go," the man said. "Show you where he lives, where he eats, where he gets his ashes hauled. Rollie Vasquez, this is your life."

Two hours later the man dropped Keller at a Ramada Inn and gave him a room key and a car key. "You're all checked in," he said. "Car's parked at the foot of the staircase closest to your room. She's a Mitsubishi Eclipse, pretty decent transportation. Color's supposed to be silver-blue, but she says gray on the papers. Registration's in the glove compartment."

"There was supposed to be something else."

"That's in the glove compartment, too. Locked, of course, but the one key fits the ignition and the glove compartment. And the doors and the trunk, too. And if you turn the key upside down, it'll still fit, because there's no up or down to it. You really got to hand it to those Japs."

"What'll they think of next?"

"Well, it may not seem like much," the man said, "but all the time you waste making sure you got the right key, then making sure you got it right side up—"

"It adds up."

"It does," the man said. "Now you have a full tank of gas. It takes regular, but what's in there's enough to take you upward of four hundred miles."

"How're the tires? Never mind. Just a joke."

"And a good one," the man said. " 'How're the tires?' I like that."

The car was where it was supposed to be, and the glove compartment held the registration and a semiautomatic pistol, a .22-caliber Horstmann Sun Dog, loaded, with a spare clip lying alongside it. Keller slipped the gun and the spare clip into his carry-on, locked the car, and went to his room without passing the front desk.

After a shower, he sat down and put his feet up on the coffee table. It was all arranged, and that made it simpler, but sometimes he liked it better the other way, when all he had was a name and address and no one to smooth the way for him. This was

36

simple, all right, but who knew what traces were being left? Who knew what kind of history the gun had, or what the string bean with the NOSCAASI sign would say if the police picked him up and shook him?

All the more reason to do it quickly. He watched enough of an old movie on cable to ready him for sleep. When he woke up, he went out to the car and took his bag with him. He expected to return to the room, but if he didn't, he would be leaving nothing behind, not even a fingerprint.

He stopped at a Denny's for breakfast. Around one he had lunch at a Mexican place on Figueroa. In the late afternoon he drove into the foothills north of the city, and he was still there when the sun went down. Then he drove back to the Ramada.

That was Thursday. Friday morning the phone rang while he was shaving. He let it ring. It rang again as he was showering. He let it ring. It rang again just as he was ready to leave. He didn't answer it this time, either, but went around wiping surfaces a second time with a hand towel. Then he went out to the car.

At two that afternoon he followed Rolando Vasquez into the men's room of the Saguaro Lanes bowling alley and shot him three times in the head. The little gun didn't make much noise, not even in the confines of the tiled lavatory. Earlier he had fashioned an improvised suppressor by wrapping the barrel of the gun with a space-age insulating material that muffled the gun's report without adding much weight or bulk. If you could do that, he thought, you ought to be able to shut up Al Bernstein.

He left Vasquez propped in a stall, left the gun in a storm drain half a mile away, left the car in the long-term lot at the airport. Flying home, he wondered why they had needed him in the first place. They'd supplied the car and the gun and the finger man. Why not do it themselves? Did they really need to bring him all the way from New York to step on the mouse?

"You said to think about my name," he told Breen. "The significance of it. But I don't see how it could have any significance. It's not as if I chose it."

"Let me suggest something," Breen said. "There is a metaphysical principle which holds that we choose everything about

our lives, that we select the parents we are born to, that everything which happens in our lives is a manifestation of our wills.
Thus, there are no accidents, no coincidences."

"I don't know if I believe that."

"You don't have to. We'll just take it as a postulate. So assum-
ing that you chose the name Peter Stone, what does your choice
tell us?"

Keller, stretched full length upon the couch, was not enjoying
this. "Well, a peter's a penis," he said reluctantly. "A stone peter
would be an erection, wouldn't it?"

"Would it?"

"So I suppose a guy who decides to call himself Peter Stone
would have something to prove. Anxiety about his virility. Is that
what you want me to say?"

"I want you to say whatever you wish," Breen said. "Are you
anxious about your virility?"

"I never thought I was," Keller said. "Of course, it's hard to
say how much anxiety I might have had back before I was born,
around the time I was picking my parents and deciding what
name they should choose for me. At that age I probably had a
certain amount of difficulty maintaining an erection, so I guess I
had a lot to be anxious about."

"And now?"

"I don't have a performance problem, if that's the question.
I'm not the way I was in my teens, ready to go three or four times
a night, but then, who in his right mind would want to? I can
generally get the job done."

"You get the job done."

"Right."

"You perform."

"Is there something wrong with that?"

"What do you think?"

"Don't do that," Keller said. "Don't answer a question with a
question. If I ask a question and you don't want to respond, just
leave it alone. But don't turn it back on me. It's irritating."

Breen said, "You perform, you get the job done. But what do
you feel, Mr. Peter Stone?"

"Feel?"

"It is unquestionably true that peter is a colloquialism for the penis, but it has an earlier meaning. Do you recall Christ's words to Peter? 'Thou art Peter, and upon this rock I shall build my church.' Because Peter *means* rock. Our Lord was making a pun. So your first name means rock and your last name is Stone. What does that give us? Rock and stone. Hard, unyielding, obdurate. Insensitive. Unfeeling—"

"Stop," Keller said.

"In the dream, when you kill the mice, what do you feel?"

"Nothing. I just want to get the job done."

"Do you feel their pain? Do you feel pride in your accomplishment, satisfaction in a job well done? Do you feel a thrill, a sexual pleasure, in their deaths?"

"Nothing," Keller said. "I feel nothing. Could we stop for a moment?"

"What do you feel right now?"

"I'm just a little sick to my stomach, that's all."

"Do you want to use the bathroom? Shall I get you a glass of water?"

"No, I'm all right. It's better when I sit up. It'll pass. It's passing already."

Sitting at his window, watching not marathoners but cars streaming over the Queensboro Bridge, Keller thought about names. What was particularly annoying, he thought, was that he didn't need to be under the care of a board-certified metaphysician to acknowledge the implications of the name Peter Stone. He had chosen it, but not in the manner of a soul deciding what parents to be born to and planting names in their heads. He had picked the name when he called to make his initial appointment with Jerrold Breen. "Name?" Breen had demanded. "Stone," he had replied. "Peter Stone."

Thing is, he wasn't stupid. Cold, unyielding, insensitive, but not stupid. If you wanted to play the name game, you didn't have to limit yourself to the alias he had selected. You could have plenty of fun with the name he'd had all his life.

His full name was John Paul Keller, but no one called him anything but Keller, and few people even knew his first and middle names. His apartment lease and most of the cards in his wallet showed his name as J. P. Keller. Just Plain Keller was what people called him, men and women alike. ("The upstairs den, Keller. He's expecting you." "Oh, Keller, don't ever change." "I don't know how to say this, Keller, but I'm simply not getting my needs met in this relationship.")

Keller. In German it meant cellar, or tavern. But the hell with that. You didn't need to know what it meant in a foreign language. Change a vowel. Killer.

Clear enough, wasn't it?

On the couch, eyes closed, Keller said, "I guess the therapy's working."

"Why do you say that?"

"I met a girl last night, bought her a couple of drinks, and went home with her. We went to bed and I couldn't do anything."

"You couldn't do anything?"

"Well, if you want to be technical, there were things I could have done. I could have typed a letter or sent out for a pizza. I could have sung 'Melancholy Baby.' But I couldn't do what we'd both been hoping I would do, which was to have sex."

"You were impotent?"

"You know, you're very sharp. You never miss a trick."

"You blame me for your impotence," Breen said.

"Do I? I don't know about that. I'm not sure I even blame myself. To tell you the truth, I was more amused than devastated. And she wasn't upset, perhaps out of relief that I wasn't upset. But just so nothing like that happens again, I've decided to change my name to Dick Hardin."

"What was your father's name?"

"My father," Keller said. "Jesus, what a question. Where did that come from?"

Breen didn't say anything.

Neither, for several minutes, did Keller. Then, eyes closed, he said, "I never knew my father. He was a soldier. He was killed in action before I was born. Or he was shipped overseas before I was born and killed when I was a few months old. Or possibly he was home when I was born or came home on leave when I was small, and he held me on his knee and told me he was proud of me."

"You have such a memory?"

"No," Keller said. "The only memory I have is of my mother telling me about him, and that's the source of the confusion, because she told me different things at different times. Either he was killed before I was born or shortly after, and either he died without seeing me or he saw me one time and sat me on his knee. She was a good woman, but she was vague about a lot of things. The one thing she was completely clear on was that he was a soldier. And he was killed over there."

"And his name?"

Was Keller, he thought. "Same as mine," he said. "But forget the name, this is more important than the name. Listen to this. She had a picture of him, a head-and-shoulders shot, this good-looking young soldier in a uniform and wearing a cap, the kind that folds flat when you take it off. The picture was in a gold frame on her dresser when I was a little kid.

"And then one day the picture wasn't there anymore. 'It's gone,' she said. And that was all she would say on the subject. I was older then, I must have been seven or eight years old.

"Couple of years later I got a dog. I named him Soldier, after my father. Years after that, two things occurred to me. One, Soldier's a funny thing to call a dog. Two, who ever heard of naming a dog after his father? But at the time it didn't seem the least bit unusual to me."

"What happened to the dog?"

"He became impotent. Shut up, will you? What I'm getting to is a lot more important than the dog. When I was fourteen, fifteen years old, I used to work after school helping out this guy who did odd jobs in the neighborhood. Cleaning out basements and attics, hauling trash, that sort of thing. One time this notions store went out of business, the owner must have died, and we were cleaning out the basement for the new tenant. Boxes of junk all over the place, and we had to go through everything, because part of how this guy made his money was selling off the stuff he got paid to haul. But you couldn't go through all this crap too thoroughly or you were wasting time.

"I was checking out this one box, and what do I pull out but a framed picture of my father. The very same picture that sat on my mother's dresser, him in his uniform and his military cap, the picture that disappeared, it's even in the same frame, and what's it doing here?"

Not a word from Breen.

"I can still remember how I felt. Stunned, like 'Twilight Zone' time. Then I reach back into the box and pull out the first thing I touch, and it's the same picture in the same frame.

"The box is full of framed pictures. About half of them are the soldier, and the others are a fresh-faced blonde with her hair in a pageboy and a big smile on her face. It was a box of frames. They used to package inexpensive frames that way, with photos in them for display. For all I know they still do. My mother must have bought a frame in a five-and-dime and told me it was my father. Then when I got a little older, she got rid of it.

"I took one of the framed photos home with me. I didn't say anything to her, I didn't show it to her, but I kept it around for a while. I found out the photo dated from World War Two. In other words, it couldn't have been a picture of my father, because he would have been wearing a different uniform.

"By this time I think I already knew that the story she told me about my father was, well, a story. I don't believe she knew who my father was. I think she got drunk and went with somebody, or maybe there were several different men. What difference does it make? She moved to another town, she told people she was married, that her husband was in the service or that he was dead, whatever she told them."

"How do you feel about it?"

"How do I feel about it?" Keller shook his head. "If I slammed my hand in a cab door, you'd ask me how I felt about it."

"And you'd be stuck for an answer," Breen said. "Here's a question for you: Who was your father?"

"I just told you."

"But *someone* fathered you. Whether or not you knew him, whether or not your mother knew who he was, there was a particular man who planted the seed that grew into you. Unless you believe yourself to be the second coming of Christ."

"No," Keller said. "That's one delusion I've been spared."

"So tell me who he was, this man who spawned you. Not on the basis of what you were told or what you've managed to figure out. I'm not asking the part of you that thinks and reasons. I'm asking the part of you that simply knows. Who was your father? What was your father?"

"He was a soldier," Keller said.

Keller, walking uptown on Second Avenue, found himself standing in front of a pet shop, watching a couple of puppies cavorting in the window.

He went inside. One wall was given over to stacked cages of puppies and kittens. Keller felt his spirits sink as he looked into the cages. Waves of sadness rocked him.

He turned away and looked at the other pets. Birds in cages, gerbils and snakes in dry aquariums, tanks of tropical fish. He felt all right about them; it was the puppies he couldn't bear to look at.

He left the store. The next day he went to an animal shelter and walked past cages of dogs waiting to be adopted. This time the sadness was overwhelming, and he felt its physical pressure against his chest. Something must have shown on his face, because the young woman in charge asked him if he was all right.

"Just a dizzy spell," he said.

In the office she told him that they could probably accommodate him if he was especially interested in a particular breed. They could keep his name on file, and when a specimen of that breed became available . . .

"I don't think I can have a pet," he said. "I travel too much. I can't handle the responsibility." The woman didn't respond, and Keller's words echoed in her silence. "But I want to make a donation," he said. "I want to support the work you do."

He got out his wallet, pulled bills from it, handed them to her without counting them. "An anonymous donation," he said. "I don't want a receipt. I'm sorry for taking your time. I'm sorry I can't adopt a dog. Thank you. Thank you very much."

She was saying something, but he didn't listen. He hurried out of there.

" 'I want to support the work you do.' That's what I told her, and then I rushed out of there because I didn't want her thanking me. Or asking questions."

"What would she ask?"

"I don't know," Keller said. He rolled over on the couch, facing away from Breen, facing the wall. " 'I want to support the work you do.' But I don't know what their work is. They find homes for some animals, and what do they do with the others? Put them to sleep?"

"Perhaps."

"What do I want to support? The placement or the killing?"

"You tell me."

"I tell you too much as it is," Keller said.

"Or not enough."

Keller didn't say anything.

"Why did it sadden you to see the dogs in their cages?"

"I felt their sadness."

"One feels only one's own sadness. Why is it sad to you, a dog in a cage? Are you in a cage?"

"No."

"Your dog, Soldier. Tell me about him."

"All right," Keller said. "I guess I could do that."

A session or two later, Breen said, "You have never been married?"

"No."

"I was married."

"Oh?"

"For eight years. She was my receptionist. She booked my appointments, showed clients to the waiting room. Now I have no receptionist. A machine answers the phone. I check the machine between appointments and take and return calls at that time. If I had had a machine in the first place, I'd have been spared a lot of agony."

"It wasn't a good marriage?"

Breen didn't seem to have heard the question. "I wanted children. She had three abortions in eight years and never told me. Never said a word. Then one day she threw it in my face. I'd been to a doctor, I'd had tests and all indications were that I was fertile, with a high sperm count and extremely motile sperm. So I wanted her to see a doctor. 'You fool. I've killed three of your babies already, so why don't you leave me alone?' I told her I wanted a divorce. She said it would cost me."

"And?"

"We've been divorced for nine years. Every month I write an alimony check and put it in the mail. If it were up to me, I'd burn the money."

Breen fell silent. After a moment Keller said, "Why are you telling me all this?"

"No reason."

"Is it supposed to relate to something in my psyche? Am I supposed to make a connection, clap my hand to my forehead, and say, 'Of course, of course! I've been so blind!' "

"You confide in me," Breen said. "It seems only fitting that I confide in you."

Dot called a couple of days later. Keller took a train to White Plains, where Louis met him at the station and drove him to the house on Taunton Place. Later, Louis drove him back to the train station and he returned to the city. He timed his call to Breen so that he got the man's machine. "This is Peter Stone," he said. "I'm flying to San Diego on business. I'll have to miss my next appointment and possibly the one after that. I'll try to let you know."

He hung up, packed a bag, and rode the Amtrak to Philadelphia.

No one met his train. The man in White Plains had shown him a photograph and given him a slip of paper with a name and address on it. The man in question managed an adult-book store a few blocks from Independence Hall. There was a tavern across the street, a perfect vantage point, but one look inside made it clear to Keller that he couldn't spend time there without calling attention to himself, not unless he first got rid of his tie and jacket and spent twenty minutes rolling around in the gutter.

Down the street Keller found a diner, and if he sat at the far end, he could keep an eye on the bookstore's mirrored front windows. He had a cup of coffee, then walked across the street to the bookstore, where two men were on duty. One was a sad-eyed youth from India or Pakistan, the other the jowly, slightly exophthalmic fellow in the photo Keller had seen in White Plains.

Keller walked past a wall of videocassettes and leafed through a display of magazines. He had been there for about fifteen minutes when the kid said he was going for his dinner. The older man said, "Oh, it's that time already, huh? Okay, but make sure you're back by seven for a change, will you?"

Keller looked at his watch. It was six o'clock. The only other customers were closeted in video booths in the back. Still, the kid had had a look at him, and what was the big hurry, anyway?

He grabbed a couple of magazines and paid for them. The jowly man bagged them and sealed the bag with a strip of tape. Keller stowed his purchase in his carry-on and went to find a hotel.

The next day he went to a museum and a movie and arrived at the bookstore at ten minutes after six. The young clerk was gone, presumably having a plate of curry somewhere. The jowly man was behind the counter and there were three customers in the store, two checking the video selections, one looking at the magazines.

Keller browsed, hoping they would clear out. At one point he was standing in front of a wall of videos and it turned into a wall of caged puppies. It was momentary, and he couldn't tell if it was a genuine hallucination or just some sort of flashback. Whatever it was, he didn't like it.

One customer left, but the other two lingered, and then someone new came in off the street. The Indian kid was due back in half an hour, and who knew if he would take his full hour, anyway?

Keller approached the counter, trying to look a little more nervous than he felt. Shifty eyes, furtive glances. Pitching his voice low, he said, "Talk to you in private?"

"About what?"

Eyes down, shoulders drawn in, he said, "Something special."

"If it's got to do with little kids," the man said, "no disrespect intended, but I don't know nothing about it, I don't want to know nothing about it, and I wouldn't even know where to steer you."

"Nothing like that," Keller said.

They went into a room in back. The jowly man closed the door, and as he was turning around, Keller hit him with the edge of his hand at the juncture of his neck and shoulder. The man's knees buckled, and in an instant Keller had a loop of wire around his neck. In another minute he was out the door, and within the hour he was on the northbound Metroliner.

When he got home, he realized he still had the magazines in his bag. That was sloppy. He should have discarded them the previous night, but he'd simply forgotten them and never even unsealed the package.

Nor could he find a reason to unseal it now. He carried it down the hall and dropped it into the incinerator. Back in his apartment, he fixed himself a weak scotch and water and watched a documentary on the Discovery Channel. The vanishing rain forest, one more goddamned thing to worry about.

"Oedipus," Jerrold Breen said, holding his hands in front of his chest, his fingertips pressed together. "I presume you know the story. He killed his father and married his mother."

"Two pitfalls I've thus far managed to avoid."

"Indeed," Breen said. "But have you? When you fly off somewhere in your official capacity as corporate expediter, when you shoot trouble, as it were, what exactly are you doing? You fire people, you cashier divisions, close plants, rearrange lives. Is that a fair description?"

"I suppose so."

"There's an implied violence. Firing a man, terminating his career, is the symbolic equivalent of killing him. And he's a stranger, and I shouldn't doubt that the more important of these men are more often than not older than you, isn't that so?"

"What's the point?"

"When you do what you do, it's as if you are seeking out and killing your unknown father."

"I don't know," Keller said. "Isn't that a little farfetched?"

"And your relationships with women," Breen went on, "have a strong Oedipal component. Your mother was a vague and unfocused woman, incompletely present in your life, incapable of connecting with others. Your own relationships with women are likewise out of focus. Your problems with impotence—"

"Once!"

"—are a natural consequence of this confusion. Your mother is dead now, isn't that so?"

"Yes."

"And your father is not to be found, and almost certainly deceased. What's called for, Peter, is an act specifically designed to reverse this pattern on a symbolic level."

"I don't follow you."

"It's a subtle point," Breen admitted. He crossed his legs, propped an elbow on a knee, extended his thumb, and rested his bony chin on it. Keller thought, not for the first time, that Breen must have been a stork in a prior life. "If there were a male figure in your life," Breen went on, "preferably at least a few years your senior, someone playing a paternal role vis-à-vis yourself, someone to whom you turn for advice and direction."

Keller thought of the man in White Plains.

"Instead of killing this man," Breen said, "symbolically, I am speaking symbolically throughout, but instead of killing him as you have done with father figures in the past, you might do something to *nourish* this man."

Cook a meal for the man in White Plains? Buy him a hamburger? Toss him a salad?

"Perhaps you could think of a way to use your talents to this man's benefit instead of to his detriment," Breen went on. He drew a handkerchief from his pocket and mopped his forehead. "Perhaps there is a woman in his life—your mother, symbolically—and perhaps she is a source of great pain to your father. So, instead of making love to her and slaying him, like Oedipus, you might reverse the usual course of things by, uh, showing love to him and slaying her."

"Oh," Keller said.

"Symbolically, that is to say."

"Symbolically," Keller said.

A week later Breen handed Keller a photograph. "This is called the thematic apperception test," Breen said. "You look at the photograph and make up a story about it."

"What kind of story?"

"Any kind at all," Breen said. "This is an exercise in imagination. You look at the subject of the photograph and imagine what sort of woman she is and what she is doing."

The photo was in color and showed a rather elegant brunette dressed in tailored clothing. She had a dog on a leash. The dog was medium-sized, with a chunky body and an alert expression. It was the color that dog people call blue and that everyone else calls gray.

"It's a woman and a dog," Keller said.

"Very good."

Keller took a breath. "The dog can talk," he said, "but he won't do it in front of other people. The woman made a fool of herself once when she tried to show him off. Now she knows better. When they're alone, he talks a blue streak, and the son of a bitch has an opinion on everything from the real cause of the Thirty Years' War to the best recipe for lasagna."

"He's quite a dog," Breen said.

"Yes, and now the woman doesn't want people to know he can talk, because she's afraid they might take him away from her. In this picture they're in a park. It looks like Central Park."

"Or perhaps Washington Square."

"It could be Washington Square," Keller agreed. "The woman is crazy about the dog. The dog's not so sure about the woman."

"And what do you think about the woman?"

"She's attractive," Keller said.

"On the surface," Breen said. "Underneath, it's another story, believe me. Where do you suppose she lives?"

Keller gave it some thought. "Cleveland," he said.

"Cleveland? Why Cleveland, for God's sake?"

"Everybody's got to be someplace."

"If I were taking this test," Breen said, "I'd probably imagine the woman living at the foot of Fifth Avenue, at Washington Square. I'd have her living at Number One Fifth Avenue, perhaps because I'm familiar with that building. You see, I once lived there."

"Oh?"

"In a spacious apartment on a high floor. And once a month," he continued, "I write an enormous check and mail it to that address, which used to be mine. So it's only natural that I would have this particular building in mind, especially when I look at this particular photo." His eyes met Keller's. "You have a question, don't you? Go ahead and ask it."

"What breed is the dog?"

"As it happens," Breen said, "it's an Australian cattle dog. Looks like a mongrel, doesn't it? Believe me, it doesn't talk. But why don't you hang on to that photograph?"

"All right."

"You're making really fine progress in therapy," Breen said. "I want to acknowledge you for the work you're doing. And I just know you'll do the right thing."

A few days later Keller was sitting on a park bench in Washington Square. He folded his newspaper and walked over to a dark-haired woman wearing a blazer and a beret. "Excuse me," he said, "but isn't that an Australian cattle dog?"

"That's right," she said.

"It's a handsome animal," he said. "You don't see many of them."

"Most people think he's a mutt. It's such an esoteric breed. Do you own one yourself?"

"I did. My ex-wife got custody."

"How sad for you."

"Sadder still for the dog. His name was Soldier. Is Soldier, unless she's changed it."

"This fellow's name is Nelson. That's his call name. Of course, the name on the papers is a real mouthful."

"Do you show him?"

"He's seen it all," she said. "You can't show him a thing."

* * *

"I went down to the Village last week," Keller said, "and the damnedest thing happened. I met a woman in the park."

"Is that the damnedest thing?"

"Well, it's unusual for me. I meet women at bars and parties, or someone introduces us. But we met and talked, and then I ran into her the following morning. I bought her a cappuccino."

"You just happened to run into her on two successive days."

"Yes."

"In the Village?"

"It's where I live."

Breen frowned. "You shouldn't be seen with her, should you?"

"Why not?"

"Don't you think it's dangerous?"

"All it's cost me so far," Keller said, "is the price of a cappuccino."

"I thought we had an understanding."

"An understanding?"

"You don't live in the Village," Breen said. "I know where you live. Don't look surprised. The first time you left here I watched you from the window. You behaved as though you were trying to avoid being followed. So I took my time, and when you stopped taking precautions, I followed you. It wasn't that difficult."

"Why follow me?"

"To find out who you are. Your name is Keller, you live at Eight-six-five First Avenue. I already knew what you were. Anybody might have known just from listening to your dreams. And paying in cash, and the sudden business trips. I still don't know who employs you, crime bosses or the government, but what difference does it make? Have you been to bed with my wife?"

"Your ex-wife?"

"Answer the question."

"Yes, I have."

"Jesus Christ. And were you able to perform?"

"Yes."

"Why the smile?"

"I was just thinking," Keller said, "that it was quite a performance."

Breen was silent for a long moment, his eyes fixed on a spot above and to the right of Keller's shoulder. Then he said, "This is profoundly disappointing. I hoped you would find the strength to transcend the Oedipal myth, not merely reenact it. You've had fun, haven't you? What a naughty boy you've been. What a triumph you've scored over your symbolic father. You've taken this woman to bed. No doubt you have visions of getting her pregnant, so that she can give you what she cruelly denied him. Eh?"

"Never occurred to me."

"It would, sooner or later." Breen leaned forward, concern showing on his face. "I hate to see you sabotaging your therapeutic progress this way," he said. "You were doing so *well*."

From the bedroom window you could look down at Washington Square Park. There were plenty of dogs there now, but none were Australian cattle dogs.

"Some view," Keller said. "Some apartment."

"Believe me," she said, "I earned it. You're getting dressed. Are you going somewhere?"

"Just feeling a little restless. Okay if I take Nelson for a walk?"

"You're spoiling him," she said. "You're spoiling both of us."

On a Wednesday morning, Keller took a cab to La Guardia and a plane to St. Louis. He had a cup of coffee with an associate of the man in White Plains and caught an evening flight back to New York. He took another cab directly to the apartment building at the foot of Fifth Avenue.

"I'm Peter Stone," he said to the doorman. "Mrs. Breen is expecting me."

The doorman stared.

"Mrs. Breen," Keller said. "In Seventeen-J."

"Jesus."

"Is something the matter?"

"I guess you haven't heard," the doorman said. "I wish it wasn't me who had to tell you."

"You killed her," he said.

"That's ridiculous," Breen told Keller. "She killed herself. She threw herself out the window. If you want my professional opinion, she was suffering from depression."

"If you want *my* professional opinion," Keller said, "she had help."

"I wouldn't advance that argument if I were you," Breen said. "If the police were to look for a murderer, they might look long and hard at Mr. Stone-hyphen-Keller, the stone killer. And I might have to tell them how the usual process of transference went awry, how you became obsessed with me and my personal life, how I couldn't dissuade you from some insane plan to reverse the Oedipus complex. And then they might ask you why you employ an alias and just how you make your living. Do you see why it might be best to let sleeping dogs lie?"

As if on cue, Nelson stepped out from behind the desk. He caught sight of Keller and his tail began to wag.

"Sit," Breen said. "You see? He's well trained. You might take a seat yourself."

"I'll stand. You killed her and then you walked off with the dog."

Breen sighed. "The police found the dog in the apartment, whimpering in front of the open window. After I identified the body and told them about her previous suicide attempts, I volunteered to take the dog home with me. There was no one else to look after him."

"I would have taken him," Keller said.

"But that won't be necessary, will it? You won't be called upon to walk my dog or make love to my wife or bed down in my apartment. Your services are no longer required." Breen seemed to recoil at the harshness of his own words. His face softened. "You'll be able to get back to the far more important business of therapy. In fact," he indicated the couch, "why not stretch out right now?"

"That's not a bad idea. First, though, could you put the dog in the other room?"

"Not afraid he'll interrupt, are you? Just a little joke. He can wait in the outer office. There you go, Nelson. Good dog . . . oh, no. How *dare* you bring a gun. Put that down immediately."

"I don't think so."

"For God's sake, why kill me? I'm not your father, I'm your therapist. It makes no sense for you to kill me. You have nothing to gain and everything to lose. It's completely irrational. It's worse than that, it's neurotically self-destructive."

"I guess I'm not cured yet."

"What's that, gallows humor? It happens to be true. You're a long way from cured, my friend. As a matter of fact, I would say you're approaching a psychotherapeutic crisis. How will you get through it if you shoot me?"

Keller went to the window, flung it wide open. "I'm not going to shoot you," he said.

"I've never been the least bit suicidal," Breen said, pressing his back against a wall of bookshelves. "Never."

"You've grown despondent over the death of your ex-wife."

"That's sickening, just sickening. And who would believe it?"

"We'll see," Keller told him. "As far as the therapeutic crisis is concerned, well, we'll see about that, too. I'll think of something."

The woman at the animal shelter said, "Talk about coincidence. One day you come in and put your name down for an Australian cattle dog. You know, that's quite an uncommon breed in this country."

"You don't see many of them."

"And what came in this morning? A perfectly lovely Australian cattle dog. You could have knocked me over with a sledgehammer. Isn't he a beauty?"

"He certainly is."

"He's been whimpering ever since he got here. It's very sad. His owner died and there was nobody to keep him. My goodness, look how he went right to you. I think he likes you."

"I'd say we're made for each other."

"I believe it. His name is Nelson, but you can change it, of course."

"Nelson," he said. The dog's ears perked up. Keller reached to give him a scratch. "No, I don't think I'll have to change it. Who was Nelson, anyway? Some kind of English hero, wasn't he? A famous general or something?"

"I think an admiral. Commander of the British fleet, if I remember correctly. Remember? The battle of Trafalgar Square?"

"It rings a muted bell," he said. "Not a soldier but a sailor. Well, that's close enough, wouldn't you say? Now, I suppose there's an adoption fee and some papers to fill out."

When they handled that part she said, "I still can't get over it. The coincidence and all."

"I knew a man once," Keller said, "who insisted there was no such thing as a coincidence or an accident."

"Well, I wonder how he would explain this."

"I'd like to hear him try," Keller said. "Let's go, Nelson. Good boy."

DAVID ELY

DEAD MEN

Regular readers of short mystery fiction have come to expect the most unusual concept from David Ely's all-too-infrequent stories. In the thirty-two years since winning an MWA Edgar for "The Sailing Club," he has proven himself to be one of the most original writers around. You have only to dip into his half-dozen novels and two collections of stories, Time Out *and* Always Home, *to find yourself in a world both familiar and strange.*

W ell, here's another one," said Detective Sergeant Knowles as Inspector Bates approached the group of men standing at the corner of Ninth and Park streets. Knowles's assistant, Dunphy, was squatting beside the body. The ambulance was easing up to the curb, its red lights whirling.

Inspector Bates, a big man with heavy shoulders and powerful arms, stood watching, his hands in his pockets and his hat tipped back on his head. The victim had been shot through the heart at close range. The pistol was probably fitted with a silencer. There wouldn't be any witnesses—not in this place, a downtown area deserted after dark.

Sergeant Knowles and Dunphy were going through the dead man's effects while the medics eased the body onto a stretcher. "They sure didn't do it for robbery," said Knowles, examining the wallet. "The guy was carrying two hundred bucks plus his gold watch."

Inspector Bates took a last look at the corpse before it was lifted into the ambulance. Its face bore an expression of frozen surprise, the eyes wide with wonder.

Knowles put the wallet into the evidence bag with the man's watch, keys, and pen. "This makes nine of them," he remarked.

Inspector Bates swept his flashlight beam across the blood-smeared sidewalk. There were more than nine, he knew. Nine this month—but he'd been going back through the files, and there were several last month that fit the pattern, and maybe some before that.

Would there be more to come?

Bud Bates was an ex-marine, a onetime amateur boxer. He considered himself a hard man—hard, but fair. He didn't make the rules, but he lived by them—the rules of society, of God, of common decency and custom—and he expected others to live by them too. If they didn't, they had to be caught and made to pay the penalty.

But if they couldn't be caught—?

He was restless and moody at home that evening. It was mid-July and the air was muggy. After he took his Irish setter for a walk, he sat in the darkened living room drinking beer in front of an electric fan, going over the cases in his mind.

At first he hadn't thought there was any connection. A body here, a body there. Every big city had them—murders that led nowhere, isolated crimes without obvious motives, without suspects.

Besides, the weapons were different. Some bullets were .38 caliber, some .45, but no two had been fired through the same barrel.

Still, he had come to sense—somehow he *knew*—that there was a connection somewhere.

If he could find it.

He had studied the victims' backgrounds without coming across anything that struck him as significant. Not that these men were saints. Some had police records, but for petty things—assault, domestic violence, drunken driving, evasion of family support orders. Nothing out of the ordinary. And whenever the police had homed in on a suspect—a business rival or a jealous lover—there proved to be a solid alibi.

It's got to be some nut, he thought. Some crazy bastard with a gun collection who goes around shooting people down for no reason.

A serial killer.

A light went on in the hall. It was Clara, his wife, going to the bathroom. On her way back she paused to look into the living room, then went on without saying anything. Bates heard her close the door to her room and snap the lock.

Sergeant Knowles came into the inspector's office early the following Tuesday, filling the doorway with his bulk. "We got something on this one," he said. There had been another murder the night before. "Shoe prints. They're kind of smeared, so we can't tell much from them."

"One of the cops probably made them," said Inspector Bates.

"Not this set. I was there first with Dunphy, and he saw them."

"But you can't tie them to the killer."

"No, not for sure, but those prints were made last night after it rained, and whoever made them, he was standing about the right distance from the body—about ten feet."

"That's not much to go on."

"Wait a minute. We found a second set."

"A *second* set?"

"They were in some mud about thirty yards away, and there were lots of them mixed up, like the guy had gone back and forth. You know. Like a lookout."

"A lookout?"

"Sure," said Knowles. "Why not? Makes sense, don't it?"

"Nothing makes sense," said Inspector Bates. He was troubled. He'd never heard of serial killers who worked in pairs.

It was raining that night, but Bud Bates was a man of habit and went out at the regular time with his dog to make their customary four-block circuit. He couldn't stop thinking about the murders. Were the victims chosen at random? It looked that way. They were virtually a cross section of society: rich, poor, and in-between; lawyers, construction workers, bartenders, accountants.

The only thing they seemed to share was the way they were killed.

"It's crazy," the inspector muttered. "The whole damned thing's crazy." This was a cop's nightmare. How long could it go on before he got a break—a witness, a solid lead, something definite to go on? The superintendent and the police board were riding him hard, demanding daily reports. The only piece of luck so far was the fact that the media had treated the killings as unrelated events, but this couldn't last long. Every morning he expected to see headlines: MURDER WAVE SWEEPS CITY or NIGHT KILLER STUMPS COPS.

A block from home, Inspector Bates let the setter off the leash. The dog went bounding ahead the rest of the way, where it circled the house, butted its way through a dog door onto the back porch, and waited for him to let it in. Bates shook some dry food into the dog's bowl, and then went to the kitchen for a can of beer. There was only a bottle of orange soda in the refrigerator. He cursed and turned away. No beer? Hell, that was *her* job. Why hadn't she put it on the shopping list? He'd looked forward to that beer. He'd *expected* it. Just one goddamned beer, was that too much to ask? She knew he wanted it—needed it—deserved it after putting in a long and frustrating day at work. Why, it was enough to drive a man over the edge, the worry and strain he had, and then a wife who didn't bother to see that he had enough beer, going off to her craft classes and her damned support group, women's stuff, and what about *him*, the guy who paid the bills—what kind of support did *he* get?

He had a daily conference with Knowles and Dunphy, who supervised the background checks and family interviews. Sometimes other plainclothesmen would be called in to report on various aspects of the investigations.

But they found nothing, knew nothing, didn't know in what direction to turn. All they could reasonably be sure of was what it wasn't.

It wasn't robbery. It wasn't drugs, either. Several victims had been casual users, and one was probably a small-time dealer, which might conceivably explain his murder—but not the others.

One victim had a Mob connection—and again, while he might have been a gang target, none of the others would have been.

There had to be a motive that fit them all. Otherwise it was mere coincidence, and Inspector Bates found that hard to believe.

But what was left?

"It's got to be thrill-killers," said Sergeant Knowles. "They get juiced up and cruise around, and when they see some guy alone they waste him."

"Could be crackheads," said Dunphy, a lean, sharp-eyed detective who was the best rifle marksman in Indiana and had a shelf of trophies.

"Crackheads wouldn't leave the money," said Inspector Bates.

"Well, maybe it's like Murder Incorporated," said Dunphy. "They do it for a price, and you pay them out of the insurance."

Inspector Bates shook his head. "Most of these guys weren't insured."

"So if it isn't crackheads and it isn't insurance, what the hell is it?" said Sergeant Knowles. "Maybe it's nothing. We got a string of murders, the only thing they got in common is we don't know who did them, so we figure they've got to be connected—but maybe they aren't."

"There's a connection, all right," Inspector Bates said, but he said it to himself later, after Knowles and Dunphy had gone and he sat alone in his office staring at the stack of files.

Was he going at this the right way? he wondered. And with the right tools? Knowles and Dunphy were hard workers—they'd done a lot of night and weekend duty—but they were the kind of cops who did best on standard procedures, giving suspects a working-over, digging up witnesses, that kind of thing. Knowles had crossed the line a few times, using rough stuff on people to get the truth out of them, and Dunphy, too, had been in hot water for what the police board called "excessive zeal," but fundamentally they were good, loyal men, and you could count on them to hammer their way through the tough cases.

Except these cases went beyond tough.

* * *

The inspector usually went to the police gunnery range once a month, but lately he'd been going two and three times a week. Firing weapons was a release. He liked the smell of the guns, liked their power and racket. It took him out of himself; he could forget his troubles there, even though the silhouette targets reminded him of the murder victims. Why couldn't he come up with the answer? What was it he wasn't seeing?

When he finished his turn, he went to the back to watch the others. Dunphy was there, showing off his skills. He could shoot with either hand; even with quick-draw unaimed fire, he always hit a vital part of the silhouette. Dunphy's sister, a policewoman, was almost as good, and some of the other female officers scored high, too. Bates had tried to get Clara interested in shooting — police wives had range privileges — but she never would. She was afraid of guns. She said they made her jumpy. Well, she was jumpy anyway. If Bates entered the room suddenly she'd give a start and pull back — but hell, he was good to her, compared to the way most men he knew treated their wives. All he insisted on was that she do her job. A wife had duties. If she didn't perform them, it was a violation of the marriage vows, and the husband had a right to make her do what God and custom intended a woman to do to satisfy a man's needs.

That's all he'd done.

And then two months ago she had moved into the spare room and put the lock on the door.

Thirteen this month — fourteen — fifteen. One was shot in an elevator, another in a deserted downtown parking lot late at night. The fifteenth was killed outside a motel. And still no witnesses, still no clues.

The inspector went through the files again, trying to make sense out of them. There had to be a pattern, he thought. Even one of those crazy patterns in which the victims had the same first name or were left-handed or had gone to the same high school.

There was no pattern, though. None that he could see. All he had were the spent bullets, the bodies, and those smeared shoe prints.

"The shooter and the lookout," the inspector mused. "Two guys."

"Maybe three guys," Sergeant Knowles said.

"Three?"

"Well, there could be a driver. A job like that—hit fast and get out—there's bound to be a driver."

"Why not an accountant, too?" said Inspector Bates sarcastically. "Somebody to keep the score?" But the idea of three killers working together lodged in his mind.

The sixteenth murder of the month took place the following night—and it introduced a new element.

The victim, a businessman, was shot to death in his apartment, apparently after he opened the door to the murderer. The body was found in the front hall by the man's wife and a neighbor woman when they returned from the movies. There had been no robbery; nothing was taken.

It was the first time a man had been shot down in his own home.

"It's got to be unrelated," said Sergeant Knowles. "Some crook figures nobody's home, and then the door opens, so he panics and shoots the guy."

But Inspector Bates suspected that whoever had killed the others had killed this one, too.

Which would mean it was planned.

They knew the man would be alone.

And what about the rest?

Bates had looked for indications of premeditation before, with scant success, but now he returned to the interviews and reports in the files. Had the others, too, been stalked and followed, their movements studied?

Some, he saw, might have been. Victim number fourteen worked late every Thursday. By the time he got to the parking lot where he was shot, it was bound to be deserted. Whoever killed him could have known that. Number seven went to the American Legion Hall now and then in the evenings. It was close to his house, so he walked, unless the weather was bad. Had someone watched him and figured out that he would have walked home that night? Number ten, killed in the park, was an evening jogger—but the report couldn't establish the direction of the shot. It could have come from the street—but it could have come from the shrubbery, if someone had waited there, someone who knew he'd be coming along.

So . . . if these victims weren't just unlucky bastards who happened to be in the wrong place at the wrong time, but had been *chosen*—

Furiously he shoved the pile of folders aside and left the office, cursing and muttering as he drove through the nighttime streets. There had to be a reason. *What reason?* On the way he thought he saw Knowles's car up ahead, an unmarked cruiser. It turned off before he could be sure, but he knew that Knowles and Dunphy were as obsessed with these murders as he was, and they'd be out somewhere, probably prowling the streets half the night.

His own house was dark. He thought maybe Clara was out at a support group meeting, until he realized it would be too late for that. She'd be in bed by now. He stumbled against a chair in the living room, and knocked a table over. "Can't we have any lights in this goddamned place?" he shouted, but she didn't answer. Fuming, he got the leash and took the setter out for the evening walk, but this didn't calm him. The murders walked with him, taunting him in the shadows of the street, making the blood beat in his ears, bringing his breath up quick. He let the setter loose and watched it dart ahead. At home again, he let the dog in from the back porch, and went into the kitchen. There was beer in the refrigerator, but he didn't want beer. He went along the hallway to her room and stood there, his fists clenched. How long had it been? Eight weeks? Nine?

She knew he was out there. He heard her suck in her breath and hold it, waiting to see what he would do.

He kicked the door until the lock broke. Then he entered the room.

July ended, and August began—with another murder. This time there was a witness, but the inspector didn't know whether this was a piece of luck or another source of confusion.

The witness, a young man in his late teens, saw not the killing but what was apparently the getaway car, which sped from the scene shortly before the youth came across the victim's body. He didn't get the numbers on the license plate—it was too dark for that, and besides, he wasn't suspicious then. But he was unshakable on one point.

It wasn't an Indiana plate.

Bates sat alone in his office for some time, trying to absorb this piece of information. Out of state? What the hell did that mean? Did it mean anything?

He lifted the telephone receiver and began punching numbers.

First he called his counterpart in Springfield, Illinois, and tried to be casual as he described his problem, playing it down as he spoke. Did the Springfield man have anything similar going on in his jurisdiction?

"Unsolved murders?" said the Springfield detective chief. "Well, sure, we always got some of those. You know, guys shot down. Maybe a few more this summer—five or six, say. How many you got?"

"Oh, a little more than that," said Inspector Bates.

He made other calls to law enforcement men in nearby states. Some reported an increase in murders; some didn't.

Inspector Lundgren of the Akron, Ohio, police told Bates there'd been fifteen such killings in recent weeks. No clues, no suspects, no apparent motives.

"Different weapons each time?" asked Bates.

"Oh, you got that, too?" said Lundgren.

Bates got similar reports from acquaintances in Louisville, Columbus, and Peoria. And his second cousin, Johnny Bates of the Grand Rapids, Michigan, police, told him they'd had six shooting deaths in July and three already in August. "You tell me, Bud," he said. "What's going on?" Inspector Bates said he was damned if he knew, but at least the newspapers hadn't done much with it, which maybe wasn't so strange, because there were 20,000 murders in the U.S. every year, so a few dozen more wouldn't make a big difference.

Except he knew it might be more than a few dozen. A lot more. He thought of calling other cities—Seattle, Boston, El

Paso—lots of places. But he decided not to. Not now. He really didn't want to know.

That night he broke into Clara's room again.

The next day he went to the superintendent and offered his resignation. "I don't know what this thing is, Jack," he said. "All I know is I can't handle it. You'd better get somebody else in here."

"Easy, Bud," the superintendent said. "What do you need? Extra men?"

"Damned if I know what I need. Every time I think I got part of the answer, something comes along that turns it upside down." Bates sat in the chair on the other side of the superintendent's desk. "All I've got is pieces, but I can't make them fit." He gripped the edge of the desk so hard his fingers whitened. "And now there's this out-of-state angle. What does that mean? They come in from the outside and do it?"

"That kid who saw the license plate? That's just one little thing."

"The way I figure it, Jack—and I'm guessing now—maybe it's the way the Mob used to operate. You know. Some people from Illinois or Michigan come here to do a job for the locals, and the locals, they go there to do one, back and forth like that, trading off, and they're all hooked up somehow. Some kind of network."

"Hold on, Bud. You're building a lot on a little. If you're saying it's the Mob, we'd have known it by now."

"It isn't the Mob. The Mob leaves signatures. These people don't leave anything."

The superintendent shook his head. "I know you're under pressure, but the idea of an interstate murder racket—you've got nothing to back that up. Hell, that would take a really professional outfit. I don't buy it. It doesn't add up. You don't even have a motive."

"Not yet."

"No motive, no suspects, nothing. And the victims—"

"What about them?"

"There's nothing that ties them together. No link. They've got nothing in common."

"They're all dead," said Inspector Bates.

He didn't see the note right away. The house was dark. He supposed Clara was at one of her support group meetings again. These women. Why didn't they stay home and take care of their husbands? He fed the setter and took a look in the refrigerator. Nothing to eat except last night's leftovers or a frozen dinner. He went to the bathroom to wash, and saw the note taped to the mirror. Clara had gone to her mother's in Peoria. She didn't say when she was coming back.

He ripped the note from the mirror and crushed it into a ball. Yes, her toilet articles were missing. He strode down the hall to her room. Her overnight bag was gone. So were some of her clothes. And she'd taken her alarm clock and that stupid stuffed bear she kept on the night table. He knocked the table over with a sweep of his hand. Damn her! She had no right to leave without his permission! He stood breathing hard, suspicions racing through his mind. She didn't get along too well with her mother. Maybe that was just a story. Suppose she'd gone somewhere else?

He thumbed through the address book beside the telephone in the hall and found her mother's number. She must have left that morning. Peoria was five or six hours away, so she ought to be there by now, unless—

It was Clara who answered his call. He felt a surge of relief through his anger. At least she hadn't lied.

"Clara—it's Bud. How come you—"

"I don't want to talk to you now."

"Wait a minute. I get home and all I find is this note, and—"

"It's too late, Bud."

"Too late, hell." He burst out in fury. "You can't get away with this! I'll give you exactly one day to get back here, understand? And then I'm coming to get you!"

"It's too late," she repeated, and hung up.

Inspector Bates stood glaring at the receiver. Sweat broke out on his face, his chest. In the kitchen the clock chimed. It was ten o'clock. Time to walk the dog. Still trembling with anger, he snapped the leash on the setter's collar and left the house. The air was cool; the quiet night soothed him. He was tired, though. His steps were heavy. He tried not to think of Clara, tried not to think of the murders.

A block from the house on his return, he loosed the dog, which bounded ahead, racing for the dog door on the back porch. It would be waiting for him: loyal and obedient. Devoted to him. Dogs could teach people a thing or two. Once a dog was yours, you could do no wrong. That was love. Clara's mother didn't like the dog; didn't like him, either. She and Clara had their differences, but they'd stick together now. Damned women; they'd gang up against a man.

A car passed by, slow. It pulled over to the curb up ahead. Its motor was still running; its parking lights were on. Maybe it was Knowles and Dunphy waiting for him. Could be another murder had happened. Another victim; another man.

Hell, he thought. Weren't they *all* men? That's what they had in common. They were all dead—and they were all men.

But there was still the *why*. He didn't know why.

No, it wasn't Knowles's car. Besides, it had a Michigan plate—and those two people getting out of the back were women, not men.

One of them was coming toward him.

Strangers in town, he thought. Probably lost, needing directions.

He'd never seen the woman before. There was a strange, apprehensive look on her face. Must be nervous about approaching a strange man on the street at night, he thought, even though there was her friend standing by the car and another one in the driver's seat.

"Inspector Bates?"

"That's me," he said, and he supposed she must be someone from Clara's group—but then he remembered that it was an out-of-state car.

She reached into her purse as he watched her, puzzled. *How come she knew his name? How could she know?* She was taking something out. It must be a different support group, he thought. Out-of-state. Women who got his name somehow. Got it from

Clara, got it from Clara's group. Knew his name, knew about him, knew where he'd be and when.

He stared at what she had in her hand, stared at if as if it were the answer to what he'd been searching for, stared at the pistol pointed his way.

So this was how it happened. Except—

He managed to utter the one word: "Why?"

The woman's hand was trembling, then steadied and held firm. "Rapist," she whispered, and she fired.

EDWARD D. HOCH

A TRAFFIC IN WEBS

Since it seemed to be a good year for series characters, I decided to try a new one—department store publicist Susan Holt.

It was during her college days that Susan Holt first encountered Walter Pater's essay on Leonardo da Vinci, with its celebrated evocation of the Mona Lisa. One phrase read: "She . . . has been a diver in deep seas, and keeps their fallen day about her; and trafficked for strange webs with Eastern merchants." That last part especially stuck in her mind. She did not know exactly what it meant, but she knew, like Mona Lisa, that it was something she wanted to do—to traffic for strange webs with Eastern merchants.

Careers often move in strange directions after graduation, and for Susan her course in art appreciation led somehow to a job in retailing, in the promotions section of Manhattan's most famous department store. She'd been there seven years, handling a good bit of the Christmas promotions and the displays that went with them, when Saul Marx, the head of the department, entered the office on the first working day after Christmas.

"Time to get started on next year's planning," he said, as he always did right after Christmas. "We've got to top this year."

"That'll take some doing," Mike Brentnor said from his desk opposite Susan's. "Got any ideas?"

Saul Marx always had ideas. That was why he was head of the department. "I've been reading about something really spectacular in Tokyo this Christmas. One of their big stores has a display of spider webs that—"

This was too much even for Brentnor. "Spider webs! I can find some up at our country place if you really want them."

"I'm serious," Marx assured him. "In fact, I want you to fly over there while the display is still in place. These aren't your ordinary spider webs. They're said to be bizarrely beautiful, almost like works of art. Once you see them I want you to phone me. If they're as wonderful as I've heard, we'll make the artist an offer to show them here next Christmas."

"The artist?" Mike Brentnor scoffed. "You mean the spider who wove them? What would I offer him—ten thousand flies?"

"There's a Japanese professor who creates them by feeding various drugs to the spiders—LSD, pot, that sort of thing."

"My God! We'd have the SPCA on our necks!"

Strange webs, Susan thought, and suddenly remembered that phrase from her college reading of Walter Pater: "trafficked for strange webs with Eastern merchants." "I'll go," she said almost without thinking. "Let me go to Tokyo."

Saul Marx turned to stare at her, as if only then remembering she was in the room. "You, Susan? Do you think you could handle something like this?"

"I arranged last year's spring show of exotic flowers, and I handled negotiations for the Best of Britain promotion two years ago," she reminded him. "You sent me to London for that."

He thought about it, but not for long. It was obvious Mike Brentnor wasn't enthused with the idea, and the only other person to send was on vacation till after New Year's. "I want someone to see these webs on display in the Tokyo store," Saul said. "They come down after New Year's, so it has to be this week. Are you up to that, Susan?"

She glanced at Brentnor, who was sinking into his pouting mode. "You bet I am!"

"Very well. See me in my office at two and we'll go over the details."

That evening she broke the news to Russell, an off-and-on live-in boyfriend who was rehearsing for a play down in SoHo. Arriving at the loft where the actors were just finishing their run-through, she got him aside. "Bad news, Russell. I can't make Nell's New Year's party. I have to fly to Tokyo for the store."

"What? Tokyo?" His face showed disappointment and the beginning of anger. "I was counting on it, Susan. What happened?"

"Brentnor doesn't want to do it and I'm next in line. I have to catch a display while it's up and negotiate to bring it to New York for next Christmas."

"Tokyo, for God's sake! There's no chance you can get back in time?"

"Today's the twenty-seventh already. I'm flying over Wednesday but it'll be late Thursday their time when I get in. That gives me Friday to see the display, and that's New Year's Eve. Even if everything went perfectly, it would be Saturday night or Sunday before I could get back. You can tell Nell how sorry I am."

"I don't know that I want to go alone."

"Why not? You know everyone."

"It's not the same going alone on New Year's Eve."

My God, she thought, *he's pouting just like Mike Brentnor at the store.* "I'm sorry," she said firmly. "It can't be helped. It's my job." He turned to walk away and she added, "What about tonight?"

He gestured toward the others. "I'm rehearsing. That's my job."

She nodded. "You can use the apartment while I'm gone if you wish. You still have the key, don't you?"

"It's around somewhere."

She turned away, trying to mask her annoyance. "I'll be back next week. You can call me."

"Sure."

Susan caught the Wednesday morning flight to Tokyo, settling in with her laptop computer for the long journey ahead. The trip took about fourteen hours, and Tokyo was fourteen hours ahead of New York time. Her eleven A.M. flight from New York would land her at Tokyo's Haneda Airport at three o'clock Thursday afternoon. It was a day lost to her, and there was little consolation in the fact that part of it would be regained on the return flight.

The airport was on the southern fringes of the city, and the newer Narita Airport was even farther away. Something she noticed in the terminal after landing was that she was taller than most of the Japanese men. Back in New York she rarely thought about her height. Suddenly one of these Japanese men was right in front of her, bowing from the waist. "Miss Susan Holt?" he asked in perfect English.

"I— Yes, that's me."

"I am Takeo Keio, manager of Fuji Star. I have come to meet you and guide you around our city."

"How nice!" She shook his hand. "This is my first visit to Tokyo. I was worried about finding my way around."

"We will claim your luggage and pass through customs. Then I will deliver you to your hotel."

"Thank you, Mr. Keio."

His limousine was long and white, like one that might be rented for a wedding back home. She settled into the plush leather seat, anxious for her first glimpse of the sprawling city. "Tokyo extends over nine hundred and thirty square miles," Mr. Keio explained as they headed away from the airport on the expressway into the central city. "Yet everything is crowded. It is a very confusing city to a visitor."

"New York is crowded, too," she assured him.

"Ah, but not like Tokyo. I have been to New York many times. Your stores are always a great inspiration to us."

"I understand Mr. Marx spoke to you on the phone about our interest in the webs display."

"Yes, yes! Professor Hiraoka has performed a miracle. Wait until you see his webs!"

"I'm anxious to get a look at them."

"Fuji Star is open late tonight if you care to—"

Susan glanced at her watch. It was after four already and she wanted nothing so much as a warm shower and a bed. "I'd better wait till morning," she pleaded. "The long flight really exhausted me."

"Very well." He spent the rest of the drive pointing out the sights to her, and when she remarked on a large structure that looked like the Eiffel Tower he announced proudly, "It is fifty-nine feet higher than the Eiffel. Our Tokyo Tower is for radio and television transmission. We have four major commercial rivals here—Fuji TV, which has no connection with our store, Nippon TV, Tokyo Broadcasting System, and TV Asahi. You may view them all on the set in your room. And that large building just ahead is your hotel. It is across the square, only a five-minute walk from Fuji Star."

"Thank you so much for the tour, Mr. Keio."

"I will look for you in the morning then? We will be closing early for the New Year's holiday, so I suggest you arrive before noon."

"I'll be in your office by ten," she promised.

Susan knew virtually no Japanese, so she spent little time with the network stations on her TV. She ordered dinner in her room and relaxed with a channel showing English-language news. Presently she stretched out on the bed to get more comfortable and fell asleep almost at once. When she awoke it was dark outside. She turned off the television and noted that the time was just after midnight. Then she took the shower she'd promised herself and went back to bed, sleeping restlessly until around five in the morning.

Looking out at the wakening city, Susan was surprised at the amount of early-morning activity. By the time she went down to breakfast at seven, the streets resembled a New York rush hour. The hotel restaurant served a passable Western breakfast. Back in her room she wrapped a small gift she'd brought for Keio, remembering that unwrapped gifts were considered rude in Japan. When she left the hotel just after nine, she noticed a Japanese youth follow her out.

As she waited for the traffic light to change, she suddenly had the impression of being shoved in the small of her back, but it happened so quickly she couldn't call it a deliberate act. Then she was falling, her leather briefcase flying from her grasp, just as a speeding taxi bore down on her. She landed on her hands and knees, feeling the pain, bracing for the instant impact of the taxi. Then a dozen hands were on her, yanking her out of harm's way as the driver slammed on his brakes.

"I— Thank you," Susan managed to gasp, looking down at her skinned and bleeding knees.

"Here, let me help you," a kindly British voice said. She looked up to see a slim man in a gray topcoat reaching out his hand to help steady her. "Are you staying at the hotel?"

"Yes." She grimaced in pain.

"I'll help you back inside and we'll see about those knees. You almost got yourself killed."

"The crowd just seemed to push me—"

Inside the lobby the Englishman issued a quick command in Japanese. "It doesn't look serious, but you should get it cleaned off. I've asked that someone escort you to your room."

She flexed her knees and both of them seemed to work properly despite the pain. "Thanks so much."

He presented his card. "I'm Geoffrey Peters, Miss Holt. With the British trade delegation. Please call me if I can be of further service."

She smiled at him, brushing the loose grime from her hands. "I will. Thanks again."

Upstairs she bathed her sore knees and put on a fresh pair of pantyhose. Luckily she still had time to reach the store by ten. It was not until she was halfway across the street, remembering the kindness of Geoffrey Peters, that she wondered how he had known her name.

Takeo Keio was awaiting her in his office on the seventh floor of Fuji Star, a massive department store filled with wonders Susan could barely imagine. After exchanging traditional gifts and sipping tea served by Rumiko, his pretty secretary, they set off to tour the store together.

"Did you take the escalator to my office?" Takeo asked.

"I was running a little late," she admitted. "I took the elevator." She told him about falling in the street.

"That is terrible! You could have been seriously injured or even killed! People here are so thoughtless at times with their pushing. You must avoid our subway tubes at all costs, especially during the rush hour when people are jammed together like cattle." He took her arm gently, as if to protect her. "But come—the first wonder of Fuji Star is at our escalators."

As they approached she saw a small Japanese woman dressed in a traditional kimono standing next to the moving staircase. The woman bowed politely and said something in Japanese. Only then did Susan realize that she was looking at a robot, an automaton equipped with an audiotape to supply information. "What did she say?"

Keio smiled proudly. "The ones at the escalators warn women to lift their kimono sleeves so as not to get them caught. Others around the store inform shoppers of special products and sales. I will admit we borrowed the idea of the automatons from Mitsukoshi, our largest competitor."

"It's wonderful!"

"Something for New York, perhaps?"

"Well—the bowing is what gives them charm, and that wouldn't be suitable in American stores."

"Ah yes!" Takeo Keio said. "A different culture."

It was obvious he was withholding the webs for the tour's finale, and they finally reached a small softly lit gallery on the top floor, not far from Keio's office. The sign next to the entrance was in both Japanese and English: THE STRANGE WEBS OF PROFESSOR HIRAOKA.

Susan entered slowly, seeing at first only a dozen glass-covered cases positioned on the walls, their contents shrouded in shadow. Then the spotlights went on, all at once, and she stood stockstill, frozen by the beauty and wonderment of what she saw. "These are exquisite," she said softly, as one might speak in church. Each of the cases held a single large spider web, its strands glistening with something like dew. The first web seemed perfect in all respects, the second off-center a bit. They seemed to grow more bizarre, of wilder formation, as she moved around the gallery. Here was one with two centers, and another with a dead fly caught at the end of a funnel-shaped tunnel. All of them glistened in the spotlights, shimmering magically. Susan stood for a moment at each one, even the most outrageous, as if expecting the web's maker to appear in one corner, carefully inching its way toward that dead fly.

"You are impressed?" the Japanese asked her with a proud smile.

"I must have these for New York. They are works of art."

"I cannot negotiate for America. You must speak directly with Professor Hiraoka. I know the prime minister himself has promised to come if he shows the webs in Tokyo next Christmas."

"Where can I find him?" she asked, unable to shift her gaze from the mesmerizing webs.

"He has been coming in every few days to tend to the webs, but tomorrow is the final day of the exhibit. The webs will be packaged carefully and returned to him."

"What tending do they need?"

"These glass fronts lift open and the professor sprays a special moisturizer on the webs. That accounts for their shimmer and the dewlike effect."

"Where does he live?"

"Professor Hiraoka teaches at Waseda University here in Tokyo and lives near the campus with his wife and family. If you wish to arrange an appointment it would be my pleasure to place my limousine and driver at your disposal."

"That's very kind of you," Susan replied. "I hate to bother him over the holiday weekend. Do you think it would be all right?"

"Certainly. For most of our people New Year's is a more important holiday than Christmas, but Professor Hiraoka is a Christian. I expect he will spend tomorrow working in his study like any other day."

"I'm surprised you celebrate Christmas at all in a Shintoist and Buddhist country."

He smiled slightly. "It is a secular holiday here. We have a place for Santa Claus if he helps to sell merchandise."

"Fuji Star has other stores around the country, do you not?"

He nodded. "Twenty-seven in all, although this is the largest. It is a publicly held corporation. I manage only this store, which has enough problems for me these days."

Susan glanced at her watch and did some quick mental arithmetic. Noon in Tokyo meant that it was ten P.M. the previous night in New York. Saul Marx had told her to phone him at home after she'd seen the webs, but it might be a bit late. Better to wait

till later and call him at the office. By that time she would have
spoken to Professor Hiraoka. "If you would give me the professor's phone number, I could call him for an appointment now."

"Certainly. I have it in my office."

Keio placed the call for her and said a few words in Japanese
to the professor. Then he turned the telephone over to her.
"Hello, Professor Hiraoka. My name is Susan Holt. I'm from
America."

The voice on the other end was strong, with a good command
of English. "Miss Holt, it's my pleasure! Takeo has told me
about you and your interest in my webs. I feel honored that a
great New York store would send someone over here to see
them."

"I'd like to speak to you about them, Professor. I know it's the
New Year's weekend—"

"Would you be free to come out here this afternoon?"

"Well—yes, of course. Mr. Keio has loaned me his car and
driver, so I should have no trouble finding the place."

"Very good. About three o'clock?"

"Perfect. I'll be there."

Professor Hiraoka lived on the outskirts of the city, in a pleasant
area where the crush of people and places, railways and high-
ways, finally began to abate. Keio's driver pulled up in front of
the house and said he would wait for her. The residence itself was
modest, and the door was answered by a young man of around
twenty who seemed vaguely familiar. He ushered her into a small
study where Professor Hiraoka awaited her.

He was tall for a Japanese, taller than Susan, and wore a black
silk kimono that was tied loosely in front, revealing pants and a
dress shirt beneath it. He bowed slightly and accepted the
wrapped gift she'd brought along. "How kind of you," he told
her. "This is my son, Yoichi."

Yoichi bowed too, and in that instant Susan remembered
where she had seen him before. He was the young Japanese in her
hotel lobby that morning, the one who had followed her outside
just before she was pushed into the street.

Yoichi left them and Professor Hiraoka settled down behind

his desk. He was nearly bald and wore tinted glasses that lent a scholarly yet mysterious look to his face. "I consider it a great honor that you have come here to my home."

"Your webs are creations of real beauty. How do you achieve it?"

He smiled. "By trial and error. I read of some experiment in which LSD was given to spiders and caused them to spin fantastic webs. I experimented in my basement workroom with all sorts of drugs and over time worked out the correct combinations for maximum results. I am aware that some people have an intense dislike for spiders, but no one can fail to appreciate the beauty of a magnificent web. Come, I will show you my workroom."

She followed him out to the kitchen, where his wife was beginning to prepare dinner. She was a small, pretty woman who hardly looked old enough to have a son of Yoichi's age. "Beware of the spiders," she cautioned Susan as they started down the cellar steps. Obviously her husband's work was something of a family joke.

The Hiraokas' home was one of the rare Tokyo houses with a basement. Professor Hiraoka switched on the lights and Susan found herself surrounded by more of the glass wall cabinets she'd seen at the store. "You'll notice we have airholes, and little pegs along the sides to encourage the spiders to start their webs. The pegs can be placed closer together if necessary, though naturally I like the webs to be as large as possible. Once they are spun I spray them with this special solution which causes them to glisten in the light and also strengthens the web somewhat."

"Could they be flown to America in these display cases?"

He hesitated for a moment. "I believe so, if they were well padded and insulated against the cold. A ship might be a bit smoother but it has the disadvantage of taking much longer. The webs should be inspected and sprayed every few days."

"Do the spiders accompany them?"

"No, no," he said with a chuckle. "Their work is finished. But I should go with them. Would this be a problem?"

"Of course not. We were planning on it. Certainly we'd want

you to supervise their installation and lighting, just as any artist would."

"The spiders are the artists. You might say I am merely their manager."

She turned from the webs and inspected the rest of the basement. On one wall was a locked cabinet, and he opened it for her. "I obtain the hallucinogens through the university. When I am away I return them. I take no chances on a burglary."

They discussed financial considerations, and Professor Hiraoka was quite reasonable. "How long would you want to show my webs at your New York store?"

She took a small calendar from her briefcase. "In our country the Christmas shopping season really starts the day after Thanksgiving. Naturally we have decorations in place before that, but Friday, November twenty-fifth, would be the opening day for the display. It would remain in place until Christmas, which is one month. Of course you would need time on both ends to prepare the display and then dismantle it. I would guess six weeks in all. In addition to your fee for the display we would pay living expenses for you and your wife in New York during that time. Would your son be coming too?"

"No, he has other interests."

"This evening I'll phone New York and have them fax me the agreement. I'm sure there'll be no problem over the terms."

They returned to his study. "I will look forward to this. My wife and I have been to New York only once before, many years ago, when I spoke at Columbia University."

Susan was warming to the whole idea. "I'm certain we can get you on some of the television talk shows. You must have humorous stories about spiders getting loose in the house."

"A few," he admitted with a smile.

"You said you read something about spiders on LSD. Is it possible that you also read the English writer Walter Pater? He wrote an essay on the Mona Lisa in which he mentioned trafficking for strange webs, and that's exactly what I'm doing."

"I never read Pater," he admitted, going to a section of his bookcase containing English-language volumes. "But I did read another Englishman, Jonathan Swift. Are you familiar with *Gulliver's Travels?*"

"Of course," answered Susan, who hadn't read it since freshman year in college.

"You may remember, here in the third part, when Gulliver visits the Academy of Lagado, he encounters a professor who fills his room with cobwebs of various hues, achieved by feeding colored flies to the spiders that spin them. He also feeds them gums and oils to strengthen the webs. The professor's object is to replace silkworms with spiders capable of producing colored silk strands strong enough to be made into clothing." He handed her the open volume.

The book was an 1865 edition of *Gulliver's Travels* with illustrations by Thomas Morten. It had been published by Cassel, Petter, and Galpin in London. The illustration did indeed show a man with sparse long hair, a beard, and glasses, wearing a ragged kimono, greeting visitors to his cobweb-covered room. Spiders could be seen in many of the webs. The man seemed to be Oriental and looked a bit like Professor Hiraoka.

"I'm surprised Swift's satire would be of interest to you."

Professor Hiraoka smiled at her. "And why shouldn't it be? After all, the only nonmythical country visited by Gulliver was Japan."

Susan phoned the store from her hotel room just before midnight. "It's almost the new year here," she told Saul Marx. "I'm celebrating all alone with a glass of champagne."

"Good for you," he grumbled. "We've got another fourteen hours to go. How are you doing with the webs?"

"Perfect! They're really beautiful things. We'll have pictures in every New York newspaper and half a dozen national magazines."

"You met the man who produces them?"

"Professor Hiraoka, yes. He's very nice and most cooperative. He and his wife are looking forward to visiting New York." Quickly she ran over the terms of the financial agreement. "Does that sound reasonable from your end?"

"What about the shipping expenses for the webs? You'd better check into that from your end."

"I already have." She gave him the figures. "And I assume our standard liability policy will cover insurance."

"We usually add a rider for special exhibitions like this."

"Fine. Could you type up the necessary agreement and fax it to me here at the hotel? I'll get Professor Hiraoka's signature on it tomorrow." She gave him the number of the fax machine in her room.

"It'll be waiting for you when you wake up in the morning. You've done a fine job with this, Susan."

"Thanks. I appreciate that. And happy new year."

"Happy new year to you, too."

She glanced at the bedside clock as she hung up the phone. It was still ten minutes before midnight. Suddenly the phone rang, and her first thought was that Saul Marx was calling her back about something.

"Hello?"

"Miss Susan Holt?" asked a male voice with a British accent.

"Yes?"

"I wonder if you remember me. We met outside your hotel this morning. My name is Geoffrey Peters."

"Oh, yes."

"I know it's very late, but I assumed no young American woman would retire before seeing in the new year. I'm downstairs in the bar and I wonder if I might buy you a drink."

"I was just getting ready for bed," Susan replied, "but I appreciate the invitation. Thank you. Perhaps another time."

His voice dropped slightly and the tone changed. "It's very important I speak with you about what happened this morning. It was not an accident but a deliberate attempt to kill you."

"I'm sure you must be mistaken," she said, but an image of Professor Hiraoka's son following her out of the hotel loomed large.

"Your life is in danger, Miss Holt. We must talk."

For a split second she considered inviting him up to her room, but immediately dismissed the thought. For all she knew, the debonair Geoffrey Peters could be a robber or a rapist. "I'll be down in fifteen minutes," she decided, "but only for one drink."

He was waiting in the bar, seated alone in a corner booth. The television set had finished proclaiming the new year, and the bar's few customers were beginning to settle down. Most seemed to be Europeans, though there were a few Americans, too. Peters wore a gray suit with a brightly striped vest. Earlier she'd only had the impression of a slim British gentleman. Now she saw that he was probably in his late thirties, with a bit of a twinkle in his eye. Seeing that, she wondered if this was all an elaborate ploy to get her into bed with him.

"So glad you could come," he said loudly enough for anyone who might be interested. "Would you join me in a champagne toast to the new year?"

She saw the open bottle with two glasses. "I just had one in my room, but I suppose another wouldn't harm me."

He agreed, and poured her a glass. "As I told you on the phone, I'm sorry to disturb you so late. But I believe it is vital that you know your life is in danger." His voice had dropped much lower.

"I hope you're just exaggerating."

"I wish I were. You were pushed in front of that taxi this morning by a young Japanese man. I believe he did it deliberately."

She took a sip of the champagne. "Let's start at the beginning, Mr. Peters."

"Please call me Geoffrey."

"All right, Geoffrey. Why were you watching me this morning?"

"I didn't say I was."

"You knew my name. You were watching me just as he was. How do I know it wasn't you who gave me a push?"

He ignored her question and said, "The young man who pushed you is Yoichi Hiraoka, the professor's son."

"I suspected as much," she admitted. "I recognized him when I visited their house today. But why? He didn't even know me."

"Japan has many of the same problems as Germany these

days—a resurgence of the kind of right-wing factions that helped bring on the Second World War. Hiraoka's son is active in such a group."

She remembered his father saying simply that he had other interests. "But why would he try to kill me? He'd never even met me. And what business is it of yours?"

The Englishman said quietly, "We were advised of your mission. So was Yoichi's group."

"Mission? What mission?" Susan was growing angry now. "I'm over here to arrange an exhibition of Professor Hiraoka's webs for next Christmas, back in New York."

"How long are you staying?"

"The store is faxing me the agreement overnight. If I can obtain Professor Hiraoka's signature tomorrow, I'll take a plane out of here the next day."

"They don't want that agreement signed. That's why an attempt was made on your life."

"What you're saying doesn't make any sense," she argued. "Why should a rightist group care about those webs and what happens to them?"

"We don't know. The only thing certain is that Fuji Star department store has become a focus of their activities. Group members under surveillance are often seen to enter the store and browse around, though they rarely buy anything."

"Are they shoplifting?"

"No. They've been watched very carefully, and they do nothing suspicious."

"Do you work for the Japanese government?"

He smiled slightly. "I'm doing some antiterrorist work for them under contract. That's all you need to know."

Susan finished the champagne. "Thank you for warning me about Yoichi. I'll be on my guard. Good night, Mr. Peters."

He stood up as she left the table. "Happy new year, Miss Holt."

She slept a bit later the following morning, and when she awoke she was surprised to see so many people on the street, even on New Year's morning. Many of the stores appeared to be open.

On her way down to breakfast she picked up the contract that had been faxed to her room and reviewed it while she ate. When she was satisfied it was in order she used her fax machine to make several more copies.

Susan could see the Mitsukoshi department store from her hotel, and she decided to visit it. Tokyo's largest, it boasted a multistoried entrance hall and a grand staircase with a huge sculpture representing the goddess of sincerity. The escalators, as in Fuji Star, had bowing automatons warning about kimono sleeves. She bought a small gift, a blue cotton *yukata*—a loose-fitting garment that went over the head and tied around the waist, to be worn after bathing or at the beach. It would look good on Russell, if he'd gotten over his anger at her sudden business trip.

On the street Susan was very careful not to stand too near the curb and she kept an eye out for Professor Hiraoka's son, but there was no sign of the young man. With some time to kill before she returned to the professor's home for his signature on the contracts, she decided to return to Fuji Star on the off chance that Takeo Keio might be at work, even on a Saturday that was New Year's Day. Japanese managers, after all, were notorious for hard work and long hours.

The store was about as crowded as Mitsukoshi's had been, and she was sorry now that she hadn't bought her gift here. She made her way to Keio's office on the top floor and asked his secretary, Rumiko, if he was in.

"Yes," she replied with a smile. "He had a visitor who brought him a New Year's gift, but I believe he's free now. Let me see."

She went to the door of his office, knocked, and opened it. Her short, startled cry brought Susan to her side at once. Takeo Keio was slumped over his desk, his head resting in a pool of blood. He'd been shot through the left temple.

The police took charge quickly. Rumiko, sobbing at her desk, told them what little she knew. A young Japanese man had arrived to see Takeo Keio at eleven that morning, saying he had a New Year's gift for him. There was indeed a gift, a small hand-carved Buddha that sat on the desk just at the edge of the blood from Keio's fatal wound. Rumiko had heard nothing unusual from the office, indicating that a silenced pistol had probably been used.

"They were together about ten minutes," Rumiko said. "Then I went over to the files. As I returned to my desk I saw the young man walking away toward the elevator."

Susan watched while the police searched the office carefully. "A silenced pistol is usually an automatic," the detective in charge explained to her. "We want to find the ejected cartridge case, if the killer didn't take it with him." He spoke good English and smiled to put her at ease. Only his eyes were cold. He'd said his name was Sergeant Shimane.

There was nothing on the desktop except the Buddha and a few of Keio's papers. The wastebasket was empty this early in the day. They went over the carpeted floor and found nothing at first, until one detective felt around the leg of a chair and came up with the cartridge case. Sergeant Shimane examined it carefully and dropped it into a plastic evidence bag.

"Now tell me what you were doing here, Miss Holt," he said.

"I had business with Mr. Keio. I'd seen him yesterday, and I returned to speak with him again today."

"On New Year's?"

"I took a chance he'd be here, since the store was open."

The detectives had finished their examination of the office without finding anything else the killer might have left. Photographers and fingerprint men moved in, and Sergeant Shimane escorted her outside. Rumiko had recovered enough to telephone the store's main office with news of the killing. Shimane questioned Susan some more, noted the hotel where she was staying, and advised her to contact him before she left the country. Then she was free to go.

With Keio's limousine no longer available, Susan took a taxi out to Professor Hiraoka's residence. The professor's wife answered the door, and Yoichi was nowhere to be seen. The professor came out of his study to greet her. "I have been looking forward to your arrival," he said, seeming genuinely pleased.

"Before you sign the agreement, I'm afraid I must tell you some bad news. I've just come from Fuji Star. Takeo Keio has been shot to death in his office."

"What? What's this you're saying?" He seemed startled by the news. "Who could do such a thing?"

"The police are looking for a young man. I know nothing more about it."

He shook his head. "Terrible, terrible—"

Susan removed the contract from her briefcase. "Professor, there are one or two questions I must ask you."

"Go ahead."

"Have you received any recent threats regarding the display of your webs? Is there anyone who didn't want them shown in America?"

"There've certainly been no threats. Are you implying that Keio's murder is somehow connected with my webs?"

"I don't know. It's a possibility."

"The only one opposed to showing the webs in America is my son, Yoichi, who has strange nationalistic ideas at times."

"Is Yoichi here now? I'd like to see him."

"He left early this morning to meet friends."

The professor's wife had been hovering near the study door. Now she entered, to his great displeasure. "Naomi—do not interfere in this!"

But she wouldn't be silenced. "What is this about my son?" she asked. "What has he done?"

"I don't know," Susan said. "I just want to talk to him."

"Those people," she muttered, then switched to Japanese.

They talked, or argued, for some minutes. Finally Naomi left the room and Susan turned to the professor. "What is the trouble?"

"She fears Yoichi is a member of a militant group bent on violence."

"Do you think it is true?"

"I know it is true," he said with a deep sigh.

"I hope we won't have any trouble in New York," Susan said. She produced the contract. "Please sign these. I'll explain anything you don't understand."

He started reading the contract, pausing now and again for the meaning of some word or phrase. Finally satisfied, he affixed his signature to three copies just as they heard the front door open.

"Whose taxi waits outside?" a voice yelled. She knew it was Yoichi.

He entered the room and saw her, throwing down the heavy jacket he'd been wearing. His face twisted with fury as Professor Hiraoka tried to calm him. "You have signed the contract, Father! You have signed my death warrant!"

Naomi Hiraoka appeared behind him, trying to grab her son's shoulders. He fought her off, and the professor shouted something in Japanese. It was an angry scene, and Susan wished she was out of there. She felt like one of those helpless flies, trapped in a web she couldn't comprehend.

Yoichi broke free of his mother's grasping hands and ran out of the house with his father's voice shouting after him. He'd left his heavy jacket on the floor and Susan picked it up without thinking. She felt the weight in the pocket and immediately imagined a small gun, the weapon that had killed Takeo Keio. It was not a gun but some sort of remote-control device.

"What's this?" she asked his parents. "Is it for a garage door?"

But Professor Hiraoka and his wife continued arguing, ignoring her for the moment. She dropped the gadget into her purse.

"I must go," she told them, scooping up the signed contracts.

They ceased their argument and Professor Hiraoka tried to regain his composure. "You must excuse us. Being the parents of a rebellious son is not always easy in today's Japan."

"Nor in today's America," Susan sympathized. "Did he know Takeo Keio?"

"He'd met him at the opening of my webs exhibit, of course. Yoichi is often at Fuji Star, for whatever reason."

"Has he been in trouble with the police?"

"I fear so. He has been arrested in demonstrations at the airport and the university."

"What did he mean about this contract being his death warrant?"

"I do not know. He wished me to exhibit the webs at a celebration next December marking the hundredth anniversary of our victory in the Sino-Japanese War, but I was against the idea from the beginning. My webs are works of art, not militaristic celebrations."

Susan stuffed the contracts into her briefcase. "My taxi is waiting. I must be on my way. A copy of the contract will be returned to you together with the advance payment agreed upon. We will be in touch about the shipping dates for the webs."

"I would like to travel with them, on the same plane if possible."

"I think we can arrange that. I'll look forward to greeting you and Mrs. Hiraoka in New York next November. And I hope your personal problems are resolved."

He bowed. "Thank you, Miss Holt."

Susan went back to her hotel and ordered a sandwich from room service. The contracts were signed; her job was done. She could be on a flight to New York in the morning. The murder of Takeo Keio was no concern of hers, whether or not Yoichi Hiraoka had pulled the trigger.

Still . . .

She opened her purse for a tip when the room-service waiter arrived and saw Yoichi's remote-control device resting there. She'd forgotten all about it. Pointing it toward the window, she pressed the button on top.

Nothing happened.

She pointed it toward the room's television set and nothing happened.

She sat down and ate her sandwich.

Was it something connected with Fuji Star? Yoichi frequented the store, and Geoffrey Peters had told her that other members of the rightist group did too. Susan walked to the window and stared across the square at it.

One last time, one last visit, she decided. She left the briefcase and contracts in the room but took the remote-control unit with her. Nervously crossing the wide street, expecting to see Yoichi lunging toward her at any moment, she made it to the store without incident. As she entered a greeter was telling customers in Japanese and English, "We will be closing in thirty minutes because of the holiday."

She took the escalator up to the top floor and noticed that a police officer stood guard at the door to Keio's office. Walking down the aisle toward the furniture department, she pressed the remote-control gadget in her pocket. Nothing happened.

This is foolish, she decided. If the purpose of the device was to set off some sort of explosive, she might blow herself up by accident. She headed for the down escalator. The waiting automaton bowed and the mouth on the white doll-like face began voicing a warning about kimono sleeves. She pressed the button in her pocket as if to zap it.

Instantly the voice was cut off, overridden by another message in Japanese. Strange.

Customers were beginning to leave the store, streaming down the escalators with their bags. Clerks were cashing up for the day. She waited until no one was near and approached the bowing figure again, activating the remote control in her pocket. Once again the substitute message came from the bowing figure.

"We are closing now," an employee told her, hurrying past.

"Thank you."

She turned, not knowing what to do, when suddenly she saw the Englishman Geoffrey Peters coming from the direction of the furniture department. "What are you doing here?" she asked.

"I heard about Keio's death and came as soon as I could. I understand you found his body, along with his secretary?"

"That's right, and I may have discovered why he was killed. You told me this store seemed to be a focal point for activity by young rightists."

"Yes," he agreed, staring at the remote-control gadget she produced from her pocket. "What's that?"

"I found it in the pocket of Yoichi Hiraoka's coat. Watch this!"

The bowing figure voiced her special message and Peters was taken aback. "This unit overrides the standard taped message with a special message. These rightist youths have been coming here for instructions, triggering this device when no one else was within earshot." He took the gadget and tried it himself.

"Keio was seen doing this, and someone killed him."

"Perhaps," Peters said a bit uncertainly.

"What does the message say?"

" *'Meet me in the gallery after the store closes.'* "

"That's now!"

"I just came from that area and I saw no one."

"Come on," she urged.

He followed her back to the furniture department, to the gallery entrance, and the spotlights came on as they walked past the sign announcing Professor Hiraoka's wonderful webs. Stretched out on the floor beneath the first case was the body of Yoichi Hiraoka.

"He's been shot," Geoffrey Peters told her, kneeling to examine the body. "We're too late."

"The killer can't be far."

It was clear to her now. She knew what had to be done. "I'll get the police," Peters said, leaving her for a moment.

Susan walked past a white-faced automaton that bowed in her kimono and announced a sale on the second floor. She hurried on, ignoring it. Another blocked her path, bowing, starting to speak as she came out of her bow, and Susan saw the silenced pistol slide from the sleeve of her kimono, coming up fast toward Susan's face.

Then she heard a deafening gunshot behind her as Peters fired and the figure toppled backward, blood gushing from her shoulder.

"My God!" Susan gasped, frozen with fright.

"It's all right," Peters said, kicking the gun away from the traumatized fingers. "I'll get some of this paint off the face and we'll see who it is."

"I already know who it is," Susan managed to tell him. "It's Takeo Keio's secretary, Rumiko."

Sergeant Shimane and his men were still in Keio's office when they heard the shot and came running. Susan's legs were a bit wobbly as she sat down on one of the chairs. "Call an ambulance!" Shimane ordered one of his men. "What happened here?"

"She killed Yoichi Hiraoka," Peters said, "and she tried to kill Miss Holt here. Yoichi's body is in the gallery."

"Keio's secretary?" the detective asked, unable to believe it. "I just finished questioning her an hour ago!"

"She killed Keio, too," Susan assured them. "No doubt with this same gun. We should have known her story about the young visitor with the gift for Keio was a lie. The little Buddha was sitting alone on the desk. When you searched for the cartridge you found nothing else on the floor, and the wastebasket was empty." Shimane and Peters both looked blank. "Don't you see? There was no wrapping for the gift! In Japan gifts are always wrapped—it's rude not to! If the killer bothered to bring a gift at all, it would have been wrapped. If he took the wrapping with him he'd have taken the gift too. Rumiko lied about the visitor. After she killed Keio she left the Buddha on his desk to bolster her story, forgetting that she should have left a wrapping, too. She's the one who's been doctoring these automatons so they'd deliver special messages to members of the youth group. It was a perfect method of getting instructions to them quickly without the danger of using a tapped telephone."

"And Keio discovered what she was doing?" Sergeant Shimane asked.

"Of course. That's why she had to kill him. The group wanted Professor Hiraoka's webs to be displayed in Tokyo next year because"—even as she spoke, the whole plot was unfolding in her mind—"because the prime minister himself had promised to visit them. There would be an assassination attempt, a bomb planted by Yoichi in one of his father's wooden frames, a signal for an uprising. When the contract was signed and Yoichi knew he had failed, he came here to report to Rumiko. He knew even without his remote-control unit that she'd be waiting in the gallery. She figured his death would be blamed on the stranger who shot Keio, so she used the opportunity to kill him. As Yoichi must have feared, the organization had no further need for him once he'd failed in his mission to win his father's exhibit for the Sino-Japanese centennial. Rather than a co-conspirator, he had become a danger to them."

"She was clever," Peters agreed. "The kimono and the face paint allowed her to pose as one of the automatons if someone came along while she was waiting for a meeting. When she recovers from her wound I think she'll be ready to talk about the others involved."

Susan felt suddenly tired. She'd run down at last. At that moment she only wanted to be out of there and on her way home. As it turned out, she stayed on for Yoichi's funeral service and helped to comfort his parents. Geoffrey Peters was there too, perhaps to comfort her. Trafficking with Eastern merchants hadn't been at all what she'd expected.

D. A. McGUIRE

WICKED TWIST

This novelette, complete with map, is told from the viewpoint of a twelve-year-old boy who knows a great deal about clamming along the Cape Cod seashore. As the first published mystery of author Diane A. McGuire, it's a most impressive debut. Mystery Writers of America named it the winner of the Robert L. Fish award as the best first mystery story of 1993.

What's your name again . . . kid?"

I hadn't liked him from the start, this obnoxious, tobacco-chewing cop. Imagine that, a cop chewing tobacco, a thick brown wad of it. I didn't think that very professional, or the way his fat belly poked out over a worn brown belt. It didn't match his pants, and that told me something right away: He'd gotten to fat for the belt that did match his policeman's uniform. As my friend Mr. Hornton would have said, this cop was not "a man of detail."

But I was. Even though I wasn't exactly a man, not yet. Me, I *saw* detail, I lived and breathed detail. So no cop was going to brush me off so easily; after all, it was *me* who found the body.

"Herbie Sawyer," I answered respectfully. But I didn't say "sir" because I didn't think he deserved it. I was sure of it when he answered, sneering as he did.

"Herbie? As in Herbert? Hell of a thing, naming a kid Herbert." He was writing this down on a clipboard that stuck out of his fat side. It was obvious he wasn't accustomed to this, to standing on a muddy bank, one foot propped in the sand, the other on a dune that was slowly sinking under his immense weight. If he didn't move soon, he was going to tumble right down the bank and into the inlet.

I would have liked to have seen that.

"It was my father's name," I said sharply.

"Oh, that a fact?" Another sneer down his long, fat nose. Italian, probably. Figured. Then I shot that thought out of my head as fast as it had entered it. My mother wouldn't have liked it.

The cop turned, spat a thick brown curd of tobacco juice into the grass, then moved quickly before he could tumble down the little incline. There were four people down there now, in addition to the body. The first was a fellow in a pale sport jacket—he must have been the medical examiner. They'd had to wait for him; supposedly he'd been getting ready to go out fishing. Tough luck for him, but with this heavy fog it probably would be better to wait. Then there was another cop, dressed a lot more professionally than this fat one. He was kind of on his knees, holding a plastic tarp, probably to cover the body with. There was a woman down there with them; she was black and neatly dressed, in civilian clothes, jeans, and a red sweatshirt, but I got the feeling she was a cop, too. She was photographing the body, the sandbar it was stuck on, and the immediate area—marsh, banks, even the mouth of the inlet facing out to the bay. And there was a third man; he was the most interesting of the group. He wasn't dressed like a cop either, but I knew he had to be one. He seemed to be in charge, what with the way he talked to the others and then stood back to let them do their jobs. After a few minutes he moved in, motioning to the woman to take some extra shots. He was wearing dark pants and a pale shirt and was a bit on the heavy side but had something about him called "presence."

Yes, that's how my mother would have put it: The man had presence, like Burt Lancaster or Kirk Douglas—my mother was hopelessly stuck back in the fifties.

And now this man was starting to walk up toward us. As he did, I gave the fat cop my address, my mother's name and employer, and information on how I'd found the body. "You the kid who called us?" the other man said, the one with "presence," as he came up the incline. Maybe he was some kind of detective, or just a cop called out of bed at five-thirty on a Sunday morning. No, he would have put on a uniform if he had one. He was a detective. I had him pegged right from the start. I also had him pegged as someone I was going to like a hell of a lot better than the tobacco-spitting, rude cop.

"Yes, sir," I said quickly, balancing my bike against my leg. I swear both legs were going to sleep; I felt like *I* wanted to go to sleep. The bait in my bike basket was starting to reek, and I wanted nothing more than to forget my traps, go home and sit out on the porch, and maybe read some comic books.

Except I'm sure I wouldn't have seen the pages, or the characters in them, or any of the writing, half of which I skipped over anyway. I would have seen her, just *her*. The body of the woman down there, the one they were covering up now. The body I'd seen that other cop, the uniformed one holding the tarp, get sick over. The body the medical examiner, if that's who he was, was shaking his head over as he dictated something into a cassette recorder attached to his belt.

The body of the woman I'd found in the early-morning fog down in the inlet.

"Herbie Sawyer, age twelve," the fat cop said, showing the clipboard to the other man. "Haven't finished getting a complete statement from him yet. I don't think he can tell us very much, just a kid out here chubbing—has some traps over there in the marsh. Ain't that right, Herbie?"

"Yeah, I was chubbing," I answered directly.

"You didn't touch anything, did you, Herbie?" the other man said, a man who would later introduce himself to me as Jake Valari, a detective sergeant and the only detective we had on the small police force here in Manamesset Village.

"No. Who'd want to?" I answered, making a disgusted face. "I mean, no, sir, of course not. I came running up here and went to Old Man Miller's shack and called the police."

At the mention of Old Man Miller, both men smiled. The fat, rude one snickered. Old Jedadiah Miller had been of absolutely no use. When I'd told him about the body, he'd nearly fallen across his tiny kitchen and pulled a half-empty bottle of Jack Daniel's off the counter. It was me who'd called the police, dialed 911 like I was supposed to.

And in a way that part had been exciting, watching the ambulance come tearing up, then the police cars. Exciting for a while.

And then a drag, waiting up here until they got the medical examiner out, then waiting some more as they located the town police chief. Turned out he was on an overnighter on Martha's Vineyard and it would be a while until he could get a ferry out. Planes were all fogged in. So that's probably why this other cop, this Detective Valari, was in charge.

Anyhow, they'd told me to wait up with the old man (he was sleeping, dead drunk) until they got around to me.

But it was me who found her, the body down in the inlet, on the gray muck and sand, at about five-fifteen this morning, with the tide still going out. It was now seven-fifteen. The sky was brightening up a bit, the fog drifting off, though it would be nearly noon before it'd all be gone. We'd had three days of this heavy morning fog. It rolled out around noontime, drifted back in by early evening. Sometimes it was like that down here on the southernmost tip of Cape Cod, at Manamesset Bay.

"Can I go soon, sir?" I asked the detective. I bumped against my bike meaningfully. I didn't usually drag it down through the dunes and up to the bank, but I hadn't trusted leaving it down by the road. Some of the summer kids thought nothing of taking a local's bike, driving it down into the marsh, thought it was a big joke. Anyhow, I wanted these two to see how anxious I was to go.

The detective just looked at me a moment. Like I said, he was on the heavy side, but he had a different carriage from the other man. That's how my mother would have put it: He carried himself well. This man's weight came from good living. I was sure of it, from playing cards and passing around the snacks as he did so, or from going out fishing with his buddies and eating out at good restaurants. Maybe even from making his own food— pasta. Yeah, I could imagine him stirring a big pot of pasta, making up his own sauce. The other fellow, his weight came from beer. I'd have known that sloppy, overlapping belly anywhere.

I also knew the smell.

"If you've given us all the information we need, then you can go. We may still want to talk to you again later, Herbie." He also had steadier feet, up here on the uncertain edge of the bank. And as he looked around and across the marshy inlet, then up toward the pale gray sands of Gray Tides Beach, he asked, "Come out here very often, Herbie?"

"To chub, sir? Sometimes, but all of that—" I pointed in the direction he was looking, across the marsh, most of which lay on the other side of the inlet. It was the inlet, a hundred feet from side to side at its mouth, where it emptied into Manamesset Bay, that broke this stretch of coastline into two beaches, Gray Tides to the north, and Miller's behind us where we stood. But we could see barely a quarter of the way up Gray Tides; fog obscured the rest. Boothby Harbor was in that direction, and Boothby shores, Boothby Village. "It's private, I mean, it's all bird sanctuary. I . . . we never go in there, sir."

I was lying; he knew I was lying, too. I could tell by his face. Still, he smiled, then fished inside his shirt pocket for a pack of cigarettes. The other one, the one I didn't like, had shifted his weight again So he was no longer in imminent danger of falling down the bank. Too bad.

"Gray Tides Bird Sanctuary and Preserve, yes, I know. You don't usually see too many people down here."

Was that a question? I answered like it was. "No, sir. There are too many other beaches around here, nicer beaches with lifeguards and the rocks and seaweed all cleared away. I mean, especially up at Boothby. The tourists don't come here much. It's too wild. We sometimes see a few birdwatchers, maybe some scientists, you know? From Woods Hole, or people studying green flies. There's boxes all through there."

"Boxes?"

"To catch the flies in. I guess they count them. I"—I shrugged; there'd been flies, just a few, on her body—"don't really know."

"But I think you do," Sergeant Valari hadn't lit his cigarette yet. He was studying me in a way I didn't exactly like. "I think you do know, quite a lot, that is. Maybe we *can* have a little chat now, what do you say?"

Why did I get uneasy then? Because something about a cop, a smart cop, always makes a kid uneasy?

"How about up there?" He motioned to the shack behind us up the shore aways, then lit his cigarette. It was Old Man Miller's shack—and Old Man Miller was still up there, sleeping off all the booze he'd drunk over the last two hours.

"Sure." I shrugged and gently lowered my bike back onto the sand.

He got rid of the fat one with an "I'll finish up with him here" and a passing of the clipboard. We watched him slip and slide down the bank toward the inlet. Then we just stood there a minute, me and this smart cop, and I watched the scene below while he read the information Officer Carleton had written down about me.

And what I had found. How I had come down to check my chub traps, two hours before low tide. How I'd seen something bright red there, lying on the small sandbar that had formed this summer in the middle of the inlet. It was new, that sandbar, and strange, fixed behind a pile of old crates that must have fallen off a boat somewhere out in the bay. The tides, or a storm, had brought them in, broken them up a bit, then fixed them in the muck, right in the middle of the little waterway near its mouth. They wouldn't last long; the next storm, hurricane, whatever, would pry them loose, or the water itself would rot them out. It didn't matter to a sandbar; sandbars are a temporary kind of thing. They form behind anything for any length of time. This one had formed long enough to catch a dead body on it.

Wearing a red shirt, brown checked knee-length shorts, and a rope belt tied around them. Remember that, I said to myself. It's a detail. And there were sneakers on her, too, an old fashioned Keds style that so many adults were wearing today. So that wasn't really unusual, the sneakers I mean, except for the fact that there were holes in them—right at the toes, both of them.

She had blond hair, long and untied. And her hands were stretched out ahead of her. In fact, she'd looked like one of those Muslims, bent over and praying toward the bay. At first I'd thought it was just a woman, a live one, doing some crazy exercises on the little bar that barely broke the water as the tide went rushing out. Then, as I got closer, I thought maybe she was digging for clams; with the fog so thick it was hard to see just exactly *what* she was doing. But when I got close enough and could hear the buzz of green flies—they flew off in a green cloud as I splashed through the water toward her—I knew she was dead. Just lying there, dead. She wasn't moving, just lying kind of on her side, both arms spread forward, her face turned sideways and away from me. One leg was stretched out straight; the other was kind of bent and pointing down into the sand. Anyhow I figured she had to be dead, lying there in half an inch of water, so still. Only the tips of her hair were moving, swaying back and forth in the water like seaweed pulsing in shallow water.

So I splashed my way through the water—the tide was going out, and the water on both sides of the bar was about ten inches deep. I could feel it pulling me as I walked, then I was up on the bar with her. I couldn't see her face, not yet, but I could feel my heart thumping in my chest. I was wondering if I should cry out, except who would hear me? Maybe I should have jumped back in the water right away, climbed the bank, and run up to Old Man Miller's shack. Of course, that's what I soon did do, but I suppose a lot of people would have done that right off; they never would have gone down to . . . well, look her over.

But then, part of me was saying, What if she *is* alive? And just hurt? Well? What about *that*? So even though my heart was going crazy a mile a minute, and I was starting to feel queasy in my stomach, I looked down at her. I was absorbing details.

The clothes. The hair. The rope belt—it looked like clothesline twine. The sneakers. And her fingernails: long and colored a pale pink, except most were broken and cracked. Some had a dark black line stuck deep beneath them, near the flesh. I could see all this only on her left hand; it was turned in an awkward position down on the sand. Her other one was partly in the mud. But on her left: thumbnail broken; index and middle finger, too. Black lines under the index, middle, and ring fingers. And something white, like a glob of sea foam, jabbed right on the nail of her little finger.

That's when I walked around her, carefully, like she might suddenly jump up and bite me. I saw her face—two glassy, blackish eyes where the green flies were landing—and watched in strange fascination as a fiddler crab crawled out of her open mouth.

The cop had said something to me; I guess I wasn't paying attention. I turned to him.

"Sorry, sir, I was . . . daydreaming. What did you say?"

"You're damned polite for a kid your age. What's with all this 'sir' stuff? Who taught you to be so polite, or is it all an act, Mr. Herbie Sawyer?" He took a long drag on his cigarette.

"My mother, sir," I answered stiffly. But I had a question of my own suddenly. Down on the other side of the inlet the cop who'd gotten sick earlier was unrolling something that looked like yellow tape off a spool. The fat cop was picking up some sticks. Bending over wasn't easy for him; he was grunting and groaning as he did and making the other cop run around like crazy. I guessed they were going to put the sticks in the marsh, and up and down the inlet, to kind of cordon off the area.

"What are they doing?" I asked, then, remembering, added, "Sergeant."

"Just a formality, son, to keep the reporters away, and anyone else who comes nosing around later. And they will. They always do." A sigh as he watched with me. "To keep them from disturbing the area—you must watch TV, don't you?"

"Yes, I do," I said. "But the area's going to be disturbed real soon anyhow, isn't it? And you won't be able to do a thing about it, will you?" I turned to look at him, adding, "Sir."

"What do you mean by that?"

"The tide, sir, the tide will be on its way back. It's dead low at seven oh-two. Right about now. So it'll be turning around and coming back in, and that'll disturb the crime scene, won't it?"

"Dead low?" he said with a frown, as though it should already have occurred to him. And then: "Crime scene? What do you mean, 'crime scene'?" He sounded irritated suddenly. "We don't know any crime has been committed, Mr. Herbie Sawyer. Now, let's get on up there and have ourselves a little talk."

"You live at Eleven Falmouth Hill Drive. Pretty classy address, Herbie." Sergeant Valari spread the clipboard and sheets on his lap. We were up on Old Man Miller's porch, or what passed for a porch. It was really kind of a sloping platform facing the waterside. In the flattest corner near the house was a pile of junk— wire baskets, diggers and trowels, frayed bits of rope, and a pile of buoys, some wood, some Styrofoam. There was also a box filled with horseshoe-crab shells, whelk egg cases, pieces of drift-wood, old shoes, sneakers, and other stuff. The whole "porch" was actually nothing more than an oceanic junkyard, just as his house was really no more than a shack—sticks and boards pasted together, a temporary cabin sitting up on a shifting, manmade beach that someday, and soon, would tear it down and take it out to sea.

"The next hurricane'll do it," the old man had told me once, and I believed it.

Inside, behind us in the house, we could hear Jedadiah Miller's deep snores. Sergeant Valari said he'd get "Mr. Miller's statement" later.

So now I sat on the sloping boards, my feet in the sand, staring at this cop as he sorted through my "statement" concerning how I'd found the body, what I'd been doing in the marsh at that time of morning, where I lived.

"We don't live there all the time," I said respectfully. So the man had forgotten about the tide; I forget things, too. It's just that a kid my age, who lives so close to the marsh and the tides, thinks it's pretty odd when others don't take it into consideration.

But maybe he had. Maybe at the start of our "relationship" or "friendship" or whatever you like to call it, Jake Valari and I were simply underestimating each other. We hadn't yet figured out that where his knowledge as a police officer and mine as a kid who tramped these marshes and knew their tides and currents like the back of my hand, where these two "areas of expertise" (as one of my teachers would say) overlapped, maybe it would be there that we'd find an answer.

Some kind of answer to the body of the woman lying down on the sandbar in the inlet.

"Oh? Where do you live—most of the time?" he asked.

"Wherever my mother can find a place. We rent. Except in summer. We live at Eleven Falmouth Hill free in the summer. It's right behind Rock of the Bay Inn. My mother works there."

"What does she do?" Now he was writing.

"She's a . . . a maid. Makes up beds and . . ." I let my head hang, then turned away. I didn't want to see any pity on this

man's face. I'd decided I liked him. I focused on a wire basket
dropped in the sand, a trowel and a digger sticking out of it.

"I see. You stay there, rent-free, for the summer?"

"Yeah, but we got the best floor. It's a three-story, real old.
We're on the ground floor and it's got two bedrooms *and* a
porch, screened in." I turned back to look at him. "Above us the
kids live."

"Kids?"

"College kids. Two lifeguards—pool guards—another chambermaid, and a couple of waitresses. My mother takes care of
the whole house, makes sure they don't have wild parties, that
kind of thing. You know? Teenagers." I said the last word with
the same scorn my mother would. She called them all teenagers,
even though two were in their twenties.

But he understood, said, "Yeah, I know teenagers. Got two of
my own,"

"Do you, sir?"

"Listen, Herbie." He clapped the clipboard down on his heavy
thighs and stared straight at me. The morning sun was coming
in stronger now, trying to force itself through the thick and stubborn swatch of fog still hugging the beach. There were gulls flap-
ping across the shore, landing not twenty feet from us. Old Man
Miller threw out scraps to them; they were waiting there, not
knowing us from the old man snoring his brains out behind us.
Some of the gulls had already given up, were now winging their
way out to a series of sandbars just visible now that the tide was
out. The bars ran in a series of parallel lines to the beach; the
closest one you could walk to and barely get your feet wet.

"Yes, sir?" I finally said.

"Quit calling me sir, will you? My own kids don't treat me as
good as you do." A quick smile and he killed his cigarette in the
sand. I looked at it, thinking it was not a very wise thing to do.
Shouldn't someone be looking over this whole area? Looking for
. . . evidence?

Still, I liked his smile and decided he rather liked me, too. That
was good, didn't hurt for a kid my age to have a cop as a friend.
Might come in handy someday.

"So this is your temporary address, but your address for the summer, am I right?"

"Right . . . sir."

He smiled again, shook his head, and started to write again. "You came out this morning to check your chub traps, found the body. You told Officer Carleton you didn't touch it."

"That's correct. I told him that."

He picked up the tone in my voice, gave me a clever, sidelong glance. "You don't like Officer Carleton, do you? Don't worry about it, not many people do." He turned back to the clipboard. "You came up here, used Mr. Miller's phone—" He turned to look at the house with a weary, if somewhat confused, look. "Hard to believe he's even got a phone."

"Got electricity, too. See there?" I pointed out where the two lines snaked across the upper beach on rickety poles. "They fall down all the time, but he always gets someone out here to put 'em back up. Got to have his TV, you know."

"Strange old fella, living out here—a bad storm'll wash him right out to sea."

There he betrayed himself at last. He was a Cape Codder; I knew it in the expression, the wistfulness of his eyes. I also knew something else right away: If that coroner or whoever down in the inlet decided that there was any way at all that woman had been *murdered,* then the first and most natural suspect would be poor old Jedadiah Miller, snoring about twenty-five feet behind me in his cabin.

And this cop knew it, too, and that was the reason for the sudden and confused wistfulness on his face.

Swiftly, I added, "Yes, sir, and so he says himself. But no one's getting him off this beach before his time, preserve or not. It starts here, you see, I mean it will, when he's dead, or his house gets blown down. His family owned all this side before they sold it to Lady Brant, she owned the other, and now it all belongs to the government—the *federal* government."

"Not yet it don't," he corrected me gently. "Not for another five years, because if'n it did"—he was teasing me, and I smiled—"you'd be setting here talking to a *federal* agent and not some little backwoods Cape Cod police sergeant."

"Yes, sir, I understand how you mean. They say Lady Brant didn't want to see no more development along here. Or so says Old Man Miller. He says she felt guilty for what her family did— she was a Boothby, did you know? Anyhow, when they dredged the harbor, Boothby Harbor I mean, they dumped all the sand and dirt and rocks here. They buried most of the marsh, filled it all in. Except for that little bit, and it's coming back; I heard some Woods Hole people talk about it in school."

He just looked at me like he was studying me. He didn't ask any questions, neither did he interrupt. So I went rambling on.

"Anyhow, Old Man Miller, he can stay here until he's gone, or his house, then this whole section goes over to her family and they'll pass it on as part of the preserve. I think that's how it happens. He can't rebuild either, even if a hurricane blows him down and takes him out to sea. It's too bad, isn't it?"

"Let's forget about old Jedadiah Miller for a minute. After you called the police, you didn't go back to look at the body, did you?"

"No, sir, I waited with Old Man . . . with Mr. Miller. He finished off nearly half a bottle of . . . whisky, I think it was, while I sat there and watched some talk show out of Providence. Boring show."

He gave half a laugh. "You're a good boy, Herbie, but I think you know that. You didn't see anything else, now, did you? People? Cars? A boat?"

"No. No, I didn't."

"Then I want to tell you something, there'll be reporters down here soon enough, snooping around, trying to get information out of you and Mr. Miller. I want to know if I can depend on you."

"You can, sir. I won't say anything but the way I saw it."

"That's the problem, Herbie. I don't want you to say anything, except you found a body, then ran up here and called the police. I don't want you to say you went down near it, do you understand?"

I just sat there, grinding my feet in the sand. He went on.

"Don't describe her. I can't forbid you, but I'm asking you not to. Her family, do you understand?"

He said that in a funny kind of way, almost strained, so I ventured a guess: "Do *you* know who she is, sir?"

"I might." He started fishing for another cigarette.

"Do you think you know how it happened?"

"I don't know, Herbie. It looks like the tide probably brought her in. She could've been swimming. High tide was when? Just after midnight?"

"Twelve fifty A.M."

"Twelve fifty. So . . . maybe she was swimming. Last night, Saturday. Lots of parties out in the bay, on the boats. She might have been swimming, and in the fog . . ."

It was all wrong, and he knew it. "She wasn't wearing any bathing suit."

"Shouldn't be talking to you like this. I'm just asking you to keep quiet about her. You can run along now, go check your traps while the tide's still low; I'll tell them you can go past. Then I'm going to wait a while and try to get a statement out of . . . Mr. Miller."

I rose to my feet slowly, looking down at the man for a moment. He seemed tired then; he'd probably been roused out of a sound sleep by my call this morning.

"Or maybe it was a fishing mishap," he said, shrugging as though he hoped that's all it was. "I'm just wild-guessing while I get something official from Dr. Chados."

"She wasn't swimming, sir, and she wasn't fishing either. It looked to me like she was dressed for something else."

Regret crept over his face; tossing suggestions off me probably hadn't been a very good idea. For all he knew, I'd go and blab everything to the first reporter who showed me a new ten-dollar bill. But he didn't know me; wild horses wouldn't drag anything more out of me than what he said was okay.

"And what do *you* think she was dressed for, Herbie?" he asked, face becoming wistful again, and then something more again: He looked sad. He'd known this dead lady, of that I was sure.

"For clamming, sir." And with that I shuffled off across the sand to get my bike.

* * *

Wild horses, however, didn't take into account Mr. Hornton, because if I hadn't had him to tell, I simply would have burst wide open.

"She wasn't swimming, Mr. Hornton, I know that," I told him as I helped him mix his paint. "I'm not supposed to tell anyone. I didn't even go home. I guess I'm afraid there'll be reporters waiting there, like on TV. But she wasn't swimming, and I don't think she was fishing either. Women don't go fishing alone, not at night or early in the morning, and not in the fog."

Elmer Hornton said nothing, but he did give me a shrewd look out of the corner of his eye.

"You see, she was dressed in shorts and a shirt, and they didn't look right, you know how I mean? And she had pink fingernails, light pink, and some of them were real long but some were broken." I looked down at my own hand, my stumpy fingers, and tried to remember exactly how hers had looked. "And she was wearing a rope belt. You see what I mean? It wasn't a *belt* but a piece of twine, like clothesline twine. Her sneakers were beat-up, too, holes in the toes, and I think maybe she was wearing old clothes because . . ." That's when I wore down; I was seeing her face, her black glassy eyes, and . . .

The crab came out of her mouth. I swallowed and helped him carry the paint cans out into his gravel driveway. He was lettering a boat, a small dinghy. Mr. Hornton was a great letterer, a man of "infinite detail," as he liked to put it.

"Fell off a boat, maybe," he suggested as he pulled a crate up to the dinghy, placed his assortment of slender, fine-tipped brushes in front of him. He had holes in the crate, between his legs, and set a brush in each. "They have some pretty wild parties out there in the bay." He paused in his selection of a brush, then looked at me. "You tell your mother yet?"

"No. She'll find out on the TV, I suppose. She always has it on when she's cleaning rooms." I sat myself down on a crate at his side. The fog was gone now, earlier than I expected, not even noon yet. The sun beat down on my dark head, his white one, fiercely. It was going to be a hot one.

"The tide brought her in, Mr. Hornton, I'm sure of it. No matter how or where she died, the tide brought her in, and dumped her right there on that sandbar. It probably carried her in around one o'clock last night, I mean this morning. That was high tide, and it's a wonder she didn't float right up into the marsh. It's a full moon tide, you know."

Then I thought about it some more. The tide could have brought her in even *earlier* than that. It would be moving into the inlet and marsh as early as eight, nine o'clock at night.

But he said nothing; he was licking one of his brushes to a thin, needle-tipped point.

"You know what a full moon high tide is like? The way it rushes into the inlet? Damn, it's dangerous. A teacher at school told me it's called a rip current. Can carry you in and—"

"And can carry you out. You ain't been going down near the inlet when the tide's going out, have you? You never try to cross it then, boy. I told you what happened to Cherry Morton back in '62?"

"A dozen times." I didn't mean to be disrespectful, neither did I want to hear about Cherry Morton for the thirteenth time, so I very quickly added, "But they got their experts, the police do, and they'll tell when she died and how she died and if there were strangulation marks or gunshot wounds or if she got stabbed or—"

He cut me off just as cleanly as if I weren't talking at all. "Cherry Morton, out of the navy on leave and expecting to go back, make a real career of it, he was. Out there clamming, trying to help the family, bring in a free meal as we called it then; he was up on the Tides side. A big bar there was, rich with clams— God, small, delicate, beautiful things. Anyhow, he tried to cross over to Miller's side when the tide was going out. Fool. Must have been drinking. I say to this day, must have been drinking. I don't know what he could have been thinking. The tides pulled him out, and the very next day they brought him back in again."

"It's not really the tide that takes you out," I corrected the old man carefully. "The current forms like this . . ." I grabbed a brush he wasn't using and a piece of scrap cardboard, and began to carefully draw a picture for him. "Here's the inlet"—I drew a U-shape—"and here's the beaches, Miller's side and Tides side.

If two longshore currents meet, right there at the mouth of the inlet, they push each other out, away from the beach. *Then,* if the tide is going out, too, and the currents all meet together, then you got one powerful rush of water sweeping out into the bay. My teacher at school said the way to escape a rip current is to—"

"Damn, it's a rip*tide,* no matter what some teacher at school tells you. The tide emptying out of that inlet is what sucks you out, boy. The inlet is damned deep farther in—hell of a lot of water rushing out when the tide's moving, especially at full moon. Anyone stuck in *that* ain't gonna get out, no matter what some teacher says. You just suck water and sink."

"You suppose that's what happened to this lady I found? She sucked water and—"

"I don't know what happened to her, but Cherry Morton was a damned fine swimmer, was in training to be a frogman, boy, a *navy* frogman. But he got pulled out, and *I was there.* I saw him get pulled out, and then he just went under. He wasn't more than waist-deep when he just got . . . sucked under." He scratched his head, stared at me. "Tide took him out and a bunch of us went looking for him, from a boat. Gibby Swenson, he went in to look around for Cherry, but we barely got *him* back into the boat alive. He was cursing and swearing when we did, said he never saw anything like it, and it felt like the maw of some giant thing, just sucking everything right out into the bay. 'Course Gibby was liable to exaggerate now and then, but anyhow, we didn't see Cherry again until next day, lying up there in the marsh, just like your dead lady. So, no, I don't know what happened to *her,* but I can tell you this . . ." He drew in nearer me, taking my diagram as he did. "Jedadiah Miller. Nothing happens on his beach without him taking notice of it. Who do you think calls the police every time they get them nude sunbathers on the preserve? Him, I bet, after he gets a good look-see through his binoculars first." A laugh, a belch, and then he looked off, embarrassed, staring at the dinghy he was supposed to be lettering.

He got good money for putting stupid names on rich people's boats. This one was going to be called the *Honey Pot.*

"Think I should go tell Sergeant Valari that?"

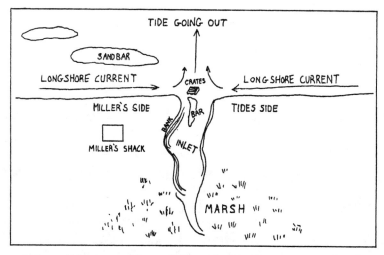

"You tell him anything you like, Herbie. But you're right, they got their experts, and not only fellas who'll tell them when and how she died and all of that, but about tides and currents and such. They'll figure it all out—you wait and see."

"But he forgot about the tides. I think he remembered them when we were sitting there and talking. I think he knew her, too. He looked awful strange when I mentioned them . . . like he'd forgot and when I said something about them . . ."

"So maybe his mind is twisting and turning the same way yours is," the man said agreeably enough, now that his mind was off Cherry Morton and how he'd died.

"And maybe she was shot, too, by a jealous husband and pushed off a boat," I said a bit glumly, recalling the plot of some inane television show I'd seen a few nights before. "But if you did that, you'd want to weight the body down, wouldn't you? So it wouldn't bob up, right?"

"You have a ghoulish streak in you, my boy. It worries me, it does." But he was smiling. "Why don't you plan to stick around a while, have some lunch with me? And if you like, I'll call and speak to your mother so she knows where to find you."

He was thinking the same as me: This story had probably broken on television by now; it was nearly eleven. And if it had, my mother'd already seen it.

"Thanks, Mr. Hornton, I'd appreciate it an awful lot if you would."

There wasn't anything on the Boston station about the woman yet, which figured. But on a Providence station, Channel 8, we found this:

"Tragedy struck a prominent Cape Cod family, the Brants of Boothby Shores, early today. This morning the body of Cynthia Allan Brant, wife of well-known attorney Steven Brant, was found washed up on the beach at Gray Tides Bird Sanctuary and Wildlife Preserve. It appears that Mrs. Brant might have been trying to cross the lower bay in the fog between seven and eight last night and fell from her skiff, the *Wicked Twist Two*. Mr. and Mrs. Brant's sailing yacht, the *Wicked Twist*, was moored in Manamesset Bay just off the wildlife preserve. Police will reveal few details at this time, but the Coast Guard has joined in the search for the missing skiff." A picture came on the screen of a small green dinghy, lettered on the stern *Wicked Twist*[2]. And as I stared at it, I realized I'd seen it before, out in Boothby Harbor, tied up alongside a magnificent sailboat, a forty-footer, the *Wicked Twist*.

"We will return in our broadcast to update you on any further developments. . . ."

I stopped eating at that point, spoon in midair, then plopped it back in my bowl of chowder. Elmer Hornton made the best clam chowder of anyone around; I'd even got the recipe and given it to my mother, but it hadn't come out the same. Now I was turning to look at him; he'd put aside his chowder and crackers, too, and was walking to the phone.

While he dialed, I rapidly checked other stations with the remote control. By sheer luck I landed on another, similar report. They were showing pictures of the boat, a beautiful sailboat of red mahogany with black and gold trim. The cameras panned in quickly, skipping across the words, *Wicked Twist*, painted on the stern in gilt-edged black script.

"Did you do that one, Mr. Hornton?" I asked, but he was already on the phone, asking to speak to Mrs. Sawyer at the Rock of the Bay Inn. I pushed my chowder away and looked back at the TV; they were already on another story.

"No, no, they didn't say Herbie's name on Channel 8, but Jesus, those reporters, they'll get a hold of it somehow. You just tell Emily Sawyer I'll keep her boy here with me today. Yeah, yeah, same to you, Joe." Then he hung up.

Apparently he hadn't been able to reach my mother, had been talking to Joe McSween, the assistant manager of the inn and a local man.

Mr. Hornton came back to his TV tray. We'd set up two on his small front porch to watch his portable color set.

"I'm not afraid of any reporters," I assured him.

"*She*"—all the emphasis was on that word as he thrust a spoon at me—"was an important lady you found."

"Yeah." I picked up my glass of root beer and sank back a little in the wicker chair.

They were doing the weather now. "I guess she was."

I didn't do much the rest of the afternoon. I helped Mr. Hornton with some of the painting, cleaned some brushes, mixed some more paint, helped him tip a small rowboat onto some sawhorses so he could strip it down. That was a whole job: The owner wanted a new coat of paint, a new name, the works. All for a lousy little rowboat. It was going to be called the *Lemmon Drop*.

"Stupid name," I said. And stupid color, too. We were mixing a bucket of lime-yellow paint.

But the *Wicked Twist Two*, or actually *Wicked Twist*², that was *not* a stupid name for a skiff. Actually quite clever. It seems Cynthia Brant, my dead lady, had been a math teacher before she married rich attorney Steven Brant. Yeah, that was pretty clever, I thought. They'd told more about her—and him—on the radio; we kept it on as we worked in the yard. They still hadn't found it, the *Wicked Twist*², that is.

"Man's name is Hardy Lemmon, and don't you be making fun of my regular, paying customers. This one, this Hardy Lemmon fellow, he gives me work every year, sends his friends over, too. Last year this little boat was the *Lemmon'ade*, and the year before that the *Lemmon'n Lime*. Man's got imagination, I'll tell you that."

"Sure," I grunted, which prompted him to reach out and give me a fake punch to the head. I laughed and ducked away. Even if I didn't have much to do, I was probably more in his way than any help. At least it kept me busy.

I was worried, you see, but mostly about my mother. Sooner or later we'd hear the phone ring; sooner or later I'd have to explain everything all over again to her. She'd be worried, scared, upset, all for nothing. It hadn't been my fault that Mrs. Cynthia Allan Brant had decided to drown and drift into the inlet with the tide.

"What's the name of his big boat, this Mr. Hardy Lemmon fellow?" I asked as he poured more yellow into his mixture to brighten it up a bit. Last year the boat had been a happy, gaudy sunflower yellow; apparently Mr. Hardy Lemmon was going for a more subdued look this year.

"Lemmon'n Lorraine."

"That's stupid."

"His wife's name is—hell, never mind." He continued to stir the paint. As he did I noticed the drawing I'd done, there on the gravel drive under a can of paint like it was some old piece of newspaper. I picked it up and stared at the picture I'd drawn of the inlet, the two beaches, the two longshore currents meeting, pushing each other out, and when the inlet was emptying, the tides. . . .

Except now there were black paint drops all over my sandbars and the beach I'd marked "Miller's Side."

"Did you letter *their* boat, the *Wicked Twist?*" I asked the old man.

"No, Jimmy Woodman did, I think, up Boothby Village. I think I recognized his work. He's a good letterer, got a very fine touch." He was still mixing paint. "Now, you gonna help me, boy, or—"

That's when the phone rang up inside the house. I looked at him, not wanting to answer, wanting suddenly for him to do this for me. Sometimes even kids my age will do that, retreat back into little children, ready to let an adult do something for them they don't want to do.

"I'll talk to her, invite her over for some supper if she likes. That way neither of you'll be home."

"Thanks" was all I could think to say. Then I pulled up a crate to sit on and studied my picture some more.

"These are fine clams, Mr. Hornton, you really oughtn't to do this for Herbie and me." That was my mother, respectful, courteous-till-it-hurt, and always full of gratitude. When life knocks you around a lot, you're grateful for every crumb you get. In fact, this small gesture was just about to overwhelm her: There were tears in her large blue eyes. I knew what she'd do next, but unfortunately wasn't quick enough to get out of her way. She was already there, arms around me, kissing the top of my head.

I'd been right about her. When Joe McSween had broken the news to her, that her twelve-year-old son had found Cynthia Brant's body down on Gray Tides Bird Sanctuary and Wildlife Preserve, not *on* the beach, as the television newsman erroneously reported, but *in* the inlet, stuck on a sandbar at its mouth, well, she'd just fallen apart. You would have thought it was *my* body they found down there. And even though Mr. Hornton had pretty much reassured her on the phone, she couldn't go back to work. McSween, never a very generous sort but not looking for any negative publicity either, had let her leave, and she'd come straight over to Mr. Hornton's house; she'd been in tears most of the afternoon. Poor old Mr. Hornton, he hadn't known what to make of it at first, even though he'd known my mother for years.

So he'd put her to work rinsing some steamers he'd picked up from a friend for a lettering job he'd done. A lot of the locals who had small fishing boats, dinghys, and the like sometimes couldn't afford to pay Mr. Hornton what he got from the richer summer people, so he was always telling them, "Don't worry about it," and "I skin the summer folks well enough to make up for it."

But of course they never did forget about it. All summer long he got "favors." A bucket of clams, which he'd steam, tasted great, or maybe a handful of small quahogs that he'd down raw, with just a dash of lemon or Tabasco sauce. Other times it might be bluefish that he'd barbecue on his little hibachi. Wonderful stuff.

That afternoon it was clams, small, sweet, soft-shelled clams. Dug from somewhere up near the marsh, I bet, because they had a gray color to their shells. They weren't the pure white of clams dug out of sandier shores like you usually see at fish markets.

"Hell, Mrs. Sawyer, Herbie'll do all right. He did all right already," Mr. Hornton said, still trying to convince her my life wasn't in imminent danger. "Called the police and that was that. His name's not been on the TV, and you can thank our local police for *that*."

"Oh, I know," she said, crushing me to her. She was a tiny woman, but strong. And I felt stupid being held like that, but I didn't move, not yet. Better to let her get it out of her system. "But my Herbie's never even seen a dead body, Mr. Hornton. I can't even imagine how frightening it must have been for him."

"Mom, it was nothing," I tried to insist, but she kept squeezing and squeezing me.

"And if that poor woman was . . . murdered? Well, I hate to say it, but what if she was? And Herbie's seen something he shouldn't have? I think of these things, I do, ever since Mr. McSween told me—"

Mr. Hornton just out and interrupted her. "Now, there you go, you're imagining things, Emily. The lady drowned, terrible as it was, but just drowned, and your son happened to find the body. That's what they said on the TV and—"

Her turn to interrupt him, surprisingly so, too; she was always so well-mannered. "But do they *know* everything yet? About her death? What do those television people know except what the police tell them? It's just like that actress, so many years ago. Out there in California. They say she fell off a boat, but to this day there are a lot of people who have second thoughts. . . ." Then her arms dropped limply off me. "Rich people, out there in the bay in their fancy boats. I see them every day, drinking and partying, and one wonders where *their* children are? Away to some fancy summer camp, I guess. But I see them, they come in for drinks and they meet their friends and then they're out on their boats doing lord knows what. You know, I love the summer because the rent is free and the work is regular, but I hate it, too. I hate those summer people. They're irresponsible and reckless and look what it's got one of them. Falling off a boat? She must have been drinking, don't you think? Or worse?"

"Mom, Mrs. Brant wasn't a summer person; neither is her husband. She came from somewhere 'round here; I heard it on the radio, and Mr. Brant is from Boothby, too."

She just stared at me blankly, as though she hadn't heard me. Was she going to cry again? Was she upset because somehow these people she depended upon—these rich and self-centered people who gave her her livelihood—had suddenly hurt, no, had *corrupted* her son? Yes, and that I had seen the other side of that world she existed in, the side she took such pains to keep me from seeing. I'd been so innocent until then, or so she believed I'd been, until I'd found the body in the inlet.

"My Lord," she said with a sudden deep breath. "I really went off, didn't I? I guess this whole thing has gotten me terribly worked up."

Mr. Hornton's turn to step in again, calm her down. With a very gentle touch around her shoulders, he said, "Why don't you go sit on the porch awhile? Watch some TV? Herbie and I'll set the table and get those steamers ready."

Strangely, but with effusive gratitude, my mother nodded her head and agreed.

We ate grand that night, steamers and hot bread, fresh beans from Mr. Hornton's garden slathered over with butter. We had some stuffed quahogs, courtesy of a nice lady down the road, a Mrs. Minnie Drew, and there was even some chowder left over, which my mother raved about.

Well, my mother doesn't exactly *rave*, but her compliments were heavy and genuine. She liked chowder. She had a more difficult time with the steamers. Originally from Springfield, Massachusetts, my mother hadn't been raised on seafood like I had been. My father had been a Cape Codder, insisted on fish and shellfish as a regular part of his diet. Mom had complied, but reluctantly.

"The steamers I see at the inn," she said as she ate her third, then delicately put the shell into a tin plate Mr. Hornton had set on the table for that purpose, "are a little different from these, Mr. Hornton, though these are quite . . . delicious." She wiped dripping butter from her bottom lip and smiled at me. She was calming down.

"Well, how do you mean, Emily?" Mr. Hornton asked politely back. He'd had a dozen or more already, stripping them from their shells, peeling back the long black membrane from what we called the neck, but which I knew—from school—was more accurately called a siphon. Then he dipped the little loose body into the butter and popped it in his mouth whole.

Only way to eat a steamer.

"The shells. Are they a different variety? The ones served at the inn have a very pale white shell. These look the same, but . . ."

"Shell's gray. That tells you where Manny Souza picked 'em up, don't it?" Mr. Hornton grinned. "Down on Gray Tides, I'll bet. Probably early in the morning, when there's a low tide. He digs 'em up before anyone can come along and tell him he can't." Then he frowned, noticing the silence between my mother and me at the mention of Gray Tides. " 'Course, Manny got these Friday or Saturday morning; he gave them to me yesterday afternoon. Still fresh, though. They'll keep awhile if you keep 'em cold."

I didn't feel like eating for a minute; I just stared at my plate. It was true, what Mr. Hornton said. I often saw Manny Souza down on the sandbars, and between them, but only when low tide came early in the morning. He hadn't been there this morning, else he'd have been the one to run and ring the alarm. Besides, I seldom saw Manny as far down the beach as the inlet, and never on Miller's side. Too much trouble to haul his buckets of clams up the long beach. Too much risk of getting caught, too.

"Shell's gray, Mom, because," I found myself automatically saying, "they're dug out of Gray Tides. That's how it got its name—the sand has a grayish tint to it, I mean if you dig into it a few inches. The whole area was a marsh that got covered up when they dredged Boothby Harbor. Anyhow, the sand is often gray up near a marsh; the organic material in the sand makes it dark, and sometimes it's old dunes, too, buried there. Dune sand tends to be gray because of the extra hornblende, that's a black mineral in the sand, and . . ." I bit my lip and grabbed another hunk of bread.

"My boy's smart, isn't he?" My mother beamed.

"I learned it in school, Mom. We had a minicourse in ocean science last term." I sighed and reached for the butter. Mr. Hornton used real butter; the man was practically a gourmet.

"Well, wherever they came from, they're delicious." She reached for one more, but she really didn't want it. Good old Mom, she was just being polite.

There wasn't much more about Cynthia Brant's "tragic drowning" on the news that night, except that the Boston stations had picked it up and repeated the facts we'd heard earlier, plus one more interesting one: The skiff had been found. Some kids fishing for flounder off the shallows below the preserve had found it washed up between some rocks. Its little outboard motor had run out of gas.

They had a few quick shots of Attorney Brant leaving his home up in Boothby with members of his family. None of them looked particularly happy, and no one spoke to any of the reporters hanging around.

My mother watched with me long enough to make sure my name still wasn't being mentioned; then she went off upstairs to check on the "kids" who lived above us. It was strangely quiet up there, for a Sunday evening that is, but she came back to tell me that two of them were working and the other three had gone out to a party.

After making sure I was all right—for the hundredth time that day—she went off to read in her bedroom. Mr. McSween had told her she could have Monday off if she "felt like she had to," but I was a big boy and told her I'd stay with Mr. Hornton or go over to one of my friends if it would make her feel better. She said she'd give it some thought, then nervously went to check the doors and windows for the fourth or fifth time.

I watched some more television, played a video game a friend had lent me, and watched more TV. I scouted around the kitchen, found some Doritos, chocolate ice cream, and a bottle of cream soda. Then I went out to our little porch, propped myself up on an old couch, and watched Arsenio Hall on some awards show while I dipped chips in chocolate ice cream. Best dip there is.

But even that bored me after a while, and I found myself flipping channels—local channels—looking for stories about Cynthia Brant. I wanted to know *the whole story*. If she had fallen off the skiff, the *Wicked Twist*[2], and how and why and when. I found one station where a reporter was interviewing a couple who supposedly had their boat moored fairly close to the *Wicked Twist*. They both claimed to have heard loud shouts and a lot of arguing around seven o'clock last night. Police were investigating their story, according to the reporter.

I thought about that for a minute. She and her husband had been arguing? Had they been drinking, too, like my mother believed all rich people did? But what about the condition of the body? There'd been no mention about it. Had there been marks or bruises? I hadn't seen any, but I hadn't seen all of her.

And what about the time of death? The police wouldn't say, they didn't have "enough information yet," according to the reporter on another station who was trying to pry answers out of the police chief, finally back from Martha's Vineyard.

"No, I'm sorry I can't help you folks out there," good old Chief Harrington, all five foot two of him, was saying to a pair of persistent reporters. "But we'll be issuing a statement soon—very soon. Right now we're treating this as an accidental death, death by drowning. Yes, we did recover the skiff and . . ."

And what time had she died? At what time so that high tide would wash her into the inlet and deposit her like a lifeless doll on that strange little sandbar?

But sometimes news people, for all their perseverance, can't get the detailed information that they—or I—wanted. I'd need to buy a newspaper, first thing tomorrow morning. And keep the

TV on, and the radio—several radios—all set to different stations.

So I ate and flipped channels and stumbled by mistake on a local channel, a Cape station out of Hyannis.

The house had cable TV hooked up to it, but we only got the "basic," the stuff you usually got for free. We were there for only a few months, so my mother never bothered to get any of the good stations, like MTV or HBO, or even the Disney Channel. Besides, we could never afford it. But we did get Hyannis-One, on Channel 61, and right there on Channel 61 was my marsh and both sides of the inlet, Tides side to the north, Miller's side, and Miller's shack as the camera swept toward the south. Long after all the big-city reporters had come and gone, a dinky little outfit out of Hyannis was doing a story on Cynthia Brant.

". . . and this is the beach the body was discovered on, by a local youth, early this morning . . ."

A shot of the sandbar but no body. The tides had come and gone and wiped it clean, smooth, flat. I remembered my drawing; I'd left it at Mr. Hornton's house.

". . . It was only a mile farther down this coast"—the speaker, a pale young woman with strawberry-red hair that was blowing in all directions, gestured past the shack and down the shoreline. There was a slow, mistlike fog rolling in; this must have been taped late that afternoon—"that the skiff, *Wicked Twist Two*, was found by some children up against the rocks. It is now believed,"—she was walking across the small patch of dunes toward Old Man Miller's shack—"that shortly after Mrs. Brant and her husband, Steven Brant, returned to their yacht from digging clams along this beach they had a fight aboard their boat." A dramatic turn to the fogswept coast, a profound look on the woman's face.

But I was stuck, barely listening as she mentioned the fact that the fight had been overheard by a couple on a nearby boat. Barely hearing as she went on to mention the police theory that Cynthia Brant had then left the yacht in the skiff with the intention of returning to her home in Boothby Village.

No, I was stuck, the Dorito in my hand turning to a brown,

chocolaty slop. Cynthia Brant and her husband had been clamming? Along the Tides?

I nearly leaped off the couch. If they had been clamming on
Saturday afternoon . . . My head began to do quick, careful calculations. I could look for my tide chart, but usually I figured
tides in my head.

High tide. Twelve fifty A.M. The tide that carried her in, then
or possibly earlier. The police had to have figured *that* by now.
So when had she and her husband been "clamming"? Low tide
on Saturday afternoon—or evening—had been about six thirty-
eight. Still light at that time. But foggy. Too foggy for clamming?
No, they'd probably been digging clams late in the afternoon.
Full moon low tide, certainly low enough for clamming. Yes,
they'd been out there clamming late in the afternoon. It explained her clothes.

Old clothes. A rope belt. Worn sneakers. The costume of the
Cape Cod clammer. Her fingers had been bare—most women
took off all the jewelry they wore when they went digging for
clams. Except maybe a wedding ring.

"Steven Brant had admitted to a 'disagreement. . . .' "

But all I could see was two people digging for clams. And the
tide rushing out. The rip current, made by two longshore currents that met, pushing each other away from shore. And then
with the tide going out . . .

I thought of Cherry Morton.

"I passed the time of day with them." Old Man Miller, only a
little unsteady on his feet, was there on the TV, talking to the
red-haired reporter. "We had a few beers, and they took some
clamming gear. He's a good boy, that Stevie, even if'n his last
name is Brant. I used to see him up and down this beach as a
kid, chubbing, dragging for crabs, catching eels. Hell"—a short,
gruff laugh—"kid was a marvel at catching eels, though what the
hell for, I used to ask. Nobody I knows eats eel round here."

I put aside my mushy chips, my melted ice cream, and moved
nearer the television. The reporter was asking him questions.

The old man was scratching his head. "Gone over this a dozen
times with the police, but I think they were out there about five,
maybe six o'clock? They took a basket and a couple of diggers

and went off. I did tell them the Tides side was showing finer clams. It's all a preserve, you know, but him being Stevie Brant, well, hell, I'm going to tell him *he* can't dig here?" Another gruff laugh.

I shut my eyes, raced back to earlier this morning. Five-fifteen? Yes, and how I ran, half-falling up the bank to Jedadiah Miller's shack, to tell him, to have him call the police. What had *he* done?

He'd made a choking sound, had already been up, was moving around his tiny bathroom. Then he came out and dived for a bottle of whisky sitting there on the counter. I hadn't even told him whether the body had been a man's or a woman's. Just: "Mr. Miller?" I had hardly banged on his flimsy screened door, just burst right in. "I think you should call the police, sir. I just found a dead body down in the inlet."

That's when he had dived for the bottle. Jack Daniel's.

Jack Daniel's. Not cheap stuff. Half-empty bottle. Damn!

I looked back at the TV as the reporter, looking very remorseful, moved away from the still-unsteady Jedadiah Miller. "Police are still investigating this tragic incident. It is a story filled with ironies, for this was the beach Steven Brant played along as a child. Now it has become the final resting place of . . ."

Garbage now. Besides, I had to do some serious thinking.

And talking. I ran into the living room and picked up the phone.

"It isn't just anyone I'd do this for, Herbie, but you told the night duty officer you had something important to tell me, something that couldn't wait till morning." He was trying to be severe, but a smile was unfolding across Sergeant Valari's round, good-natured face as he came into the house.

"My mother's asleep, sir," I said softly. "Can we talk out on the porch?"

"Well, why the hell not, Herbie?" he answered in the same tone. "Not every day I get to talk police business with a budding twelve-year-old detective." Then he paused and eyed me warily. "That's not all this is, is it? You're not dragging me up here on some wild-goose chase?"

"I'd never bother you, sir, if I didn't think it was important, or if it could wait. And I don't think it can."

He grunted some kind of agreement, and we went out onto the porch. I carefully shut the door, put on a light, turned off the TV, and started.

But to each suggestion I made, he shot me down:

"They *were* arguing, Herbie. We found two boats, close by, heard them, right around seven o'clock. That's *after* they left Gray Tides and got back to their boat."

And: "Why didn't she change her clothes? Hell, Herbie, I can't explain everything, and neither do I have to. She was drinking. He was drinking. Jedadiah Miller can attest to the fact that they all were drinking. That probably didn't end when they got back to their boat. I don't say it's right, to drink and be out on a boat. In fact, it's a damned stupid thing to do. But they did. She had a blood alcohol level of 0.12, and that I can tell you because it'll be in the papers tomorrow. I hate to think you dragged me way up here . . ." He shook his head. "You told Officer O'Brien you'd found some new evidence up here, but I don't see any signs of it, Herbie. I hate to tell you, but you've disappointed me, boy."

"The Jack Daniel's?" I asked frantically. I was reaching for straws, and he knew. I was also being made to look like a fool, and we both knew it.

"Hell, I don't know where Jed got *that*. Maybe the Brants did bring it for him, but if they did, so what? It's more likely Jed went down to the nearest liquor store and bought it for himself."

"They got him drunk, sir. No. *Steven Brant* got him drunk; he liquored him up and waited for him to go to sleep. That's what Old Man Miller always does when he gets drunk—he sleeps. I know it. And Steven Brant would know it, too."

"How would Steven Brant—"

"It was on the news tonight. Channel 61, the red-haired—"

"Oh, that snoopy, know-it-all reporter? She was out harassing Jed this afternoon—"

I interrupted again, rude as it was. "She said Steven Brant knew the whole area, that he'd played there as a kid. Mr. Miller even said so on TV. Makes sense; his grandmother owned all of the Tides side. So he knew about Jed, do you see?"

He frowned at me but suddenly had no quick rebuttal. That was when I realized this man, this smart cop, was playing a game with me, a game of deriding every single thing I said, just to find out what I knew, what I might have to share with him.

It scared me suddenly; of course no cop would come out in the middle of the night to talk to a twelve-year-old kid, not if Cynthia Brant had died of accidental drowning. Of course not. They were investigating this as something else.

They . . . the police . . . him. Accidental drowning they call it, the press, too. Accidental drowning until you have enough facts or evidence to call it something else.

"I don't know what to say. But you're right about that. And we had a tide analysis done, currents and tides and so on. Had a Woods Hole expert come down to the station, though I could have read everything right off a tide chart if I wanted to. Anyhow, he explained to me about riptides and all that. But the fact is, a tide or current did carry her body in—her *dead* body. She had a fight with her husband, got mad, and jumped in the dinghy to go back to shore. The last he saw of her was her in the dinghy, moving off in the fog toward shore. She'd been drinking; he feels terrible now for letting her go. That was sometime after seven, which more or less confirms what the coroner thinks. She'd been dead between ten and twelve hours when you found her."

"You think she died around seven o'clock—last night?"

"Steven Brant says he last saw her at about seven fifteen, but he's not positive of the time. Went below deck to watch 'Evening Magazine,' which comes on at seven-thirty, right after. Fell asleep and stayed there the rest of the night."

"I think she died closer to six, sir."

"Herbie, what I'm telling you I shouldn't, but it will be in the papers and . . ." He sat back heavily in the wicker chair and started shuffling for a pack of cigarettes.

"My mother doesn't like people to smoke in the house, sir."

"Listen, Herbie—" A sudden lunge forward, as though he'd liked to have lunged for my neck. He slapped both hands down on his knees instead. "Everything fits, just like he says it happened. That's all I can tell you. The poor lady, drunk, in the fog, she lost her balance somehow, fell overboard and . . ."

"She died around six. I know she did. She died in the rip current, just like Cherry Morton back in—"

" 'Sixty-two? That story still going around?" He gave a hollow-sounding laugh. "Herbie Sawyer, I do admire your persistence. But, boy, if you've got nothing else to offer me . . ." He began to stand.

"Why did you come out here, sir?" I looked up at him, trying not to appear too desperate. "I mean, if you didn't have doubts of your own?"

"Oh, hell, Herbie, I always have doubts. And you were right about Cynthia Brant. I knew her. She went to school with me up in Sandwich, except she was three years younger than me." He shoved the package of cigarettes back in his pocket.

"How'd she die? Do you know? Were there bruises? Did he beat her up?"

He just stared down at me.

"Because he didn't, did he? She just clean drowned—no rocks out there to bang around against, at the mouth of the inlet, I mean. She just drowned. She never went back to the *Wicked Twist* with her husband. He let her drown, then he went back alone and staged a fight, real loud, cursing, whatever those people heard. Then he turned on the outboard motor on the little boat and just set it off—to the south—in the fog. Made it look like she took off on him."

He was still staring at me, and I knew the look in his eyes even though it was fairly dim out there on that porch.

"Do you know, sir, on the wire baskets Old Man Miller has, well, he attaches a piece of line to them, old fishing line, string, anything, and to the end of that he puts a piece of old buoy or wood. Sometimes the buoys are Styrofoam. It's to mark the basket in case you set it down where the water's fairly deep. 'Course you wouldn't do that if you were clamming, but for scalloping, later in the fall, you would need to mark your basket; you'd be out in deeper water, you see."

"What are you getting at, Herbie?"

"She . . . the body, I mean, Mrs. Brant . . . she had something white stuck to one of her nails. She also had dirt deep under them where being in the water hadn't cleaned 'em yet. That's not so strange, I guess. You might be so mad you'd not bother to clean your hands, but she had nice hands—I mean, long nails, painted. Yeah, you might be so mad you wouldn't change your clothes or clean up your hands, but would a lady leave Styrofoam stuck to her nails?"

"How did you know that's what it was?" This was his most vicious moment yet, if the man could be called vicious. He just had this sound to his voice, this sudden anger, but it wasn't directed at me. He thought someone had talked . . . too much. "Did they mention that on that Hyannis news show? Damn, wait till I get ahold of Carleton—"

"No, sir," I said quickly. "No one told me. I saw it. And I think I know how it all happened. She was struggling to get clear of the current. She was probably carrying the basket, or trying to carry it across the mouth of the inlet, about six last night. I think she was on Miller's side, and her husband, he was probably over on the Tides. The tide was low but still going out. She could have been waist-deep in water and thought nothing of it . . . at first."

And I thought of Cherry Morton, a swimmer, a man going into training to be a navy diver, a frogman. It had killed him, and deposited his body *on the next high tide* up in the marsh. "He might even have been in the dinghy, calling her over—and she walked right across the inlet and into the current that sucked her out. Could she swim, sir?"

He was answering in spite of himself. "Not very well."

"And she was drinking, too. I think if you drag at the mouth of the inlet, side to side and out to about a hundred, maybe a hundred and fifty, feet, you'll find Old Man Miller's clam basket . . . and maybe some of the clams she dug, too."

"Hell, you're wrong, Herbie. You're dead wrong." He sat back on the edge of the chair. "I thought of all that, too. Don't you think I thought of that? She got her hand caught, or tried to grab onto a Styrofoam float, whatever, but . . . hell, Herbie, we went down into the galley of the *Wicked Twist* and looked into the refrigerator there, and what do you think we found?" A pause, to let it sink in. "A basket of clams, Herbie, a big wire basket of clams."

"Maybe they had two baskets, sir."

"No. Jed Miller says they borrowed only one."

"Maybe the Brants had one of their own."

"Herbie . . ."

"Maybe they took a second basket when Jed was sleeping. You do see why Steven Brant wanted him to be sleeping? So he wouldn't hear when Cynthia started to cry out. " I felt sick suddenly. My brilliant line of reasoning had been shot down, and with such brutal and inarguable simplicity.

I thought I'd known. Thought I could explain all of it: why Jed Miller had to be gotten drunk; why there was a glob of sea spit under her nail, which turned out to be Styrofoam; why she hadn't changed her clothes, filed and cleaned her nails; and why the same forces that had carried her out and drowned her had brought her back.

Back to nearly the very same spot where she had died.

He looked at the floor, big hands clenched together. "Jed said it was one of his, the basket on the *Wicked Twist*. We let the bastard keep his clams." He regretted saying that, looked quickly off the porch in the direction of the road. "So it's as he said: She went off mad, she fell off the boat in the fog, and she drowned. That's all it is. It was foggy, and she was not a good swimmer. That's all."

"Sir?"

He turned slowly to look back down at me. I could hear my mother moving around inside now, her soft, almost plaintive "Herbie?"

I ignored her. "What color were those clams?"

He frowned, then answered roughly. "What the hell color do you think they were? Damn it, Herbie, they were white, of course."

"Of course, but if they came from Tides Preserve they should be gray." I could feel my heart beating in my throat. Would this man know the difference? Did he call all clams white, without thinking? "And he told you those were the clams he got from the preserve?"

He was frowning, but thinking, too. My mother came to the door timidly, fearfully, in her pink housecoat.

"He bought those clams, the ones you saw, sir. I'm sure of it. He had to. Because when you go clamming, you never know."

"You never know?"

"You never know if you're going to get any. It's almost always a hit-or-miss deal, sir. But Steven Brant, he *had* to have some, in case he and his wife didn't get any. So you'll either find a basket of white clams, which he got or bought somewhere else, or you'll find a mixture of white *and* gray-tinted clams, which would be the ones he bought and the ones he and his wife dug. You see, he had to have *some* clams in his refrigerator . . . for *you* to see."

"And if they're all gray?"

"He still could have killed her, but you'll have to find some other way to prove it. "

"Herbie?" My mother's voice was an anguished whisper.

"Just make sure he admits *those* are the ones he and his wife dug. Get him to admit that, sir."

"Christ—" He looked off as my mother came onto the porch.

"It'd be a guaranteed drowning, sir. No marks, no bruises. He didn't have to hold her head under or hit her, knock her out. Nothing. The current would do it all for him."

"Jesus H. Christ," he muttered again.

There was no new information on Cynthia Brant's drowning for the next two days. The police were holding off from their "official statement" until Wednesday. So until then we heard the same story.

Except that someone did get hold of my name, and reporters did come to our house. I avoided them, though: out the back door as they came in the front. My mother handled them fairly well, in her vague, unfocused way. They'd get impatient and leave.

One paper did try a different angle, focusing on the "tragic irony" of it all, how the Brants had been clamming on the very beach where her body was later found. Another paper made mention of the tides and currents—complete with diagrams. The Woods Hole expert was quoted. The story appeared by way of explaining how the body got carried into the inlet, not how she died.

But though Woods Hole experts are fine, no one knows an area like a person who lives in it does. I knew the area. So did Steven Brant. He knew that tide was powerful—he'd probably heard the story of Cherry Morton more times than he could count. He knew if anyone were trying to swim—or walk—across the mouth of the inlet as the tide was going out . . . well, unless you knew how to get out, you just sucked water and sank. Cynthia Brant hadn't known the area. She'd been drinking. And carrying clams. It was foggy, and the only person who might have helped her was lying dead drunk up in his shack.

She probably trusted her husband, too.

So when Sergeant Valari called me Wednesday morning to tell me three things, then made me swear not to tell anyone—the full story was breaking at noontime—I didn't. Not Mom. Not Mr. Hornton. No one.

This is what the sergeant told me:

One: Steven Brant, under questioning, did admit to giving Jedadiah Miller the bottle of Jack Daniel's for "old times' sake" and to thank him for the use of his clamming gear. But he insisted he took one basket—and only one—and it was the one found aboard the *Wicked Twist*.

Two: The police did drag the area at the mouth of the inlet. And they found another wire basket, which Jedadiah also identified as his, but he couldn't explain how it had gotten there, about ninety feet beyond the mouth of the inlet.

And three: The police went back to the galley of the *Wicked Twist* one more time. The clams were still there, but by this time the whole ship was being held, pending a further investigation and the results of an inquest. Steven Brant insisted the clams in the basket were the ones he and his wife had dug . . . all of them, and couldn't understand the fuss everyone was making over them.

That's probably when Sergeant Valari read him his rights. I like to think it was. Because every clam in that wire basket was white, you see.

White as sea foam.

MIRIAM GRACE MONFREDO

THE APPRENTICE

Miriam Grace Monfredo is the author of two excellent histor-
ical mysteries, Seneca Falls Inheritance *and* North Star Con-
spiracy, *dealing with women's rights and slavery in the years*
before the Civil War. She has also written historical mysteries
for Ellery Queen's Mystery Magazine; *in fact, "The Appren-*
tice" is the first of her contemporary mysteries to appear there.
It is a strange and wonder-filled tale, certainly the most uncon-
ventional whodunit of the year.

The child huddled on narrow concrete steps that led from the
basement of an Eighth Street brownstone. Above her the sidewalk shimmered with heat. Although Kelsey didn't think anyone
could see her, she wriggled down one more step—but now she
couldn't see anyone coming. Sweat made her T-shirt stick to her
skin; she stretched out the neckband to blow on her bare chest.
It had been cooler in the brownstone. But she couldn't go back
inside yet. She laid her cheek against the cold iron railing. And
wished she would stop crying.

When she inched up one step for a quick look, a man with a
beard was rounding the street corner. Kelsey stiffened and
ducked, and her stomach fluttered like a snared bird. She ground
her fists into her eyes, pushing hard against the tears. But then
she thought of something: That might be the *sorcerer* coming.

Cautiously poking her head up between the black bars of the
railing, Kelsey peered through it. The bearded man walked
toward the brownstone across the street, and now that she could

see him clearly, Kelsey grinned. Yes, it was the sorcerer. She pushed red wisps of hair away from her eyes so she could watch him.

He didn't look much like a sorcerer. But she decided she might not know exactly how real sorcerers did look. She had seen drawings of wizards with tall pointed hats and purple cloaks covered with curved moons and stars. They always had long gray beards. *He* had a short black beard and wore a brown raincoat. Mostly he looked to her like a regular person. Of course, the Wizard of Oz looked like a regular person, too—but he wasn't a very good wizard.

She felt better now. Summer dampness had turned to drizzle, and the headlights of cars were round yellow eyes staring at her through the grayness. Kelsey crouched in the stairwell, listening to tires slicking over wet pavement. Exhaust and gasoline mixed with the thick, rich smells of stores and restaurants and the hotdog stand around the corner.

She waited while the sorcerer went into his brownstone. Then she scampered up the basement steps and ran across the street. She rang his doorbell with the secret signal—two long and one short—he had taught her to use. When he opened the door, he had already taken off his raincoat and was pulling a black sweater over his head. His face looked sharp and pale between the sweater and his black hair. Kelsey thought his nose was like the curved beak of a bird. He drew her inside, closed the door, and locked it.

"Does anyone know you're here?" he said, looking down at Kelsey with dark, careful eyes.

"No," she said. "I didn't tell anyone."

He nodded and walked toward a kitchen—at least Kelsey thought it must be a kitchen because it had a microwave. She followed him, smelling orange and cinnamon tea in the mugs he put on the desktop.

He pulled a chocolate bar, lumpy with nuts, from his pocket and held it out to her. Kelsey took the bar, broke it in half, and handed his piece back to him, then slid onto a chair and watched him pour boiling water from the microwave into the mugs. He set one down on the desk in front of her.

She let the chocolate melt in her mouth, but she didn't want the tea. It took too long to cool. "Can we do it?" she asked him.

"Right this minute?" he said, his black eyebrows lifting like wings. Then, "Where are your father and mother?"

"They've gone. Took my aunt Lucy and uncle John, and my grandmother and grandfather Crane home. They won't be back for a while. Please, can we do it now?" she said, slipping off the chair to stand close in front of him.

"Go over there," he said, pointing to a black sofa. He switched on the lamp that cast a circle of yellow light.

The great river rocked in the cradle of its banks, as slowly it moved south to the sea. Willows poured green-leafed falls into the river, and the summer sky overhead was so blue. . . .

"Blue as yer eyes, Miss Kelsey," called Huck.

Kelsey heard him just as her head broke the surface of the water. Huck sat cross-legged on a raft of rough logs. Standing beside him, a tall black man poled past the shallows. Kelsey drifted beside the raft and listened while Huck told about when he and Jim set off downstream, running away, both of them, from their own particular slavery.

Huck puffed little clouds from his corncob pipe. He told her about the lickin's, and the time he'd had to set up all night with a gun on his lap, 'cause he was scared his pap was gonna kill him with a knife.

Kelsey liked most of Huck's story, but not the parts about lickin's and knives.

"Why do children get lickin's?" asked Kelsey.

"Appears like you don't know a whole lot, do you, girl?" said Huck. "Well, big people lick li'l kids—'cause they's kids, I'd reckon."

"Is that fair?"

"It ain't a case of fair, Miss Kelsey. It's a case of size. A case of size fer sure! Hey, ain't *you* ever bin licked?"

Kelsey felt her stomach flutter. "Are you and Jim going to ride on this river forever?" she asked.

Huck nodded. "Reckon it sure beats gettin' civilized. But you *sure* you ain't been licked?"

"I need to go now," Kelsey said.

"Okay. Jim," he said to the silent man with the pole, "Jim, we got to pull in to shore."

Kelsey felt the water suddenly swell, lifting her toward the sky.

"Hey there," yelled Huck, "don't go flyin' off. Grab hold of the raft now, y'hear?"

Kelsey looked down and saw the sorcerer sitting under a willow in an arc of sunlight.

The autumn afternoon without wind was like magic, Kelsey decided; the trees let go and their leaves fell down straight and soft as golden snow. By the next day they would cover the sidewalk like an enchanted carpet.

Her stomach had stopped hurting, but her face felt cold. She pulled her sweatshirt down, then yanked the hood up over her head. While she waited, she sniffed at the sharp fall air—like the red spaniel that lived down the street.

The sorcerer walked toward her through the leaf snow, his head and shoulders flecked with gold stars. Kelsey remembered when she had first found out for certain about him.

"Why is this spiky tree growing here inside your house?"

"It is a hawthorn tree," he had said, as though that explained everything.

And it did. When Kelsey found "hawthorn tree" in her father's encyclopedia, the entry ended with: "It is still believed by some that ancient sorcerers stood under hawthorn trees to cast their spells."

Well, of course.

Now, while he brushed the leaves from his coat, Kelsey told him about the funeral. Her aunt Lucy had died. Kelsey had had to sit quietly in the church pew between her father and mother; the funeral service went on forever and ever.

After forever, all the relatives gathered at her grandmother and grandfather Crane's house to eat and cry. Kelsey saw her uncle John, his eyes red and swollen, holding the hand of her cousin Melissa. Now Melissa had no mother. Kelsey wondered what it would be like not to have a mother—what a horrible girl she must be to wonder that! No wonder her stomach hurt.

Kelsey had gone to stand beside the front door. She had wanted to go home.

While she told him this, the sorcerer had been silent, watching her with his careful eyes. Now he asked her, "Does your stomach still hurt?"

She realized she'd been rubbing herself. "No!" she said quickly. "No."

The sorcerer kept watching her as he said, "Shall we do it again?"

Kelsey nodded. "But not the river this time. I don't want to hear about children getting lickin's. It's not right, is it?"

The sorcerer leaned down until his face was close to hers. "What do *you* think?"

"I think it's not right," Kelsey said. She remembered the enchanted leaves on the sidewalk. "This time, can we go on a flying carpet?"

The sorcerer led her toward the sofa in front of the bookcase; a beam of light appeared over his fringed rug—just before it soared into the air.

Sunbeams slanted through the pink marble arches of the palace courtyard. Under every arch was a fountain. The water leapt in the sun and fell with a tinkling sound on fronds of huge-leafed palms. The air smelled of sugared dates and spices.

All the other children clustered together on marble steps, but Kelsey floated just above a silk cushion. She reached down to finger its long tassels. On other cushions sat Ali Baba and Sinbad, Aladdin, and Princess Buddir al-Buddoor.

Under a purple-fringed canopy, Scheherazade knelt on a pink cloud and told wondrous tales, weaving threads of the stories together like the strands of silk running through Kelsey's hands.

Scheherazade told of Ali Baba and the cavern of forty thieves; of Aladdin and his powerful genie with a voice like thunder; of Sinbad enslaved by corsairs, almost eaten by a one-eyed giant, and carried through the air by an enormous bird.

When she ended the story of Sinbad's adventures, Scheherazade said in a flutelike voice, "And so Sinbad escaped the most terrible circumstances by his quick wit and his courage."

Sinbad jumped up and bowed low. Kelsey thought his billowing pants looked like the legs of the elephants he had ridden. How could he be so brave? He was so small.

Kelsey drifted on the magic carpet up through the long, misty corridor. The sorcerer, from far away, said to her, "What did you think about Aladdin's uncle, the evil magician, who beat the boy and buried him alive under a great stone?"

"The genie in the lamp saved Aladdin," said Kelsey. "Do you think I could find a genie?"

"That is not an answer to the question I asked," said the sorcerer, his voice now so close Kelsey wanted to cover her ears.

"Well, *my* uncle isn't an evil magician," she said, after she'd thought hard about his question. "My uncle John is Melissa's father. And he's a nice man."

The sorcerer looked at her intently. "Are you sure about that?" he said softly.

Kelsey concentrated on the snowflakes hitting the windowpane, trying not to hear the baby wailing in the bedroom. It wasn't that she disliked the new baby. But there wasn't much to like. At least, not yet.

Her mother was tired. But as long as Kelsey could remember, her mother had been tired. She almost always stayed in her bedroom, sipping from a flower-shaped glass.

The worst thing about the baby arriving was all the people who arrived with it. Kelsey was glad to see her granny Stuart from Rhode Island, who was her father's mother, and a widow. But the cousins and aunts and Uncle John, and her grandmother and grandfather Crane who lived across town—it seemed there was always someone who shouldn't be there in the brownstone every day.

There was noplace to hide. But sometimes, she would sneak out and run across the street to the sorcerer's house. If only she weren't so small. She wished the sorcerer would turn her into a ferocious red lion. But probably he wouldn't. He thought she should be a girl.

One silent white afternoon she ran out of the brownstone, pulling on her jacket and mittens. She crossed the street and waited on the sidewalk, watching birds swooping over snow-shrouded trees and crying into the wind.

She saw the birds' beaks open and close against the sky, but there was no sound. Why couldn't she hear the birds? Maybe it was true: Maybe if she told something bad, she would never hear anything again.

Then the sorcerer came down the brownstone steps, and they walked together into the park and sat on a stone bench. He handed Kelsey a chocolate bar. She inched closer to him and heard the pigeons murmuring at their feet.

Startled birds scattered as the horse's hoofs click-clacked over the cobblestoned London street. Kelsey hovered just above a young man driving a carriage, who pointed out bleak factories looming into the sky. Smoke and soot hung in the air. The smell from the gutters along the street made Kelsey's eyes water.

She heard a high-pitched whining sound. It became one great keening voice, and scores of children tumbled out of the factories' doors as though they had been spewed from dark open mouths.

Kelsey stared at their rags, their thin, hungry look. They blended somehow into the street so that it seemed the very cobblestones were moving.

"What were they doing in those places?" she asked the young man.

"Working," said Oliver. His face was tight and closed as he motioned the coachman to stop the carriage.

Kelsey watched the children run off down the dozens of narrow alleyways growing like twisted arms from the trunk of the main thoroughfare. "Who takes care of them—where are their mothers and fathers?" she asked. "Where do they live?"

"For some, the streets are their families. They sleep in the alleys, the thieves' kitchens, and the night shelters."

"You don't," said Kelsey.

"I used to," Oliver said harshly, twisting on the seat to watch a man emerging from the shadows of the building. "Fagin," he muttered.

Kelsey saw a shriveled old man running bony white fingers

through his matted hair. He grinned hideously, and his long fingers never stopped moving, turning and twisting around one another.

"Who *is* he?" she whispered to Oliver.

"Watch," he said.

Several children ran up to the man, gave him something, then darted away into the shadows like small brown birds. One boy, shaking his head, stretched out an open hand, then drew it back.

Fagin hit him. Hard. The boy doubled over and rolled groaning into the filthy gutter.

Kelsey tried to fly away, but she couldn't. And she couldn't stop looking at the man's long white hands, constantly moving, never still. . . . Her grandfather Crane always had dirty fingernails. Kelsey hated that.

"No, please." She was trying not to cry. "I want to go away from here. Please." Her eyes cast frantically over the dark street.

The sorcerer appeared at the corner, holding the horse's reins.

Kelsey was quiet as she rode up through the foggy cobblestoned corridor. Back in the sorcerer's house, she said, "That boy . . . I think that man hurt him. And the boy didn't even do anything bad—did he?"

The sorcerer looked his careful look and shook his head.

Kelsey said, "It's a very lucky thing that Oliver grew up."

"But sometimes," said the sorcerer, "if a child does not know she is being hurt, she might never grow up."

Kelsey walked slowly, head down, sneakers scuffing the new spring grass growing in the sidewalk cracks. Her report card was stuffed in her jeans pocket. The teacher hadn't said anything, just handed her the envelope with a frown. When Kelsey opened it in the girls' room stall, she felt a kind of disappointment, as though she had lost something important that she thought was hers. She threw up in the toilet, but she didn't feel better afterward.

She stopped walking to hitch up her jeans and pull her belt a notch tighter. She had to go home. Granny Stuart was visiting again from Rhode Island, but she would be disappointed with Kelsey, too.

* * *

Kelsey stood just outside the door of her mother's bedroom. Did they know she was still there? She probably shouldn't listen.

"Adrienne, something's *wrong* with that girl!" It was Granny Stuart's voice.

"What do you mean—wrong, Mother Stuart?" asked Kelsey's mother.

"I've told you before, she's not the same grandchild I knew a year ago, when you lived in Providence."

"Well, now, Mother Stuart, you don't see her all the time. Just on your visits. So, of course she looks different to you. For one thing she's older. . . ."

There was a long silence, so Kelsey squatted in front of the door to look through the keyhole.

Her grandmother was just staring at her mother. "*Older* has nothing to do with her thinness, her withdrawn look, that tenseness," Granny Stuart said. "The child I knew in Providence was outgoing. Friendly. And bright. Look at this report card. Her grades are below average. Something's very wrong with her, Adrienne!"

Kelsey pulled away from the keyhole. She shouldn't listen—they were talking about someone else. Some other girl.

But she could hear her mother's voice scale upward. "So why don't you talk to her father? He's what's wrong. Your son, Mother Stuart, is never home. He stays at the university almost every night. I feel so alone. Talk to *him* about what's wrong. . . ."

Her voice trailed off in a whisper. Kelsey couldn't hear any more. But she was scared for the girl Granny Stuart had been talking about. What if the girl couldn't tell what was wrong? What if she didn't know?

Beneath a ray of sunshine streaming into his hole, the White Rabbit rolled off the edge of the chessboard. He scurried to safety just before the scepter crashed down.

"Off with your head," screamed the Red Queen.

"Off with *yours*," Kelsey said, glaring at the creature. Then she drew back, suddenly frightened. What had she said? She bit her lip and whirled around to look for the sorcerer. He floated up through the hole, but she had glimpsed his face.

Why was his mouth twitching?

A week before, Granny Stuart had had to go home. Kelsey cried, and wanted to go with her to Rhode Island, and even though Granny Stuart said, "Yes," her father had said, "No—why would Kelsey want to leave her family?"

And now it was the Fourth of July. Her grandmother and grandfather Crane always had a picnic on the Fourth. This year's had begun in the early afternoon, and Kelsey, in the crush of people, had lost her mother and father. Now she ran out of the house to look for them. When she found her father, he was standing with her uncle John and others who had gathered in the backyard.

"Can we go now?" Kelsey asked him. "Can we go home, please?" She felt frightened and confused, and her stomach ached. She thought she might throw up.

Kelsey heard her father's voice from so far away she had to strain to hear him answer, "We have to stay for the fireworks. But why do you want to leave? Do you feel all right, Kelsey?"

She thought her father looked at her anxiously. But she knew that he wouldn't take her home. "I'm okay," she said.

"You seem flushed. It's hot out here. Why don't we go in the house where it's cooler?" Her father reached out his hand toward her.

"No!" She backed away from him.

He looked surprised, then angry. "Kelsey, what's the matter with you? You act like you're afraid of me."

Kelsey shook her head, the confusion closing around her like a giant hand. She wanted to say—something. But she didn't know what to say.

Her father turned to answer something Uncle John asked him. Kelsey waited as long as she could, then slipped away from him into the shadow of trees surrounding the house.

She looked back. No one was watching. She reached the front sidewalk and started running.

* * *

"I want to do it right now," she told him, pressing her stomach — she could feel it trying to climb into her throat. Probably from running up the steps.

"Where are your mother and father?" asked the sorcerer.

"At the picnic."

"How did you get back here alone?"

"I walked to the subway."

"You must never, *never* do that again. It's not safe for you."

"Who cares? No one . . . no one cares about me. But I'm not bad — am I?"

He shook his head, while his dark eyes studied her; they had an expression Kelsey had never seen before. "Where was the picnic?" he said softly.

"You know where it was." Did he know? *Did he know?*

"Yes. I know."

She hugged herself, shivering in the July heat. "I want us to do it. Right now."

"Yes," he said. "I think this is the time."

They watched the little girl in a red hooded cape pick wildflowers in the deep green woods.

"How old is she?" Kelsey asked the sorcerer.

"She could be any age," he answered as they followed the little girl through the trees.

"Where is she going?" Kelsey said.

"To her grandparents' house."

Kelsey felt the flutter, as if a soft-winged bird had flown inside her, hovered a moment, and then flown on.

Outside the woods the sun shone brightly; but inside, the trees grew so thick, so tall, that the light was dim and shivery. Suddenly they came to a circle of sunlight over a grassy clearing. A tiny house stood in the clearing. Carrying her flowers, the little girl ahead of them climbed the steps and went inside.

The sorcerer motioned to Kelsey. "Follow her. Go and see what is inside."

Kelsey hung back, shaking her head. The soft-winged bird had returned and stayed.

"Go inside," said the sorcerer. "Look for the girl in her grand-mother's bedroom."

He gave her a nod, but Kelsey hesitated. Again the sorcerer nodded, and touched her shoulder. Kelsey bit her lip and looked up at him. When he nodded again, she slowly climbed the steps and entered the house.

It seemed very quiet inside. The front room was bare, as was the long hall beyond. Kelsey heard a murmur of voices and fol-lowed the sound down the hall. She came to a small room and stopped just inside the door.

The little girl stood talking to her grandmother, who was sit-ting in a large bed. The grandmother's head was turned away and covered by a white ruffled cap, so Kelsey couldn't see her face.

The little girl talked softly; Kelsey could hardly hear her until she said, "But, what big hands you have, Grandmother."

The bird inside Kelsey began to beat its wings faster. The grandmother climbed out of bed, the large figure covered by a long nightgown. A deep voice said, "My hands are big to hold you better."

The hands reached toward the little girl and pushed back the red hood. They unbuttoned the cape, and it dropped to the floor.

Kelsey felt strong wings beating inside her. "No," she whis-pered to the little girl. "No. Run away." But she couldn't run.

The big hannds held the child's shoulders; then they began to move. The child whimpered and tried to pull away, but the hands gripped her tightly. The grandmother's white ruffled cap fell back from her face.

A face with a gray beard.

Kelsey felt the scream in her stomach fly to her throat, but the room remained silent. She squeezed her eyes closed. And felt the big hands move again. Now Kelsey could hear the scream; she stumbled out of the room and ran, while the sound of fear raced ahead of her down the endless hall.

The door . . . where was the door? The door was gone!

Crying, she beat on the walls with her fists, the hurt and shame as thick as the walls. "Let me go. Let me go or . . . or I'll tell. *I'll tell.*"

The walls disappeared.

The house around her vanished.

The man with black hair and the nose of a bird sat in his circle of light. Kelsey jumped off the sofa and ran to him.

"Who has been hurting you?" he said. "Tell me."

"It was . . . I can't tell," she cried.

His arms went around her, holding her cries. He wiped her eyes with the tissue from a box on his desk, then said with great care, "Evil things have been done to you. You *have* to tell."

Kelsey struggled against the tears. "I don't know if I can—he told me not to."

"He won't hurt you anymore," the sorcerer said, "if you can tell me, Kelsey. *Tell me*."

"It wasn't . . . wasn't Grandmother in the bed."

"Who else would be in Grandmother's bed?"

"You *know*." She hit his chest with her fists. "You know it was Grandfather Crane!"

"Yes, now I know," he said. "And you have to tell."

"I just told you."

He shook his head. "You must tell your Grandmother Stuart in Rhode Island. She will help you—she promised me she would."

Kelsey pulled away and looked up at him. "Then you're not a sorcerer—at least not all the time—are you?"

She thought she'd said something he didn't like; his mouth twitched, but then it curved upward. Kelsey had never before seen him smile.

He put the volume of fairy tales back in the bookcase, and while he telephoned, Kelsey stood close beside him. She heard Granny Stuart say, "Hello?"

"Mrs. Stuart? This is Dr. Sorensen. We have the answer to what you and I . . ." He stopped when Kelsey held out her hand. "Do you want to tell her, Kelsey?" he asked.

Kelsey nodded slowly and reached for the phone.

BILL PRONZINI

BURGADE'S CROSSING

Another series sleuth new to these pages—and new to most mystery readers, too—is Bill Pronzini's Quincannon, a former U.S. Secret Service agent who is now a partner in a San Francisco detective agency that might one day rival Pinkerton's. The year is 1895 in this particular story, which takes Quincannon to a ferry crossing on the Sacramento River where the plaintive sounds of a calliope are heard as he waits in a storm to protect a man marked for murder. Quincannon has appeared previously in two novels and at least one short story. We expect to see more of him in the pages of the new Louis L'Amour Western Magazine.

Quincannon heard the calliope ten minutes before the Walnut Grove stage reached Dead Man's Slough. The off-key notes of "The Girl I Left Behind Me" woke him out of a thin doze; he sat up to listen and then peer through the coach's isinglass window. He saw nothing but swamp growth crowding in close to the levee road. Sounds carried far here in the river delta, particularly on cold, early-winter afternoons such as this one. And the rusty-piped sound of the calliope was familiar even at a distance: The *Island Star* had drifted downriver and tied up at Burgade's Crossing, just as he'd expected.

The stage's only other passenger, a mild little whiskey drummer named Whittle, lowered the dime novel he'd been reading and said tentatively, "Sounds festive, doesn't it?"

"No," Quincannon growled, "it doesn't."

Whittle hid his face again behind the book. It was plain that he was intimidated by a man twice his size who wore a bushy, gray-flecked freebooter's beard and was given to ferocious glowers when in a dark mood. He was pretending to be a drummer himself, of patent medicines, and Whittle had tried to engage him in brotherly conversation by telling a brace of smutty stories. Quincannon had glowered him into silence. Ordinarily he was friendly and enjoyed a good joke, but today he had too much on his mind for frivolous pursuits. Besides, Whittle's stories were graybeards that hadn't been worth a chuckle even when they were new.

The *Island Star*'s calliope stopped playing for a time, started up again with the same tune just before they reached the north-bank ferry landing at Dead Man's Slough. The coach's driver clattered them off the levee road, down an embankment steep enough to cause the rear wheels to skid and the brake blocks to give off dry squeals. Quincannon had the door open and was already swinging out when the stage came to a halt.

A chill wind assailed him. Overhead, dark-edged clouds moved furtively; the smell of rain was heavy in the air. The coming storm would break before the passenger packet *Yosemite*, bound upriver from San Francisco, reached Burgade's Crossing at midnight. There were possible benefits in a stormy night, Quincannon thought bleakly, but the potential dangers far outweighed them.

He took a pipe from the pocket of his corduroy jacket, packed and lit it as he surveyed his surroundings. He had seen Burgade's Crossing from a distance several times, from the deck of one or another of the Sacramento River steamers, but he had never been here before. It was a sorry little backwater, with no attractions for anyone except the misguided souls who chose to live in or near it.

There was nothing on this side but the road and ferry landing; the town's buildings were all on the south bank. The ferry ran across Dead Man's a few hundred yards from where the slough merged with the much wider expanse of the Sacramento. West of the ferry, on the river, was a steamboat landing; east of the ferry, on the slough next to a continuation of the levee road, stood Burgade's Inn—a long, weathered structure built partly on solid ground and partly on thick pilings over the water. The rest of Burgade's Crossing ran east in a ragged line to where the slough narrowed and vanished among tangles of cattails and swamp oaks choked with wild grapevine. Its sum was a dozen or so buildings, a dozen or so shantyboats and houseboats tied to the bank, and a single sagging wharf.

The *Island Star,* Gus Kennett's store boat, was moored at the wharf. The calliope on her foredeck was again giving forth, monotonously, with "The Girl I Left Behind Me." The music had drawn a small crowd; Quincannon could see men, women, a few children clustered on the gangplank at the battered little steamer's waist.

He shifted his attention to the broad, flat-bottomed ferry barge. It had been tied on the south side, and at the stage driver's hail the ferryman had come out of his shack and was now winching it across. The scow was held by grease-blackened cables made fast to pilings on a spit of northside land a hundred yards upslough. The current pushed the ferry across from shore to shore, guided by a centerboard attached to its bottom and by the ferryman's windlass.

When the barge nudged the bank, the ferryman quickly put hitches in the mooring ropes, collected the toll, then lowered the approach apron. The stage driver took his team of four aboard, their hooves and the coach's wheels clattering hollowly on the timbers. Quincannon, scowling and puffing on his pipe as if it were a bellows, followed on foot. A minute later the cable whined thinly on the windlass drum and the scow began moving again, back across.

The wind was stronger on open water, sharp with the smells of salt and swamp and impending rain. It made the slough choppy, which in turn caused the ferry to buck and squirm even with its heavy load. Again, Quincannon felt worry at what lay ahead tonight. Why the devil couldn't Noah Rideout have been sensible and spent another night—or better yet, another week—in San Francisco?

He touched the pocket where he'd stowed the telegram that had arrived for him in Walnut Grove this morning. Its contents were what had thrust him into his bleak mood:

EFFORTS HERE STILL FRUITLESS STOP NJR RETURNING TONIGHT
ON YOSEMITE STOP COULD NOT DISSUADE HIM COMMA STATES
BUSINESS HERE FINISHED AND IS NEEDED AT HOME STOP LS
ACCOMPANYING HIM BUT NO ONE ELSE COMMA REFUSED
BODYGUARDS STOP URGENT YOU MEET HIM AT BURGADES
CROSSING AT MIDNIGHT STOP

SC

"NJR" was Noah J. Rideout, of course. "LS" was Leland
Stannard, the foreman of Rideout's huge Tyler Island farm. And
"SC" was Sabina Carpenter, the other member of Carpenter and
Quincannon, Professional Detective Services.

There were still some narrow-minded dolts who questioned
the wisdom of a former U.S. Secret Service operative entering
into private partnership with a woman, even though Sabina had,
like Kate Warne before her, worked for several years for Allan
Pinkerton. The truth of the matter was, she was the equal of any
man at detective work. In fact, Quincannon admitted grudgingly
to himself, if never to Sabina or anyone else, she was not only his
equal but in many ways his better. If her efforts in San Francisco
were continuing to prove fruitless, then there was nothing to be
found there.

The weight of the case was now all on his shoulders. And it
was a dual burden: to find out, if he could, who wanted Noah
Rideout dead; and to prevent, if he could, the act of murder from
taking place. There had been one bungled attempt in San Francisco—that was what had led Rideout to hire Carpenter and
Quincannon, Professional Detective Services—and he was certain there would be another tonight. The one lead he and Sabina
had uncovered had led him to Walnut Grove, and that lead had
preceded him here to Burgade's Crossing: Gus Kennett, owner
of the *Island Star,* who was rumored to be the man hired as
Rideout's assassin.

The ferry trip took less than ten minutes. And five minutes
after the barge landed on the south bank, the stage was on its
way along the levee road to Isleton—empty now, for Whittle was
stopping here, too. The two men, Quincannon carrying his old
war bag, the drummer lugging a heavy carpetbag, trudged uphill

to the inn without speaking. Inside, a bearded giant who identified himself as Adam Burgade took three dollars from each of them. The fee entitled the weary traveler to a meal and a room.

Burgade had at least two other guests at present. They were in the common room, and an odd pair they were: a young nun, dressed in a black habit, sitting before the glowing potbellied stove; and an old man with a glass eye and a fierce expression, standing with his hands on his hips before Burgade's liquor buffet.

Whittle stood blinking at the nun. Then, jerkily, he tipped his hat and said, "Good afternoon, Sister. Will you take offense if I say I am surprised to find you here?"

"Not at all, sir. I'm surprised myself to be here."

The old man glared with his good eye. "An outrage, that's what I call it. A damned outrage."

Burgade said, "Watch your language, Mr. Dana. I won't tell you again."

"This is no place for a nun," Dana said. "Besides, I'm a veteran—I served with McClellan's Army of the Potomac in the War Between the States. I'm entitled to a drink of whiskey when I have the money to pay for it."

"The buffet is temporarily closed," Burgade explained to Whittle and Quincannon.

"You hear that?" Dana said. "Temporarily closed. Not a drop of good spirits sold while that woman is in the house. And me with a parched throat. It ain't right, I tell you, Burgade. I ain't Catholic. I ain't even religious."

"Well, I am."

The nun seemed embarrassed. "Really, Mr. Burgade, as I said before, you needn't close your buffet on my account. I don't mind others using alcohol in moderation."

"Mr. Dana don't use it in moderation," Burgade said. "It's best this way, Sister Mary."

"Bah," Dana said.

"Mr. Whittle here is a whiskey drummer," Burgade told him. "Maybe he has a bottle in his grip that he'll sell you."

"I would, and gladly," Whittle said, "but I've no samples left. This is my last stop, you see, Mr. Dana—"

"Bah."

Burgade said, "Gus Kennett's store boat is in, tied up at the wharf. He'll have a jug of forty-rod for sale, if you don't mind paying his price."

"I'll pay any price. But can I bring it back here to drink?"

"No. Burgade's Inn is a temporary temperance house."

"Temporary temperance house. Bah." Dana started for the door, stopped abruptly when he passed Quincannon, and turned back to face him, scowling. "Well, looky here. A Johnny Reb."

"Johnny Reb?"

"That's right. Southerner, ain't you?"

"I was born in Baltimore," Quincannon admitted, "but I've lived in California for fifteen years."

"Once a Johnny Reb, always a Johnny Reb. Spot one of you a mile away. Only good Reb's a dead one, you ask me."

"The Civil War has been over for thirty years, Mr. Dana."

"Tell that to my right eye. It's been pining for the left one for more'n thirty years. Damned Reb shot it out at Antietam."

He clumped out and banged the door behind him.

"Don't mind him, gents," Burgade said. "Nor you either, Sister. He's only like that when he's sober and on his way upriver to the doctor. His bark's worse than his bite."

Whittle said, lowering his voice, "We *can* do business, can't we, Mr. Burgade? Even though the inn is a temporary temperance house? I've some fine buys on Kentucky sour mash—"

"In the kitchen, Whittle, in the kitchen."

The two men went through a door next to the buffet. Rich aromas wafted out, reminding Quincannon that he hadn't eaten since a sparse breakfast. No time now, though; he could have supper later. As for the closing of the buffet, it was of no consequence to him. He had given up the use of spirits when he had entered into partnership with Sabina two years ago.

He found his way down a central corridor at the rear, to the room he'd been given. It was not much larger than a cell, windowless, furnished with a narrow bed and a washstand. He stayed there just long enough to deposit his war bag on the mattress and to double-check the loads in the Remington Navy revolver he carried under his coat.

Outside, the wind pushed him along a muddy branch of the levee road toward the wharf. The *Island Star*'s calliope was mercifully silent, and the number of customers had dwindled to a handful as dusk approached. The little steamer was old and weatherbeaten, her brasswork greening from lack of polish, her short foredeck cluttered with crates and barrels. She was one of a handful of store boats that prowled the fifteen hundred square miles of sloughs and islands between Sacramento and Stockton, peddling everything from candy to kerosene to shantyboaters, small farmers, field hands, and other delta denizens.

Gus Kennett had more profitable sidelines, however. He bought and sold stolen goods, a crime for which he had been arrested twice and convicted once, and was rumored to be involved in a variety of other felonious activities, including robbery and assault. Murder, too, if what Quincannon had heard rumored was true.

As he drew abreast of the gangplank, the old man, Dana, came hurrying out of the lamplit cargo hold, clutching a bottle of forty-rod whiskey. Dana glared at him in passing, muttered something, and scooted off to find a place to do his solitary drinking. He was evidently the last of Kennett's customers. No one was visible in the hold, and the decks were deserted except for a deckhand who lounged near the rusty calliope.

Quincannon sauntered across the plank, entered the hold. It had been outfitted as a store, with cabinets fastened around the bulkheads, a long counter at one end, and every inch of deck space crammed with a welter of sacks, bins, barrels, boxes, tools, and other loose goods. Gus Kennett was perched on a stool behind the counter, a short-six cigar clamped between yellow horse teeth. He was a barrel of a man, Kennett—no, a powder keg of a man—with short, stubby arms and legs; a small head; and a huge, powerful torso.

"Afternoon," Kennett said around the stump of his cigar. "Help you with something, friend?"

"A plug of cable twist, if you have it."

"Don't. Never had a call for it."

"What kind of pipe tobacco do you sell?"

"Virginia plug cut and Durham loose."

"The plug cut, then."

Kennett produced a sack of cheap tobacco and named a price that was half again what it would cost even in Walnut Grove. Quincannon paid without protest or comment.

"Don't believe I've seen you in Burgade's Crossing before," Kennett said. "Big gent like you, nice dressed, I wouldn't forget."

"I've never been here before."

"Passing through?"

"On business."

"What kind of business?"

"Patent medicines," Quincannon said. "Dr. Wallmann's Nerve and Brain Salts, guaranteed to cure more afflictions and derangements than any other product made. I don't suppose I might interest you in a bottle?"

Kennett laughed. "Do I look like I need nerve and brain salts?"

"No, sir, you don't. But some of your customers might."

"Got my own supplier for patent medicines."

Quincannon feigned a sigh. "Little enough business for me here, it seems. Or anywhere in these backwaters. I believe I'll catch the next steamer for Sacramento. There is one due tonight, isn't there?"

"I couldn't say, friend. Ask Adam Burgade."

"I'll do that. Doesn't appear to be much business for you here, either, if I may say so."

"Never is in Burgade's Crossing."

"So you'll be moving on soon yourself?"

"That I will," Kennett said. "Was there anything else, friend?"

Quincannon had taken the conversation to its limit; if he tried to prolong it, he would succeed only in making the store-boat owner suspicious. He said, "No, friend, nothing," and took his leave.

He was uneasy again as he left the *Island Star*. How was Kennett planning to commit murder tonight? There had been nothing aboard the store boat and nothing in Kennett's manner to provide a clue. A distant rifle shot through rain-soaked darkness was pure folly. A pistol shot or knife thrust at close quarters were more certain methods, but Noah Rideout would not be alone when he left the *Yosemite,* and the odds were short that an assassin would be identified or killed himself before he could escape. No, Gus Kennett would not risk his own neck, no matter how much he was being paid. He was sly and slippery, not bold.

Would he enlist the help of others? His deckhand, perhaps? That was another troubling thought.

As was the question of who had hired him and why.

Noah Rideout was a man of many enemies. A hard man, uncompromising in his business dealings and personal life. In his fifty-seven years he had had two wives, several mistresses, and three sons, all of whom, by his own free admission, hated him enough to want him dead. He owned much of the rich Tyler Island croplands; he had forced several small farmers to sell their land to him at low prices, and earned the hatred of others by his tireless and expensive campaign to build more levee roads as a means of flood control. And he had been a leader in the legal battle against hydraulic gold mining in the Mother Lode, the dumping of billions of cubic yards of yellow slickens that had clogged rivers and sloughs and destroyed farmland. The California Debris Commission Act, passed two years before in 1893, had made the discharge of debris into the rivers illegal and virtually put the hydraulickers known as the Little Giants out of business.

Rideout himself had been unable to narrow down the field, although it was his opinion that "one of the damned hydraulickers" was behind the murder plot. His battle with them had been long and bitter, involving bribery and intimidation of witnesses on the part of the miners, and he felt that some were not above mayhem as a means of revenge. But neither Quincannon nor Sabina had been able to find a link between Gus Kennett and one of the Little Giants, or any other evidence to support Rideout's contention.

Restlessly Quincannon prowled through the meager town, but there was nothing there to enlighten him. Full dark had closed down when he started back to the inn. The wind had sharpened and the first drops of rain iced his skin. The clouds were low-hanging now, so low that the tops of some of the taller trees in the swamp were obscured by their drift.

Diagonally across the road from the inn was a barnlike building that he took to be the livery. One of the doors was open, and a buttery lampglow shone within. The light drew him. Inside he discovered four horses in stalls, an expensive Concord buggy, and the hostler asleep in the harness room.

He had a look at the buggy. He thought it might belong to Noah Rideout, and gold monogrammed letters on its body— NJR—confirmed it. Could Kennett's plan have something to do with the rig? Or with the livery barn? Not the rig; Quincannon checked the wheels and hubs, the axle-trees, the transverse springs, even the calash folding top and under the wide leather seat, and found nothing out of order. The barn, though, was an excellent place for an ambush. He would have to keep that in mind.

The rain was gathering momentum as he came out of the livery. Thunder rumbled faintly; so did his empty stomach. He hurried across to the inn.

Sister Mary had the common room to herself. She was still sitting before the stove, working now with cloth and thread on a sampler. He nodded to her and sat down at the long puncheon table.

She asked, "Has it begun to storm?"

"It has."

"I thought I heard thunder. Will it rain heavily tonight, do you think?"

"From all indications. Are you waiting for the midnight packet, Sister?"

"No, I'm going downriver. I'll be leaving in the morning."

"It's unusual for a nun to travel alone, isn't it?"

"Yes. My brother in Isleton is ill."

"I'm sorry to hear that. Seriously ill?"

She nodded gravely. "I am afraid so."

A Chinese waitress entered and Quincannon asked for supper. It turned out to be a plate of fried catfish, potatoes, corn, and a cup of bitter coffee. He wolfed it all down and requested another helping, after which he found room for a slab of peach pie. His appetite had always been prodigious. He had inherited all of his father's lusty appetites, in fact, along with his genteel southern mother's love for cultural pursuits.

Sabina had once remarked that he was a curious mixture of the gentle and the stone-hard, the sensitive and the unyielding. He supposed that was an accurate assessment. And the reason, perhaps, that he was a better detective than Thomas L. Quincannon, the rival of Pinkerton in the nation's capital during the Civil War. He knew his limitations, his weaknesses. His father had never once admitted to being wrong, considered himself invincible—and had been shot to death while on a fool's errand on the Baltimore docks. John Frederick Quincannon intended to die in bed at the age of ninety. And not alone, either.

In his room, he lit his pipe and tried to read one of the books of poetry he habitually took along for relaxation on field investigations. But he was too keyed up to relax tonight. And the verses by Whitman and Wordsworth made him yearn for Sabina. It was a sad but true fact that she had become more than a business partner to him. He had made numerous advances to her that were only partly of a lustful nature; she had rejected each gently but firmly. "We work splendidly together, John," she'd said. "If we were to become lovers, or more, it might damage our professional relationship."

He didn't agree with this, and he was ever willing to put the matter to the test. There were times when he felt that she cared deeply for him and that she was weakening; at other times he was convinced she would never weaken. It made his life difficult, and at the same time highly stimulating.

After a while the restlessness drove him back to the common room. Sister Mary had retired, and there was still no sign of old man Dana. He watched Whittle and Burgade play chess. Burgade was surprisingly good at the game; the whiskey drummer made a poor opponent. Eventually Whittle wearied of losing and went to his room, and Quincannon took his place at the board.

He played an excellent game himself in normal circumstances, but his mind kept slipping away to Gus Kennett and Noah Rideout's imminent arrival. Burgade won three matches and they played a fourth to a draw. Outside, rain hammered on the inn's roof and the wind moaned and chattered ceaselessly. A foul night. And a foul deed no doubt planned for it.

But a deed that would not be done. No, by Godfrey, not with

a fee balance of one thousand dollars yet to be collected from Mr. Rideout.

It was just eleven-thirty by his stemwinder when he left the inn. Burgade registered surprise at his departure, and to forestall questions, Quincannon explained that he was meeting an acquaintance on the *Yosemite* and felt the need of some fresh air before the packet arrived. A bit lame, but Burgade accepted it without comment.

In the wet darkness he pulled the brim of his hat down and the collar of his slicker up to keep water out of his eyes and off his neck. Visibility was no more than a few yards. He could barely make out the daubs of lantern light that marked the ferryman's shack and steamboat landing. Wind gusts constantly changed the slant of the rain so that it was like a jiggling curtain against the night's black wall.

Shoulders hunched and body bowed, he set off along the muddy road toward town. The surface was still solid along the edges, but if the rain continued to whack down with such intensity, by morning this track and the levee road would be quagmires.

Faint scattered lights materialized as he neared the town buildings, but none shone at the wharf. At first he thought the *Island Star* had slipped out of Dead Man's Slough under cover of the storm. But no, she was still moored there, the bumpers roped to her strakes thumping against the pilings as the rough waters rolled her from side to side. All dark as she was, she looked like a ghost boat. There was no sign of Gus Kennett or his deckhand. No sign of anyone in the vicinity.

Quincannon heeled around, started back toward the inn. He had gone only a few yards when a lull between gusts brought a sound to his ears. It was faint and far off, an odd hollow chunking. He paused, straining to hear over the storm's wailings and moanings. There it was again . . . and again. It seemed to be coming from on or across the slough, but he couldn't be certain. He waited to hear it another time—and heard only the wind, the harsh slap and gurgle of the water as it punished the bank below.

He plowed ahead, bypassing the inn and then the ferryman's

shack. The steamer landing, he saw as he approached it, was deserted. He veered off to check behind the landing's rickety lean-to shelter, to peer among the willows and cottonwoods that leaned over the river nearby. He startled a bird of some sort, a snipe or a plover, and sent it whickering off through the swamp growth. Nothing else moved there except the storm.

He stood shivering under the lean-to, his hand still resting on the butt of his revolver, alternately watching the river and the road down from the inn. It wasn't long before he heard the first shrill blast of the *Yosemite*'s whistle: She was on schedule despite the foul weather. Less than a minute later her three tiers of blurred lights appeared; and at almost the same instant lamp-glow spilled out through the front door of the inn and a slicker-clad figure emerged. Quincannon tensed, drawing back against the shelter wall.

The figure came down to the landing, not hurrying, tacking unsteadily through the mud and rain. Whittle? No, it was the old man with the glass eye, Dana. He didn't see Quincannon until he was almost upon him. And when he did, he started so violently that he came close to losing his balance and toppling into the river.

"Hellfire!" he shouted when he recovered. He leaned close to peer at Quincannon's face, breathing whiskey fumes at him. "Is that you, you damn Johnny Reb? What're you lurking here for?"

"I'm not lurking. I'm waiting for the *Yosemite*."

"Sacramento bound, eh?"

"No. Meeting someone."

"Another Copperhead, no doubt. Say, you got relatives fought at Antietam?"

"No."

"Reb that shot my eye out looked just like you."

Dana belched, moved off to stand at the far side of the shelter. He watched the *Yosemite*'s approach with his good eye, and Quincannon watched him.

The packet's captain was experienced at landing in the midst of a squall. He brought the *Yosemite* in straight to the landing, her whistle shrieking fitfully, and held her there with her stern buckets lashing the river while a team of deckhands slung out a gangplank. As soon as the plank was down, two men wearing slickers and toting carpetbags hurried off. After which Dana, with a one-eyed glare at Quincannon and a muttered "Damn all Johnny Rebs," staggered on board. The deckhands hauled in the plank and the steamboat swung out toward midchannel again. The entire operation had taken no more than a minute.

When Quincannon recognized Noah Rideout as one of the disembarkees, he stepped forward and identified himself. Rideout peered up at him; he was half a head shorter and had a habit of standing with his feet spread wide, a pose that was both belligerent and challenging. He reminded Quincannon of a fighting cock.

"What are you doing here?" Rideout demanded.

Quincannon told him in brief, clipped sentences. Rideout was neither concerned nor impressed.

"Well, let this man Kennett come ahead with his dirty work. I am armed and so is Leland. So are you, I trust. That makes three guns against one."

"Kennett may not be planning to use guns. And he may have help, for all we know."

"What sort of ambush could he be planning, then?"

"I haven't a clear idea. The man is shrewd and unpredictable. I suggest we get inside as quickly—"

"Inside? Inside where?"

"The inn, of course."

"That rathole," Rideout said contemptuously. "I wouldn't spend five minutes in Adam Burgade's house."

"It's the only place here to stay the night."

"I am not staying in Burgade's Crossing. I'll sleep in my own bed."

Quincannon stared at him. "You mean you're thinking of traveling home in this weather?"

"Not thinking of it," Rideout said, "about to do it."

"Sir, I strongly advise—"

"I don't care what you advise. Why should I stay here, if this is where some blackguard plans to assassinate me?"

"He could just as easily make the attempt on the road, with the rain and dark to conceal him. It would be safer at the inn."

"Damn the inn. If this rain keeps up, the levee road will be impassable tomorrow. I refuse to stay in Burgade's Crossing one night, let alone two, when I can be home in three hours." He turned to Leland Stannard, a dark, heavyset man who sported mutton-chop whiskers. "Enough of this shilly-shallying. Leland, go up to the livery barn and fetch the buggy and team."

"Right away, Mr. Rideout." Stannard started off.

"Quincannon, you go with him, give him a hand."

"No, sir, I'm staying with you."

"I don't need a bodyguard."

"You hired my firm to prevent your death and that is exactly what I intend to do. If it means accompanying you to your home tonight, then there will be three in your buggy, not two."

"Stubborn, aren't you?"

"No more than you, sir."

Rideout seemed to want further argument, but changed his mind when the wind gusted sharply, pelting him with stinging rain. He shouted, "Have it your way," and stomped off toward the ferryman's shack.

Quincannon followed, grumbling to himself. He would have to leave his war bag at the inn; Rideout wouldn't go with him to pick it up, and he wouldn't let the farmer out of his sight for a minute until they reached his Tyler Island farm. A charge for the inconvenience would be added to Rideout's bill.

The burly ferryman did not take kindly to being wakened from a sound sleep, and even less kindly to a crossing on such a night as this. It was dangerous, he said; the wind was a she-devil, the current was flood-fast—

Rideout cut him off with a curt word and a gold coin that flashed in the light from the ferryman's bug-eye lantern. There were no more protestations. The ferryman had the landing apron down and was making ready with the windlass when Stannard drove the Concord buggy down the embankment.

The two horses were skittish; it took all four men to coax them onto the rocking barge. Stannard set the brake and then swung down to help Rideout hold the animals while the ferryman hooked the guard chain, cast off the mooring ropes, and bent to his windlass. Quincannon braced himself against the buggy's off rear wheel, scanning as much of the shore and slough as he could make out through the downpour. He thought he saw someone up on the road near the inn, a shape like a huge-winged vulture, but he couldn't be sure. If they *were* being watched, whoever it was stood still as a statue.

Progress was slow, the barge rolling and pitching on the turbulent water. They were less than halfway across when Quincannon heard a moaning in the storm's racket—a split of wind on the ferry cable, he thought, or the strain on the scow produced by the load and the strong current. Then all of a sudden the barge lurched, made a dancing little sideslip that almost tore loose Quincannon's grip on the buggy wheel.

The ferryman shouted a warning that the wind shredded away. In the next instant there was a loud snapping noise, and something came hurtling through the wet blackness, cracking like a whip. One of the cables, broken free of its anchor on the north bank.

Swirling water bit into the scow, drenched Quincannon to the knees as it sluiced up across the deck. The ferryman was thrown backward from the windlass; the drum spun free, ratcheting. He shouted again. So did Rideout, who was clinging to the horse on Quincannon's side. The barge, floating loose now and caught by the current, heaved and bucked toward the dark sweep of the river.

The terror-stricken horses reared, and a hoof must have struck Stannard; he screamed in pain and was gone into the roiling slough. Quincannon felt the deck canting over, the buggy beginning to tip and slide away from him. He lunged toward Rideout, caught hold of his arm. In another few seconds the buggy would roll, and the weight of it and the horses tumbling would capsize the scow. There was nothing to be done but to go into the water themselves, try to swim clear while they were still in the slough.

The ferryman knew it, too. He yelled a third time—"Jump, jump!"—and dived over the guard chain. But Rideout fought against going overboard. He clawed desperately to free himself, to cling to the side rail, all the while shouting, "I can't swim! I can't swim!"

Quincannon was bigger and stronger, and there was no time

left for such concerns. He wrenched the little farmer around, locked an arm about his waist, and jumped both of them off the tilting deck.

Rideout's struggles grew frenzied as the chill water closed over them. Quincannon nearly lost his grip on the man's slicker, managed to hold on and to kick them both up to the surface. Rideout continued to flail and sputter in panic, which left Quincannon no choice in this matter either. He rapped the farmer smartly on the chin with a closed fist, a blow that put an abrupt end to the scuffling.

The current had them by then, but it was not half as powerful here as it would be in the river. Quincannon shucked one arm out of his slicker, shifted his grasp on Rideout, and then worked the other arm free; without the dragging oilskins, he could move more easily in the water. It took him a few seconds to get his bearings, to pick out the faint light on the ferryman's shack. Then, towing the unconscious man, he struck out toward the bank.

The wind and the current battled him at every stroke, bobbing the pair of them like corks. Once an eddy almost took Rideout away from him. His right leg threatened to cramp; the cold and exertion numbed his mind as well as his body. The bank, the light, seemed far away . . . then a little closer . . . and closer still . . .

It might have been five minutes or fifteen before his outstretched arm finally touched the shore mud. He got his feet down, managed to drag himself and his burden up through the silt. Lay there in the pounding rain waiting for his breath and his strength to return.

Shouts penetrated the storm, roused him. He sat up weakly. At his side Rideout lay unmoving. Three men were sloshing toward them along the edge of the embankment, Adam Burgade in the lead. Behind him were the burly ferryman and the drummer, Whittle.

When Burgade helped him to his feet, Quincannon said, "Look after Rideout. I'm all right."

Burgade squatted to examine the farmer. "He's alive but he's swallowed a quart or two. I'll get it out of him." He rolled

Rideout onto his stomach, straddled him, and began forcing the water out of his lungs.

Quincannon turned to the ferryman, who was sodden but appeared none the worse for his own hard swim. "The other man on the barge—Stannard?"

"Drowned, looks like. There's no sign of him."

So Gus Kennett would stand trial for murder after all.

Whittle asked, "What happened out there?"

"Cable snapped," the ferryman said. "Don't know how—'twas new enough, and strong the last I checked it."

Quincannon knew how. Even the strongest cable could not withstand the blade of an ax. The odd, hollow chunking he'd heard earlier had been ax blows. Kennett must have known of Rideout's stubborn refusal to spend a night at Burgade's Inn, that he would put his buggy on the ferry barge even in a squall; and he must have rowed a skiff over to the spit anchor and cut most of the way through the cable, leaving just enough for the ferry to be winched out into midstream before it snapped. A diabolical plan. Kennett might have killed four men for the price of one, and evidently without qualms.

He said nothing of this now; there would be time enough later for explanations. He watched the innkeeper finish emptying Rideout, stand and hoist the limp form into his giant's arms.

"He'll live," Burgade said, "if pneumonia don't set in."

"Same might be said for all of us."

Quincannon was still shaky-legged; the ferryman had to lend an arm as they trudged back along the bank, up the steep incline to the road. He was able to walk then under his own power. The ferryman veered away to his shack for dry clothing; the rest of them slogged to the inn.

Sister Mary was waiting anxiously inside. She clasped her hands at the damp front of her habit when she saw Rideout cradled in Burgade's arms. "Is he dead?"

"No, Sister. But he come pretty close."

"Do you think he'll live?"

"Chances are. Say a prayer for him."

Burgade carried the farmer into one of the rear rooms. Quincannon followed, helped strip off Rideout's soggy clothing and get him into bed.

"Hot coffee," he said then, "and plenty of it."

"Whiskey's better for taking off a chill. This is no longer a temperance house, nun or no nun."

"Just coffee for me," Quincannon said, and went out and down the hall to the room he'd occupied earlier. His war bag was still on the bed. A good thing, after all, that he hadn't been able to come back for it before boarding the ferry. He shucked out of his own soggy clothing, noticed then, for the first time, that he'd lost his Remington Navy in the slough. Rideout would pay for a replacement, he thought darkly, and no argument. New clothing and a new slicker, too.

He rubbbed himself dry, dressed, and returned to the common room. Burgade and Whittle were alone there, sitting at the puncheon table with steaming mugs of coffee in front of them. A third cup waited for Quincannon.

"You sure you don't want a shot of Whittle's rotgut to go with it?" Burgade asked him.

"Rotgut?" Whittle was offended. "Mr. Burgade, you know very well—"

Quincannon cut him off. "Where's Sister Mary?"

"Gone to minister to Rideout," Burgade said. "She said she— Hey! What's got into you?"

Quincannon had turned and was running back along the corridor. He yanked open the door to Rideout's room—and just in the nick of time. The woman in the black habit was bending over the bed, a pillow clasped tightly in both hands and pressed down over Rideout's face. The farmer was conscious enough to grapple with her, but too feeble to save himself.

Quincannon rushed in, tore the pillow from her grasp, and flung it aside. She clawed at him, cursing, then tried to ruin him with her knee. He put an end to this lethal behavior by swinging her around and bear-hugging her from behind, pinning her against his body.

"Here, what do you think you're doing?" Whittle said from the doorway. His tone was outraged. "How dare you treat a nun that way!"

"She isn't a nun. Listen to what she's saying, drummer. No nun ever used such language as that."

The woman continued to curse and struggle, trying now to backkick Quincannon's shins; he sidestepped nimbly. Her hood had come askew and strands of bright hennaed hair poked free.

Rideout pushed up onto one elbow, staring at her in dull-witted confusion. "Melissa?" he said.

"You know her, eh? I thought so. Who is she?"

"Melissa Pelletier. She—I knew her in Sacramento last year."

"Knew me?" the woman shouted. "You promised to marry me, damn you. Instead you left me to die with scarlet fever."

"Scarlet fever? I never knew you were ill . . ."

"Nearly a year before I recovered. A year! I swore I'd make you pay dearly—and I would have, if Gus Kennett wasn't a blundering fool. And if this"—she called Quincannon a colorful name—"hadn't stopped me just now."

Quincannon was remembering the tune the *Island Star*'s calliope had played over and over today: "The Girl I Left Behind Me." Coincidence? Perhaps, but he didn't think so. Melissa Pelletier had likely paid Kennett for that bit of satisfaction, too.

Burgade had pushed past Whittle. "What in blazes is this all about?" he demanded of Quincannon. "And what does Gus Kennett have to do with it?"

"Help me put this, ah, lady where she can't do any more harm and I'll explain."

Together they locked Melissa Pelletier in one of the other rooms. Then they returned to Rideout's room, where the farmer was now sitting up in bed with a mug of coffee in one hand. With the other he gingerly rubbed a large bruise on his chin.

"I'll thank you for saving my life," he said to Quincannon, "not once but twice tonight. But dammit, man, was it necessary to crack my jaw?"

Not only necessary, Quincannon thought, *but a pleasure.*

He proceeded to tell his tale to Burgade and Whittle. The innkeeper took an angry view of such goings-on in his town; he was all for rushing down to the *Island Star* with rifle and pistol and either shooting Gus Kennett or placing him under citizen's arrest. Quincannon dissuaded him. He had neither the desire nor the stamina for any more heroics tonight. Even if Kennett realized he had been found out and managed to slip away in his boat, he would not get far. The sheriff of Walnut Grove and the law elsewhere in the delta would see to that.

"You seemed to know Sister Mary wasn't Sister Mary," Whittle said. "What made you suspect her?"

It had been more than one thing. She had told him her brother was seriously ill in Isleton and she was bound there to visit him; yet she had remained in Burgade's Crossing to wait for passage on tomorrow morning's downriver packet, rather than taking the stage from Walnut Grove that had brought him and Whittle here this afternoon. Then there was the figure he'd seen watching the ferry as he and Rideout boarded it. It had resembled a huge-winged vulture, the very shape a woman dressed in black robes with a slicker held fanned out over her head would make. He had known she'd been outside, too, because of the dampness of her habit. And there was no reason for her to have stood watching in the rain unless she knew what was about to happen and wanted to see it done.

Quincannon did not articulate any of this. Nor would he to anyone but Sabina, who would properly appreciate such clever deductions—and, he very much hoped, properly reward him. Instead he smiled an enigmatic smile.

"Detective work, gentlemen," he said. "That is all I can say. A man in my profession must never reveal his secrets."

JULIAN RATHBONE

SOME SUNNY DAY

Julian Rathbone has been writing novels of suspense and intrigue for almost thirty years, specializing in the sort of thrillers that helped establish the reputations of Graham Greene and Eric Ambler. Lately he has launched a most unusual series of short stories, featuring Basilia "Baz" Holmes and Dr. Julia Watson. That's right—a female Holmes and Watson! The Holmes in question is said to be Sherlock's great-niece, with her first name derived from that of Basil Rathbone, a relative of the author. This latest Holmes and Watson story has the unique distinction of winning the first award ever presented by England's Crime Writers' Association for the best short story of the year.

On more than one occasion Baz has abused her great reputation as a criminal investigator for very dubious ends. The "murder" of Don Hicks was a case in point. On our return from Las Palomas we quarreled quite bitterly on the subject. Then, as she has also done on subsequent occasions, she produced a line of reasoning, which, were it not put into practice with remarkable results, I would find endearingly old-fashioned—a naïve amalgam of Hobbes and Nietzsche with a few other "philosophers" like de Sade filling in the harmonies.

Standing with her back to the forty-eight-inch TV screen which plays continuously but always silently in her living room, and which serves the social purpose of an open fire, she rocked back and in her Tibetan snow leopard slippers came on like a pompous don.

"My dear Julia," she said, full of smug self-satisfaction because things had gone so well, in spite of my efforts to put them right, "there is only one personal morality that deserves more than a moment's consideration. Follow your own individual star, the promptings of your innermost soul—be true to that and nothing else—"

I interrupted as mockingly as I could: "Do it my way?"

Baz went on, unruffled.

"The morality you appeal to, the communally shared sense of what is right and wrong, is a fiction, a tissue of lies invented by man in his social aspect to allow society to function, to regulate the transactions we make one with another in our social lives." She sipped ice-cold Russian vodka—neat with a scatter of freshly ground black pepper. "My dear Julia, you are not ill-educated, and you are trained in the social sciences; you are therefore perfectly well aware that all societies hold their own moralities to be the only good ones, yet all societies swiftly and hypocritically change their moralities as soon as their survival is threatened if they do not—"

I attempted an interruption: "I cannot recall a society which condoned or encouraged wholesale robbery on the scale perpetrated by your friend Hicks."

She froze, then gave me that long cold stare which she knows I hate because of its element of Olympian scorn for the foolishness of a mere mortal.

"You forget Ruskin's truism that the wealth of Victorian England was built on the loot of empires."

"And you forget," said I, pleased to find a rejoinder on the spot and not halfway down the stairs, "that he also said you cannot put an unearned sovereign in your own pocket without taking it from someone else's."

Well, enough of that; I leave the reader to judge between us.

I am well aware that Hicks's demise was well aired in the media at the time, and that a couple of hacks have since cobbled together books about the whole affair, but I am also aware that such sensations are less than seven-day wonders, and the more intelligent readers of these memoirs will have quite rightly by now forgotten all but a hazy outline of the sordid business. If, however, you have the sort of mind that does retain in detail the trivia of what passes for news, then I suggest you skip the next page.

In 1970 a gang of three evil hoodlums carried out the Grosswort and Spinks bullion robbery. In the process they killed a security guard but got clean away with £30 million worth of gold bars which were never recovered. Their getaway van had been stolen for them by a petty south London car thief called Don Hicks, who also drove it in the second stage of the robbery. He was arrested for the car theft and later accused of being an accessory—but the prosecution on the major charge was later dropped and he went down for only two years. The three hoodlums were arrested almost certainly on evidence supplied by Hicks, and they got twenty years each.

When Hicks came out he sold up his south London assets, a garage and a terrace house in Tooting Bec, and opened a small car workshop in Marbella, where he claimed to be providing an essential service a Spaniard could not supply—talking English to the English residents who needed their cars fixed.

Six months later he met and married María Pilar Ordoñéz, who was working as a hotel maid and cleaner. Two months after the wedding they moved into a luxury pad in Las Palomas, the smartest little bay between Marbella and Gibraltar. They had won the big one, the fat one the Spaniards call it, the Christmas lottery—six million in sterling at the then rate of exchange. No one believed them, nobody doubted that the money was the Grosswort and Spinks bullion, but no one could prove it, least of all Detective Inspector (as he was then) Stride, who had been in charge of the case. He was furious at this outcome—that Hicks should get off lightly for turning Queen's evidence was one thing, that he should end up seriously wealthy was quite another.

Sixteen years of well-heeled contentment followed, but then Hicks's paradisaical life took two nasty knocks. First, his first wife, Sandra, went to Stride and said she was prepared to tell him all about Hicks's part in the Grosswort and Spinks robbery, including how he had masterminded the whole thing, but most important of all, where what was left of the bullion was, and so on. Second, the three hooligans he had shopped were let out. No one had any doubt at all they would head straight for Las Palomas—in the dock eighteen years before, they had promised Hicks, in song, that don't know where, don't know when, we'll meet again some sunny day. The only question was: Would Stride get there first?

It turned out not to be a coincidence at all that Holmes and I were also on our way, club class BA Gatwick to Málaga. I passed her the plastic ham from my plastic tray and she gave me her orange.

I asked her, "Why?"

"Because," she said, smoothing her immaculately glossy, sleek black hair behind her small but perfect ear, "Don is a very old friend. A very good friend."

"You made a friend out of a robber?"

"He has wit, charm, and he is very, very clever."

"But I thought you occupied yourself with putting criminals behind bars."

"I occupy myself solving human problems whose ironic intricacies appeal to the intellectual side of my personality."

And she terminated the conversation by turning her head slightly away from me so the bony profile of her remarkable nose was silhouetted against the flawless empyrean of space at thirty thousand feet.

We were met at Málaga airport by an urchin in an acid house T-shirt which also carried the slogan "Don't Worry, Be Happy." He wore jeans and trainers and looked every inch a Spanish street Arab until you saw his eyes which, beneath his mop of black hair worn fashionably stepped, were deep-set and blue. He shook hands very politely with me, but to my surprise was awarded with a kiss on both cheeks from Baz.

"¡Madrina!" he cried. "¿Cómo estás?"

" 'Madrina'?" I asked, as he picked up our bags.

"Godmother," Baz replied.

I was stunned. I was even more stunned when Juan Hicks ("Heeks") Ordoñéz led us out to the car park, threw our bags into the trunk of a large silver-gray open-top Merc, and himself settled, with keys, into the driver's seat. I made rapid calculations.

"Baz," I said, "this lad cannot be more than sixteen."

"Sixteen next September."

"But he's driving. Isn't that illegal?"

"Yes. No doubt it would become an issue if he were involved in an accident. He bears this in mind and drives very well."

You could have fooled me. I was sitting directly behind him, with Baz on the other side. For most of the way Juan steered with his left hand, lay back into the corner between door and front seat with his right hand draped over the back of it. That way he was able to keep up a lengthy and animated conversation with Baz, shouted over the roar of the horn-blasting diesel lorries he successively passed.

Baz's Spanish is fluent and perfect—she spent three years of her adolescence there, studying guitar with Segovia amongst others—while mine hardly goes beyond the *"Un tubo de cerveza, por favor"* level, but I picked up some of it, and pieced together the rest from subsequent events—enough to offer the reader an approximate and much truncated transcription.

"How's Dad, Juan?"

"Not good. Very upset indeed. He's left the house and gone on the boat. He's there on his own, refuses to have anyone with him. He says the moment he sees either Stride or McClintock, Allison or Clough coming out after him, he'll start the engine and make for the open sea."

"What good will that do him?"

"None at all. But the boat's very fast. And very maneuverable too. He reckons he can get through the straits and out into the Atlantic before anyone catches him—unless they are prepared to rocket or shell him."

"What then?"

Juan shrugged, head forward on his neck, left hand twisted palm up.

"That's it. *Adíos* Papa."

Baz thought, then said, "A bad scene, Juan."

"Very bad."

"What does your mother think of it all? And the rest of the household?"

"The household shifts from catatonic trance to histrionic hysterics. Especially the girls, and all my cousins. The servants too. But Mama is doing the full dignified matriarch bit. Clytemnestra when she hears about Iphigenia, you know? But if he goes she'll probably throw herself off the quay. Anyway, she'll try to, but I shall be on hand to stop her."

"You won't be strong enough."

He shrugged. "Maybe your fat friend should be there too to help me."

After about twenty miles we swung off the *autovía* and into the hills between it and the sea. The hills were covered with urbanizations—small villas in lots of a hundred or more, all in each group exactly identical to its neighbors. They all had rosebushes and bougainvillea and tiny swimming pools; all were painted white, had red-tiled roofs which clashed with the bougainvillea, and heavy wrought-iron gates, multi-padlocked.

The radio phone bleeped and Juan picked up the handset without slowing down. Indeed, after the briefest exchange he was accelerating with the thing still in his hand.

"Yes?" asked Baz.

"Stride's arrived. We have a friend in the Guardia Civil Cuartel and he says they're planning to move on the stroke of midday, in ten minutes' time. We might well be late."

The next five minutes were a hell of screeching tires and a blaring klaxon. I was thrown from side to side, and when I held on to the fairing of the rear passenger door I lost the straw hat I had bought in Liberty the day before. It had a broad paisley-pattern silk band and streamers and cost £39.99, and that was the sale price.

Presently the view opened up and improved enormously. A small unspoiled fishing village huddled round a little harbor, set within a wider cover. There was a small marina beside the harbor, and about fifteen larger boats at anchor in the bay. The hillsides round the bay were dotted quite sparsely with large houses in varying styles of architecture, though 1970s Moorish predominated. The whole area was fenced, but very discreetly;

only as you approached the red-and-white-striped barrier with its big notice proclaiming *Zona Particular y Privada*, etc. did you see the ribbon of twelve-foot fencing snaking over the hillside amongst the olives. An armed security man heard us coming—he would have had to be deaf not to—and had the barrier up just in time. I have no doubt Juan would have crashed it if he had not.

Juan had to slow a bit—the streets were narrow and crowded, the car rumbled over cobbles and occasionally clanged against sharp corners. Then the bay opened up; we zipped along a short promenade of palm trees, oleanders, and cafés and out on to the mole that separated the harbor from the marina.

There was quite a crowd at the end. Three green Guardia Civil jeeps with the officers dressed in full fig for the occasion—black patent hats, yellow lanyards, black belts and gun holsters, the men in combat gear with automatic weapons. There was a black unmarked Renault 21, and Chief Inspector Stride was leaning against it. There were two television crews and about twenty journalists with cameras and cassette recorders. Above all there was the household. All the adults were dressed in black, but magnificently, especially three dolly-birds—no other word will do—in flouncy tops, fanny pelmets, and sheer black stockings. Eight children, uneasily aware of crisis but bored too, played listlessly while nannies and servants clucked over them if they went too near the water's edge. But above all was Mother—Señora María Pilar Ordoñéz, a veritable pillar of a woman indeed—tall, pale, handsome with an aquiline nose, heavy eyebrows beneath her fine black mantilla; it was impossible to believe she had ever been a chambermaid.

All eyes were fixed on a large but powerful-looking cabin cruiser at anchor in the roads between the headlands. One could discern the Spanish flag on the forearm, the Blue Peter at the yard, and the red duster of the British mercantile marine over the stern. A little putter of sound came across the nacreous water that just rose and fell with a small swell not strong enough to break the surface, and bluish-white smoke swirled behind the exhaust outlets. Hicks had the engine running, was ready to slip his anchor.

When Stride, a big man in a suit he'd grown too fat for, big pursy lips above turkey jowls, saw us, he lifted his hat and big, arched, bushy eyebrows. He's head of the City of London Police Serious Fraud Squad now and has often clashed with Baz, knows her well. He had been given the job of arresting Hicks, dead against all rules and precedents, solely because he was the last officer still operational who had actually worked on the Gross-wort and Spinks bullion robbery back in 1970.

I expect he was about to say something too boringly obvious to be worth recording, when the village church clock struck twelve, the notes bleeding across the air above the water. A Guardia Civil colonel, no less, touched his elbow and he and a party of Guardias began a slow descent down stone steps to a smart little cutter that was waiting for them. As they got to the bottom the village clock began to strike twelve again.

"In case you didn't count it the first time," Holmes murmured.

"Aren't you going to do anything for your fine friend?" I asked.

She shrugged with unusual stoicism, and sighed.

"I fear this time for once, my dear Watson, we are too late."

As the last note bled away into silence the cutter edged out from the quay and began to pick up speed. At the same time a figure appeared on the bow of the cabin cruiser and we saw him fling the anchor rope into the sea. He disappeared into the glassed-in cockpit; the cabin cruiser began to move, accelerated, began a wide turn, throwing up a brilliant gash of bow-water against the black-blue of the sea and then . . . blew up. Blew up really well, into lots of little pieces that went soaring into the immaculate sky only to rain down again within a circle fifty meters across. The bang reverberated between the cliffs and seabirds swooped up and away in a big soaring arc. It was not impossible to believe the soul of Don Hicks was amongst them.

Doña María Pilar, at least, thought so. With her hand to her throat she stifled back a cry of grief and moved with determination toward the unfenced edge of the quay. Her purpose was clear. I launched myself across the intervening space and grasped her round the waist at the last moment, causing her, and myself, to fall heavily on a cast-iron bollard and cobbles.

Naturally, she was the first to be helped to her feet. She looked down at me and said, in Spanish which Holmes was good enough to translate for me later:

"Who the fuck is this great fat scrotum, and what the fuck does he think he's doing?"

"We know," she said, two hours or so later, "who did it. What Señora Basilia has to do is prove it. If"—and she waved a fork from which long strands of spaghetti still hung—"you can prove it so well that the police here will lock up McClintock, Clough, and Allison for ten years or more, then I shall pay you twenty million pesetas."

Well, at that time, just before the British economy went into what will probably turn out to be terminal decline, that was one hundred thousand pounds.

We were all, and I mean all, about fifteen of us, in the big dining room in Casa Hicks. This was a spendid room, the central feature of which was a big, heavy, well-polished Castilian oak table with matching chairs—up to twenty could be found, for the Hicks family entertained often and lavishly, in the old style. The ceiling was coffered cedar. Three walls were done out with tiles to waist height, the patterns reproduced from the Alhambra. Above these were alcoves filled with arum and madonna lilies. Persian carpets hung between the niches, except on the wall opposite Doña María Pilar, at the far end of the long table, where the carpet space was filled with a full-length painting of Don Hicks done eight years earlier in the style of Patrick Proctor, possibly by Patrick himself. It portrayed him full length in a wet suit, with a harpoon gun in his right hand, while his left held a three-foot shark just above the tail so its nose rested on the floor. Hicks, done thus, was a striking figure, a very handsome, broad, tanned face set off by a leonine mop of silver hair, the suit concealing the no doubt well-padded shoulders, the swelling tum, and the varicose veins.

The remaining wall was glass onto a verandah with a view of the harbor, but on this occasion rattan blinds were drawn on the outside and looped over the wrought-iron balcony, probably to cut out the mid-afternoon sun and heat while allowing air to circulate, possibly also because none of those assembled were prepared to look down on the spot of oily water, still with some debris floating, where their lord and master had suffered his demise.

"I have already determined to do so," said Baz, "and only required your permission before initiating my inquiries."

There was a murmur of appreciation from all those around the table who were silently or not so silently weeping. It was not a household in which one could readily grasp the relationships unless or until one accepted the unacceptably obvious. María Pilar ruled a harem, or more properly I should say a seraglio. There were her own three children—Juan, who had driven us from the airport, his younger brother, Luis, and Luis's twin sister, Encarnación. Then there were three—well, I'm sorry, but there's only one wrd for it—concubines: Dolores (or Lola), Carmen, and Purificación (or Puri). Lola and Puri were curvaceous and very, very feminine, Lola with deep red hair, Puri's black and gypsyish, both worn long. Carmen was tall, athletic, with natural dark-honey blond hair worn short above green eyes. Between them all they had, I later gathered, six more children whose ages ranged from one to thirteen, though only the older three or four were with us for lunch.

What was even more scandalous was that Baz herself was apparently to some extent responsible for these arrangements. María Pilar had approached her fourteen years earlier with a problem: After the birth of her twins the doctors had told her more children would kill her. Since she was deeply Catholic, this posed a problem: Don Hicks had not risked a lifetime in prison in order to end up a celibate on the outside. María Pilar's pride was such that she could not accept his having clandestine affairs, nor would she tolerate the gossip and innuendoes that would arise if he did. Baz proposed the solution: concubines. María would remain in control and in charge, the locals would have nothing to be sly about because it would all be in the open, and so on. It had been difficult to begin with but once Lola's first child arrived and Carmen moved in, it had worked beautifully— María Pilar finding great fulfilment in playing the role of supermum to the whole household. As a sociologist I have to say I approve—since it works. As a strongly anti-Catholic feminist I'm not so sure. . . .

"As soon as the shops reopen," Baz continued, "I shall be grateful if Juan will be good enough to take me to the nearest reliable shop selling underwater equipment—I imagine the one his father used to use is reliable—and tomorrow, weather and the police permitting, I shall examine what is left of the wreck."

"You will charge the expenses to Don's account."

Baz inclined her head in acceptance of this offer.

"Meanwhile," she asked, "I need to know when McClintock, Clough, and Allison arrived here."

Luis, an attractive lad, fairer than Juan, chipped in. "They were first seen only yesterday morning. But they went straight to one of the smaller villas on the other side of the bay. It had been booked and prepared for them in advance, so it is likely they have confederates already working in the area."

"In any case," said Baz, "twenty-four hours would have been ample [she pronounces the word "ah-mpull," an irritating affectation] for them to have put a bomb in place, or more probably a mine. What very few people are aware of is that Brian McClintock is a member of the IRA and no doubt learned the technology that blew up your father from those who did much the same to poor dear Louis."

The meal over, I declined a second opportunity to enjoy Juan's driving skills and pronounced myself eager, as eager as one appropriately could be in a house suddenly plunged into mourning, for a siesta. I was shown to a room at the back of the house, which yet had good views of the distant sierra above the olive and almond groves, and which shared a bathroom with the room on the other side, which had been allocated to Baz. My luggage was there ahead of me, and unpacked—a service I always find mildly impertinent on the rare occasions it happens to me.

However, sleep did not come easily—the excitements of the day had been too intense—and presently I pulled on my Bermuda shorts with the passionflowers and a plainer but comfortably loose orange top, and set off for a quiet and, I hoped, discreet exploration of the property. In truth I was hungry, too. No doubt out of consideration for both the dead and bereaved,

María Pilar had allowed lunch to consist only of the spaghetti, which normally would have been the first course merely, and fruit, and the so-called breakfast on the plane had been so relentlessly aimed at carnivores that I had not been able to take on board as much as I like to at the beginning of the day.

I padded down the corridors and stairs I had already climbed, into the spacious circular hall with a glass dome. For the most part the house was silent—the ghastly tragedy that had occurred may have stifled appetites for food, but not apparently for sleep. Though I was surprised at one point to hear two girls giggling behind a door, and then again *sevillanas* played quite loudly on Radio Málaga with castanets added in real. Servants, I supposed, less moved by their master's death than they appeared to be in front of his family.

In the hall, also tiled and with alcoves filled with roses this time, there was no mistaking the door to the kitchens and similar offices: It was slightly ajar, lined with green baize, and the stone steps led down. I now entered a quiet and blissfully cool world of larders and pantries lit only by small grills near the ceilings. It was all very clean and neat too—one could imagine that María Pilar's influence was as strong in these partially subterranean halls as everywhere else. Presently I was in the kitchen, hung with whole sets of copper pans, with assorted knives in racks, and, precisely what I had hoped to find, a row of blackish-brown sheep cheeses, one of which had already been cut. The cheese was almost pure white, a sort of creamy marble, and crumbly—in short, *à point,* or as the Spanish have it, *al punto.* It was with me the work of a moment to cut myself enough to fill a half *barra.* I wondered where the wine was kept. Such a good cheese deserved a fruity red.

At that moment I heard a totally indescribable noise. Nevertheless I shall do my best. It was a sort of rhythmical combination of squelching and slapping, each beat ending with a brisk noise somewhere between a squeak and the noise of torn cloth. It happened about twelve times, then stopped.

Of course I was petrified. Fat people, and I am very fat, live in constant dread of the ridicule which is provoked by the situation I was then in. Nevertheless, curiosity, and a loyal feeling too that

Holmes should be aware of anything untoward that was going on in the house, prompted me presently to move in the direction from which the sounds had come. I passed through an open but bead-curtained doorway into a short narrow defile between white walls from which the sun's glare was instantly blinding. I waited until I could see—of course I had not brought my shades with me—and followed it into a wide sort of patio. It was clearly used by the gardener as a marshaling yard for potted plants—there were rows and rows of them, mostly pelargoniums in all their wonderful variety ranging from the brilliant simple vermilion people call geranium red, to wonderful concoctions in purples and mauves that to all but the most overeducated taste rival orchids for exotic beauty.

The floor was of polished terrazzo chips. Pools of water lay round the bases of the flowerpots, which, in spite of the adjustable rattan roofing which shielded the plants from direct sunlight, steamed gently in the heat. So too did the strangely shaped splodges of water which tracked, arrow-shaped, pointing away from the door of what was obviously a potting shed, across the yard, and out on to a gravel walk, and finally a steep slope of dried grasses and immortelles that dropped beneath olives to the sea—and I mean the sea, not the bay, for the house was set on the headland between the two. Unable to make anything of this, I returned to my room and ate my *bocadillo,* little mouthful. A little duty-free Scotch with water helped it down *faute de vin,* and soon I felt able after all to have a zizz.

"I hope, Julia, you have brought your long spoon with you."

"We are then, my dear Holmes, invited to sup with the Devil?"

"Precisely so. You know I do not readily indulge in hyperbole or other forms of linguistic excess, so you will heed me when I tell you the invitation came from one of the most evil men I have ever had to deal with."

Generally speaking, Baz's opinion of the male sex is low. We were then to dine with the lowest of the low. I was relieved, however, to learn that dining was at least on the agenda.

"The Devil has a name?"

"Brian McClintock. And I imagine Frank Allison and Malcolm Clough will be in attendance."

The bad news was that, Spanish-style, dinner would not be served till ten. We were invited for drinks at half-nine.

I asked Baz if her shopping trip to Málaga had been successful.

"Indeed yes. And apart from the underwater equipment, I bought one or two other odds and ends which will help us in our endeavors." From her silk-and-wool shoulder bag, woven in Samarkand, she pulled a small black plastic bag. It was sealed with black plastic tape.

"This," she said, "is a radio transmitter, part of an eavesdropping device of exceptional accuracy and power. While we are dining, I shall attach the microphone and microtransmitter to the underside of the dining table. Later you will go to the ground-floor toilet, which is in a vestibule off the main hall and close to the dining-room. I know all this, my dear Watson, because I also went to the agent who manages the villa our evil trio has rented. All I ask of you this evening is that you simply place this package in the cistern. The microtransmitter will send its signal to the RT in the cistern, which will then relay whatever it picks up to the Guardia Civil Cuartel in Las Palomas."

"What if they frisk us on the way in?"

"I don't think they will. But if they offer to we shall plead our sex and go home. Not much will be lost; this is simply a backup to my main strategy."

"I think they will. In their position I would."

"Ah, but what you do not understand is that they believe we are on their side. In fact they have already paid me a retainer."

"My dear Holmes, this is too much!"

"Isn't it just? But it will work out, you'll see."

The evil trio's villa, on the other side of the bay, was perhaps one of the nastiest buildings I have ever been to. Built some ten years earlier, probably on the cheap, it was already showing marked signs of wear. The outside wall by the front door was streaked with orange stains, and the stucco rendering was coming away off the corners to expose ill-laid cheap brick. The door itself was made of pine simulating oak, studded with nailheads and with a cast-iron grill simulating a convent gate. The varnish was lifting. Fortunately we could not see much of the garden, as the dusk was already upon us, but there was the inevitable bougainvillea clashing with a profuse variety of nicotiana.

We were welcomed into a hall, where black mold grew up the outside wall, by Frank Allison, a tall dark man once handsome and strong, now a ruin of himself. He offered us what must once have been a con man's charm and was now the wheedling flattery of a conniving ex-con. The only good argument for the death penalty, and not one I would discount until the situation is re-formed, is what long prison terms in our appalling prisons do to the inmates. I write as one who has been a Prison Visitor.

The interior he took us into had been furnished to appeal to the lowest common factor in taste and had sunk below even that. There were stained-glass lanterns over the lights; others were lac-quered brass fittings from which the lacquer had peeled. The up-holstered furniture was covered in grubby, ill-fitting loose covers of a wishy-washy design. The upright chairs were made from turned pine with stick-on moldings, painted black. Cracked leatherette simulated leather. On a wall table a large bowl of opalescent glass in the shape of a stylized swan held English lilac which was no longer factory fresh. Worst of all was a painting of a gypsy girl pretending to sell sardines, but really it was her boobs that were on offer, heavily framed in a bright, shiny gilt above a false fireplace that the occupants had been using as an ashtray.

"Lovely, isn't she?" said Brian McClintock, coming in behind us. He was a short, compact, tough-looking man, with a pale pock-marked face, and eyes the color of year-old ice. He ran his fingers over the gypsy girl's boobs. "Original, see? You can feel the impasto. Glad you could make it, Holmes. And your friend. I don't think I've had the pleasure."

I took the gray claw he proffered and repressed a shudder at its chill. No shudder though for the chill of the strong g-and-t, well iced, that came after it, accompanied by canapés of anchovy on Ritz biscuits, cream cheese with tiny pearl onions. Really, one might as well have been in Balham, though I doubt the drinks there would have been served so strong.

Incidentally, all what he called "the doings" were handed around (and probably had been prepared) by the third of the evil trio: Malcolm Clough. He was fat and bald but with forearms and fists still solid and strong, the skin not gone loose, supported by muscle as well as fat. He affected a slightly camp style that went with the apron he was wearing. I got the impression that he supplied the muscle, Allison the mean, low cunning, but that McClintock was the leader—in terms of pure nastiness he had the edge on the others.

After the one drink, taken with the five of us standing and remarking on the continuing brightness of the weather and the possibility of thunder by the end of the week, Malcolm declared his paella would be sticking and would we be so kind as to go through. He showed us to places round an oval table with cracked veneer, dressed with plastic mats and Innox cutlery. Before he "dashed" he used a Zippo lighter on the single red candle set in a tiny tin chamber pot bearing the legend "A Present from Bognor Regis." The place settings were already filled with bowls of gazpacho—which, I have to say, I found perfectly acceptable. Allison filled wineglasses with a semisweet, which was not. McClintock lifted his to Holmes.

"Cheers. Well, Baz. How's it going?"

"Early days yet, Bri, early days. I'm still not quite sure how it was done, but tomorrow I shall find out. Or the next day."

"We saw you was in Málaga," commented Allison, "and bought the underwater gear. Have much trouble explaining why you wanted it?"

"None at all," replied Baz. "You will recall that the other side has retained me to fit you up as Hicks's assassins. In order to do that they expect me to recover faked evidence from the ocean floor. Little do they realize that I shall in fact use the opportunity to discover how Hicks got away from the boat in the second or so between when he was seen on the deck and the moment of the explosion. The evidence has to be there somewhere."

"But we retained you to locate the bastard. Not figure out how it was done."

"Of course, Bri. But since I am sure he has not returned to Casa Hicks, figuring out how it was done will provide essential clues as to how far he has got. And in what direction. So it is important that I should work out just how he did get away. From that we should be able to deduce how far he was able to get in whatever he was using as a getaway vehicle. I already feel fairly sure that it was a heavily armored midget submarine of Russian design. We know some of your bullion turned up on world markets via the Eastern bloc. If I am right, and there will be cleats on the hull of his cruiser and a hatch to link the two, and these are what I shall be looking for tomorrow, then I think we can safely say he got no further than Tangier, or the coast nearby. In fact, I already have people working for me there, scouring the souks and bazaars, the pubs, and above all the male brothels. Did you know Hicks was that way inclined?"

"I'd believe any filth of a creepy cunt like Hicks," said Allison.

"Come, come," said Clough, returning to serve the paella, "nothing wrong with a bit of bum every now and then."

After the paella there was whisky-soaked bought-in ice cream gâteau, and as it was served I felt the pressure of Baz's foot on my own. From that I understood that the microphone stroke microtransmitter was in place, and that the ball was in my court as regards the more powerful transmitter. In fact this was a great relief, since the cold of the ice cream hitting the oily glutinous mass of rice, mussels, and prawns had provoked a reaction that brooked no delay. It had become a problem—for if I went the once, how would I explain a second "visit" so soon after?

" 'Scuse I," I said, and pushed back my chair. Fortunately a glance at Baz's stony face brought me to my senses just in time, and I managed the obvious question I had been about to omit out of foreknowledge. "Where is it?"

"The ladies' room? Upstairs, second on the right," said Malcolm Clough.

I looked a question at Baz and received a tiny shrug which seemed to say go ahead anyway.

Up there, I popped the bag in the cistern—it was a high-level one but I was able to manage just by lifting the lid—unclipped my braces, negotiated the satin-edged cover on the seat, and then thought again. I did not fancy that the Civil Guard headquarters in Las Palomas should hear the first effects of *tarta al whisky* on paella. I rehoisted the nether garments and stood on the seat—necessary now because the bag had sunk to the bottom of the cistern. The seat, thin pink plastic, shattered. I retrieved the bag, pushed it outside the door, and contrived, with some haste now, and in spite of the shards of broken plastic, to answer one of nature's more peremptory calls, perched on the cold porcelain pedestal. Then I retrieved the bag from the landing. *But,* I thought, *when they discover the broken seat they may guess I stood on it and for why.* I placed it instead in another pink plastic receptacle instructing ladies in terms so coy I cannot recall them to deposit tampons and sanitary towels in here and not down the loo. On my way back down I pondered some of what had happened, and had been said, and came to the conclusion that Baz was playing a pretty fishy game.

"Baz," I said, on the way home, "you're playing a pretty fishy game."

"So it may seem to you, dear Julia, so it may seem to you."

"And that bag you gave me, it's in the upstairs loo. Does that matter?"

"I think not."

We were wending our way down the short drive to the electronically controlled gate. The garden of the evil trio's rented villa was of course untended, and branches of hibiscus and plumbago brushed my face.

"It would be fairer for me, and render me more likely to play my part properly, if you told me the truth."

"Julia, so far you have performed magnificently, and as for the truth, remember, he who tells it is sure to be found out—but, as they say, hist!"

Her sudden movement banished from my lips my riposte to her secondhand epigram and she pulled from I know not where, for she was wearing a single-piece, pocketless garment cut like a boiler suit but made out of yellow wild silk, a small but powerful pencil torch. Its beam, as if laser-guided, fell instantly on the head of a woman standing pressed up against a cypress tree. As the light fell on her she flung up an arm to cover her face, but not before we had both recognized the tall, athletic, and sullenly beautiful Carmen—the second of Hicks's concubines.

"We shall ignore her," said Baz, extinguishing the torch and taking my arm. "She has served her purpose. I imagine, too, she has the means of opening the gate we are approaching and hopefully has left it open for us."

This turned out to be the case.

Baz was never an early riser, her preferred hours of alertness and work being from midday until two, then from ten at night to five in the morning. She therefore engaged to be on the Hickses' second cruiser, with her underwater gear, no earlier than half-eleven—an arrangement which the Hicks family, being Spanish by birth or habit, found perfectly acceptable.

I, on the other hand, wake at seven and have to be up and doing by eight at the very latest, and that was the hour that found me next morning again padding about an almost perfectly silent house, bored and hungry. This time I felt no compunction about going straight to the kitchen: A hostess who cannot provide breakfast for her guests at a reasonable time must not be surprised if they fend for themselves. I found coffee in a filter jug, which I reheated, milk in a big fridge, and a pack of four croissants in a cupboard. I found the means of heating them through, and I speedily got outside the lot. The moment then arrived which I dread—it is precisely as I pour my second cup of coffee that I most feel a dreadful urge to smoke again. I gave up five years ago, but still the only way to keep myself from a mad scramble for the nearest fag is to resort to displacement activity.

I recalled the extraordinarily handsome pelargoniums in the gardener's patio outside and resolved to pinch a few cuttings while no one was about. I supplied myself with several sheets of kitchen roll soaked in water and a pair of kitchen scissors, and stepped out into the already hot sunlight. I took my time selecting them, for I felt it would be impractical to take more than eight.

I had just snipped the fourth when I heard noises from the kitchen, much the same sort of noises as I had made a half hour earlier. What to do? Some people can be surprisingly shirty when they catch you taking cuttings, especially if they are of hybrids they have themselves created, as well might have been the case in this instance. I decided to hide in an alcove where there was a stone sink and a coiled hose, and wait until whoever was in the kitchen had gone. I gathered up my impedimenta, did just that, turned to face outward, and found I was looking across the patio at the man who had to be the gardener himself. He was tall but old, with short white hair and a big white mustache and a big white beard, both stained with yellow. He was dressed in an orange mono splashed with mud and perhaps cement, wore heavy-duty gardening boots.

"¡Hola!" I offered. "¡Buenas días!"

He said nothing, which is unusual for a Spaniard when offered the time of day, but unbuttoned his breast pocket, took out a pack of Ducados, shook one out, and lit it. The smell recalled painfully just why I had been caught so obviously in flagrante delicto. Then as he expelled the first puff, sandaled feet tick-tocked out of the kitchen and there was Lola, in a short and transparent nightie as well as gold sandals, carrying a tray with a bowl of coffee and a large chocolatina.

She didn't see me, but put the tray down on a large upturned flowerpot, perched up on to her toes, and gave the gardener a big kiss.

"¡Hola, Papa, crossantes, no quedan. No sé por qué . . . !"

So. The gardener was Lola's father—not an unlikely arrangement. I put down my stolen cuttings and sidled away, muttering apologies in mixed Spanish and English, which they ignored.

At midday then we were all out in the bay on the Hickses' second major craft, an elegant reproduction of a Victorian steam yacht, but with modern engines, radar and so on, and just over the spot where his more conventionally modern cruiser had been blown up. Presently Holmes and Juan appeared from below, clad in wet suits. On the deck they hoisted oxygen cylinders on to their backs, fixed masks, all that scene—one has seen it a thousand times on TV—and finally to the manner born toppled backwards over the taffrail.

When I say "all" I mean all—not only María Pilar and her

children, the concubines including the strange and at the moment clearly agitated Carmen, and their older children, but also Stride, and the Colonel of the Civil Guards, again in full fig, black hat, black mustache, Sam Browne, and the rest. Twenty minutes or so went by during which we all watched the rise and plop of bubbles through the oily water. After a time a brown scum crept by on which floated panty pads and used contraceptives. I was amused that the efforts of the *ayuntamiento* de Las Palomas to cast a cordon sanitaire round their unspoiled haven were vitiated by the sea—the flotsam of the Costa del Sol, recently renamed Costa del Mierda, could not be so easily kept at bay. During all this Holmes apparently kept up a laconic conversation with the colonel by phone.

Suddenly a big break of bubbles through the heaving scum heralded a shout of triumph. The colonel stood up and explained, in Spanish of course but the gist was clear: "She's got it."

An underling in round, peaked cap strode across to the small funnel that rose in front of the staterooms, and yanked on a small lever. A shiny copper or brass horn near the top of the funnel emitted two short blasts and a long one that echoed across the bay. Our attention was drawn to the villa the evil trio had rented and its purlieus. It was nearer the water and nearer our boat than I had expected. What one saw was a platoon of Guardias, in full combat gear, snaking up over the terraces towards the house. A PA system boomed incomprehensibly, presumably calling upon the occupants to surrender. It was answered by the crackle of small arms, and tiny puffs of blue smoke drifted across the frontage. The Guardias replied and most of the villa's windows, shutters and all, disintegrated in the firestorm. Five seconds and a white flag was waved. Clough and Allison appeared on the terrace, their hands on their heads.

At this moment Carmen uttered a cry expressing horror and despair and jumped for the taffrail. Undeterred by my effort the previous day, I again launched myself at her, but she was too quick for me and I fell on my boobs and face on the spot where she had been standing. She was last seen doing a powerful crawl through the filth of the bay and out to sea. No one, apart from me, seemed bothered to try to stop her.

A familiar voice behind me: "Well, you could have got us up a bit smarter than that. We've missed all the fun." And Holmes, followed by Juan, both holding black plastic bags, squelched and smacked past me toward the companionway. I looked at the frog footprints they left, arrow-shaped but pointing back to the rail they had climbed over, and all fell into place.

Lunch on board was, I have to say, magnificent though served as a finger buffet—a system that I normally find unsatisfactory: besides various hams and chicken and so on that I can't take there were giant prawns, calamares romana, Canary potatoes in hot cumin sauce, Russian salad, six other salads, and a huge cold sea bass. There was French champagne and the best in Spanish brandy. Oh yes, I almost forgot, there was cream Catalan, Pyjama ice-cream, watermelon, peaches, loquats, and so on. And unlimited coffee.

When it was over we were all called into the main stateroom. A table had been set across one end beneath a second portrait of Hicks, this time one of him steering the boat we were on. Behind the table sat Holmes, Stride, and the colonel of the Civil Guards. The rest of us sat if we could, or stood in a crowd at the back. The colonel opened the proceedings and Juan, whose English could be as good as his father's, whispered what he said in my ear.

The gist was simple. Condolences to the bereaved family delivered somewhat perfunctorily. Then congratulations to Holmes for so speedily sorting out and proving by whom and how the dreadful deed had been done. Three criminals with an unjustified grudge against Hicks had mined his boat and detonated their explosives by a remote control device, blowing him into bite-sized pieces. They had been assisted by Carmen, a close friend of Hicks, but who had also developed a grudge against him. She had been caught on the other side of the headland and confessed all. Meanwhile Holmes had recovered evidence of how the mine was detonated from the seabed, and the device used to transmit the signal would shortly be discovered in the villa. The Guardias under his command had attempted a peaceable arrest of the three murderers but they had resisted. One of them, Brian McClintock, had been shot dead.

Applause.

Stride took the floor. He was, he said, very grateful indeed to his colleague of the Spanish Guardia Civil, so long a force for law and order respected all over Europe and the world, for this magnificent achievement. Speaking on behalf of the English equivalents, his senior officers in Scotland Yard and in the Special Branch, he would like to say how pleased he was that these three nasties had been wrapped up for good, especially McClintock who was known to have had a hand in the assassination of Lord Mountbatten, even though he had been in prison at the time. No doubt the lefties back home would bleat as they usually did, as they had after the Gibraltar affair, at summary justice executed against known terrorists, but he was confident that Spain's handling of the whole business would be unequivocally endorsed by HMG.

He paused, sipped water, dropped his voice by an octave. He was, he said, saddened by the death of Don Hicks. He had always had a sneaking admiration for the man and had regretted quite deeply the duty that had brought him to these shores—namely to arrest him for a crime nearly twenty years old. So in a way it was a relief not to have to do this, and a great relief to be able to write once and for all finis to the Grosswort and Spinks bullion case. He had no reservations at all about adding his condolences to the colonel's and offering them to the bereaved family.

Applause.

"Hang on," I said. My voice squeaked but I was determined. "This won't do, you know. Don Hicks is alive and well and living in his garden shed—"

"Julia!" Holmes's voice was like frozen prussic acid, but I plowed on.

"Those three men were villains, I know, but this time they have been fitted up—"

"Watson!"

"I saw Hicks this morning. Lola, Dolores, over there, she

brought him his breakfast. In the garden shed. Yesterday I saw his frogman footprints—"

María Pilar intervened this time: "If no one else will silence that fat scrotum, I shall." And she came for me with a knife.

I don't know why she calls me that. I know I wear mannish clothes, but she can't really believe I'm a man. . . .

On the way back to the airport, Juan driving, my remonstrations with Holmes were again interrupted by a bleep on the radio phone. Juan passed the handset to Holmes.

"It's for you."

Holmes listened, then said, "I'll ask her."

She turned to me and her eyes, deep violet, dilated by the drugs she often uses at the successful outcome of a case, seemed to penetrate the inner recesses of my soul.

"Julia, the police cannot find the radio transmitter that detonated the bomb, and which you hid for me in the cistern of the upstairs toilet of the villa. Please tell me where it is."

Defeated, I told her.

A shadow of a smile crossed her lips though not her eyes.

"I imagine that being men they preferred not to look for it there."

One last footnote. When I got back home I found eight pelargoniums, fully grown, of real magnificence, delivered by a florist who is on the Designer Living Card list, of which more anon in a later tale. The card read "Gratefully yours, DH." They are very lovely and I cherish them. But plants bought ready grown never give the same pleasure as those one has reared from stolen cuttings—do they?

BRUCE HOLLAND ROGERS

ENDURING AS DUST

Bruce Holland Rogers is a relatively new writer residing in Illinois, but few people reading this story will doubt that he's well versed in the Washington scene. Is it really a crime story? You're darn right it is, and it earned an Edgar nomination from Mystery Writers of America!

I drive past the Department of Agriculture every morning on my way to work, and every morning I slow to a crawl so that I can absorb the safe and solid feel of that building as I go by. The north side of Agriculture stretches for two uninterrupted city blocks. The massive walls look as thick as any castle's. Inside, the place is a warren of offices and suboffices, a cozy organizational hierarchy set in stone. I've often thought to myself that if an H-bomb went off right over the Mall, then the White House, the Capitol, the memorials and the reflecting pools would all be blown to ash and steam, but in the midst of the wreckage and the settling dust, there would stand the Department of Agriculture, and the work inside its walls would go securely on.

I don't have that kind of security. The building that houses the Coordinating Administration for Productivity is smaller than our agency's name. The roof leaks. The walls are thin and haven't been painted since the Great Depression.

That I am here is my own fault. Twenty years ago, when I worked for the Bureau of Reclamation, I realized that the glory days of public dam building were over. I imagined that a big RIF wave was coming to the bureau, and I was afraid that I'd be one of those drowned in the Reduction in Force. So I went looking for another agency.

When I found the Coordinating Administration for Productivity, I thought I had found the safest place in Washington to park my career. I'd ask CAP staffers what their agency did.

"We advise other agencies," they would say.

"We coordinate private and public concerns."

"We review productivity."

"We revise strategies."

"We provide oversight."

"But clearly, clearly, we could always do more."

In other words, nobody knew. From the top down, no one could tell me precisely what the administrative mission was. And I thought to myself, I want to be a part of this. No one will ever be able to suggest that we are no longer needed, that it's time for all of us to clear out our desks, that our job is done, because no one knows what our job is.

But I was wrong about the Bureau of Reclamation. It hasn't had a major project for two decades, doesn't have any planned, and yet endures, and will continue to endure, through fiscal year after fiscal year, time without end. It is too big to die.

The Coordinating Administration for Productivity, on the other hand, employs just thirty civil servants. We're always on the bubble. With a stroke of the pen, we could vanish from next year's budget. All it would take is for someone to notice us long enough to erase us. And so, as I soon learned, there was an administrative mission statement after all: Don't Get Noticed.

That's why we never complained to GSA about the condition of our building, why we turned the other cheek when FDA employees started parking in our lot and eventually took it over. That's also why no one ever confronted the secretaries about the cats named Dust. And above all, that is why I was so nervous on the morning that our chief administrator called an "urgent meeting."

I sat waiting outside of the administrator's office with Susana de Vega, the assistant administrator, and Tom Willis, Susana's deputy. "I don't like this," Tom said. "I don't like this one damn bit."

Susana hissed at him and looked at the administrator's secretary. But Roxie wasn't listening to us. She was talking, through an open window, to the cat on the fire escape. The cat was a gray tom with the tattered ears of a street fighter. He backed up warily as Roxie put the food bowl down. "Relax, Dust," she said. "I'm not going to hurt you."

It was January, a few days before the presidential inauguration, and the air coming in through the window was cold, but nobody asked Roxie to close it.

"When has Cooper ever called an *urgent* meeting?" Tom continued in a lower voice. "Hell, how many times has he called a meeting of any damn kind? He's up to something. He's got to throw his goddam Schedule-C weight around while he still has it to throw."

Throwing his weight around didn't sound like Bill Cooper, but I didn't bother to say so. After all, Cooper was a political appointee on his way out, so whether he threw his weight around or not, Tom's underlying point was correct: Cooper was a loose cannon. He had nothing to lose. Intentionally or not, he might blow us up.

Roxie waited to see if the cat would consent to having his chin scratched, but Dust held his ground until the window was closed. Even then, he approached the food warily, as if checking for booby traps.

Susana told Tom to relax. "Two weeks," she reminded him. "Three at the outside."

"And then God only knows what we'll be getting," Tom said, pulling at his chin. "I hate politics."

Roxie's intercom buzzed, and without turning away from the cat she told us, "You can go in now."

I followed Susana and Tom in, and found Cooper nestled deeply in his executive chair, looking as friendly and harmless as he ever had. His slightly drooping eyelids made him seem, as always, half asleep. He waved us into our seats, and as I sat down, I realized how little he had done to personalize his office in the twelve years of his tenure. Everything in the room was government issue. There weren't any family pictures or the usual paperweights made by children or grandchildren. In fact, there wasn't anything on the surface of his desk at all. It was as if Cooper had been anticipating, from the day he moved in, the day when he would have to move out.

There was *some* decoration in the room, a pen-and-ink drawing on the wall behind Cooper, but that had been there for as long as I had been with the CAP. It showed an Oriental-looking wooden building next to a plot of empty ground, and I knew from having looked once, maybe fifteen years ago, that the drawing wasn't just hung on the wall. The frame had been nailed into the paneling, making it a permanent installation.

"People," Cooper said from deep inside his chair, "we have a problem." He let that last word hang in the air as he searched for what to say next.

Susana, Tom and I leaned forward in our chairs.

"An impropriety," he went on.

We leaned a little more.

"A mystery."

We watched expectantly as Cooper opened his desk drawer and took out a sheet of paper. He studied it for a long time, and then said, "You people know my management style. I've been hands-off. I've always let you people handle the details," by which he meant that he didn't know what we did all day and didn't care, so long as we told him that everything was running smoothly. He tapped the sheet of paper and said, "But here is something that demands my attention, and I want it cleared up while I'm still in charge."

And then he read from the letter in his hand. The writer represented something called the Five-State Cotton Consortium, and he had come to Washington to get advice on federal funding for his organization. He had taken an employee of the Coordinating Administration for Productivity to lunch, picking her brain about the special appropriations process as well as various grant sources. The woman had been very helpful, and the letter writer just wanted Cooper to know that at least one member of his staff was really on the ball. The helpful staffer's name was Kim Semper.

At the sound of that name, I felt ice form in the pit of my stomach. I stared straight ahead, keeping my expression as plain as I could manage. I knew some of what Cooper was going to say next, but I tried to look genuinely surprised when he told us what had happened after he received the letter.

"I wanted to touch base with Ms. Semper and make sure that the citizen hadn't actually paid for her lunch. You people know as well as I do that we don't want any conflict-of-interest cases."

"Of course not," said Susana. "But I don't see how there could be any such conflict. We don't actually make funding decisions."

"We don't?" Cooper said, and then he recovered to say, "No, of course not. But you people will agree that we wouldn't want even the *appearance* of impropriety. And anyway, that doesn't matter. What matters is that in my search for Kim Semper, I came up empty. We don't have an employee by that name."

Trying to sound more convincing than I felt, I said, "Maybe it's a mistake, Bill. Maybe the letter writer had the name wrong, or sent the letter to the wrong agency."

"Hell, yes!" Tom said with too much enthusiasm. "It's just some damn case of mistaken identity!"

But Cooper wasn't going to be turned easily. "I called the citizen," he told us. "No mistake. Someone is posing as an officer of our agency, a criminal offense."

I said, "Doesn't there have to be intent to defraud for this to be a crime?"

Cooper frowned. "The citizen did buy lunch for this Kim Semper. She benefitted materially." He shook the letter at me. "This is a serious matter."

"And one we'll get to the bottom of," Susana promised.

"I want it done before my departure," Cooper said. "I don't want to saddle my successor with any difficulties," by which he meant that he didn't want to leave behind any dirty laundry that might embarrass him when he was no longer in a position to have it covered up.

Susana said again, "We'll get to the bottom of it."

Cooper nodded at Tom. "I want a single point of responsibility on this, so the personnel director will head up the investigation."

With Cooper still looking at him, Tom looked at me expectantly, and I felt compelled to speak up. "That would be me," I said. "Tom's your deputy assistant."

"Of course," Cooper said, covering. He turned to me. "And you'll report to him." Then he added, "You aren't too busy to take care of this matter, I assume."

"It'll be tight," I said, thinking of the Russian novel I'd been wading through for the last week, "but I'll squeeze it in."

Outside of Cooper's office, Susana patted Tom's shoulder, then mine, and said with complete ambiguity, "You know what to do." Then she disappeared down the hall, into her own office.

Roxie's cat was gone, but Roxie had something else to distract her now. She was reading a GPO publication called *Small Business Administration Seed Projects: Program Announcement and Guidelines*. She didn't even look up when Tom hissed at me, "Sit on it!"

"What?"

"You know damn well what I mean," Tom said through his teeth. "I don't know what this Kim Semper thing is all about, and I don't want to know! This is just the kind of problem that could blow us out of the goddam water!"

I said, "Are you telling me to ignore an assignment from the chief administrator?"

I could see in Tom's eyes the recognition that he had already been too specific. "Not at all," he said in a normal voice, loud enough for Roxie to overhear if she were listening. "I'm telling you to handle this in the most appropriate fashion." Then he, too, bailed out, heading for his own office.

I found my secretary, Vera, trying to type with a calico cat in her lap. The cat was purring and affectionately digging its claws into Vera's knee.

"Damn it, Vera," I said, surprising myself, "the memo specifies feeding only. Everybody knows that. You are not supposed to have the cat inside the building!"

"You hear that, Dust?" Vera said as she rubbed behind the cat's ears. "It's back out into the cold with you." But she made no move to get up.

"Hold my calls," I growled. I went into my office and closed the door, wishing that I had a copy of the legendary memo so that I could read chapter and verse to Vera. It was bad enough that the secretaries had distorted the wording of the memo, issued well over twenty years ago, that had allowed them to feed a stray cat named Dust, "and only a cat named Dust." It seemed like every so often, they had to push beyond even the most liberal limits of that allowance, and no manager was willing to make an issue of it, lest it turn into a civil service grievance that would bring an OPM investigation crashing down around our ears.

I didn't stew about the cat for long. I still had Kim Semper on my mind. It took me a few minutes to find the key to my file cabinet, but once I had the drawer open, there weren't many folders to search through before I found what I wanted. I untaped the file folder marked PRIVATE and pulled out the letter. It was addressed to me and sported an eleven-year-old date. "After failing to determine just who her supervisor is," the text began, "I have decided to write to you, the Director of Personnel, to commend one of your administrators, Miss Kim Semper." The story from there was pretty much the same: A citizen had come to Washington looking for information, had stumbled across the Coordinating Administration for Productivity, and had ended up buying Semper's lunch in exchange for her insights on the intricacies of doing business in the Beltway. Though he had been unable to contact her subsequently, her advice had been a big help to him.

After checking the personnel files, I had called the letter writer to tell him that he'd been mistaken, that there was no Kim Semper here at the CAP. Maybe, I suggested, he had gone to some other agency and confused the names? But he was sure that it was the CAP that he had consulted, and he described our building right down to the tiny, nearly unreadable gray lettering that announced the agency's name on the front door.

In a government agency, a mystery, any mystery, is a potential bomb. If you're not sure of what something is, then you assume that it's going to blow up in your face if you mess with it. At the CAP, where everything was uncertain and shaky to begin with, the unknown seemed even more dangerous. So I had buried the letter.

Now maybe it was coming back to haunt me. I wondered if I

should cover my tail by Xeroxing my letter and bringing Cooper a copy right now. "Hey, Bill. I had to check my files on this, to make sure, but would you believe . . ." Maybe that would be good damage control.

But maybe not. After all, Cooper seemed to think this was an urgent matter. I had known about it for eleven years and done nothing. And my letter was so old that I probably didn't have to worry about it hurting me if I didn't bring up its existence. By now, the writer himself might not even remember sending it to me. Perhaps the man was even dead. If I kept my mouth shut, it was just possible that no one would ever know about my Kim Semper letter. And if that was what I wanted, then it would help my cause to do just what Tom had urged: to sit on the investigation, to ignore Kim Semper until the executive branch resignations worked their way down, layer by layer, from the new president's cabinet to our agency, and Cooper was on his way.

Either option, hiding the letter or revealing it, had its dangers. No matter how I played it out in my mind, I couldn't see the safe bet. I returned to what I'd been doing before the meeting with Cooper, and I should have been able to concentrate on it. Napoleon was watching this Polish general, who wanted to impress him, trying to swim some cavalry across a Russian river, but the horses were drowning and everything was a mess. It was exciting, but it didn't hold my attention. I read the same page over and over, distracted with worry.

At the end of the day, there was no cat in Vera's lap, but there was a skinny little tabby begging on the fire escape. At her desk, Vera was pouring some cat food into a bowl labeled, "Dust."

"Sorry I snapped earlier," I said.

"Bad day?" Vera said, opening the window.

"The worst," I told her, noticing the stack of outgoing mail on her desk. "Is that something I asked you to do?"

"Oh, I'm just getting some information for the staff library," she said.

I nodded, trying to think of something managerial to say. "You're self-directed, Vera. I like to see that."

"Oh, I've always been that way," she told me. "I can't stand to be idle." She opened the window to feed the cat and said, "Here you go, Dust."

Cooper called another meeting for Thursday of the next week. It was the day after the inauguration, and he must have felt the ticking clock. Before the meeting, Tom called me.

"How's your investigation coming?" he said.

"Slowly."

"Good. That's damn good. See you in the old man's office."

For once there wasn't a cat on Roxie's fire escape. Cooper's door was open, and I walked right in. Susana and Tom were already there, and Cooper motioned me to a seat. Cooper didn't waste any time.

"What have you got?"

I opened my notebook. "First, I double-checked the personnel files, not just the current ones, but going back twenty-five years." I looked at Cooper grimly. "No one by the name of Kim Semper has *ever* worked for the Coordinating Administration for Productivity."

"Yes, yes," Cooper said. "What else?"

"I called over to the Office of Personnel Management. There is not now, nor has there ever been, anywhere in the civil service system, an employee named Kim Semper." I closed the notebook and put on the face of a man who has done his job well.

Cooper stared at me. I pretended to look back at him earnestly, but my focus was actually on the framed pen-and-ink behind him. If I had to give it a title, I decided, it would be, "Japanese Shed with Empty Lot."

At last Cooper said, "Is that all?"

"Well, Bill, I haven't been able to give this my full attention."

"It's been a week, a *week* since I brought this up to you people."

"And a hellish week it's been," I said, looking to Tom for help.

"That's true," Tom jumped in. "The inauguration has stirred things up. We've had an unusually, ah, unusually heavy run of requests." Cooper frowned, and I could see Tom's hands tighten on the side of his chair. He was hoping, I knew, that Cooper wouldn't say, "Requests for what? From whom?"

Susana saved us both by saying, "I'm ashamed of the two of

you! Don't you have any sense of priorities? And, Tom, you're supposed to be supervising this investigation. That means staying on top of it, making sure it's progressing." She turned to Cooper. "We'll have something substantial next week, Bill."

"I don't know, people," Cooper said. "Realistically, something like this is out of your purview. Maybe it calls for an outside investigator."

Cooper was almost certainly bluffing. Any dirt at the bottom of this would cling to him like tar if we brought in the consul general's office. He wanted to keep this internal as much as we did.

Even so, Susana paled. She played it cool, but it was a strain on her. "Why don't you see what we come up with in seven working days? Then you can decide."

Minutes later, in the hallway, Tom said, "So what now?"

"Don't look at me," Susana told him without breaking stride. "I pulled your bacon out of the fire, boys. Don't ask me to think for you, too." Then over her shoulder, she added, "You'd just better appear to be making progress by our next little get-together."

Before he left me standing alone in the hallway, Tom said, "You heard the lady, Ace. Let's see some goddam action."

In my office, with the door closed behind me, I finished another chapter of the Russian novel and then got right on the case. I cleared space on the floor and laid out the personnel files for the last eleven years. It made sense to assume that "Kim Semper" was an insider, or had an inside confederate who could arrange her lunchtime meetings. And I knew that Ms. Semper had been working this free-lunch scam since at least the date of my letter. I figured that I could at least narrow down my suspect pool by weeding out anyone who hadn't been with the CAP for that long.

Unfortunately, that didn't narrow things much. Even Cooper, by virtue of three straight presidential victories for his party, had been with the CAP for longer than that.

So what did I really have to go on? Just two letters of praise for Kim Semper, dated eleven years apart. The letter writers themselves had met Kim Semper, but there were good reasons for not calling them for more information. After all, I wanted to keep my letter buried to preserve my plausible deniability. And Cooper's letter writer had already been contacted once about Kim Semper. If I called again and grilled him, he might resent it, and I could use up his goodwill before I even knew what questions to ask. Also, he might get the impression that the Coordinating Administration for Productivity didn't have its act together, and who knew where that could lead? I didn't want a citizen complaining to his congressional rep.

What I needed was another source, but there wasn't one.

Or was there?

I arranged the personnel files on the floor to look like an organizational hierarchy. If someone were to send a letter praising an employee of the CAP, where might that letter go?

To the top, of course. That was Cooper.

And to the Director of Personnel. That was me.

But what about the space between these two? What about the Assistant Administrator and her Deputy? That is, what about Susana and Tom?

Outside of Susana's office, her administrative assistant, Peter, was preparing to feed a black cat on the fire escape. Almost as soon as he opened the window, Peter sneezed.

"Susana in?"

"Yes," Peter said, "but she's unavailable." He set the cat bowl down and closed the window. Then he sneezed again.

"If you're so allergic," I said, "how come you're feeding the kitty?"

"Oh, I like cats, even if they do make my eyes swell shut." He laughed. "Anyway, feeding Dust is the corporate culture around here, right? When in Rome . . ."

From the other side of Susana's door, I could hear the steady beat of music.

I watched the stray cat as it ate. "I'm surprised, with all the cats on our fire escapes, that it isn't just one continuous cat fight out there."

"They're smart animals," Peter said. "Once they have a routine, they stay out of each other's way."

I nodded, but I wasn't really paying attention. Over the beat of the music, I could hear a female voice that wasn't Susana's counting "One-and-two-and-three-and—"

I went to her door and put my hand on the knob.

"I told you," Peter said, "Susana's unavailable. If you want to make an appointment . . ."

"This can't wait," I said. I opened the door.

Susana was in a leotard, and I caught her in the middle of a leg lift. She froze while the three women on the workout tape kept on exercising and counting without her.

"I told Peter I wasn't to be disturbed," she said, still holding her leg up like some varicolored flamingo.

"This won't take but a minute," I said. "In fact, you can go right on with your important government business while we talk."

She stopped the tape and glared at me. "What do you want?"

"To get to the bottom of this Kim Semper thing. And if that's what you really want too, then you can't be throwing me curve balls."

"What are you talking about?" She pushed the audiovisual cart between two file cabinets and threw a dust cover over it.

"I'm talking, Susana, about sitting on information. Or call it withholding evidence. I want your correspondence file on Kim Semper."

Susana circled behind her desk and sat down. Ordinarily, that would have been a good gesture, a way of reminding me that she was, after all, the assistant admin, and this was her turf I had invaded. But it was a hard move to pull off in a leotard. "Just what makes you think I even have such a file?"

That was practically a confession. I fought down a smile. "I'm on your side," I reminded her. "But we've got to show some progress on this. Cooper is on his last official breath. Dying men are unpredictable. But if we hold all the cards, how dangerous can he be?"

She stared over my head, no doubt thinking the same thoughts I had about my own Kim Semper letter. How would Cooper re-act to knowing that she'd had these letters in her files all along?

"You've got the file where, Susana? In your desk? In one of those cabinets? If I close my eyes," I said, closing them, "then I'll be able to honestly tell Cooper that I don't know *exactly* where my information came from. It was just sort of dropped into my lap."

It took her a minute of rummaging, and then a folder fell into my hands. I opened my eyes. The three letters ranged from two to ten years old.

"Read them in your own office," she said. "And next time, knock."

On my way out, I noticed that Peter was reading something called *America's Industrial Future: A Report of the Presidential Colloquium on U.S. Manufacturing Productivity for the Year 2020 and Beyond.* A thing like that wouldn't ordinarily stick in my mind, except that Tom's secretary, Janet, was reading the same report. She was also holding a mottled white-and-tan cat in her lap. I didn't bother to confront her about it—that was Tom's fight, if he wanted to fight it. I just knocked on Tom's door and stepped into his office.

He swept a magazine from his desk and into a drawer, but he wasn't fast enough to keep me from noting the cover feature: "The Girls of the Pac Ten." "What the hell do you want?" he growled.

"A hell of a lot more than I'm getting," I barked back. "Damned little you've done to help this investigation along, Willis. Enough bullshit. I'm up to here with bullshit. I want your goddam Kim Semper correspondence file."

"Like hell." Tom glowered, but a little quiver of uncertainty ran across his lowered eyebrows. He wasn't used to being on the receiving end of such bluster.

"Cut the crap, Tom. This goddam Semper bullshit will toss us all on our asses if we don't give Cooper something to chew on. So give."

A little timidly, he said, "I don't know what you're—"

"Like hell," I said, waving de Vega's letters. "Susana came across, and I'd sure as hell hate to tell Cooper that you're the one stalling his goddam investigation."

He bit his lip and took a file cabinet key from his desk drawer. "Jesus," he said. "I've never seen you like this."

"You better hope like hell you never see it again," I said, which was probably overdoing things, but I was on a roll.

As I read it in my office, the first of Tom's letters cheered me considerably. One was twenty years old, which altered my suspect list quite a bit. From my array of files on the floor, I removed anyone who hadn't been with the CAP for the last two decades. That left just myself, Tom Willis, and Tom's secretary, Janet. I picked up Janet's file and smiled. *Kim Semper,* I thought, *you have met your match.*

And then I read Tom's other letter, the most recent one of all, excepting Cooper's. It praised *Mr.* Kim Semper, for *his* dedication to public service.

No, I thought. *This can't be right.*

Unless there was more than one Kim Semper.

I sat down behind my desk. Hard. And I thought about the cat named Dust, who came in a dozen variations, but who, by long tradition, was always Dust, was always considered to be the same cat, because the ancient memo had allowed for the feeding of a cat named Dust, "and only a cat named Dust."

I picked up the phone and dialed the number of the man who had written to praise Mr. Semper. "Mr. Davis," I said when I had him on the line, "one of our employees is in line for a service award, and I just want to make sure it's going to the right person. You wrote a letter to us about a Mr. Kim Semper. Now, we've got a Kim Semple on our staff, and a Tim Kemper, but no Kim Semper. Could you do me the favor of describing the man who was so helpful?"

As lame stories go, this one worked pretty well. It sounded plausible, and it didn't make the CAP look bad. And it brought results. Davis was only happy to make sure Semper or Semple or Kemper got his due. The description fit Peter to a T.

I tried the next most recent letter, but the number had been disconnected. The next one back from that—I changed Tim Kemper to Lynn—brought me a good description of Roxie. The third call, the one that cinched it, paid off with a description that could only be my own Vera.

That's when I buzzed Vera into my office.

"I want a copy of the cat memo," I told her.

"The cat memo?"

"Don't fence with me. If you don't have a copy of it yourself, you know how to get one. I want it within the hour." Then I lowered my voice conspiratorially. "Vera, I don't have anything against cats. Trust me on that."

She had a copy in my hands in five minutes. When I looked at the date, I whistled. Dust the cat had been on this officially sanctioned meal ticket for more than forty years, much longer than I had supposed. The memo also named the secretary who had first started feeding Dust. After a phone call to OPM, I was on my way to Silver Spring, Maryland.

The house I stopped in front of was modest, but nonetheless stood out from all the other clapboard houses on that street. There were abstract, Oriental-looking sculptures in the garden. The white stones around the plum trees had been raked into tidy rows, and there was a fountain bubbling near the walkway to the front door.

A white-haired woman holding a gravel rake came around the side of the house, moving with a grace that belied her eighty years.

"Mrs. Taida?" I said. She looked up and waved me impatiently into the garden. As I opened the gate, I said, "I'm the one who called you, Mrs. Taida. From the Coordinating Administration for Productivity."

"Yes, of course," she said. As I approached, she riveted me with her gaze. Her eyes were blue as arctic ice.

"You are Janet Taida, yes?"

"You expected me to look more Japanese," she said. "Taida was my husband's name. Sakutaro Taida. The artist." She waved at the sculptures.

"I see," I said, then reached into my pocket for the photocopied memo. "Mrs. Taida, I want to talk to you about the cat named Dust."

"Of course you do," she said. "Come inside and I'll make some tea."

The house was furnished in the traditional Japanese style, with furniture that was close to the floor. While Mrs. Taida started the water boiling in the kitchen, I looked at the artwork hanging on the walls. There were paintings and drawings that seemed vaguely familiar, somehow, but it wasn't until I saw the big pen-and-ink on the far wall that I knew what I was looking at.

"There's a drawing like this in the administrator's office," I said when Mrs. Taida came into the room with the teapot.

"A drawing *almost* like that one," Mrs. Taida said. She waved toward a cushion. "Won't you sit down?" she commanded. She poured the tea. "That's a Shinto temple. It has two parts, two buildings. But only one stands at a time. Every twenty years, one is torn down and the other is rebuilt. They are both present, always. But the manifestation changes."

"The drawing at work shows the other phase," I said, "when the other building is standing and this one has been torn down."

Mrs. Taida nodded. A white long-haired cat padded into the room.

"Dust?" I said.

Taking up her teacup, Mrs. Taida shook her head. "No, there's only one Dust."

I laughed. "But like the temple, many manifestations." I unfolded the memo. "This memo, the Dust memo, mentions you by name, Mrs. Taida. You started it, didn't you? You were the administrator's secretary when the secretaries received their sanction to keep caring for, as it says here, 'a cat named Dust.' "

"Once we began to feed one, it was very hard to turn the others away. So I read the memo very carefully."

"Mrs. Taida, cats are one thing, but . . ."

"I know. Cats are one thing, but Kim Semper is far more serious, right?" She lowered her teacup. "Let me explain something to you," she said. "The Coordinating Administration for Productivity was commissioned over fifty years ago. They had a clear wartime purpose, which they completed, and then the agency began to drift. Your tea is getting cold."

She waited until I had picked it up and taken a sip.

"A government agency develops a culture, and it attracts people who are comfortable with that culture. After its wartime years the CAP attracted ostriches."

I opened my mouth, but she held up her hand.

"You can't deny it," she said. "For forty years, the CAP has been managed by men and women who wanted to rule over a quiet little fiefdom where nothing much happened."

She sipped her own tea.

"Do you have any idea what it's like to be a secretary under conditions like that?" She shook her head. "Nothing happens. There's too little to do, and the day just crawls by. You can't have any idea how hard it was, at the end of the war and with a Japanese husband, to get a government job. And then to have to sit on my hands all day, doing nothing . . ."

"Mrs. Taida—"

"I am not finished speaking," she said with authority, and I felt my face flush. "As I was saying, working at the CAP was like being a sailor on a rudderless ship. Have some more tea."

I held out my cup, as commanded.

"What endures in a government agency?" she asked as she poured again. "The management? The support staff? Job titles shift. Duties change. But the culture remains. It's like the tradition of a secretary feeding a stray cat at ten in the morning. The secretary may retire, but another will come, and if there's a tradition of feeding the stray cat at ten, then the person who takes the job will likely be someone who likes cats anyway. The cat may die or move on, but another will appear before long. The feeding goes on, even if who is fed and by whom changes over time."

She put the teapot down. "Administrators come and go, but the culture endures. And Kim Semper endures. When a citizen calls the agency for help, he isn't referred to management. No one at that level knows anything. No, the citizen is referred to Kim Semper. And for the pleasure of the work itself, of knowing things and being helpful, the secretaries do the job of the Coordinating Administration for Productivity. And they do a very good job. How many of those people who are helped by Kim Semper bother to write letters, do you suppose? And how many of the letters that are written actually end up in the hands of CAP administrators? Kim Semper provides good answers to hard questions about productivity and legislative action. I gave the CAP a rudder, you see. It operates from the galley, not the bridge."

"There's the question of ethics," I said. "There's the matter of lunches paid for by citizens, of benefit derived by fraud."

She looked at me long and hard. It was a look that said everything there was to say about collecting a GS-13 salary working for an agency where the managers were fuzzy about how they should fill their days. She didn't have to say a word.

"Well, what am I supposed to do then?" I said. "Now that I know the truth, what do I say when the administrator asks for my report?"

"You didn't get to where you are today without knowing how to stall," Mrs. Taida said. "You do what you do best, and let the secretaries do what *they* do best."

"What about *after* Cooper is gone?" I said. "This is a bomb just waiting to go off. This is the kind of thing that can sink a little agency like ours."

"The Coordinating Administration for Productivity is a fifty-year-old bureaucracy," Mrs. Taida said, "with a little secret that no one has discovered for forty years. You're the only one who threatens the status quo." She picked up our teacups and the pot. "If you don't rock the boat, I'm sure the CAP, along with Dust and Kim Semper, will endure for time without end. And now, if you don't mind, I have things to do."

I drove back to the office slowly. I knew what I had to do, but I didn't know exactly how to get it done. At least, not until I got as far as the Department of Agriculture. There, I pulled into the right lane and slowed to a crawl.

Size, I thought. The thing that comforts me about the Department of Agriculture is its size. It is big and white and easy to get lost in. That's what safety is.

I drove back and got right to work. It was a big job. I enlisted Vera and Roxie, along with Janet, Peter, and some of the secretaries from downstairs. I didn't explain in great detail what we were doing or why it was important. They understood. In a week, we had generated the very thing that Bill Cooper had called for.

"Results," I announced, shouldering between Susana and Tom to drop my report onto Cooper's desk. It landed with a thud. Cooper blinked slowly, then opened the heavy white binding to the first page. *A Report on Personnel and Operational Disloca-*

tion at the Coordinating Administration for Productivity, it read. "Everything you need to know about Kim Semper is in there."

Cooper nodded. "It's, ah, impressive. You people really knocked yourselves out."

"Yes, sir," I said. "I can't take all the credit. Susana and Tom were instrumental, really."

Neither of them looked up. They were still staring at the report.

Cooper began to scan the executive summary, but his eyes began to glaze when he got to the paragraph about operational location as a time- and institution-based function not contingent upon the identity of the individual operator. "So can you summarize the contents for me?"

"Well," I said, "it's a bit involved. But you can get the gist of it in the summary that you're reading."

Cooper kept thumbing through the summary. It went on for ninety-three pages.

"To really get a complete sense of the situation," I said, "you'll need to read the complete report. Right, Susana?"

She nodded. "Of course."

"Tom?"

"You bet your ass. It's all there, though. Every damn bit of it." He said it with pride, as though he really had made some contribution.

"It took a thousand pages to get it said, Bill. And it really takes a thousand to make sense of it all. So, you see, I can't just give it to you in a sentence."

"I see," Cooper said, nodding, and he was still nodding, still looking at the four-inch volume, when Susana and Tom and I left the room.

"You're a goddam genius is what you are," Tom said. And Susana told me, "Good work."

And when Cooper cleared out for good, he left the report behind. It's there still, taking up space on his successor's desk. Sometimes when I see it sitting there, I think to myself that a bomb could go off in that room, and everything would be blown to hell but that plastic-bound, metal-spined, ten-pound volume of unreadable prose. It wouldn't suffer so much as a singed page.

It gives me a safe and solid feeling.

PETER TREMAYNE

MURDER BY MIRACLE

"Peter Tremayne," author of fantasy novels, police procedurals, and even a 1981 Raffles novel, is really Peter Berresford Ellis, noted biographer and Celtic historian. Last year, when he decided to launch a new series detective based on his Celtic scholarship, he did so in a spectacular manner. Four novelettes about a seventh-century Irish nun named Sister Fidelma were published almost simultaneously in four different mystery anthologies. You'll find all four stories listed on the honor roll at the back of this book. Choosing just one to reprint here was a difficult task. I finally chose "Murder by Miracle," possibly because of its island setting and the nature of the crime encountered there. In any event we'll be watching for the first Sister Fidelma novel, Absolution by Murder, *due this year from Headline Books in England.*

As the boat rocked its way gently against the natural granite quay, Sister Fidelma could see her welcome committee standing waiting. The committee consisted of one young, very young, man; fresh-faced and youthful, certainly no more than twenty-one summers in age. He wore a noticeable expression of petulance, coupled with resolution, on his features.

At the boatman's gesture, Sister Fidelma eased herself into position by the side of the vessel and grabbed for the rope ladder, hauling herself quickly up on to the gray granite quay. She moved with a youthful agility which seemed at odds with her demure posture and religious habit. To the young man watching her perilous ascent, her tall but well-proportioned figure, the rebellious strands of red hair streaking from under her headdress, the young, attractive features and bright green eyes, had not been what he was expecting when he had been informed that a *dálaigh,* an advocate, of the Brehon Court, was coming to the island. This young woman was not his idea of a religieuse, let alone a respected member of the law courts of Éireann.

"Sister Fidelma? Did you have a good trip over?" The young man's voice was slow, his tone measured, not really friendly but "correct." The phrase "coldly polite" came into Fidelma's mind and she grimaced wryly before allowing her features to break into an amused grin. The grin disconcerted the young man for a moment. It was also at odds with her status. It was an urchin grin of frivolity. Fidelma gestured wordlessly to the seas breaking behind her.

With the late autumnal seas running, dirty gray and heavy with yellow-cream foamed caps, the trip from the mainland had not been one that she had enjoyed. The wind was cold and blustery and whistling against this serrated crag of an island which poked into the wild, angry Atlantic like the top of an isolated hill that had been severed from its fellows by a flood of brooding water. Approaching the island, the dark rocks seemed like the comb of a fighting cock. She had marveled how anyone could survive and scratch a living on its seemingly inhospitable wasteland.

On her way out the boatman had told her that only 160 people lived on the island, which, in winter, could sometimes be cut off for months with not even a deftly rowed currach being able to make a landing. The island's population were close-knit, introspective, mainly fisherfolk, and there had been no suspicious deaths there since time immemorial.

That was, until now.

The young man frowned slightly and when she made no reply he spoke again.

"There was no need to bother you with this matter, Sister Fidelma. It is quite straightforward. There was no need to bring you out from the mainland."

Sister Fidelma regarded the young man with a soft smile.

There was no disguising the fact that the young man felt put out. Sister Fidelma was an outsider interfering with his jurisdiction.

"Are you the *bó-aire* of the island?" she asked.

The young man drew himself up with a posture of dignity in spite of his youth.

"I am," he replied with a thinly disguised air of pride. The *bó-aire* was a local magistrate, a chieftain without land whose wealth was judged by the number of cows he owned; hence he was called a "cow chief." Some communities, such as those on the tiny islands off the coast, were usually ruled by a *bó-aire* who owed allegiance to greater chieftains on the mainland.

"I was visiting Fathan of the Corca Dhuibhne when news of this death reached him," Fidelma said softly.

Fathan of the Corca Dhuibhne was the chieftain over all these islands. The young *bó-aire* stirred uncomfortably. Sister Fidelma continued:

"Fathan requested me to visit and aid you in your inquiry." She decided that this formula was a more diplomatic way of approaching the proud young magistrate than by recounting the truth of what Fathan had said. Fathan knew that the *bó-aire* had only just been appointed and knew, too, that the matter needed a more experienced judgment. "I have some expertise in inquiry into suspicious deaths," Fidelma added.

The young man bit his lip sullenly.

"But there is nothing suspicious about this death. The woman simply slipped and fell down the cliff. It's three hundred feet at that spot. She didn't have a chance."

"So? You are sure it was an accident?"

Sister Fidelma became aware that they had both been standing on the quay with the wind whipping at them and the salt sea spray dampening their clothing. She was wet in spite of the heavy wool cloak she had put on for the crossing from An Chúis on the mainland.

"Is there somewhere we can go for shelter? Somewhere more comfortable to talk this over?" She posed the second question before the young man could reply to her first.

The young *bó-aire* reddened at the implied rebuke.

"My *bóthan* is up the road here, Sister. Come with me."

He turned to lead the way.

There were one or two people about to acknowledge the *bó-aire* as he passed and to cast curious glances at Sister Fidelma. The news of her arrival would soon be all over the island, she thought. Fidelma sighed. Island life seemed all very romantic in the summer, but even then she preferred life on the mainland, away from the continually howling winds and whipping sea spray.

In the snug gray stone cabin of the *bó-aire*, a smoldering turf fire supplied a degree of warmth, but the atmosphere was still damp. A young woman of the *bó-aire*'s household provided an earthenware vessel of mead, heated with a hot iron bar from the fire. The drink put warmth and vigor into Fidelma.

"What's your name?" she asked as she sipped the drink.

"Fogartach," replied the *bó-aire* stiffly, realizing that he had trespassed by neglecting to introduce himself properly to his guest.

Sister Fidelma felt the time had come to ensure the proud young man knew his place.

"Well, Fogartach, as local magistrate, what qualification in law do you hold?"

The young man's head rose a little in vanity.

"I studied at Daingean Chúis for four years. I am qualified to the level of *dos* and know the *Bretha Nemed* or Law of Privileges as well as any."

Sister Fidelma smiled softly at his arrogance.

"I am qualified in law to the level of *Anruth*," she said quietly, "having studied eight years with the Brehon Morann of Tara."

The *bó-aire* colored, perhaps a little embarrassed that he had sounded boastful before someone who held a degree that was only one step below the highest qualification in the five kingdoms of Éireann. Little more needed to be said. Sister Fidelma had, as gently as she could, established her authority over the *bó-aire*.

"The matter is straightforward enough," Fogartach said, a little sulky. "It was an accident. The woman slipped and fell down the cliff."

"Then the investigation should not take us long," replied Sister Fidelma with a bright smile.

"Investigation? I have my report here."

The young man turned with a frown to a sheaf of paper.

"Fogartach," Fidelma said slowly and deliberately, "Fathan of the Corco Dhuibhne is anxious that everything is, as you say, straightforward. Do you realize who the woman was?"

"She was a religieuse, such as yourself."

"A religieuse? Not just any religieuse, Fogartach. The woman was Cuimne, daughter of the High King."

The young man frowned.

"I knew her name was Cuimne and that she carried herself with some authority. I did not realize she was related to the High King."

Sister Fidelma grimaced helplessly.

"Did you also not realize that she was the Abbess Cuimne from Ard Macha, personal representative of the most powerful churchman in Éireann?"

The young *bó-aire*'s face was red with mortification. He shook his head silently.

"So you now see, Fogartach," went on Fidelma, "that the chieftain of the Corco Dhuibhne cannot allow any question to arise over the manner of her death. Abbess Cuimne was an important person whose death may have ramifications at Tara as well as Ard Macha."

The young *bó-aire* bit his lip, seeking a way to justify himself.

"Position and privilege do not count for much on this little windswept rock, Sister," he replied in surly fashion.

Fidelma's eyes widened.

"But they count with Fathan of the Corco Dhuibhne, for he is answerable to the king of Cashel and the king of Cashel is answerable to the High King and to the archbishop of Ard Macha. That is why Fathan has sent me here," she added, now deciding the time had come to be completely brutal with the truth.

She paused to let the young man consider what she was saying before continuing.

"Well, take me through what you know of this matter, Fogartach."

The *bó-aire* sat back uneasily, bit his lip for a moment, and then resigned himself to her authority.

"The woman . . . er, the Abbess Cuimne arrived on the island four days ago. She was staying at the island's *bruighean*, the hostel run by Bé Bail, the wife of Súilleabháin, the hawk-eyed, a local fisherman. Bé Bail has charge of our island hostel. Not that we have much use for it; few people ever bother to visit our island."

"What was Abbess Cuimne doing here?"

The *bó-aire* shrugged.

"She did not say. I did not even know she was an abbess but simply thought her to be a member of some community come here to find isolation for a while. You know how it is with some religieuses? They often seek an isolated place to meditate. Why else should she be here?"

"Why indeed?" Fidelma echoed softly, and motioned the young man to continue.

"She told Bé Bail that she was leaving the island yesterday. Ciardha's boat from An Chúis would have arrived about noon. She packed her satchel after breakfast and went off to walk alone. When she didn't return at noon, and Ciardha's boat had left, Bé Bail asked me to keep a lookout for her. The island is not so large that you can get lost.

"Well, a little after lunch, Buachalla came running to me—"

"Who is Buachalla?"

"A young boy. A son of one of the islanders."

"Go on."

"The boy had spotted Abbess Cuimne's body below Aill Tuatha, that's the cliffs on the north of the island. I organized a couple of men together with the apothecary—"

"An apothecary? Do you have a resident apothecary on the island?" Fidelma interposed in surprise.

"Corcrain. He was once personal physician to the Eóganacht of Locha Léin. He had a desire to withdraw to the island a year ago. He sought solitude after his wife's death but has become part of our community, practicing his art for the good of the islanders."

"So, a couple of islanders, the apothecary, and yourself, all followed the young boy Buachalla?"

"We found the body of Abbess Cuimne at the foot of the cliffs."

"How did you get down to it?"

"Easy enough. There's a stony beach under the cliffs at that point. There is an easy path leading down to it. The path descends to the stretch of rocks about a half mile from where she fell. At the point she fell, incidentally, cliffs rise to their highest point. It was just under the highest point that we found the body."

"Did Corcrain examine her?"

"He did so. She was dead, so we carried her back to his *bóthan* where he made a further examination and found—"

Sister Fidelma held up her hand.

"I'll speak to the apothecary shortly. He will tell me what he found. Tell me, did you make a search of the area?"

The *bó-aire* frowned and hesitated.

"Search?"

Sister Fidelma sighed inwardly.

"After you found the body, what then?"

"It was obvious what had happened. Abbess Cuimne had been walking on the edge of the cliffs, slipped, and fell. As I said, it is three hundred feet at that point."

"So you did not search the top of the cliff or the spot where she fell?"

Fogartach smiled faintly.

"Oh, her belongings, such as she carried, were with Bé Bail at the hostel. She carried little else save a small satchel. You must know that religieuses carry but little with them when they travel. There was no need to look further. I have her belongings here, Sister. The body has already been buried."

Sister Fidelma bit her tongue in exasperation at the ignorant conceit of the young man.

"Where do I find Corcrain, the apothecary?"

"I'll show you," said the *bó-aire,* rising.

"Just point me in the right direction," Fidelma replied sarcastically. "I promise not to get lost."

The young *bó-aire* was unable to prevent an expression of irritation from crossing his face. Fidelma smiled maliciously to herself. She suspected that the young *bó-aire*'s arrogance was due to the fact that he considered her unworthy of her office because of her sex. Some of the island people, she knew, adhered to curious notions.

Corcrain's *bóthan,* or cabin, stood only two hundred yards away across the rising ground, one of many well-spaced stone buildings strung out across the slopes of the island like rosary beads. The slopes rose from the sea to stretch toward the comb like rocks forming the back of the island which sheltered the populated area from the fierce north winds.

The apothecary was nearly sixty, a swarthy man, whose slight frame still seemed to exude energy. His gray eyes twinkled.

"Ah, so you are the female Brehon that we have all been hearing about?"

Fidelma found herself returning the warm guileless smile.

"I am no Brehon, merely an advocate of the Brehon Court, apothecary. I have just a few questions to ask you. Abbess Cuimne was no ordinary religieuse. She was sister of the High King and representative of the Archbishop of Ard Macha. This is why Fathan, chieftain of the Corco Dhuibhne, wants to assure himself that everything is as straightforward as it should be. Unless a proper report is sent to Tara and to Ard Macha, Abbess Cuimne's relatives and colleagues might be prone to all sorts of imaginings, if you see what I mean."

Corcrain nodded, obviously trying to disguise his surprise.

"Are you a qualified apothecary?"

"I was apothecary and chief physician to the Eóganacht kings of Locha Léin," replied Corcrain. It was just a matter-of-fact statement without arrogance or vanity.

"What was the cause of Abbess Cuimne's death?"

The old apothecary sighed. "Take your pick. Any one of a number of the multiple fractures and lacerations whose cause seems consistent with a fall down a three-hundred-foot granite cliff on to rocks below."

"I see. In your opinion she slipped and fell down the cliff?"

"She fell down the cliff," the apothecary replied.

Sister Fidelma frowned at his choice of words.

"What does that mean?"

"I am no seer, Sister. I cannot say that she slipped nor how she came to go over the cliff. All I can say is that her injuries are consistent with such a fall."

Fidelma watched the apothecary's face closely. Here was a man who knew his job and was careful not to intrude his own interpretation on the facts.

"Anything else?" she prompted.

Corcrain bit his lip. He dropped his gaze for a moment.

"I chose to withdraw to a quiet island, Sister. After my wife died, I resigned as physician at the court of the Eóganacht and came here to live in a small rural community to forget what was going on in the outside world."

Fidelma waited patiently.

"It has taken me a full year to become accepted here. I don't want to create enmity with the islanders."

"Are you saying that there was something which makes you unhappy about the circumstances of Abbess Cuimne's death? Did you tell this to the *bó-aire*?"

"Fogartach? By the living God, no. He'a a local man. Besides, I wasn't aware of the 'something,' as you put it, until after they had brought the body back here and I had begun my examination."

"What was this 'something'?"

"Well, there were two 'somethings' in reality, and nothing from which you can deduce anything definite."

Fidelma waited while the apothecary seemed to gather his thoughts together.

"The first curiosity was in the deceased's right hand, which was firmly clenched. A section of silver chain."

"Chain?" Fidelma queried.

"Yes, a small silver chain." The apothecary turned, brought out a small wooden box and opened it.

Fidelma could see in it that there was a section of chain which had obviously been torn away from something, a piece no more than two inches in length. She picked it up and examined it. She could see no artisan's marks on the silver. It had been worked by a poor, provincial craftsman, not overly proud of his profession.

"Did Abbess Cuimne wear any jewelry like that? What of her crucifix, for example?"

"Her own crucifix, which I gave to the *bó-aire,* is much richer, and worked in gold and ivory. It looked as if it were fashioned under the patronage of princes."

"But you would say that when she fell she was clutching a broken piece of silver chain of poor quality?"

"Yes. That is a fact."

"You said there were two 'somethings.' What else?"

The apothecary bit his lip as if making up his mind before revealing it to Sister Fidelma.

"When a person falls in the manner she did, you have to expect a lot of bruising, contusions . . ."

"I've been involved in falls before," Sister Fidelma observed dryly.

"Well, while I was examining the body I found some bruising to the neck and shoulders, the fleshy part around the nape of the neck. The bruising was slightly uniformed, not what one would expect from contact with rocks during a fall."

"How would you decipher those marks?"

"It was as if Abbess Cuimne had, at some time, been gripped by someone with powerful hands from behind."

Fidelma's green eyes widened.

"What are you suggesting?"

"Nothing. It's not my place to. I can't even say how the bruising around the neck and shoulders occurred. I just report what I see. It could be consistent with her general injuries, but I am not entirely satisfied it is."

Fidelma put the piece of silver chain in the leather purse at her waist.

"Very well, Corcrain. Have you prepared your official report for the *bó-aire* yet?"

"When I heard that a Brehon from the mainland was coming, I thought that I'd wait and speak with him . . . with her, that is."

She ignored his hasty correction.

"I'd like to see the spot where Abbess Cuimne went over."

"I'll take you up there. It's not a long walk."

The apothecary reached for a blackthorn walking stick, paused, and frowned at Sister Fidelma's sandals.

"Do you not have anything better to wear? The mud on the path would destroy those frail things."

Fidelma shook her head.

"You have a good-sized foot," observed the apothecary, meditatively. He went to a chest and returned with a stouter pair of leather round-top shoes of untanned hide with three layers of hide for the sole, stout shoes such as the islanders wore. "Here, put these on. They will save your dainty slippers from the mud of the island."

A short time later, Fidelma, feeling clumsy but at least dry in the heavy untanned-leather island shoes, was following Corcrain along the pathway.

"Had you seen Abbess Cuimne before the accident?" Fidelma asked as she panted slightly behind her guide's wiry, energetic form as Corcrain strode the ascending track.

"It's a small island. Yes, I saw and spoke to her on more than one occasion."

"Do you know why she was here? The *bó-aire* did not even know that she was an abbess. But he seems to think she was simply a religieuse here in retreat, to meditate in this lonely spot away from distraction."

"I didn't get that impression. In fact, she told me that she was engaged in the exploration of some matter connected with the island. And once she said something odd. . . ."

He frowned as he dredged his memory.

"It was about the bishop of An Chúis. She said she was hoping to win a wager with Artagán, the bishop."

Sister Fidelma's eyes widened in surprise.

"A wager. Did she explain what?"

"I gathered that it was connected with her search."

"But you don't know what that search was for?"

Corcrain shook his head.

"She was not generally forthcoming, so I can understand why the *bó-aire* did not even learn of her rank; even I did not know that, though I suspected she was no ordinary religieuse."

"Exploration?" Sister Fidelma returned to Corcrain's observation.

Corcrain nodded. "Though what there is to explore here, I don't know."

"Well, did she make a point of speaking to anyone in particular on the island?"

The apothecary frowned, considering for a moment.

"She sought out Congal."

"Congal. And who is he?"

"A fisherman by trade. But he is also the local *seanchaí,* the traditional historian and storyteller of the island."

"Anyone else?"

"She went to see Father Patrick."

"Who?"

"Father Patrick, the priest on the island."

They had reached the edge of the cliffs now. Sistser Fidelma steeled herself a little, hating the idea of standing close to the edge of the wild, blustery, open space.

"We found her directly below this spot," Corcrain pointed.

"How can you be so sure?"

"That outcrop of rock is a good enough marker." The apothecary indicated it with the tip of his blackthorn.

Fidelma bent and examined the ground carefully.

"What are you looking for?"

"Perhaps for the rest of that chain. I'm not sure."

She paused and examined a patch of broken gorse and trodden grass with areas of soft muddy ground. There were deep imprints of shoes, which the faint drizzel had not yet washed away. There was nothing identifiable, just enough remaining to show that more than one person had stood in this spot.

"So this area is consistent with the spot she must have gone over from?"

The apothecary nodded.

Fidelma bit her lip. The marks could well indicate that more than one person had left the path, which was two yards away from the edge of the cliff at this point, and stood near to the edge of the cliff. But the most important thing about the cliff edge here was the fact that it was at least six feet away from the worn track. There was surely no way that the Abbess Cuimne could go over the cliff by accident while walking along the path. To fall over, she would have had deliberately to leave the pathway, scramble across some shrub and gorse, and balance on that dangerous edge. But if not an accident . . . what then?

There was something else, too, about the cliff edge. But she did not wish to move too close, for Fidelma hated high, unprotected places.

"Is there a means of climbing down here?" she suddenly asked Corcrain.

"Only if you are a mountain goat, I reckon. No, it's too dangerous. Not that I am saying it is totally impossible to get down. Those with knowledge of climbing such inaccessible spots might well attempt it. There are a few caves set into the face of the cliff along here and once some people from the mainland wanted to go down to examine them."

"At this spot?"

"No. About three hundred yards along. But the *bó-aire* saw them off, declaring it was too dangerous. That was last year."

Fidelma took off her short woolen cloak, which she wore to protect her from the almost continuous drizzle of the island's gray skies, and put it down near the cliff edge. Then she knelt down before stretching full-length on it and easing forward to peer over the edge. It was as the apothecary said: Only someone skilled in the art of climbing, or a mountain goat, would even attempt to climb down. She shivered for a moment as she stared down to the rocky beach three hundred feet below.

When she had stood up and brushed down her cloak she asked Corcrain, "Where do I find this man Congal?"

Congal was a big man. He sat before a plate piled with fish and a boiled duck's egg. Though he sat at table, he still wore his fisherman's clothes, as if he could not be bothered to change on entering his *bóthan*. Yet the clothes simply emphasized his large, muscular torso. His hands, too, were large and callused.

"Sad, it is," he growled across the scrubbed pine table to where Sister Fidelma sat with a bowl of sweet mead which he had offered in hospitality. "The woman had a good life before her, but it is a dangerous place to be walking if you don't know the ground."

"I'm told that she was exploring here."

The big man frowned.

"Exploring?"

"I'm told that she spoke with you a few times."

"Not surprising that she would do so. I am the local *seanchaí*. I know all the legends and tales of the island." There was more than a hint of pride in his voice. Sister Fidelma realized that pride went with the islanders. They had little enough but were proud of what they did have.

"Is that what she was interested in? Ancient tales?"

"It was."

"Any subject or tale in particular?"

Congal shifted as if defensively.

"None as I recall."

"What, then?"

"Oh, just tales about the ancient times, when the druids of Iarmuma used to hunt down the priests of Christ and kill them. That was a long time ago, even before the Blessed Patrick came to our shores."

"You provided her with some of these tales?"

Congal nodded.

"I did so. Many priests of Christ found a refuge on this island during the pagan times. They fled from the mainland while the king of Iarmuma's men were burning down the churches and communities."

Sister Fidelma sighed. It did not sound the sort of subject Abbess Cuimne would be interested in pursuing. As representative of the archbishop, she had, as Sister Fidelma knew, special responsibility for the uniform observances of the faith in Ireland.

"But no story in particular interested her?" she pressed.

"None."

Was Congal's voice too emphatic? Sister Fidelma felt an uneasy pricking at the back of her neck, that odd sensation she always felt when something was wrong, or someone was not telling the full truth.

Back at the cabin of the *bó-aire,* Sister Fidelma sorted through the leather satchel which contained the belongings of the dead abbess. She steeled herself to sorting through the items which became objects of pathetic sentiment. The items proclaimed the abbess to have some vanity, the few cosmetics and a jar of perfume, her rosary and crucifix, a splendidly worked piece of ivory and gold, which proclaimed her rank, as sister to the High King, rather than her role as a humble religieuse. The rosary beads were of imported ivory. There were items of clothes for her journey. All were contained in the leather shoulder satchel which traveling monks and nuns carried on their journeys and pilgrimages.

Sister Fidelma sorted through the satchel twice before she realized what was worrying her. She turned to the impatient *bó-aire*.

"Fogartach, are you sure these are all the Abbess Cuimne's possessions?"

The young magistrate nodded vehemently.

Sister Fidelma sighed. If Abbess Cuimne was on the island to carry out some search or investigation, surely she would have had a means of recording notes? Indeed, where was the pocket missal that most religieuses of rank carried? Over a century before, when Irish monks and nuns had set out on their missions to the far corners of the world, they had to carry with them liturgical and religious tracts. It was necessary, therefore, that such works were small enough for missionaries to carry with them in special leather satchels called *tiag liubhar*. Therefore the monks engaged in the task of copying such books began to reduce their size. Such small books were now carried by almost all learned members of the church. It would be odd if the abbess had not carried even a missal with her.

She drummed her fingers on the tabletop for a while. If the answer to the conundrum was not forthcoming on the island, perhaps it might be found in the wager with Artagán, the bishop of An Chúis on the mainland. She made her decision and turned to the expectant *bó-aire*.

"I need a currach to take me to An Chúis on the mainland at once."

The young man gaped at her in surprise.

"Have you finished here, Sister?"

"No. But there is someone I must consult at An Chúis immediately. The boat must wait for me so that I can return here by this afternoon."

Bishop Artagán rose in surprise when Sister Fidelma strode into his study at the abbey of An Chúis, after being ceremoniously announced by a member of his order. It was from here that Artagán presided over the priesthood of the Corco Dhuibhne.

"There are some questions I would ask you, Bishop," she announced as soon as the introductions were over.

"As a *dálaigh* of the Brehon Court, you have but to ask," agreed the bishop, a flaccid-faced though nervous man of indeterminable age. He had led her to a seat before his fire and offered hospitality in the form of heated mead.

"The Abbess Cuimne—" began Fidelma.

"I have heard the sad news," interrupted the bishop. "She fell to her death."

"Indeed. But before she went to the island, she stayed here in the abbey, did she not?"

"Two nights while waiting for a calm sea in order to travel to the island," confirmed Artagán.

"The island is under your jurisdiction?"

"It is."

"Why did the Abbess Cuimne go to the island? There is talk that she had a wager with you on the result of her visit and what she would find there."

Artagán grimaced tiredly.

"She was going on a wild-goose chase," he said disarmingly. "My wager was a safe one."

Fidelma drew her brows together in perplexity.

"I would like an explanation."

"The Abbess Cuimne was of a strong personality. This was natural as she is—was—sister to the High King. She had great talents. This, too, is natural, for the archbishop at Armagh appointed her as his personal representative to ensure the uniformity of holy office among the monasteries and churches of Éireann. I have met her only twice. Once at a synod at Cashel and then when she came to stay before going to the island. She entertained views that were sometimes difficult to debate with her."

"In what way do you mean?"

"Have you heard the legend of the reliquary of the Blessed Palladius?"

"Tell me it," invited Fidelma in order to cover her bewilderment.

"Well, as you know, two and a half centuries ago, the Christian community in Éireann was very small but, God willing, increasing as people turned to the word of Christ. By that time they had reached such a size that they sent to the holy city of Rome to ask the pope, Celestine, the first of his name to sit on the throne of Peter, the disciple of Christ, to send them a bishop. They wanted a man who would teach and help them follow the ways of the living God. Celestine appointed a man named Palladius as the first bishop to the Irish believing in Christ."

Artagán paused before continuing.

"There are two versions of the story. Firstly, that Palladius, en route to Éireann, took sick in Gaul and died there. Secondly, that Palladius did reach our shores and administer to the Irish, eventually being foully murdered by an enraged druid in the pay of the king of Iarmuma."

"I have heard these stories," confirmed Sister Fidelma. "It was after Palladius's death that the Blessed Patrick, who was then studying in Gaul, was appointed bishop to Ireland and returned to this land, where once he had been held as a hostage."

"Indeed," agreed Artagán. "A legend then arose in the years after Palladius's death: that relics of this holy saint were placed in a reliquary, a box with a roof-shaped lid, about twelve centimeters wide by six in length by five deep. They are usually made of wood, often yew; lined inside in lead and on the outside ornate with gilt, copper alloy, gold foil, with amber and glass decoration. Beautiful things."

Sister Fidelma nodded impatiently. She had seen many such reliquaries among the great abbeys of Éireann.

"The legend had it that Palladius's relics were once kept at Cashel, seat of the Eóganacht kings of Munster. Then about two hundred years ago there was a revival of the beliefs of the druids in Iarmuma. The king of Iarmuma resumed the old religion and a great persecution of Christian communities began. Cashel was stormed. But the relics were taken into the country for safekeeping, taken from one spot to another until the relics of our first bishop were taken to the islands, away from the ravages of man. There they disappeared."

"Go on," prompted Sister Fidelma when the bishop paused.

"Well, just think of it. What a find it would be if we could discover the relics of the first bishop of Éireann after all this time! What a center of pilgrimage their resting place would make, what a great abbey could be built there which would attract attention from the four corners of the world . . ."

Sister Fidelma grimaced wryly.

"Are you saying that the Abbess Cuimne had gone to the island searching for the reliquary of Palladius?"

Bishop Artagán nodded.

"She informed me that in Ard Macha, in the great library there, she had come across some old manuscripts which indicated that the reliquary was taken to an island off the mainland of the Corco Dhuibhne. The manuscripts, which she refused to show me, were claimed to contain notes of its location written at the time. The notes had been kept in an old book in the library of the monastery of Ard Macha. There were legends of priests fleeing to these islands during the persecutions of the king of Iarmuma, but surely we would have known had the sacred reliquary been taken there."

The bishop sniffed disparagingly.

"So you did not agree with Abbess Cuimne that the reliquary was on the island?" queried Sister Fidelma.

"I did not. I am something of a scholar of the period myself. Palladius died in Gaul. That much is obvious, for most records recount that fact."

"So this is why you thought that the abbess was on a wild-goose chase?"

"Indeed, I did so. The relics of Palladius have not survived the ravages of time. If they have, then they would be in Gaul, not here. It was hard to dissuade Abbess Cuimne. A strong-willed woman, as I have told you."

The bishop suddenly frowned.

"But what has this to do with your investigation into her death?"

Sister Fidelma smiled gently and rose from her seat.

"I only needed to assure myself of the purpose of her visit to the island."

On the bouncing trip back, over the harsh, choppy gray seas, Sister Fidelma sat back in the currach and reflected with wrinkled forehead. So it was logical that the Abbess Cuimne had talked about the reliquary of Palladius to Congal, the *seanchaí* of the island; why then had the man not been forthcoming about that fact? What was the big fisherman trying to hide? She decided to leave Congal for the time being and go straightaway on landing to talk with the island's priest, Father Patrick. He had been the second person whom the Abbess Cuimne had made a special effort to talk with on the island.

Father Patrick was an old man, certainly into his late mid- or even late eighties. A thin wisp of a man, who, Sister Fidelma thought, would be blown away by the winds that buffeted the island. A man of more bone than flesh, with large knuckles, a taut parchmentlike skin, and a few strands of white hair. From under overhanging brows, pale eyes of indiscernible color stared at Fidelma.

Father Patrick sat in a chair by his fireside, a thick wool shawl wrapped around his frail frame and held close by a brooch around his scrawny neck.

Yet withal, the frailty and age, Fidelma felt she was in the presence of a strong and dynamic personality.

"Tell me about the reliquary of Palladius." Sister Fidelma opened abruptly. It was a shot in the dark but she saw that it paid off.

The aged face was immobile. Only the eyes blinked once as a token of surprise. But Fidelma's quiet eyes picked up the involuntary action.

"What have you heard about the old legend?"

The rasping voice was so pitched that Fidelma was hard

pressed to hear any emotion, but there was something there . . . something defensive.

"*Is* it a legend, Father?" asked Fidelma with emphasis.

"There are many old legends here, my daughter."

"Well, Abbess Cuimne thought she knew this one to be true. She told the bishop of the Corco Dhuibhne that she was going to see the reliquary before she left the island."

"And now she is dead," the old priest observed almost with a sigh. Again the watery pale eyes blinked. "May she rest in peace."

Sister Fidelma waited a moment. The priest was silent.

"About the reliquary . . ." she found herself prompting.

"So far as people are concerned it is only a legend and will remain so."

Sister Fidelma frowned, trying to interpret this statement.

"So it is not on the island?"

"No islander has seen it."

Fidelma pursed her lips in an effort to suppress her annoyance. She had the distinct feeling that Father Patrick was playing semantic games with her. She tried another tack.

"Abbess Cuimne came to talk with you on a couple of occasions, didn't she? What did you talk about?"

"We talked about the folklore of the island."

"About the reliquary?"

The priest paused. "About the legend of the reliquary," he corrected.

"And she believed it was here, on the island, isn't that so?"

"She believed so."

"And it is not?"

"You may ask any islander if they have seen it or know of its whereabouts."

Fidelma sighed impatiently. Again there had come the semantic avoidance of her question. Father Patrick would have made a good advocate, skillful in debate.

"Very well, Father. Thank you for your time."

She was leaving the priest's cell when she met Corcrain, the apothecary, at the step.

"How ill is Father Patrick?" Fidelma asked him directly.

"Father Patrick is a frail old man," the apothecary replied. "I fear he will not be with us beyond the winter. He has already had two problems with his heart, which grows continually weaker."

"How weak?"

"Twice it has misbeat. The third time may prove fatal."

Sister Fidelma pursed her lips.

"Surely the bishop could retire an old man like that? He could go to rest in some comfortable abbey on the mainland."

"Surely—if anyone could persuade Father Patrick to leave the island. He came here as a young man sixty years ago and has never left. He's a stubborn old fellow. He thinks of the island as his fiefdom. He feels responsible, personally, for every islander."

Sister Fidelma sought out Congal again. This time the *seanchaí* met her with suspicion.

"What did the Abbess Cuimne want to know about the reliquary of Palladius?" demanded Sister Fidelma without preamble.

The big man's jaw dropped a little at the unexpectedness of her question.

"She knew it was on the island, didn't she?" pressed Fidelma, not giving the man a chance to reflect on the question.

Congal compressed his lips.

"She thought it was so," he replied at last.

"Why the secret?"

"Secret?"

"If it is on the island, why has it been kept secret?"

The big man shifted awkwardly.

"Have you spoken with Father Patrick?" he asked sullenly.

"I have."

Congal was clearly unhappy. He hesitated again and then squared his shoulders.

"If Father Patrick has spoken with you, then you will know."

Fidelma decided not to enlighten the storyteller that Father Patrick had told her virtually nothing.

"Why keep the fact that the reliquary is on the island a secret?" she pressed again.

"Because it *is* the reliquary of Palladius; the very bones of the first bishop appointed to the Irish believing in Christ, the blessed saint who brought us out of the darkness into Christian light. Think, Sister Fidelma, what would happen if it were generally known that the relics were here on this island. Think of the pilgrims who would come streaming in, think of the great religious foundations that would be raised on this island, and everything that would follow that. Soon people from all over the world would be coming here and destroying our peace. Soon our community would be swamped or dispersed. Better that no one knows about the relics. Why, not even I have seen them nor know where they are hidden. Only Father Patrick . . ."

Congal caught sight of Sister Fidelma's face and must have read its amazed expression.

"Did Father Patrick tell you . . . ? What did Father Patrick tell you?" he suddenly demanded, his face full of suspicion.

There was an abrupt knocking at the *bóthan* door and before Congal could call out the young *bó-aire* put his head around the door. His face was troubled.

"Ah, Sister, Corcrain the apothecary asks if you could return at once to Father Patrick's cell. Father Patrick has been taken ill but is demanding to see you."

Corcrain met her at Father Patrick's door.

"I doubt if he has long, Sister," he said quietly. "Not long after you left he had that third shock to the heart that I was warning against. However, he insists on seeing you alone. I'll be outside if you need me."

The old priest was lying in bed; his face was wan, with a curiously bluish texture to the skin.

The eyes flickered open, the same colorless pale eyes.

"You know, don't you, my daughter?"

Sister Fidelma decided to be truthful.

"I suspect," she corrected.

"Well, I must make my peace with God and better that you should know the truth rather than let me depart with only suspicion to shroud my name."

There was a long pause.

"The reliquary is here. It was brought by priests fleeing from the king of Iarmuma's warriors over two hundred and fifty years ago. They hid it in a cave for safekeeping. For generations, the priest officiating on this island would tell only his successor of its whereabouts. Sometimes when a priest wasn't available, an islander would be told so that the knowledge would pass on to each new generation. I came here as a young priest some sixty years ago and learned the secret from the old priest I was to replace."

The old man paused to take some deep breaths.

"Then the Abbess Cuimne came. A very intelligent woman. She had found evidence. She checked the legends with Congal, who knows a lot save only where the relics are hidden. He tried to stop her going further by telling her nothing, little short of lying to her. Then she came to me. To my horror, she had a piece of parchment, a series of jumbled notes written in the hand of no less a person than the Blessed Patrick himself. When Palladius died, Patrick had been sent by the pope to succeed him as bishop to the Irish. The parchment contained a map, directions which were meaningless unless one knew what it was that one was looking for, and the place one had to look in.

"Abbess Cuimne was clever. She had heard of the legends and found this paper tucked into an ancient book belonging to the Blessed Patrick in Ard Macha's great library. She made some educated guesses, my daughter."

"And you tried to dissuade her from continuing her search?"

"I did everything to persuade her that legends are not necessarily reality. But she was determined."

"And then?"

"Then I was honest with her. I pleaded with her to spare this island the consequence of the revelation of the news that it was the hiding place of the reliquary. I pointed out the consequences to this community if such a thing was made public. You are a woman with some imagination, Sister Fidelma. I can tell. Imagine what would happen to this peaceful little island, to this happy little community."

"Could the relics not be taken off the island?" asked Fidelma. "Perhaps they could be sent to Cashel or even to Ard Macha?"

"And then this island would lose the holy protection given to it by being the repository of the sacred relics. No. The relics were brought here for a purpose and here they must remain."

The old priest's voice had suddenly become sharp. Then he fell silent for a while before continuing.

"I tried my best to make her see what a disaster it would be. We have seen what disasters have happened to other communities where relics have been found, or miracles have been witnessed, and great abbeys have been built and shrines erected. Small communities were devastated. Places of simple pious pilgrimage have been made into places of crass commercial enterprise. Devastation beyond imagining, all the things which so repelled our Savior. Did He not chase the moneylenders and merchants from the temple grounds? How much more would He turn on those who made His religion a subject of commercialism today? No, I did not want that for our tiny island. It would destroy our way of life and our very soul!"

The old priest's voice was vehement now.

"And when Abbess Cuimne refused to accept your arguments, what did you do?" prompted Sister Fidelma, quietly.

"At first, I hoped that the abbess would not be able to decipher properly the figures which would lead her to the reliquary. But she did. It was the morning that she was due to leave the island. . . ."

He paused and an expression of pain crossed his face. He fought to catch his breath but shook his head when Fidelma suggested that she call the apothecary.

Sister Fidelma waited patiently. The priest finally continued.

"As chance would have it I saw the Abbess Cuimne on the path to Aill Tuatha, the north cliff. I followed her, hoping against hope. But she knew where she was going."

"Is that where the reliquary is hidden?" asked Fidelma. "In one of the cliff-top caves at Aill Tuatha?"

The priest nodded in resignation.

"The abbess started to climb down. She thought the descent was easy. I tried to stop her. To warn her of the danger."

The priest paused, his watery eyes now stirring in emotion.

"I am soon going to meet my God, my daughter. There is no

priest on the island. I must make my peace with you. This is by nature of my confession. Do you understand?"

Fidelma paused; a conflict between her role as an advocate of the Brehon Court and that as a member of a religious order with respect for the confessional caused her to hesitate. Then she finally nodded.

"I understand, Father. What happened?"

"The abbess started to descend the cliff toward the cave entrance. I cried out and told her if she must go down to be careful. I moved forward to the edge of the cliff and bent down even as she slipped. Her hand reached out and grabbed at my crucifix, which I wore on a silver chain around my neck. The links of the chain snapped. In that moment I grabbed for her, holding on momentarily to her shoulders and even her neck.

"Alas, I am old and frail; she slid from my grip and went hurtling down to the rocks."

The priest paused, panting for breath.

Sister Fidelma bit her lip.

"And then?" she prompted.

"Peering down, I could see that she was dead. I knelt a while in prayer, seeking to absolve her for her sins, of which audacity and arrogance were the only ones I knew. Then a thought struck me, which grew in my mind and gave me comfort. We are all in God's hands. It occurred to me that it was His intervention. He might have saved the abbess. Instead, perhaps it was His will that had been wrought, a miracle which prevented the reliquary being discovered. One death to prevent a great evil, the destruction of our community. The thought has given me comfort, my daughter. So I simply picked up my broken crucifix, though some of the chain was missing. Then I forced myself to walk back to the path, walk down to the beach, and search her. I found her missal and inside the piece of paper that had given her the clue, the one written by the Blessed Patrick. I took them both and I returned here. I was silly, for I should have simply taken the paper and left her missal. I realized how odd it must have looked to the trained eye that it was missing. But I was exhausted. My health was none too good. But the reliquary was safe . . . or so I thought."

Sister Fidelma gave a deep, troubled sigh.

"What did you do with the paper?"

"God forgive me, though it was written in the hand of the Blessed Patrick, I destroyed it. I burned it in my hearth."

"And the missal?"

"It is there on the table. You may send it to her kinsmen."

"And that is all?"

"It is all, my daughter. Yet my conscience has troubled me. Am I, in turn, arrogant enough to think that God would enact a murder . . . even for such a pious purpose? My grievous sin is not coming forward to the *bó-aire* with my story. But my main purpose was to keep the secret of the reliquary. Now I am dying. I must tell someone of the secret. Perhaps God has willed that you, a total stranger to this island, should know the truth as you had learnt part of that truth already. What is the old Latin hexameter?—*Quis, quid, ubi, quibus, auxilius, cur, quomodo, quando?*"

Sister Fidelma smiled softly at the old man.

"Who is the criminal? What is the crime? Where was it committed? By what means? With what accomplices? Why? In what way? When?"

"Exactly so, my daughter. And now you know these things. You suspected either Congal or myself of some dark crime. There was no crime. If it was, the cause was a miracle. I felt I had no choice but to tell you and place the fate of this island and its community in your hands. Do you understand what this means, my daughter?"

Sister Fidelma slowly nodded.

"I do, Father."

"Then I have done what I should have done before."

Outside the priest's cell a number of islanders had gathered, gazing at Sister Fidelma with expressions varying between curiosity and hostility. Corcrain looked quizzically at her but Fidelma did not respond to his unspoken questions. Instead she went to find Congal to tell him about the cave at Aill Tuatha. That was Congal's responsibility, not her burden.

* * *

The gulls swooped and cried across the gray granite quay of the island. The blustery winds caught them, causing it to seem as if they had stopped momentarily in their flight, and then they beat their wings at the air and swooped again. The sea was choppy and through its dim gray mist Sister Fidelma could see Ciardha's boat from An Chúis, heaving up and down over the short waves as it edged in towards the harbor. It was not going to be a pleasant voyage back to the mainland. She sighed.

The boat would be bringing a young priest to the island to take over from Father Patrick. He had fallen into a peaceful sleep and died a few hours after Sister Fidelma had spoken with him.

Fidelma's choice had been a hard one. She had returned to the *bó-aire*'s cabin and pondered all night over the young magistrate's official report in the light of what she now knew.

Now she stood waiting for the boat to arrive to take her away from the island. At her side the fresh-faced young magistrate stood nervously.

The boat edged in towards the quay. Lines were thrown and caught, and the few travelers climbed their way to the quay up the ancient rope ladder. The first was a young man, clean-featured and looking appallingly youthful, wearing his habit like a brand-new badge of office. Congal and Corcrain were standing at the head of the quay to greet him.

Sister Fidelma shook her head wonderingly. The priest did not look as if he had learned yet to shave and already he was "father" to 160 souls. She turned and impulsively held out her hand to the young *bó-aire*, smiling.

"Well, many thanks for your hospitality and assistance, Fogartach. I'll be speaking to the Chief Brehon and to Fathan of the Corco Dhuibhne. Then I'll be glad to get back to my interrupted journey back to my Abbey of Kildare."

The young man held on to Sister Fidelma's hand a fraction of a second longer than necessary, his worried eyes searching her face.

"And my report, Sister?"

Sister Fidelma broke away and began her descent, halting a moment on the top rung of the ladder. In spite of the young man's arrogance, it was wrong to continue to play the cat and mouse with him.

"As you said, Fogartach, it was a straightforward case. The Abbess Cuimne slipped and fell to her death. A tragic accident."

The young *bó-aire*'s face relaxed and, for the first time, he smiled and raised a hand in salute.

"I have learned a little wisdom from you, *Anruth* of the Brehon Court," he said stiffly. "God keep you safe on your journey until you reach your destination!"

Sister Fidelma smiled back and raised a hand.

"Every destination is but a gateway to another, Fogartach," she answered. Then she grinned her urchin grin before dropping into the stern of the gently rocking currach as it waited for her below.

DONALD E. WESTLAKE

LAST-MINUTE SHOPPING

Sometimes one finds enjoyable crime stories in unexpected places—like this little Christmas tale by one of America's top mystery writers, tucked away in the pages of The New York Times Book Review.

When O'Brien answered the doorbell, it was Officer Keenan standing there. "Oh, no!" O'Brien cried. "Not on Christmas Eve! Besides, I didn't *do* anything!"

"Take it easy, O'Brien," Keenan said. "I'm not here to arrest you."

"You're not?"

"I'd like to come in," Keenan said.

"You're in," O'Brien agreed, and shut the door behind him.

Keenan looked around the neat but sparse living room. "Huh," he said. "Crime really doesn't pay."

"Is that why you came here, to tell me that?"

"No, O'Brien," Keenan said. "We've known each other over the years."

"You've arrested me over the years, you mean. And a lot of times it didn't stick."

"I do my job, you do yours." Keenan shrugged, and said, "Now I need your help."

"I don't fink," O'Brien said.

"Oh, you would, if the circumstance was right," Keenan said, "but that's not what I want. You may not know this, but I've had a steady lady friend for a few years now."

"She hasn't done much for your personality."

"I guess not," Keenan said, "because two weeks ago we had a major fight, we broke up, that was the end of it, and it was all my fault."

"I'm sorry to hear that," O'Brien said.

"Fellow feeling. I've always liked that about you." Keenan nodded and said, "An hour ago, ten P.M. on Christmas Eve, she calls me. She's sorry we broke up, she's been thinking about me, why don't we try to get back together. Sure, that'd be great, I been miserable for two weeks, I didn't know I'd ever get another chance. She's a waitress at a place in midtown, she took the Christmas Eve shift because there wasn't anybody for her to go home to, she'll get off at eleven-thirty, she wants me to come to her place at midnight."

"An hour from now."

"That's the problem," Keenan said. "Laurie says—that's her name, Laurie. Laurie says she's been thinking about nothing but me for the last two weeks, but like a dope *I've* been trying to think about anything *except* her, making myself miserable. So what this means is, I know she's gonna have a really thoughtful terrific Christmas present for me when I get to her place, but I got nothing for her, and everything's closed, and I don't want to look like a bum when we're supposed to be making up and getting back together again."

"Tough," O'Brien said.

Keenan cleared his throat. "There's a jewelry store," he said, "called Henderson's."

"Hey, wait a minute!" O'Brien said, backing up. "We been getting along so well up to now."

"Take it easy, take it easy. I believe you know this jewelry store."

"Believe what you want," O'Brien said.

"I believe you've made a number of unofficial visits to Henderson's over the years," Keenan said.

"Prove it."

"I don't want to prove it," Keenan said. "Not now, not tonight. What I want is to get into Henderson's in the next half hour."

O'Brien looked at him.

"Not to steal anything," Keenan said. "You can't give a person stolen goods for a Christmas present."

"Oh, yeah?"

"Yeah," Keenan said. "What I want to do, I want to go into Henderson's, pick out something really nice, and leave the money for it."

"And you want *me* to get you in."

"Without busting anything. The kind of neat work you always do."

"Keenan," O'Brien said, "this is looking an awful lot like entrapment."

"I wouldn't set you up," Keenan said. "Come on, O'Brien, you know me. I've always been straight with you, and you've always been crooked with me. I'm not gonna change now. And after this, I'll owe you one. The time'll come, down the road, I'll take care of you."

"Call the owner of the store, ask him to open up."

"He's away for the holidays. You're my only hope."

O'Brien pondered. "You want me to break into Henderson's with you watching."

"I'll turn my back until the door's open."

"A cop standing right there, and I'm breaking into a jewelry store."

"It's my future happiness, O'Brien."

"And I've got no choice, do I?"

"Sure you do."

O'Brien brooded. Keenan said, "Don't you have a lady friend?"

"Yeah?"

"While we're in there, pick her up a little something."

O'Brien perked up. "I can?"

Keenan gave him a look. "And *pay* for it."

"Oh, right," O'Brien said. "You can't give stolen goods for a Christmas present."

"That's right."

"It's very hard," Keenan whispered, "to pick out a nice piece of jewelry in the dark."

"Usually in this situation," O'Brien told him, "the perpetrator just takes a couple handfuls and goes."

"This isn't the usual situation," Keenan said. "Can't we have a *little* more light from that flash?"

"You wanna spend Christmas at the precinct, explaining your love life?"

"Well, aim it better, anyway."

Keenan leaned over the counters of brooches and rings, and O'Brien leaned over Keenan, shining the flashlight at the trays. Two strips of electrician's tape on the lens left only a narrow slit for light to come through. Gold and silver and semiprecious stones gleamed murkily in that amber light.

"Maybe over on this side," Keenan said, and they bumped each other as they turned to cross the store.

More trays of underlit goodies. O'Brien whispered, "How you gonna pay for this stuff? You can't use a credit card when the store's closed."

"I got cash. I grabbed what I had, and borrowed from guys at the station."

"Plan ahead, huh?"

"Yeah. Ouch! That's my foot under your foot, O'Brien."

"Sorry."

Finally, after a longer time than O'Brien usually spent in Henderson's, Keenan chose a nice bracelet, gold filigree with garnets, a nice Christmasy glow. "Six hundred bucks," he said, reading the tag. "Good, I thought it'd be more. I'll just leave the money where the bracelet was." He did, and said, "What about you, O'Brien? Find anything for your lady friend?"

"I think over on the other side there was something. Hold the flashlight for me, okay?"

"Right. Ow!"

"Sorry."

Rubbing his shin, Keenan said, "I thought you'd be better than that, in the dark."

"You mean, get like permanent night vision? It doesn't work that way. Shine it here, will you, Keenan?"

It wasn't long before O'Brien found what he wanted, a pretty brooch. "That goes with Grace's eyes," he said. "How much is it?"

Keenan squinted at the tag. "Four fifty."

"I think I can do that." O'Brien pulled out a wad, thumbed through it. "Yep. And thirty bucks left over."

He left the money, then eased them out of the store and hooked up the alarm again. "I appreciate this, O'Brien," Keenan said.

"It was easy," O'Brien said.

When Grace opened the door, her smiling face was framed by the lustrous Christmas tree across the room. It made her look like an angel. O'Brien said, "Grace, you're beautiful."

"What a sweet thing to say," Grace said, and shut the door, and kissed him.

O'Brien took the little box out of his pocket. "Merry Christmas," he said.

Grace looked at the little box and her smile faded. "What did you do, Harry?" she asked him.

"I got you a Christmas present. It's Christmas."

"You didn't—Harry, you promised me. You didn't . . ."

"Steal it?" O'Brien laughed. "I wouldn't do that," he said. "You can't give stolen goods for a Christmas present."

"That's right." Grace opened the box and gazed in pleasure at the silver brooch with the green stones. "It's beautiful!"

"Like you."

Doubtful again, she said, "Harry? You don't have any money, I know you don't. How'd you pay for this?"

"I did some consultancy work for a cop tonight," O'Brien said, "and he paid me. He doesn't *know* he paid me, but he paid me." In his mind's eye came the memory of Keenan stumbling around in the dark, his pockets full of he couldn't be sure how much money. "The thing is," O'Brien said, as he pinned the brooch on his lady friend, "I got *great* night vision."

KATE WILHELM

REFORMING ELLIE

*Kate Wilhelm is a well-known science fiction author who has
also written fantasy, horror, and detective tales. With her husband, Damon Knight, she has been especially active in writers'
conferences and workshops, encouraging new writers of science fiction. In 1993 she published a new mystery novel and
contributed her first short story to EQMM—this memorable
tale of childhood friends.*

A relentless February rain was falling when Carol Ballinger left
work; it wasn't too bad on Amsterdam, but when she turned
onto 110th, the rain came straight at her; she was soaked and
freezing by the time she got home. Michael's jacket was dripping
from a chair back, and she had to nudge his wet shoes out of the
way. She flicked on the answering machine and began to wrestle
with her rubber boots that always pulled off her shoes, and often
her hose, half listening to calls for Michael. She straightened in
surprise at the last message.

"Carol? You there? It's Ellie. Look, I'll be in town on Wednesday night. How 'bout that! I don't guess you could meet my
plane? A joke, honey, forget it, I'll find you."

Carol listened to it again as she finished taking off her wet
clothes and hung her jacket on the other chair back, acutely aware
of the near-tremulous feeling of excitement that verged on dread
that Ellie had often aroused in her. Irritably she shrugged off the
feeling, a fossil from her childhood. She heard Michael behind
her and turned. "Did you hear the message? Ellie's coming to
visit."

"Who's Ellie?" he asked, toweling his hair. He looked cross. He hated getting wet, possibly as much as she did.

"I've told you all about her," Carol said. His blank look was not a pretense, she knew; she brushed against him on her way to the bathroom for another towel. Belatedly he moved back a step. "If you'd ever listen to anything I say," she muttered and slammed the door.

Dinner was reheated spaghetti with canned sauce.

"Where's she going to sleep?" Michael asked, as they ate.

"On the couch."

"How long?"

"You heard her message. You know as much as I do. You didn't mind when Lon Voorhees parked out on the couch for more than a month last fall."

"That was different."

"Right. He's your friend. Well, she's mine."

"Dammit, Carol, I'm not objecting."

"You should go look at your expression in the mirror."

It had been almost cute when he used to pout like that. He was large, over six feet, and broad, with curly black hair, an enviable fringe of eyelashes; the little-boy look had been unexpected and appealing ten years ago. She jerked up and away from the table and started to scrape her dish noisily.

Of course, the apartment was too small for a third person to share. Five hundred square feet—two bedrooms, the living room, with eating space, barely, a kitchen that only one person at a time could enter, the tiniest bathroom she had ever seen. The interior paint once had been neutral, a non-color, but now it was more like mustard; the furniture was brown Naugahyde and rickety, and things were everywhere because there wasn't any storage room. Books, magazines, his school notebooks, her notebooks . . . Michael used the second, cavelike bedroom as his study, where he now headed without scraping his plate, or even taking his dishes to the sink. Angrily Carol cleared the table, washed the dishes, and then listened to Ellie's drawling voice once more.

She had known Ellie Withers all her life; they had lived side by side in nearly identical houses in a subdivision outside of Tulsa, had toddled together, had gone to preschool, to kindergarten, all the way through high school together. Most people had thought they were sisters, even twin sisters. Blond, hair darkening a bit through their teens, blue eyes . . .

Ellie had asked her one night, "How do you hold your arms when you sleep?"

"I don't know. How do you?"

"Straight down at my sides. Or else crossed on my chest, like this." She demonstrated. "And you should move them once every fifteen minutes or you could get gangrene, and they have to cut off your hand."

Carol hadn't really believed her, but she had worried about it for months. She had tried to catch herself falling asleep, or coming awake, tried to check the position of her arms.

Another time, later, Ellie had said, "They know if you're bleeding. If you're ready to go all the way. They can smell the difference in you. Like cats or dogs can."

They had been twelve, approaching a corner where half a dozen adolescent boys were fooling around, and Carol had suddenly wanted to crawl into the hedge at Mrs. McKittrick's yard where they were walking.

For years she had taken two, three showers a day, immersed herself in long, scented bubble baths, used cologne lavishly, dabbed on her mother's perfume. . . .

Ellie had broken the news about Santa Claus; she had known that Miss Erenhart was pregnant and would have to drop out of teaching seventh grade. She had sworn a girl could get pregnant by French kissing, and later on said that if you stood up right after sex, you wouldn't get pregnant.

They had stayed in touch only sporadically after high school; Ellie had borrowed three hundred dollars from Carol, and had run off with Bert Lowenstein. Although Carol would have been too embarrassed, even ashamed, to ask about the loan, or demand payment, Ellie had never given her an address where she could have been reached, either. But she always knew where Carol was. There had been a card now and then, never with a return address, and a phone call now and then during which she dodged the question of where she was living. Ellie by phone, or by mail, never had roused the feeling of anxiety that her coming visit had brought on. Ellie in person was different.

Michael had begun to pace the length of the hall from his study to the living room, and back, his forehead deeply creased as he muttered unintelligibly. In fourteen weeks he would take the bar exam, and then things would be different, she told herself, as she had been doing more and more frequently, counting the months, then the weeks. Soon she would be counting the days.

She watched Michael a moment and then began to work on an article she was doing for a gardening magazine.

"Did you pick up my jacket?" Michael asked, at the entrance to the living room.

"Raining too hard."

"Get it tomorrow, will you? Another seminar at Dirac's this weekend. I'll need it."

She put down her pen. "Then why don't you get it yourself?"

He had already left and was midway down the hall. He stopped, turned to give her a puzzled look. "It's closer for you."

"By one lousy block. And it's your jacket."

"Look," he said reasonably, with that pouting look on his face, "just this once. Okay? I won't have time tomorrow."

"Neither will I," she said.

"Jesus," he said, shaking his head. "I have that paper to write, a test coming up, a tax seminar to prepare for. . . . Don't do this to me."

She knew what-all he had to do: Michael dutifully reported to her every assignment, every problem, every word said at the seminars. She shrugged and picked up her pen. After a moment, she heard his study door slam, and she put the pen down and drew in a deep breath; her hand was shaking. She had done it, she thought in wonder. She had turned him down.

Fourteen more weeks, she told herself. Just fourteen more weeks. Don't make waves now. Her lips tightened. But damned if she would fetch his jacket. After another moment she began to write: "For that shady spot between the back of the garage and the fence I put in some hostas a few years ago, but last summer I decided that wasn't quite enough, and now I'm glad. Bergenias are up in full bud, and the dicentra alba is starting to open. The cheiranthus has spread. . . ."

Ellie had not changed a bit, was Carol's first thought, even as Ellie was screaming how little *she* had changed. Then they both cried and hugged each other, and touched each other's hair — Ellie's was long, blonder than it had ever been in the past, and very frizzy; Carol's was shades darker and quite short. They hugged and kissed again, and it really was like having a sister appear after a very long absence.

Ellie was wearing ecru tights and a purple sweater, purple suede boots, and a violet jacket of suede cloth. And yes, she admitted, she was frozen, and starved.

Now, diffraction grating in long dangling earrings caught the light, broke it into a million blinding bits as she tossed her hair back, swung her head from side to side, taking in Michael and Carol alternately. "So I decided to give the big city a try, get a job, have a little fun in the Big Time. . . ."

Carol was at the stove scrambling eggs for her; Michael and Ellie were at the table. "What kind of job?" he asked, at the same instant that Carol cried, "Ellie, that's wonderful! It will be great to have you around again!"

Ellie laughed. "I thought so too."

Michael pursed his lips and stood up. "Back to the grind," he said, and headed for his study.

It was close to one-thirty before Carol got to bed, groggy with fatigue, but too keyed up to go to sleep. Michael stirred and rolled over, made room, pretending to be asleep. She knew he was pretending by the way he breathed. She pretended to believe in his sleep, and stared at the ceiling where lights from across the street made a pattern of overlapping circles, dark, light, dark. . . . She was listening to the traffic, clashes, doors slamming, sirens, squealing brakes. . . . She hadn't heard it for years; it wasn't too bad since they were on the third floor, but she imagined it must sound loud and exciting to Ellie. Carol's mother at one time had decided to reform Ellie; she had tried kindness, tried bribes, tried bullying her, tried stories of girls who went wild. . . . There had been no chance at reforming Ellie ever.

Ellie took things. Carol had been with her once when she decided she wanted a $200 sweater. Ellie had told her exactly what to do: Carol was to take a lot of garments into the dressing room, keep changing them, keep the saleswoman's eyes on her while Ellie got the sweater on, her own sweatshirt over it, and fussed at Carol for being so slow. It had worked, and Carol had confessed to her mother a week later in an agony of guilt. Most of the kids she knew had lifted things now and then, and she had done it, too—a pen, candy bars, comic books, but the things Ellie stole were different. And Carol's fears had been different.

She followed a dark circle until it changed into a light circle, and drifted inward to sleep. Then she came wide awake with the problem of where she put her arms when she slept.

When she got home on Thursday, she felt frozen. The temperature had dropped twenty degrees and a stiff wind had moved in. Ellie and Michael were in the living room where Ellie's couch-bed was still more bed than couch. Ellie was wearing Carol's nicest robe, a rose-colored silk/wool blend that her mother had sent her.

Ellie stroked the robe. "Mike's been telling me all about estate planning, how to avoid probate, how to shield yourself from too much tax."

"That's nice," Carol said, pulling off her heavy khaki jacket. Ugly as sin, was how she thought of it, but it was the warmest thing she owned. She tossed it over a chair in order to put on a pot of coffee, and in her mind she saw herself picking up the little overnight suitcase Ellie had brought, walking out the door wearing her good coat, leaving them to talk about taxes forever. Startled by the clarity of the vision, how right it felt, she snatched up her jacket and fled to change her clothes.

After dinner, when Michael left them, Carol asked what had happened to Bert Lowenstein.

Ellie looked blank for several seconds. "You remember him? I honestly had forgotten about him. We split after a week." She shrugged. "I thought for sure you'd go on through school, make a career for yourself. You know you've got roaches?"

"Plans change," Carol said, remembering more and more of

what it was like to be with Ellie. Now it came back to her that this was always one of her tactics: Touch her in a sore spot and she retaliated swiftly. She had told Ellie about her job last night, designer in a big flower shop, in a back room where she arranged flowers. Baskets of flowers. Bouquets. Corsages. "You never did say what kind of job you have in mind."

"Is there any more coffee?" Ellie asked.

Michael came to the end of the hall. "Carol, where's the cleaning ticket for my jacket? I'll pick it up tomorrow."

"I don't know," she said. "Wherever you put it."

"I put it on your purse this morning."

"Then maybe it dropped off when I picked up my purse."

He glowered at her and wheeled about, returned to his study. She got up to make another pot of coffee, ignoring the knowing look on Ellie's face. A mistake, she told herself crossly. Ellie never took things that were free. Again she was jolted by the thought that swam in her mind.

Ellie's voice dropped to a conspiratorial whisper. "What do you guys do? What do you do for fun?"

"Nothing." Fourteen weeks, she thought desperately. Fourteen weeks.

"Do they pay much for those articles you write? That looks like fun. Even if it is cheating, pretending like that."

"Hundred per article. One a month. It's a small-circulation magazine, shoestring stuff."

"Oh."

Although they talked late into the night again, she learned nothing about Ellie's plans. A job. An apartment. Low on cash right now, broke actually, could Carol spare twenty for a couple of days? Expecting a phone call tomorrow, maybe. Money coming any day. She just had that one very small suitcase, but that wouldn't slow her down, not with a closet full of Carol's things that would all fit. Carol had counted out twenty-two dollars, two dollars of it in change; she had loaned Ellie fifteen.

Sleep was a long time coming. She was too conscious of Michael's deep breathing, an occasional snore, too conscious of Ellie's question: What do you do for fun?

She could still unerringly put her finger on a sore spot, Carol thought then. Fun! Her career! She had dropped out of school when it became very evident that there was not going to be enough money for both of them to stay in. His grants, his student loans, and her small salary barely housed and fed them with her working full-time. He would get his degree, work, and she would return to finish her education was the plan in the beginning, but they had not mentioned it in years. Then the plan was for him to make a lot of money, for them to move out of the city, so she could have a house with a yard and a garden. They hadn't talked about that for years, either.

Friday morning she found the ticket for Michael's jacket, packed his bag for him, and tried to keep out of the way as he dashed about. Ellie was on the couch with the blanket over her head when Carol left.

Red and white carnations, asparagus fern, a sprig of holly, two bergenia leaves . . . If she walked over to the Broadway Mart, and then stopped for wine, it wouldn't be much out of her way. Her boss, Mrs. Bertelsen, wouldn't mind if she left early, she knew. She had to go to the bank, she remembered, another block. Four sprays of freesias, with their heady fragrance, lemon mums . . . She could be home by three-thirty, surprise Ellie, have a nice dinner with just the two of them, maybe even find out something about Ellie's life during the past decade, her plans for now, maybe even confide in her the worrisome thoughts that had been occurring ever since she heard Ellie's voice on the answering machine. Ellie the catalyst.

They had drifted apart after the sweater incident. Carol had taken a job in order to save for college. They had still ridden the same bus to school, and had gone to the same parties, the same school dances and football games, but it had changed by then. Carol's mother had been relieved; she had been a nurse, with little regard for Ellie's mother, who lived off an insurance settlement and various men who appeared in her life and vanished. Ellie's father had died in an accident at work. Carol's father had walked out when she was six months old. Two fatherless girls, growing up side by side, almost like sisters.

At ten before three Carol left work. The sharp cold air stunned her; she drew her scarf up tighter and headed for Broadway. Not many people were out walking and those who were had bundled up past recognition. Traffic was heavier than usual; visible air that smelled of exhaust and oil blasted her face. She walked fast, keeping her head down.

At the market she bought makings for burritos, and a carton of cole slaw. She paused at the door to button up her jacket again, to readjust the scarf, and facing out, seeing the traffic on Broadway, she saw Ellie in a taxi. She was in the backseat, wearing Carol's good coat, laughing.

Using her fifteen dollars for a taxi! She watched it out of sight, and then began to walk, forgetting the bank, forgetting the wine. She had given Ellie good instructions about the Broadway bus schedule, which stop to use, where the subway was, how much it would cost. A taxi. She trudged home, climbed up the three flights of stairs, disgusted at herself for giving Ellie the money she had planned to stretch out to next Tuesday.

She automatically put away her groceries and then stood in the kitchen, looking at the living-room space where Ellie's bed was rumpled and unmade, her small suitcase in the middle of the floor, Carol's nice robe half on the bed, half on the floor. The telephone rang and she picked it up simply to avoid listening to Michael's message, the caller's message.

"Oh, Ellie, glad I caught you," a man's voice, clipped and very fast. "Look, the reservation's set up, at the Mayfair Regent on Park Avenue. I gave them my credit-card number, yours will be valid by Monday. After you're settled in, call Bud—"

"Wait a minute," Carol said. "I'm afraid you've—"

"Ellie, I gotta go, like now. Take this down. Bud Castleman. He'll give you the stuff I faxed out there, and an advance if you need it for the weekend. Is that a laugh or what? Ready for the number?" He didn't wait for a response, but rattled off a telephone number that Carol wrote on the telephone pad. "Gotta go, kid, like I said. Give me a call on Monday at the office. Have fun, Mrs. Farley." He hung up.

Carol sat down abruptly, staring at the words she had written. Mayfair Regent, Park Avenue. Bud Castleman. She pushed the message button on the machine and listened to two calls for Michael, and then the same man's voice: "Harve Wannamaker calling Elinor Farley. You there, Ellie?" then Ellie's answer, the click.

She blinked hard. Ellie had said she was expecting a call, money was due, but the Mayfair Regent? She blinked again and stood up; then, eyeing the suitcase, she crossed the room and lifted it. The suitcase had a combination lock. All through school they had used each other's birthdays for the combination locks on their hall lockers. She turned the numbers to 6, 1, 7, and it sprang open. Underwear, hose . . . and a large manila envelope, thick with papers, newspaper articles, some legal documents . . . She sat on the unmade couch-bed and started to read; when she finished she replaced everything, rose dazedly, and walked from the living room to her bedroom where she sat on the side of her own bed.

Elinor Farley's husband, James, aged sixty-eight, had died in an accident last April, leaving an estate of nearly $2 million to his widow. Farley's grown son, Sutton Farley, had contested the will, and also had accused his stepmother of murdering his father.

In Carol's head a scene from the past replayed in stark clarity; they had been sixteen or seventeen. "Don't be an airhead," Ellie had said coldly, waving her hand to dry nail polish. "Mom's got the right idea, just the wrong guys. She always thinks they have money, and they never do. What you do is find an old geezer with dough, give him a few good years, and then do him in and collect. Simple, and it's not even terrible. Get one who's going to kick soon anyway, what's the big deal?"

Girl talk. Just crazy girl talk. Like you're going to snag a rock star, or be a movie star, or a model, or marry a rich old man and inherit a fortune. Two million dollars!

She didn't move when she heard Ellie return. She didn't know what to say, how to act. Ellie went to the kitchen, listened to the answering machine, made rustling sounds; then she went to the bathroom and Carol could hear water running. Finally she stood up and moved out into the hall, to the bathroom door, which was open; in the cramped space Ellie was at the sink washing something. A wig! She turned and looked startled momentarily;

her hand flew to her own hair, which was as short and as dark as Carol's. Then she shrugged, and turned back to the wig.

"Shit," she muttered. She had not immersed the wig, but was dabbing at it with a washcloth.

"I took a call for you," Carol said. "Harve Wannamaker."

Ellie stopped scrubbing the wig. "And?"

"He made you a hotel reservation."

Ellie let out a whoop and flung the washcloth down in the sink. Water splashed her and she laughed and turned to leave the bathroom. Carol stepped into the kitchen out of the way.

"What else did he say?"

Carol repeated the message and Ellie hugged herself and spun around. "An advance! He'd better come loaded! Where's your phone book? What hotel?"

Carol watched her punch in the numbers, listened numbly when she asked if there was a confirmed reservation for Elinor Farley; she banged down the receiver, and whooped again. "Come on, let's go!" Ellie cried. She ripped the note from the pad and stuffed it into the purse on the table, tossed the wig high in the air, caught it, and threw it across the room onto the couch, laughing.

"What do you mean? Go where?"

"Look, I told you I was expecting a call, money's due. Well, it's here, or will be on Monday. It was cleared too late today to be touchable until Monday, but for now I have a reservation at a snazzy hotel. Be my guest, honey. We'll have room service, whatever you want, lobster, truffles, pheasant under glass! Champagne! My God, yes!"

Watching her, Carol shivered, as if the cold air had entered her, was lodged just under her rib cage. She shook her head.

"Hey, it's for real, kid!" Ellie cried, laughing. "I told you I was married, it didn't last? He sort of made a settlement on me. It's real!"

"You did it, didn't you?" Carol whispered.

Ellie's smile vanished; her face became masklike. She looked swiftly at her suitcase, back at Carol. "You nosy bitch! Come, stay, do whatever you want. I'm outta here."

When she reached for the coat Carol grabbed it. "You can't have it," she said.

For a moment Ellie looked murderous, but shrugged, and started to walk toward the couch, then stopped, and without turning she said, "How about lending me another ten or fifteen for a cab."

"I don't have it."

Ellie faced her angrily. "Come on, after I see this Bud what's-his-face, I'll pay it back, and the other fifteen, plus interest."

"I didn't get to the bank."

Ellie's fists clenched. She was wearing Carol's best dress, and her navy shoes, and on the table where she had tossed it was Carol's navy purse, with travel brochures sticking out.

"Tell me again about the bus and subway," Ellie said furiously. "Which is quicker?"

She would never see her clothes again, Carol knew, or the fifteen dollars, or the three hundred Ellie had borrowed in the distant past. She could live without the money, but she couldn't replace the clothes. Slowly she said, "I'll go with you. You can wear the dress until we get to your room, and you collect from that man. Then you can pay me what you owe me, and I'll bring my stuff back in your suitcase. You won't want it after this, I suppose."

Ellie regarded her through narrowed eyes. "What I owe you? The fifteen bucks?"

"Plus the three hundred you borrowed ten years ago."

"And the forty I got from your mom's purse, mustn't forget a penny."

The cold was spreading all through Carol, even to her lips, which had turned too numb to speak. She nodded. She had not believed it, that Ellie had taken the money from her mother's purse. She had pleaded her case, convinced her mother that Ellie wouldn't do that to a friend.

"Okay," Ellie said finally. "Deal. I'll get my stuff from the bathroom." She walked to the bathroom, talking. "Listen, honey, I earned that money, every damn penny. And if I hadn't got it, that bastard Sutton would have. He managed to get every cent frozen as hard as the Antarctic. I had to sell everything I had just to stay alive this year. He hadn't even seen his father for fifteen years, nothing, no calls, zilch. Not when the old man had a heart attack, not when we got married, nothing. And he's got bucks he's never got around to counting. A movie producer! A goddamn movie producer! Well, it's mine now!"

Carol had read all this in the articles in the suitcase.

Ellie came out with her toothbrush and a comb, went to the suitcase and opened it, stashed her things away, tossed in the boots, picked up the wig, made a face at it, and threw it in also. She started to put on the cloth jacket.

"You can wear my heavy jacket," Carol said.

"How generous of you," Ellie said darkly, but she threw her own jacket into the suitcase, closed it, and turned the combination. Then she looked at Carol and said, "Listen, sweetie: That guy of yours is bad news. I know the type. He'll let you foot the bills until he's got it made, and then he'll find someone more suitable, a Bennington girl, or someone like that. You didn't learn a thing from your mother, did you? My God, your own mother put your father through medical school and he took a powder. Get something in writing now before it's too late."

"My mother is very happily married," Carol said stiffly.

"To a sheepherder in Australia! You call that a life?"

He wasn't a sheepherder; he was a rancher, with enough money to give her mother a good life at last. Ellie had said that her mother was in Phoenix, or Taos, or someplace like that; they hadn't been in touch for years.

The bitter cold air took away her breath when they left the apartment. Carol ducked her head against the wind and thought how wrong Ellie was about Michael. He would never leave her, she knew; he needed her. In the beginning she had found that need reassuring, even comforting; no one had ever needed her before he had come into her life, an overgrown little boy with a bashful smile, beautiful eyelashes. A little boy who clung to her and made her feel strong and capable. A little boy who confided in her, told her everything about himself, his fears, his worries, his insecurities. No, she thought almost grimly, he would never leave her. No matter what he did in school, at his seminars, it was that little boy who came home to her night after night and talked interminably about his fears, his worries, his plans.

She led Ellie to the IRT–7th Avenue subway station. At this time of day, nearly five, the bus would be jammed and slow. At the stairs Ellie hesitated; without ceremony Carol shoved her into the mass of people going down and they were swept along.

This was how fish moved in schools, she thought, how birds flew in flocks; no decisions, you just got into the swarm and went where it took you. The swarm moved down the stairs to the platform and spread out a bit as a new swarm pressed in from behind. She nudged Ellie down the platform farther, closer to the edge, and they stopped where she knew the door would open. Ellie put the suitcase down between them and Carol thought to tell her not to let go of it, but she said nothing and looked in the other direction. Let her learn the hard way. The train was coming; the roar began to shake the platform, and the people swarm pressed in harder.

Just as she turned back she saw a gloved hand jab at Ellie, while another hand grabbed for her purse as she staggered forward off-balance. Carol lunged for Ellie's arm at the same moment that someone else pushed her, and, twisting, she fell over the suitcase. Her cheek hit the platform hard; the suitcase knocked the breath out of her and she struggled for air. The roar was drowned out by one long scream.

People got her to her feet, moved her, made room around her. Someone was holding her up, telling her she was all right. People were yelling, a siren sounded too close, and through the noise she kept hearing a choking, unrecognizable voice: "She was pushed over the edge! The train was coming and she was pushed. I tried to grab her. She was pushed over."

"Take it easy, lady. Just take it easy now. Okay? Is this yours?" A lean woman in a police uniform held out the blue purse and Carol reached for it. "Okay, in a second. Did you see anyone?"

"Hands. Gloves. She was pushed over the edge! Oh God!" She choked on the words and buried her face in her hands, crying. "Oh, my God! He pushed her over the edge!"

More voices. She paid no attention. She should have warned Ellie, should have caught her, should have protected her. She sobbed harder. Then someone had her arm, moving her again. Out into the cold, into a car. She should have grabbed Ellie's arm, screamed. . . .

"What we're going to do is take you to your hotel. We called your lawyer, Mr. Castleman. He'll meet us there with a doctor. Just to make sure you're okay. Then we'll get a statement and leave you alone to get some rest."

Carol froze as the officer talked. They thought she was Ellie. Her hotel, her lawyer. She shuddered. When she opened her mouth to say that wasn't right, only a groan came out.

At the hotel the manager hovered until the officer ordered him to bring up the registration book later, to send up coffee now, send up Mr. Castleman when he arrived. She was leading Carol to the elevator when two men approached them.

"Castleman," one of them said, tall, heavy, gray-haired, with thick glasses. "This is Dr. Jervis. My God, this is terrible, Mrs. Farley. Terrible."

Again Carol opened her mouth to correct the mistake; she raised her hand in a gesture for him to stop and saw blood all over her fingers, on the back of her hand; she swayed and closed her eyes. Dr. Jervis had one hand on her wrist by then.

"Let's get her to her room and have a look," he said, and they entered the elevator and rode to the tenth floor. In the suite Dr. Jervis took her to the bathroom and cleaned her abrasions with a washcloth that was as soft as a cloud. "Just skinned up," he said cheerfully, cleaning her hand. He had her undress and put on a fluffy hotel robe and pressed her ribs, examined her shoulders and back. "Nothing time won't take care of," he said, washing his own hands at the sink. "I'll leave you a tranquilizer, and aspirins."

When he left her in the bathroom she looked at it in wonder. It was bigger than her kitchen and bath combined, and everything sparkled. And she thought, she could do it. A wave of terror buckled her knees; she clutched the edge of the sink until it passed, and then regarded herself in a wall-sized mirror and nodded. She could do it. Michael would see the short darkened hair, the ugly jacket, the dress. Ellie wouldn't be recognizable. Michael would see what he expected to see. There was a little insurance, enough to get him through the next fourteen weeks. Then he would find the Bennington girl and tell her his troubles, cry on her shoulder. Forever.

When she went back out to the sitting room, wearing the robe, holding a wet washcloth against her face, the doctor was gone. Bud Castleman and the police officer were both standing up; he was hard and mean-looking. The officer looked wary.

"Mrs. Farley," the officer said, "could you answer a question or two from Mr. Castleman, just to verify your identity?"

"How did he get here? Harve said I should call Bud Castleman, but I didn't. Not yet."

"We called him," the officer said. "I found the note with his name and number in your purse."

Castleman's grim expression eased a fraction, but he was still studying her intently. "You're not what I expected," he said after a moment. "Can you tell me your mother's maiden name?"

"My mother? Doreen Claypool."

"Mrs. Farley," the officer said when Castleman nodded slightly, "why don't you sit down here and have some coffee and tell me what happened, all you can remember." She gave Castleman a look of disgust and opened a notebook.

Carol sank down into a chair gratefully. She ached all over. "We were coming here. Harve called and said the reservation was made, and we were going to have room service bring up dinner. . . ."

She was unconscious of the watchfulness of Bud Castleman as she spoke. The manager arrived with the registration book. She signed it shakily; Castleman compared the signature to the note she had jotted earlier. When the manager left, she raised her scraped hand to her hair, and said, "Harve told you I have long blond hair. Is that it?"

"He did," Castleman admitted.

"It's in the suitcase," she said. When she started to get up, she swayed and sank back to the chair.

"What's the combination?" Castleman asked, still watching her closely.

She told him and he opened the suitcase, pulled out the wig and the little suede cloth jacket, and looked satisfied finally.

"It got dirty," she said, closing her eyes. "A pigeon, or something."

After the officer left, Bud Castleman ordered a bottle of wine from room service and began to talk about money, and she listened with her eyes closed, thinking about Ellie, and then thinking of gardens in Italy, in the south of France.

APPENDIX

THE YEARBOOK OF THE MYSTERY AND SUSPENSE STORY

THE YEAR'S BEST MYSTERY AND SUSPENSE NOVELS

Lawrence Block, *The Devil Knows You're Dead* (Morrow)
William J. Caunitz, *Cleopatra Gold* (Crown)
Mary Higgins Clark, *I'll Be Seeing You* (Simon & Schuster)
Patricia D. Cornwell, *Cruel & Unusual* (Scribners)
James Crumley, *The Mexican Tree Duck* (Mysterious Press)
Dominick Dunne, *A Season in Purgatory* (Crown)
Elizabeth George, *Missing Joseph* (Bantam)
Carl Hiaasen, *Strip Tease* (Knopf)
Tony Hillerman, *Sacred Clowns* (HarperCollins)
Peter Hoeg, *Smilla's Sense of Snow* (Farrar, Straus & Giroux)
Susan Isaacs, *After All These Years* (HarperCollins)
Sebastien Japrisot, *A Very Long Engagement* (Farrar, Straus & Giroux)
John le Carré, *The Night Manager* (Knopf)
Elmore Leonard, *Pronto* (Delacorte)

Steve Martini, *Prime Witness* (Putnam)
Ed McBain, *Mischief* (Morrow)
Marcia Muller, *Wolf in the Shadows* (Mysterious Press)
Joyce Carol Oates, *Foxfire* (Dutton)
James Patterson, *Along Came a Spider* (Little, Brown)
Bill Pronzini, *Demons* (Delacorte)
Ruth Rendell, *The Crocodile Bird* (Crown)
Scott Turow, *Pleading Guilty* (Farrar, Straus & Giroux)
Andrew Vachss, *Shella* (Knopf)
Barbara Vine, *Anna's Book* (Harmony)
Minette Walters, *The Sculptress* (St. Martins)
Joseph Wambaugh, *Finnegan's Week* (Morrow)

BIBLIOGRAPHY

I. COLLECTIONS AND SINGLE STORIES

Alcott, Louisa May. *From Jo March's Attic: Stories of Intrigue and Suspense.* Edited by Madeleine Stern and Daniel Shealy. Boston: Northeastern University Press. Nine further stories by the author of *Little Women,* from the pages of *Frank Leslie's Lady's Magazine.*

Ambler, Eric. *The Story So Far: Memories and Other Fictions.* London: Weidenfeld & Nicolson. All nine of Ambler's published short stories, with some sixty pages of new memoirs.

Avallone, Michael. *Open Season on Cops and The Arabella Nude.* Brooklyn: Gryphon Publications. Two novelettes from *Mike Shayne Mystery Magazine,* 1962–63.

Block, Lawrence. *Some Days You Get the Bear.* New York: Morrow. Twenty-one stories, three new, 1963–93, mainly from *Playboy, EQMM,* and *AHMM.* Three feature private eye Matt Scudder. (A couple of the stories are non-criminous.)

Bruce, Leo. *Murder in Miniature: The Short Stories of Leo Bruce.* Introduction by B. A. Pike. Chicago: Academy Chicago. Twenty-eight stories, all but one from the *London Evening Standard,* 1950–56. Ten feature Sergeant Beef and eight feature Sergeant Grebe.

Clark, Mary Higgins. *Death on the Cape and Other Stories.* London: Arrow Books. Eight stories from various sources, 1958–92.

Dexter, Colin. *Morse's Greatest Mystery and Other Stories*. London: Macmillan. Ten stories, five about Inspector Morse. Two stories are new and two others, listed below, appeared only in limited editions.

―――. *Neighborhood Watch*. Richmond (Surrey), England: Hartley Moorhouse. A single Morse short story in a limited edition.

―――. *The Inside Story*. London: Macmillan. A single Morse short story in a booklet published for an advertising promotion.

Doyle, Arthur Conan. *The Further Adventures of Sherlock Holmes*. Pleasantville, N.Y.: The Reader's Digest Association. Afterword by Philip A. Shreffler. An unusual collection containing all seven Holmes stories from the American edition of *His Last Bow* plus four Doyle stories not usually included in the official Holmes canon: "The Man with the Watches," "The Lost Special," "The Field Bazaar," and "How Watson Learned the Trick."

Estleman, Loren D. *People Who Kill*. Eugene, Ore.: Mystery Scene Press/Pulphouse Publishing. Nine stories, 1977–90, mainly from *AHMM*.

Garfield, Brian. *Suspended Sentences*. Eugene, Ore.: Mystery Scene Press/Pulphouse Publishing. Eight stories, 1977–87, all but one from *EQMM* or *AHMM*.

Gorman, Ed. *Dark Whispers*. Eugene, Ore.: Mystery Scene Press/Pulphouse Publishing. Eleven stories, 1983–92, one new, from various sources.

Hansen, Joseph. *Bohannon's Country*. New York: Viking. Five novelettes, three featuring rancher-sleuth Hack Bohannon. One story new, others from *AHMM* and *EQMM*.

Keating, H. R. F. *Inspector Ghote and Some Others*. Helsinki: Eurographica. A limited edition of three stories, two previously uncollected. 1991.

Kessel, John. *Meeting in Infinity*. Sauk City, Wisc.: Arkham House. Fifteen fantasy stories, a few criminous, including a private-eye fantasy, "The Big Dream." 1992.

King, Stephen. *Nightmares and Dreamscapes*. New York: Viking. Twenty stories and novelettes, three new, plus a teleplay, a nonfiction article and poem about baseball, and a brief parable. Most are fantasy-horror but at least four are criminous, including a Sherlockian pastiche.

Mortimer, John. *The Best of Rumpole*. New York: Viking. Seven novelettes chosen by the author from previous collections.

Nolan, William F. *Helle on Wheels*. Baltimore: Maclay & Associates. A single story about series detective Nick Challis, in a limited edition. 1992.

————. *3 for Space*. Brooklyn, N.Y.: Gryphon Books. Three short stories, one new, about futuristic private eye Sam Space. 1992.

Pronzini, Bill. *Carmody's Run*. Arlington Heights, Ill.: Dark Harvest. Introduction by the author. Three stories and a short novel about freelance bodyguard Carmody, 1971–75, all revised for this edition.

Sabatini, Rafael. *The Fortunes of Casanova & Other Stories*. Foreword by George MacDonald Fraser. Selected by Jack Adrian. Oxford: Oxford University Press. Twenty stories, 1907–37, mostly about rogues and adventurers but with some detection.

Stone, Richard. *Mysteries Suspended: More Early Cases of Sherlock Holmes as Chronicled by John H. Watson M.D.* Luton, England: Turnstone Press. Ten new Holmes pastiches.

Taylor, John. *The Unopened Casebook of Sherlock Holmes*. London: BBC Books. Six pastiches written to accompany a radio series.

Thomson, June. *The Secret Journals of Sherlock Holmes*. London: Constable. Seven new stories in the author's third collection of Sherlockian pastiches.

Westlake, Donald E. *Give Till It Hurts: A Christmas Story*. New York: The Mysterious Bookshop. A new Dortmunder story in a twelve-page booklet for bookshop customers.

II. ANTHOLOGIES

Ashley, Mike, ed. *The Mammoth Book of Historical Whodunnits*. New York: Carroll & Graf. Twenty-two stories, five new, and a novel by Raymond Butler, with settings ranging from ancient Egypt to the year 1910. Foreword by Ellis Peters, an afterword on old-time detection, and an appendix listing important novels and short stories.

Bloch, Robert, ed. *Monsters in Our Midst*. New York: Tor Books. Seventeen new mystery-horror stories, including one also published in Lawrence Block's collection, *Some Days You Get the Bear,* above.

Charyn, Jerome, ed. *The New Mystery.* New York: Dutton. Forty-two stories, fifteen new, from mystery and mainstream writers in several countries. Includes a few fantasies and brief excerpts from three novels.

Cody, Liza, and Michael Z. Lewin, eds. *2nd Culprit.* London: Chatto & Windus. Twenty-one new stories, three reprints, two nonfiction pieces, and other features in the second of a new series from Britain's Crime Writers Association.

Coupe, Stuart, and Julie Ogden, eds. *Hardboiled.* St. Leonards (New South Wales), Australia: Allen & Unwin. Fourteen recent stories by American writers, 1988–92. 1992.

Dibdin, Michael, ed. *The Picador Book of Crime Writing.* London: Picador. Eighty-seven excerpts from novels, stories, poems, and essays, by both mystery and mainstream writers.

Dziemianowicz, Stefan, Robert Weinberg, and Martin H. Greenberg, eds. *Nursery Crimes.* New York: Barnes & Noble. Thirty horror stories involving children, some criminous.

Fallen Angels: Six Noir Tales Told for Television. New York: Grove Press. Preface by James Ellroy. Stories by James Ellroy, Raymond Chandler, William Campbell Gault, Jonathan Craig, Cornell Woolrich and Jim Thompson, together with their screenplay adaptations as shown on the Showtime cable television channel.

Gorman, Ed, and Martin H. Greenberg, eds. *Predators.* New York: Roc Books. Twenty-one mystery and horror stories, all but one new, some fantasy.

Great British Mystery Stories of the Twentieth Century. Franklin Center, Penn.: Franklin Library. Twenty-three stories from various sources. A volume in the Franklin Library of Mystery Masterpieces. No editor given, but the suggestions of Kenneth D. McCormick are acknowledged. 1990.

Greenberg, Martin H., ed. *Crimes of Passion: Twenty-three Tales of Love and Hate.* New York: Barnes & Noble. Twenty-two stories and a novel by Ed Gorman, from various sources.

———, and Ed Gorman, eds. *Danger in D.C.: Cat Crimes in the Nation's Capital.* New York: Donald Fine. Nineteen new stories.

————, ed. *Malice Domestic 2*. New York: Pocket Books. Introduction by Mary Higgins Clark. Sixteen new stories in the second of an annual series.

————, ed. *Murder British Style: Nineteen Classic Cozy Mysteries*. New York: Barnes & Noble. Eighteen stories plus a novel, *The Three Coffins*, by John Dickson Carr.

————, and Carol-Lynn Rossel Waugh, eds. *Santa Clues*. New York: Signet pb. Twenty-one new Christmas mysteries, a few fantasy.

Haining, Peter, ed. *Great Irish Detective Stories*. London: Souvenir Press. Twenty-six stories, one new, from the nineteenth and twentieth centuries.

————, ed. *The Television Late Night Horror Omnibus*. London: Orion. Thirty-three stories adapted for various TV anthology series in England and America. A half-dozen or so are criminous, the rest fantasy.

Hale, Hilary. *Midwinter Mysteries 3*. London: Little, Brown. Ten new stories in an annual anthology series.

Hoch, Edward D., ed. *The Year's Best Mystery and Suspense Stories 1993*. New York: Walker and Company. Fourteen of the best stories from 1992, with bibliography, necrology, and awards lists.

Hutchings, Janet, ed. *The Deadliest Game: Tales of Psychological Suspense from Ellery Queen's Mystery Magazine*. New York: Carroll & Graf. Fifteen stories, all but one from 1991–93.

Jakubowski, Maxim, ed. *Constable New Crime 2*. London: Constable. Fifteen new stories and one reprint by British and American authors.

Knight, Stephen, ed. *A Corpse at the Opera House: A Crimes for a Summer Christmas Anthology*. St. Leonards (New South Wales), Australia: Allen & Unwin. Fourteen new stories by Australian writers in the third of an annual serries. See also next three titles. 1992.

————, ed. *Crimes for a Summer Christmas*. St. Leonards (New South Wales), Australia: Allen & Unwin. Sixteen new stories by Australian writers in the first of an annual series. 1990.

————, ed. *More Crimes for a Summer Christmas*. St. Leonards (New South Wales), Australia: Allen & Unwin. Sixteen new stories by Australian writers in the second of an annual series. 1991.

————, ed. *Murder at Home: A Crimes for a Summer Christmas Anthology*. St. Leonards (New South Wales), Australia: Allen & Unwin. New stories by Australian writers in the fourth of an annual series.

Mandelbaum, Paul, ed. *First Words: Earliest Writing from Favorite Contemporary Authors*. Chapel Hill, N.C.: Algonquin Books of Chapel Hill. Childhood work by forty-two authors, mainly mainstream, including fifty pages of an unfinished mystery novel by a fourteen-year-old John Updike.

Manson, Cynthia, ed. *Blood Threat and Fears: Thirty-three Great Tales of Psychological Suspense*. New York: Barnes & Noble. Stories from *EQMM* and *AHMM*.

————, ed. *Canine Crimes*. New York: Jove. Fourteen stories involving dogs, all from *EQMM* and *AHMM*.

————, ed. *Grifters and Swindlers*. New York: Carroll & Graf. Seventeen stories from *EQMM* and *AHMM*.

————, ed. *More Murder Most Cozy*. New York: Signet. Eight stories from *EQMM* and *AHMM*.

————, ed. *More Mystery Cats*. New York: Signet. Fourteen stories, mainly from *EQMM* and *AHMM*.

————, ed. *Murder on Main Street*. New York: Barnes & Noble. Forty tales of small-town crime from *EQMM* and *AHMM*.

————, and Charles Ardai, eds. *High Adventure*. New York: Barnes & Noble. A mixed collection of twenty-seven mystery, adventure, and science fiction tales, twelve of which appeared in *EQMM* and *AHMM*.

Muller, Marcia, Ed Gorman, and Bill Pronzini. *Criminal Intent I*. Arlington Heights, Ill.: Dark Harvest. Three new mystery novellas.

Murder Under the Tree. New York: Zebra Books. Six new Christmas mysteries by women writers.

Mystery Scene magazine staff, eds. *Hollywood Kills*. New York: Carroll & Graf. Twelve stories, some fantasy, and a novel by William Campbell Gault, all with Hollywood settings.

————, eds. *The Year's 25 Finest Crime and Mystery Stories: Second Annual Edition*. New York: Carroll & Graf. Introduction by Jon Breen. Twenty-five of the best stories, mainly from 1991–92.

Resnick, Mike, ed. *More Whatdunits*. New York: DAW Books.

Nineteen new science fiction mysteries, most involving alien creatures, written in response to puzzles posed by the editor.

Weinberg, Robert E., Stefan Dziemianowicz, and Martin H. Greenberg, eds. *100 Dastardly Little Detective Stories*. New York: Barnes & Noble. A hundred brief detective tales from various sources.

————, eds. *Tough Guys and Dangerous Dames*. New York: Barnes & Noble. Twenty-four tough mysteries from the pulps, 1932–50.

Williams, Alan, ed. *The Headline Book of Spy Fiction*. London: Headline. Forty-two stories and novel excerpts. 1992.

III. NONFICTION

Barer, Burl. *The Saint: A Complete History in Print, Radio, Film and Television of Leslie Charteris' Robin Hood of Modern Crime, Simon Templar, 1928–1992*. Jefferson, N.C.: McFarland & Company. A biography of Charteris's professional life, with contents of all books, synopses of all radio and television episodes, and information about the French Saint books, *The Saint Magazine*, comic strips, fan club, etc. Illustrated.

Bintliff, Russell. *Police Procedurals: A Writer's Guide to the Police and How They Work*. Cincinnati: Writer's Digest Books. A volume in the Howdunit Series for writers. See also the next listing.

Blythe, Hal, Charlie Sweet, and John Landreth. *Private Eyes: A Writer's Guide to Private Investigators*. Cincinnati: Writer's Digest Books. A volume in the Howdunit Series for writers.

Breen, Jon L. *What About Murder? 1981–1991: A Guide to Books About Mystery and Detective Fiction*. Metuchen, N.J.: Scarecrow Press. A supplement to the 1981 volume, this is more than twice as long as the original, containing a new section on mystery anthologies as well as lengthy comments on all critical, biographical, and reference books about the mystery published during the past decade.

Cassiday, Bruce, ed. *Modern Mystery, Fantasy and Science Fiction Writers: A Library of Literary Criticism*. New York: Continuum. Excerpts from critical essays, biographies, and reviews of eighty-eight well-known genre writers, fifty-four of them in the mystery field.

Collingwood, Donna, ed. *Mystery Writer's Marketplace and Sourcebook*. Cincinnati: Writer's Digest Books. A guide to novel and short-story markets as well as reference books, editors, bookstores, and agents.

Dale, Alzina Stone, ed. *Dorothy L. Sayers: The Centenary Celebration*. New York: Walker and Company. Fourteen new essays by mystery writers and scholars on various aspects of Sayers's life and writing.

Forster, Margaret. *Daphne du Maurier*. New York: Doubleday. A new biography of the author of *Rebecca*.

Freeling, Nicholas. *Criminal Convictions: Errant Essays on Perpetrators of Literary License*. Boston: David R. Godine. Essays on detective fiction in its broadest sense, including Conrad, Kipling, Dickens, and Stendhal as well as Doyle and Simenon.

Gerard, Michael C. *The Poisonous Pen of Agatha Christie*. Austin: University of Texas Press. A study of the use of drugs, poisons, and chemicals in Christie's work.

Gorman, Ed, Martin H. Greenberg, and Larry Segriff, with Jon L. Breen, eds. *The Fine Art of Murder: The Mystery Reader's Indispensable Companion*. New York: Carroll & Graf. More than 125 essays and lists, most new, by writers, editors, and critics of the mystery.

Hilfer, Tony. *The Crime Novel: A Deviant Genre*. Austin: University of Texas Press. A study of the crime fiction genre.

"Johns, Ayresome" (George Locke). *The Anthony Berkeley Cox Files: Notes Towards a Bibliography*. London: Ferret Fantasy. A limited edition, large-format booklet of some thirty pages, containing a bibliography and an original short typescript by Anthony Berkeley.

Lachman, Marvin. *A Reader's Guide to the American Novel of Detection*. New York: G. K. Hall/Macmillan. A guide to 1,314 titles by 166 authors, including a list of 100 classics in the genre. Second in a series. See also Gary Warren Niebuhr's *Reader's Guide to the Private Eye Novel*, below.

Melling, John Kennedy. *Alchemy of Murder: A Clinical Survey of Successful Women Crime Writers*. London: John Kennedy Melling. Introduction by Gwendoline Butler. A limited-edition sixteen-page monograph, privately published by the author.

————. *Gwendoline Butler—the Inventor of the Women's Police Procedural*. London: John Kennedy Melling. Introduction by Gwendoline Butler. A limited-edition thirteen-page monograph, privately published by the author.

Niebuhr, Gary Warren. *A Reader's Guide to the Private Eye Novel*. New York: G. K. Hall/Macmillan. A guide to more than 1,000 titles by ninety authors, including a list of 100 classics of the genre. Third in a series of *Reader's Guides* to mystery novels.

Palmer, Scott. *Films of Agatha Christie*. London: Batsford. A study of films derived from Christie's novels and short stories.

Peters, Catherine. *The King of Inventors: A Life of Wilkie Collins*. Princeton, N.J.: Princeton University Press. A biography of Collins, author of the first important mystery novels in English, *The Moonstone* and *The Woman in White*.

Peterson, John. *The Life of Father Brown*. Barrington, Ill.: John Peterson. Annotated versions of eight articles originally published in *Midwest Chesterton News*, 1991–92. Includes a chronology of the Father Brown stories.

Redmond, Christopher. *A Sherlock Holmes Handbook*. Toronto: Simon & Pierre. Various aspects of Sherlockiana.

Reynolds, Barbara. *Dorothy L. Sayers: Her Life and Soul*. New York: St. Martin's. A new biography covering the Lord Peter Wimsey mysteries and especially Sayers's later religious writing.

Sallis, James. *Difficult Lives: Jim Thompson, David Goodis, Chester Himes*. Brooklyn, N.Y.: Gryphon Books. Essays on the life and work of three hardboiled writers, previously published in literary quarterlies.

Salwak, Dr. Dale. *Mystery Voices: Interviews with British Crime Writers*. San Bernardino, Cal.: Brownstone Books/Borgo Press. Interviews with Catherine Aird, P. D. James. H. R. F. Keating, Ruth Rendell, and Julian Symons, each with chronology and author photograph.

Seabrook, Jack. *Martians and Misplaced Clues: The Life & Work of Fredric Brown*. Bowling Green: Bowling Green State University Popular Press. A critical biography, including analysis of all of Brown's mystery and science fiction novels and stories.

Seels, James, ed. *Lawrence Block Bibliography 1958–1993*. Mission Viejo, Cal.: A.S.A.P. A limited, signed edition listing all the books and stories Block wishes to acknowledge, with an introduction by Wendy Hornsby, foreword and short story by Bloch, appreciation by Charles Ardai, and afterword by Philip Friedman.

Server, Lee. *Danger Is My Business: An Illustrated History of the Fabulous Pulp Magazines*. San Francisco: Chronical Books. A history of adventure, detective, and fantasy pulps.

Shine, Walter, and Jean Shine, eds. *Rave or Rage: The Critics and John D. MacDonald*. Gainesville: University of Florida, George A. Smathers Libraries. Summaries of and excerpts from all reviews and commentary on MacDonald.

Siegel, Jeff. *The American Detective: An Illustrated History*. Dallas: Taylor Publishing. The evolution of the detective in American fiction, with movie stills, book jackets, and author photos.

Slide, Anthony. *Gay and Lesbian Characters and Themes in Mystery Novels: A Critical Guide to Over 500 Works in English*. Jefferson, N.C.: McFarland & Company. A detailed alphabetical guide to authors and their books, showing changing attitudes toward homosexuals in print.

Wolfe, Peter. *Alarms & Epitaphs: The Art of Eric Ambler*. Bowling Green: Bowling Green State University Popular Press. A study of all of Ambler's novels.

AWARDS

MYSTERY WRITERS OF AMERICA EDGAR AWARDS

Best Novel: Minette Waters, *The Sculptress* (St. Martin's)

Best First Novel by an American Author: Laurie King, *Grave Talent* (St. Martin's)

Best Original Paperback: Steven Womack, *Dead Folks' Blues* (Ballantine)

Best Fact Crime: Bella Stumbo, *Until the Twelfth of Never* (Pocket)

Best Critical Biographical: Burl Bayer, *The Saint: A Complete History* (McFarland & Co.)

Best Short Story: Lawrence Block, "Keller's Therapy" (*Playboy*, 5/93)

Best Young Adult: Joan Lowery Nixon, *The Name of the Game Was Murder* (Delacorte)

Best Juvenile: Barbara Brooks Wallace, *The Twin in the Tavern* (Atheneum)

Best Episode in a Television Series: David Milch, "4B or not 4B" (*NYPD Blue*, ABC)

Best Television Feature or Miniseries: Allan Cubitt, *Prime Suspect 2* (*Mystery!* PBS)

Best Motion Picture: Ebbe Rose Smith, *Falling Down* (Warner Bros.)

Grand Master: Lawrence Block

Ellery Queen Award: Otto Penzler, Otto Penzler Books

Robert L. Fish Memorial Award: D. A. McGuire, "Wicked Twist" (*AHMM*, 10/93)

CRIME WRITERS' ASSOCIATION (BRITAIN)

Gold Dagger: Patricia Cornwell, *Cruel and Unusual* (Little, Brown)
Silver Dagger: Sarah Dunany, *Fatlands* (Hamish Hamilton)
Last Laugh Award: Michael Pearce, *The Mamur Zapt & The Spoils of Egypt* (Crime Club)
Short Story Award: Julian Rathbone, "Some Sunny Day" (*Constable New Crimes 2*)
Nonfiction Award: Alexandra Artley, *Murder on the Heart* (Hamish Hamilton)
Golden Handcuffs Award: Margaret Yorke
Diamond Dagger: Ellis Peters

CRIME WRITERS OF CANADA ARTHUR ELLIS AWARDS (FOR 1992)

Best Novel: Carsten Stroud, *Lizardskin* (Bantam)
Best First Novel: Sean Stewart, *Passion Play* (Beach Holme)
Best Short Story: Nancy Kilpatrick, "Mantrap" (*Murder, Mayhem and Macabre*, Mississauga Arts Council)
Best True Crime: Kirk Makin, *Redrum the Innocent* (Viking Penguin)

PRIVATE EYE WRITERS OF AMERICA SHAMUS AWARDS (FOR 1992)

Best P.I. Novel: Harold Adams, *The Man Who Was Taller Than God* (Walker and Company)
Best P.I. Paperback Original: Marele Day, *The Last Tango of Delores Delgado* (Allen & Unwin)
Best First P.I. Novel: John Straley, *The Woman Who Married a Bear* (Soho)
Best P.I. Short Story: Benjamin Schutz, "Mary, Mary, Shut the Door" (*Deadly Allies*, Doubleday)
Life Achievement Award: Marcia Muller

BOUCHERCON ANTHONY AWARDS (FOR 1992)

Best Novel: Margaret Maron, *Bootlegger's Daughter* (Mysterious Press)

Best First Novel: Barbara Neely, *Blanche on the Lam* (St. Martin's)

Best True Crime: Barbara D'Amato, *The Doctor, the Murder, the Mystery: The True Story Behind the Bronion Murder* (Noble Press)

Best Critical Work: Ellen Nehr, *Doubleday Crime Club Compendium* (Offspring Press)

Best Short Story: Diane Mott Davidson, "Cold Turkey" (*Sisters in Crime 5*, Berkley)

Best Motion Picture: *The Crying Game* (Miramax)

MYSTERY READERS INTERNATIONAL MACAVITY AWARDS (FOR 1992)

Best Mystery Novel: Margaret Maron, *Bootlegger's Daughter* (Mysterious Press)

Best First Mystery Novel: Barbara Neely, *Blanche on the Lam* (St. Martin's)

Best Nonfiction/Critical: Ellen Nehr, *Doubleday Crime Club Compendium* (Offspring Press)

Best Short Story: Carolyn Hart, "Henri O's Holiday" (*Malice Domestic 1*, Pocket Books)

MALICE DOMESTIC AGATHA AWARDS (FOR 1992)

Best Novel: Margaret Maron, *Bootlegger's Daughter* (Mysterious Press)

Best First Novel: Barbara Neely, *Blanche on the Lam* (St. Martin's)

Best Short Story: Aaron and Charlotte Elkins, "Nice Gorilla" (*Malice Domestic 1*, Pocket Books)

INTERNATIONAL ASSOCIATION OF CRIME WRITERS HAMMETT PRIZE (FOR 1992)

Alice Hoffman, *Turtle Moon* (Putnam's)

NECROLOGY

Kobo Abe (1924–1993). Well-known Japanese novelist who occasionally dealt with criminal themes, as in *The Ruined Map* (1969).

John Brooks Barry (1938?–1993). Author of *The Michaelmas Girls*, a 1975 novel about Jack the Ripper, published only in England.

Miriam Borgenicht (1915–1992). Author of ten mystery novels, notably *A Corpse in Diplomacy* (1949).

William Brinkley (1917–1993). Mainstream novelist who wrote a single crime novel, *Peeper* (1981).

Chandler Brossard (1922?–1993). Mainstream novelist who published one crime novel, *The Wrong Turn,* as "Daniel Harper," and co-edited a collection of Poe's short stories.

Anthony Burgess (1917–1993). Well-known British mainstream novelist who also wrote as "Joseph Kell." His many works included at least four crime novels, notably *A Clockwork Orange* (1962).

Leslie Charteris (1907–1993). Famed British-American creator of The Saint, a roguish detective who starred in some 150 novels, novellas and short stories, notably *The Saint Versus Scotland Yard* (1932), *The Brighter Buccaneer* (1933) and *The Saint in New York* (1935). Virtually all the Saint stories have been filmed for movies and television, and Charteris supervised publication of *The Saint Magazine* from 1953 to 1967.

Avram Davidson (1923–1993). Well-known science fiction author and editor who won first prize in the 1956 *EQMM* contest and the 1961 short-story Edgar from MWA. He was the author of two Ellery Queen novels, *And on the Eighth Day* (1964) and *The Fourth Side of the Triangle* (1965), written from detailed plot outlines by Frederic Dannay, and a story collection, *The Enquiries of Dr. Eszterhazy* (1975).

Julia Davis (1904–1993). Author of two mystery novels under the pseudonym F. Draco, 1951–52.

Les Dawson (1933–1993). British comedian who authored a 1976 spy novel and a detective spoof, neither published in America.

Lillian de la Torre (1902–1993). Pen name of Lillian de la Torre Bueno McCue, author of books and plays about famous true crimes, and best known for her short mysteries about Samuel Johnson and James Boswell, collected in four volumes beginning with *Dr. Sam Johnson, Detector* (1946). Past president of Mystery Writers of America.

Lester del Rey (1915–1993). Well-known science fiction writer and editor who authored one crime novel, *Police Your Planet* (1956), under the pseudonym of "Erik van Lhin."

Kevin FitzGerald (1902–1993). British author of eight thrillers, 1948–66.

Lacey Fosburgh (1942?–1993). Journalist and true-crime writer who authored a single suspense novel, *Old Money* (1983).

"Janet Green" (1908–1993). Pseudonym of Victoria McCormick, British screenwriter who authored mystery novels and plays as well as short stories for *EQMM* and *AHMM*.

"William Haggard" (1907–1993). Pseudonym of British spy novelist Richard Henry Michael Clayton, author of nearly three dozen novels, many about Colonel Charles Russell, and five uncollected short stories.

"MacDonald Harris" (1921–1993). Pseudonym of Donald W. Heiney, mainstream writer who published one crime novel, *The Treasure of Sainte-Foy* (1980).

Michael Harrison (1907–1991). British novelist and noted Sherlockian who authored a dozen short pastiches about Poe's C. Auguste Dupin, collected as *Murder in the Rue Royale* (1972). He also published five mystery novels as Harrison and as "Quentin Downes."

John Hersey (1914–1993). Famed novelist and Pulitzer Prize–winner who wrote a single suspense novel, *The Walnut Door* (1977).

"Victoria Holt" (1906–1993). Pseudonym of British novelist Eleanor Alice Hibbert, who publlished thirty-two novels of romantic suspence beginning with *Mistress of Mellyn* (1961). She also published more than 150 historical romances, crime novels, and other books as "Jean Plaidy," "Philippa Carr," "Eleanor Burford," "Ellalice Tate," "Elbur Ford," and "Katherine Kellow."

Dorothy B. Hughes (1904–1993). A founding member and Grand Master of Mystery Writers of America, author of fourteen novels, notably *The Fallen Sparrow* (1942), *Ride the Pink Horse* (1946), and *In a Lonely Place* (1947). An Edgar nominee for her biography *Erle Stanley Gardner: The Case of the Real Perry Mason* (1978).

Felix Jackson (1902–1992). German-born film and TV writer who authored a single crime novel, *So Help Me God* (1955).

Fletcher Knebel (1911–1993). Well-known author whose work included nearly a dozen suspense thrillers, notably *Seven Days in May* (1962), co-authored with Charles W. Bailey II.

Tage la Cour (?–1993). Danish bibliophile and historian of the mystery who co-authored (with Harald Mogensen) *The Murder Book: An Illustrated History of the Detective Story* (1971), and wrote an Hercule Poirot parody for *EQMM*, 1/57.

Keith Laumer (1925–1993). Science fiction writer and author of a half-dozen suspense thrillers including three novelizations of "The Avengers" TV series.

Eleazar Lipsky (1911–1993). Author of six suspense novels, mainly with legal backgrounds, including *The Kiss of Death* (1947), *Murder One* (1948), and *The People Against O'Hara* (1950).

Helen McCloy (1904–1993). Grand Master and first woman president of MWA. Author of twenty-eight mystery novels (notably *Through a Glass Darkly* [1950], expanded from a prize-winning short story featuring psychologist sleuth Dr. Basil Willing) and a short-story collection. Published one mainstream novel as "Helen Clarkson."

Edith Meiser (1898?–1993). Actress and radio scriptwriter who authored a single mystery novel, *Death Catches Up with Mr. Kluck* (1935), under the pseudonym of "Xantippe."

Scott Meredith (1923–1993). Well-known literary agent who contributed to the pulps and played a large part in the editorial policy of *Manhunt*'s early years. With his brother, Sidney, he edited *The Best from* Manhunt (1958).

Chap Reaver (1935?–1993). Author of three young-adult mysteries, notably the MWA Edgar winners *Mote* (1990) and *A Little Bit Dead* (1992).

John Murray Reynolds (1901–1993). Contributor to mystery and adventure pulp magazines during the 1930s.

Arthur Roth (1925–1993). Novelist who published three mysteries, 1964–68, under the pseudonym "Slater McGurk."

Richard Sale (1911–1993). Pulp author, screenwriter and film director who published more than 400 short stories and nine suspense novels and collections, notably *Benefit Performance* (1946).

Harrison E. Salisbury (1908–1993). Well-known journalist and historian who authored a single novel of intrigue, *The Gates of Hell* (1975).

Robert Sampson (1927–1992). Short-fiction writer and pulp historian who won an Edgar for his 1985 story "Rain in Pinton County."

Julian Semenov (1931–1993). Prolific Russian crime and intrigue writer with two novels published in America. A founder of the International Association of Crime Writers.

Kay Nolte Smith (1932–1993). Author of an MWA Edgar-winning first novel, *The Watcher* (1980) and a half-dozen other novels, mainly mystery.

Julius Sprechman (1920?–1993). Hollywood writer who published his first intrigue novel, *Caribe,* in 1986.

Don Stanford (1918–1992). Author of several adventure novels and three suspense novels, beginning with *The Slaughtered Lovelies* (1950).

Ray Stanich (1927–1992). Co-author, with Francis M. Nevins, Jr., of *The Sound of Detection: Ellery Queen's Adventures in Radio* (1983).

Chris Steinbrunner (1933–1993). Co-editor (with Otto Penzler) of the Edgar-winning *Encyclopedia of Mystery and Detection*

(1976), and contributor to books and periodicals about mystery films and television, occasionally as "Peter Christian." Active in MWA for many years and longtime editor of its newsletter.

Samuel M. Steward (1909–1993). Author of two novels, 1985–89, with Gertrude Stein and Alice B. Toklas as detectives.

Ian Stuart (1927–1993). British author of nineteen crime novels, notably *Death from Disclosure* (1976), and stories in *EQMM* and elsewhere. Occasionally wrote as "Malcolm Gray." (Not to be confused with Alister MacLean, who published two novels as "Ian Stuart" in 1961–62.)

C. L. Sulzberger (1912–1993). Well-known journalist who authored one suspense novel, *The Tooth Merchant* (1973).

Andrew Tully (1914–1993). Author of a single suspense novel, *The Brahmin Arrangement* (1974).

HONOR ROLL

ABBREVIATIONS

AHMM—*Alfred Hitchcock's Mystery Magazine*
EQMM—*Ellery Queen's Mystery Magazine*
(Starred stories are included in this volume. All dates are 1993.)

Allyn, Doug, "The Sultans of Soul," *EQMM*, March
*————, "The Ghost Show," *EQMM*, December
Allyn, Jim, "The Tree Hugger," *EQMM*, mid-December
Ardai, Charles, "Nobody Wins," *AHMM*, mid-December
Bannister, Jo, "Face Value," *EQMM*, September
Bashover, Albert, "Criminal Justice," *AHMM*, mid-December
*Block, Lawrence, "Keller's Therapy," *Playboy*, May
————, "How Would You Like It?" *Monsters in Our Midst*
————, "The Merciful Angel of Death," *The New Mystery*
————, "Someday I'll Plant More Walnut Trees," *Some Days You Get the Bear*
————, "The Tulsa Experiment," *Some Days You Get the Bear*
Burke, Jan, "Why Tonight?" *AHMM*, mid-December
Chizmar, Richard, "A Capital Cat Crime," *Danger in D.C.*
Cohen, Stanley, "A Bite of Lunch," *EQMM*, August
Corwin, Steve, "Hot Oil," *AHMM*, February
Courtney, Terry, "Fate Is a Four Letter Word," *AHMM*, June
Crenshaw, Bill, "Postcards from the Ledge," *AHMM*, February

De Noux, O'Neil, "Why," *EQMM*, April

Dexter, Colin, "Neighbourhood Watch," *Morse's Greatest Mystery and Other Stories*

Douglas, Carole Nelson, "Parris Green," *Malice Domestic 2*

Ellison, Harlan, "Mefisto in Onyx," *Omni*, October

*Ely, David, "Dead Men," *EQMM*, August

Fyfield, Frances, "Cold and Deep," *Malice Domestic 2*

Gallison, Kate, "Ars Longa, Vita Brevis," *EQMM*, August

Gorman, Ed, "Anna and the Snake People," *Malice Domestic 2*

Halsted, Robert, "Fiat de Luxe," *AHMM*, June

Hansen, Joseph, "A Woman's Voice," *AHMM*, September

———, "McIntyre's Donald," *Bohannon's Country*

Harford, David K., "Calves in the Barn on a Monday Morn," *AHMM*, February

Haywood, Clyde, "The Fourth Man," *AHMM*, March

Healy, Jeremiah, "Spin-A-Rama," *AHMM*, November

Henson, Herb, "A Dead Sailor's Secret," *AHMM*, August

Hillerman, Tony, "First Lead Gasser," *EQMM*, April

Hoch, Edward D., "The Serpent and the Mongoose," *EQMM*, February

———, "The Theft of the Bald Man's Comb," *EQMM*, July

———, "Spy at Sea," *EQMM*, October

———, "Leopold's Guns," *EQMM*, November

*———, "A Traffic in Webs," *EQMM*, mid-December

Holt, Esther J., "Cemetery Flowers," *AHMM*, April

Howard, Clark, "The Long Drop," *EQMM*, February

Jones, Suzanne, "Demon Lover," *EQMM*, March

———, "Find a High Place," *EQMM*, July

———, "No Connection," *EQMM*, October

Kaminsky, Stuart M., "The Man Who Hated Books," *The New Mystery*

Lewin, Michael Z., "Rainey Shines," *EQMM*, July

———, "The Stranger," *EQMM*, September

Limón, Martin, "Lady of the Snow," *AHMM*, June

Linscott, Gillian, "Death of a Dead Man," *Midwinter Mysteries 3*

Lovesay, Peter, "Pass the Parcel," *Midwinter Mysteries 3*

Lupoff, Richard A., "You Don't Know Me, Charlie," *Hardboiled*, August

Maron, Margaret, "That Bells May Ring and Whistles Safely Blow," *Santa Clues*

*McGuire, D. A. "Wicked Twist," *AHMM*, October
*Monfredo, Miriam Grace, "The Apprentice," *EQMM*, November
Obermayr, Erich, "Marcel Sieurac's Murder," *AHMM*, mid-December
O'Daniel, Janet, "Wake the Dead," *AHMM*, May
Olson, Donald, "A Matter of Wife and Death," *EQMM*, February
———, "They'll Never Find You," *EQMM*, March
———, "Stolen Goods," *EQMM*, September
———, "Trial by Fire," *EQMM*, October
Owens, Barbara, "Who Killed Wee Winky?" *EQMM*, July
———, "All in the Eyes," *EQMM*, October
Pearce, Gerald, "Gemini," *EQMM*, March
Powell, James, "The Fixer-Upper," *EQMM*, May
Pronzini, Bill, "Shade Work," *EQMM*, November
*———, "Burgade's Crossing," *Louis L'Amour Western Magazine*, premiere issue
Rankin, Ian, "Concrete Evidence," *EQMM*, April
———, "Video, Nasty," *Constable New Crimes 2*
*Rathbone, Julian, "Some Sunny Day," *Constable New Crimes 2*
Reed, Mary, and Eric Mayer, "A Byzantine Mystery," *The Mammoth Book of Historical Whodunnits*
Richardson, D. L., "Hunter and the Sanibel Trade," *AHMM*, June
———, "G-Men and Old Loves," *AHMM*, July
Roberts, John Maddox, "Lotto," *AHMM*, December
*Rogers, Bruce Holland, "Enduring as Dust," *Danger in D.C.*
Saylor, Steven, "The Treasure House," *The Armchair Detective*, spring
———, "The House of the Vestals," *EQMM*, April
———, "The Disappearance of the Saturnalia Silver," *EQMM*, mid-December
Slesar, Henry, "Happen to Anyone," *EQMM*, November
Solomon, Stanley J., "Gift Givers," *AHMM*, August
Stevens, B. K., "Sideshow," *AHMM*, December
Stodghill, Dick, "A Clinical Interest in Murder," *AHMM*, November
Strong, Marianne, "The Shaft," *EQMM*, September
*Tremayne, Peter, "Murder by Miracle," *Constable New Crimes 2*
———, "Murder in Repose," *Great Irish Detective Stories*
———, "The High King's Sword," *The Mammoth Book of Historical Whodunnits*

————, "Hemlock at Vespers," *Midwinter Mysteries 3*

Van Ash, Cay, "Bismillah," *Constable New Crimes 2*

Walsh, Jackie, "Playland," *EQMM*, July

Wasylyk, Stephen, "The Knife," *AHMM*, January

————, "Teamwork," *AHMM*, December

————, "Anomalies," *EQMM*, October

*Westlake, Donald E., "Last-Minute Shopping," *The New York Times Book Review*, December 5

————, "Give Till It Hurts," *Give Till It Hurts*

Wheat, Carolyn, "The Black Hawthorn," *Danger in D.C.*

*Wilhelm, Kate, "Reforming Ellie," *EQMM*, December

Williams, David, "Freeze Everybody," *EQMM*, August

Winchester, Simon, "Never Knew He Had It in Him," *EQMM*, October

Zeman, Angela, "The Witch and the Fishmonger's Wife," *AHMM*, mid-December